# What Remains

## Tim Weaver

W F HOWES LTD

This large print edition published in 2015 by
W F Howes Ltd
Unit 4, Rearsby Business Park, Gaddesby Lane,
Rearsby, Leicester LE7 4YH

1  3  5  7  9  10  8  6  4  2

First published in the United Kingdom in 2015
by Michael Joseph

A CIP catalogue record for this book is available
from the British Library

ISBN 978 1 51001 219 6

Typeset by Palimpsest Book Production Limited,
Falkirk, Stirlingshire

Printe~~d~~ ~~and bound in Great Britain~~
by TJ Inte~~rnational~~ ~~Ltd, Padstow, Co~~rnwall

For Mum and Dad

# AUTHOR'S NOTE

In my second novel, *The Dead Tracks*, there's a short conversation between David Raker and Colm Healy where Healy talks about the failed investigation that's at the heart of *What Remains*. At the time I wrote the scene, I never really thought that a few lines of dialogue would eventually form the basis for an entire book. It's a consequence, I suppose, of my tendency not to work to plans: in the latter stages of *The Dead Tracks*, and then through the three novels that followed, Healy took on much more of a role than I ever would have anticipated, and that case – and his failure to solve it – began to affect him in ways that I never considered until I got there.

Because of that, eagle-eyed readers might notice a few minor changes between the case that Healy describes in *The Dead Tracks* and the version in *What Remains*. There were various reasons I felt I needed to make those alterations, but it ultimately came down to the fact that a full-length novel would have suffered without them. Where possible, though, I've tried to stay close to the details of the investigation that Healy (and, to a lesser extent, Raker) has talked about over the course of the series.

Finally, I've made some small changes to the working practices of the Metropolitan Police too, purely to service the story more effectively; as always, my hope is that it's done with enough subtlety and care for it not to cause offence.

## 16 July 2010

## BRUTAL MURDER OF FAMILY SPARKS CITY-WIDE MANHUNT

Eight-year-old twin girls and their 29-year-old mother have been found dead in what police are calling 'an unforgivable and callous attack'. Gail Clark and her daughters Abigail and April were discovered after a neighbour became concerned she hadn't seen or heard from the family in over four days.

Last night, police were calling for witnesses in and around Searle House, a twenty-storey block of flats in New Cross, south London, where the family lived on the seventeenth floor. Detective Inspector Colm Healy, leading the investigation, said a news conference would be scheduled for later today, and further details would be released to the public then. In the meantime, he appealed for information from

1

anyone who lived in Searle House or any of the surrounding estates: 'We believe Ms Clark and the two girls were murdered on Sunday or Monday this week – that's the 11th or 12th July. This was a particularly brutal crime, one of the worst I've seen in twenty-four years as a police officer, and I appeal to any member of the public who saw anything suspicious to bring that information to us without delay.'

DI Healy continued: 'We have a number of leads and I want to reassure the public and the local community that the person responsible will face the full force of the law.'

# PART I

# 14 JANUARY 2014

# CHAPTER 1

I met Colm Healy in a motel in Kew.

It was just north of the motorway, a big steel-grey building with all the aesthetic beauty of a shipping container, perforated by two long rows of identical windows. The car park was half full, slush skirting the pavements and approach road, ice-cold water cascading from broken guttering above the main entrance.

The bar was probably the best bit about the place, and not only because – with alcohol – you could eventually pretend you were somewhere else. It looked like it had recently undergone a refurbishment, and although the views only took in the car park and, vaguely, a glimpse of the Thames, the interior was smart and modern, a mix of booths and sofas, set in a semicircle around a curved counter.

I made a beeline for one of the booths, shrugging off my coat and ordering a black coffee, and then spent the time waiting for Healy by removing a series of printouts from a slipcase I'd brought with me. They were all job vacancies. I laid them out in two lines of five, all ten facing away from me, and put them into chronological order, starting with the one that had the most imminent deadline.

A few minutes later, the main door squeaked open on its hinges and Healy emerged into the stark light of the room. He nodded at me once, then headed to the bar. He was dressed in faded denims and a red T-shirt with something printed on the front of it, his hair combed but wet, his face flushed, like he'd just stepped out of the shower. I heard him ask for a Diet Coke, and then he came over. He eyed the printouts as he sat, but didn't say anything.

'Evening,' I said. 'Are you all right?'

'I guess.'

'What's wrong?'

He looked at me. 'Nothing. I'm fine.'

But I knew what was wrong. We both did.

Six days ago, on 8 January, we'd met in a café in Hammersmith after Healy had called and suggested getting together. It was the first time I'd seen him in fourteen months. In only six days, a lot had changed: not only had I paid for ten days' accommodation for him in the motel, but I'd also topped up his Oyster card, given him enough money to cover petrol, trawled recruitment agencies for work, even run him to interviews and driven him to the shops to buy food. He was uncomfortable with it – in a lot of ways I was too – but he'd got to the point where he didn't have a lot of options left.

A ghost to his family, his career as a cop a memory, he'd wiped out most of his savings and been living in a homeless shelter, what money he had left just about stretching to a mattress, a pillow and a bunk. No one else – his ex-wife, his sons, his former colleagues at the Met – knew how low he'd sunk because he was too proud, too bruised, to call them. However, he and I were different: not friends exactly, perhaps never that – which had been part of the reason he'd phoned me – but there was a connection between us. He knew I'd understand him. Perhaps more importantly, he knew I wouldn't judge him. We'd both lost those we'd loved, we'd battled some of the same demons, we'd hunted in the same shadows for the same people and confronted the same darkness in men. I never believed in fate or destiny – in most ways I still don't – but I'd begun to believe in something like it in the years since I'd known Healy. We'd gone our separate ways many times, but eventually, somehow, the paths of our lives always returned to the same point.

'What are these?' he said, looking at the jobs.

'Short-term store security gigs.'

He nodded and pulled a couple towards him.

As I watched him, I could see a shaving rash on one side of his neck, fresh blood dotted in the spaces above it; a cut that hadn't healed. There were plenty more of those where Healy was concerned, but most were better hidden. He was almost forty-nine, but he looked older.

He was overweight and out of condition, his face a little swollen, his eyes marked by crow's feet that criss-crossed so many times it was hard to see where one line ended and the next one began. His red hair fell forward as he continued reading, specks of water flecking off, on to the paper. On the front of his T-shirt, I could see what was printed: *Boys on Tour – Dublin 07*.

'Memorable trip?' I said to him.

He looked up. 'What?'

I nodded at his shirt.

He looked down at the words on his chest, cracked and worn by years of being put through the wash. 'Yeah,' he said, seeming to drift. 'I was the best man for someone. Took a group of us back to the motherland for a few days.' He stopped, a hint of a smile – and then it was gone. 'A different time, I guess.'

He turned his attention back to the printouts, clearly done talking about the trip, about returning to the city where he'd been born and grown up.

'How did the interview go today?'

He shrugged. 'Who knows?'

'What do you mean?'

'I mean, I drove all the way down to Rotherhithe, sat there and answered their questions, and they stared at me blankly and told me they'd let me know.'

'Did they say when?'

'A couple of days.'

The barman brought over Healy's Diet Coke

and set it down in front of him. Healy stayed silent, eyes fixed on the glass, but his thoughts were as clear as if inked on his face: *I don't want to be drinking this*.

When I'd offered to help him out, I'd attached a couple of conditions: one was that he had to find a job, even if only temporary, to get him back on his feet financially as soon as possible; the other was that he had to stay off the booze. The day we'd met in the café I hadn't smelled it on him, but I knew he'd been at the bottle in the weeks leading up to it. I could see it in his face, in the way it had begun to rub away at him. He'd been distressed, worn, a little bleary-eyed, the effect of the liquor still evident, clinging to him like a second skin.

'What about the other thing?' he said.

'What other thing?'

'The twins.'

I looked outside, the lights from the river blinking as sleet swept across the car park. The twins and their mother were where it had all begun; the catalyst for Healy's decline. In July 2010, he'd walked into a tower block in south London and found the three of them. He'd entered that place as one of the Met's best detectives – and now, three and a half years later, he was a homeless half-drunk, mourning a failed marriage, the break-up of his family and the self-destruction of his career. He hadn't called me six days ago because he wanted to find out how I was. He hadn't even called me because he was insolvent, jobless, homeless and desperate. He'd called me because he wanted my help in finding the man who'd murdered that family; the faceless killer that had started it all.

Nothing else mattered to him any more.

As I thought of that, of a hunt for the man responsible, something Healy had said to me in Hammersmith started playing out in my head: *I couldn't find the bastard who killed them, couldn't find a trace of that arsehole anywhere, and from there my whole life got flushed.* His voice had been unsteady, his eyes full of tears. *Now look at me. I'm living in a homeless shelter. I'm pathetic.*

'Raker, what about the twins?'

I stirred, tuning back in. He'd leaned forward in the booth, Diet Coke pushed to one side, hands together in front of him.

'Someone I know at the Met is mailing me a copy of the file,' I said to him. 'It'll be with me tomorrow. But I need to finish my current case first.'

I found missing people for a living, and my current case was a sixteen-year-old runaway from Greenwich. I'd located her, and returned her to her parents, but there were still things to be taken care of: calls to the Met to confirm she'd been found, a final meeting with the family to answer any questions, forms to sign, payment to be made. I sometimes let cases overlap at the beginning and end, but I didn't work them concurrently, because

I believed each one deserved to be treated with the same level of care. I felt a natural connection to the lost, an emotional bind I wasn't sure I could ever put into words, which made the girl every bit as important to me as Healy. More pragmatically, her family were paying me too.

In contrast, everything I'd ever done for Healy, perhaps everything I'd *ever* do, came with no financial reward. Often, it came with no reciprocation or thanks either. I'd accepted that reality a long time ago, accepted who he was, and the forces that drove him, because it felt like a lot of those forces also drove me. We were bound to one another. I'd saved his life once. He'd saved mine.

This was who we'd become.

'So you're just going to sit on their file until you're ready?' he said.

'How can I sit on something I don't have yet?'

A flicker of irritation.

'Healy, I told you the situation when we met last week.'

He didn't say anything, fingers tapping out a rhythm on the glass. After a long breath, he said, 'Fine. Why don't you give me the file when it arrives, so I can get started?'

'I don't think that's a good idea.'

'I don't need babysitting, Raker.'

'I never said you did.'

'No one knows that case better than me.'

'I know that.'

'I was *there*. It was *my* case.'

'That's exactly why it needs a fresh perspective.'

He didn't say anything else.

In the silence that followed, I started to leaf through the printouts again, trying to consider how best to engage him with the jobs, but when I looked up, his eyes weren't on me or the jobs any more, they were on the window, watching a car reverse out of its parking space. There was a sudden distance to him, as if he'd forgotten I was even here. 'I knelt down between their beds,' he was saying quietly, almost talking to himself, 'in the middle of that desperate fucking flat, their mam dead in the next room, every atom of innocence ripped from them, and I remember the forensic team left briefly, and I was alone with those girls. And I . . . and I just . . .'

Even as he faded out, I couldn't take my eyes off him, mesmerized by this flash of transparence. It was so unlike him, a moment so out of character my first thought was that something might be wrong with him. Seeing the rest of the sentence hanging there on his lips, I leaned forward, trying to hear him more clearly, but then he clocked the movement and seemed to shiver out of the lull, pulling away from its grip, and the mood changed instantly. He looked from the window to me, then to the jobs, clearly embarrassed about letting his guard down.

'Are you okay?'

He remained still, silent.

'Look,' I said, keeping my voice steady, 'I promised

you I would help you, and I meant it. But I want to take a first run at it. I want to come in fresh. There's no hidden agenda here, Healy. Don't look for the negative in this.'

A snort, but no comment.

'Healy?'

He just looked at me.

'What's the matter?'

'What do you *think's* the matter?' he said, picking up one of the printouts. 'All this shite. It's worthless. What matters is finding out who murdered those girls.'

'You need a job.'

He dismissed me with a shake of the head. 'I hate it. Filling in application forms, pretending I'm someone I'm not, having to kiss the arse of people I don't rate and won't like. But you know what? It's not even that. The thing that *really* pisses me off is that I could do any of these jobs in my sleep. I was on the force for twenty-six years, I saw things I can never wash away, I've been across the table from men so depraved they sucked the light out of the room. But according to the pile of rejection letters I've been busy collecting, I'm not even qualified enough to shuffle along shop aisles on the lookout for spotty dickheads trying to steal smartphones. I mean, the fact that I've managed to get one – *one* – two-month security gig in an entire year should tell you all you need to know. The spiel ain't working, Raker. No one wants to employ me.'

'Getting a job these days isn't eas—'

'I don't *want* a job.'

I pushed down my irritation. 'How are you going to help those girls if you're living in a homeless shelter again?'

'What'll help them is finding the person who killed them.'

'We will.'

'We won't if all we're doing is sitting around staring at pieces of paper like these.' He picked up a couple more printouts. 'Like I give a shit about any of this.'

'Healy, you get a job, you've got money. You've got money, you've got a place to stay. When you've got a place to stay, *then* you've got some firm ground to work from. If you want to do what's best by those girls and their mother – if you *really* want that – you'll apply for every one of these, and you'll do whatever it takes to get one of them.'

He sat there, staring at me, the muscles in his face taut, his fingers playing with a part of his chest which was obviously giving him some discomfort.

'You all right?' I said.

He realized I was talking about his chest. 'I'm fine.'

'Just email your CV off to these places, okay?'

No response. I'd set up an email account for him, and he was using the PCs in the business centre at the motel to send off his applications. It wasn't hard.

'Okay?'

More silence.

I sighed. 'Healy?'

'When will you be done with your other case?'

'Tomorrow afternoon.'

His fingers moved away from his chest and started playing with the edges of the printouts. Eventually, he gathered them all up and slid along to the end of the booth. 'I've got that interview at the recruitment agency at three,' he said to me. 'But after I'm done there, we can meet here if you want. You can bring the file and we can talk about the girls.'

I nodded.

'Will you bring the file?'

'If it turns up, yes.'

'Don't play me.'

'I'm not playing you, Healy.'

He shuffled out of the booth, his gaze lingering on me. But it was harder to read him this time, his eyes showing nothing, his face a blank. At the door to the bar, he paused for a second and looked back, a loneliness clinging to him.

A moment later, he was gone.

# CHAPTER 2

It hadn't always been like this.

The previous night, after I called my contact at the Met about getting hold of the murder file, I'd gone looking for Healy using Google, trying to capture a sense of who he was before it had all gone wrong. I met him in 2011, when his life was already unravelling, and had only known him as he was now. But that version of him wasn't the original. Before the twins, he'd been smart, lucid, accomplished.

History hadn't painted him as a failure.

In fact, quite the opposite.

I found countless quotes from him in relation to big cases he'd led, solved and closed. Further back, I discovered he'd won a Police Bravery Award in 2005 – something he'd never mentioned – for halting an armed robbery while off duty. There had been a photograph of him too, from 2008 – before the twins, before his marriage collapsed, before the tragic death of his own daughter – when he'd been at his heaviest. Three stone overweight, maybe more. His face was bloated, his cheeks flushed, his collar pinching at excess skin, and yet – despite the weight – there was a poise to him, a subtle confidence, a deftness and a strength that were difficult to define and harder to explain. But they were there, clear as day, as he'd been caught in the blink of that shutter.

Looking at that photo had made me wonder how it was that Healy had ended up getting the call about the twins. Was he asked because he was highly rated and his commanding officer knew he'd do his best by that family? Or was it more random? Did he just happen to be the nearest available man, or the only one in the office at the time? I imagined, if it was the second, he'd been over that moment countless times: what if he hadn't been able to take the case, or he'd been in the middle of something else? How would his life have been different? Either way, something was certain: the Met wouldn't have harboured any doubts about his competency. They'd have expected him to close the case.

Finally, my search had taken me to media accounts of the night the family were killed. Even within the confines of sanitized newspaper reports, the details had been incredibly hard to stomach, something instinctive taking flight in me as I'd read them: unease, anger; a sudden, powerful connection to Healy, as if I'd been able to sense what he must have been feeling as he'd been left there alone with the bodies, kneeling between their beds as the forensic team drifted away.

But what really brought it home wasn't any of

that. Instead, it was a YouTube video of a news conference that Healy had held on 16 July 2010, a fuzzy image of a Sky News reporter standing in front of the Scotland Yard sign, giving an introduction, talking about the case, about the family.

Thirty seconds in, Healy appeared.

He was perched behind a nest of microphones. He'd smartened up for the TV cameras: a tailored navy-blue suit, a silver-grey tie, his red hair parted at the side and combed through. He'd lost some weight in the two years between this and the photograph I'd seen of him earlier: half a stone, perhaps a bit more.

As I watched him, I realized how disconcerting it was seeing him like this – this professional, this together, the same man who'd completely fallen apart and ended up on the streets of the city. As he introduced himself and the other officers at the table, as he began reading from a prepared statement, I felt an odd kind of regret at never having met this version of him.

The feeling had lingered while I'd listened to him detailing the names of the victims, the circumstances of their deaths, the location, the viciousness of the crime. After a couple of minutes, he'd set aside the official statement and looked out at the crowd. 'I'll try and answer as many questions as I'm able,' he said, his voice clear, his Irish accent soft, 'but this is an ongoing investigation, so you'll appreciate that I can't answer everything.'

His eyes had scanned the room, fixing on

someone beyond the range of the Sky News camera, before nodding at them.

'Why were the whole family targeted?' a journalist had asked.

'At this stage, we're working from the assumption that the intended target was Gail Clark, but the investigation is fluid and that could change very quickly.'

'So the girls were collateral damage?'

Healy winced. 'I don't care for your choice of words.'

'What about the girls' father?'

There had been a pause, filled with the chatter of cameras going off and the gentle whir of rolling film. Healy's eyes lingered on the reporter who'd asked the question, and then he addressed everyone: 'Gail's former husband, and the girls' father, Kevin Sims, is deceased. He died six months after they were born. Given that, clearly he's not a line of inquiry we're pursuing. However, we would be interested in talking to a white male in his mid-to-late thirties, who was seen in Gail's company a number of times in the months before the family were killed.'

'Can you tell us anything else about this man?'

Again, Healy stopped for a moment, appearing to gather his thoughts. 'We believe he may be integral to finding out more about what happened earlier this week, so we appeal for that gentleman to come forward, or for anyone who thinks they might know anything relevant to get in touch with us immediately.'

'Was this man Gail Clark's boyfriend?'

'I can't confirm that at this stage.'

'But you already have witnesses, correct?'

'Again, I can't confirm that at this time – but as I stated previously, we have a number of leads we're pursuing.'

He'd offered nothing more and, shortly after, the footage had returned to the reporter at Scotland Yard. Five seconds after that, the video ended.

I'd continued searching online, rereading reports from the days that had followed the conference, and further soundbites from Healy. The more time that passed, the more the tone of his statements began to change, becoming terser and less engaged; he communicated less and less with the media, until he wasn't giving them anything at all. Three months into the case, despite the age of the victims and the horrific nature of the crimes, the story began fizzling out entirely, until – at the four-month mark – it became hard to find any stories on the family at all.

It had started with a press conference that Healy had hoped would zero in on the killer, and it had finished with failure, with resentment, with guilt. Maybe a man wasn't built to handle the weight of those things, even someone as world-weary as Healy had been. Maybe it was inevitable you would lose something of yourself in the middle of such carnage, finding the bodies of two children slaughtered in their sleep, but not the person who'd done it. It was bound to consume you – and do it slowly, piece by piece.

I'd felt an abrupt and genuine sense of sorrow for him then, perhaps for the first time since he'd returned to my life. Sorrow for the loss of a different, better version of him, for the waste of a good career, for the horrific deaths of the twins and their mother. And sorrow for the destruction of Healy's own family because he'd never been able to find the man responsible. As the feeling had grown, as I'd pushed aside my frustrations at him, I'd seen clearly what I had to do.

What I was always going to have to do.

I had to help him.

# CHAPTER 3

Twenty-four hours after I met Healy in the motel bar, snow began falling, drifting in from the northern fringes of the city, where black, swollen banks of cloud had gathered above the rooftops.

Having found their daughter and completed my part in the case, I left the family in Greenwich and headed west, along Blackheath Road, in the direction of New Cross. Traffic was heavy, brakes blinking in front of me, red smears against the drifting snow – but just as everything ground to a complete halt, I found the turning I'd been looking for, and pulled off the main road into Cork Hill Lane.

A few seconds later the noise of New Cross Road had vanished and a series of railway arches emerged from the night, the middle one straddling the road. On the other side of it was a sprawling council estate, endless doors embedded in a mixture of five-storey buildings and twenty-storey tower blocks. I pulled in at the kerb and switched off the engine. The radio went with it, plunging the car into silence, the falling snow adding to the lack of sound as it settled on the surrounding concrete.

I looked over my shoulder, into the back seat. A copy of the murder file sat there, pinched between the covers of a card folder and secured with an elastic band. When it had turned up in the post that morning, I'd toyed with the idea of holding it back from Healy, as motivation for him to get his life back on track. But I didn't have the stomach to use the death of a family as a bargaining chip, and as I sat here now – yards from where they'd been found – I felt another flutter of sadness for the girls, for their mother, even though I knew nothing about them; and I felt sorry for the man who'd eventually become so haunted by their deaths. In an hour, I was supposed to be meeting him back at the motel in Kew, to talk about the interview he'd had at the recruitment agency, and about some new jobs I'd sourced for him. But he wouldn't care about any of it – and being here, in the shadow of this place, maybe I understood better than ever why.

Immediately to my left, there was a small park, sitting in the space adjacent to the flats, a swing in the middle, on its own, moving gently in the wind. Everything – the grass, the swing, the blistered windowsills and fractured roofs – was being covered in a perfect, undisturbed blanket of snow.

I looked across to the tower block closest to me.

Searle House looked back.

It was twenty floors of misery, barely functioning,

and a decade past its prime. At ground level on this side, there was a huge, ugly wall – once painted white, now tagged with graffiti – dumpsters pushed against it, and black refuse bags spilling out on to the floor. As I looked at it, I recalled a moment from the day before: Healy staring out into the car park of the motel, suddenly distant, disconnected from our conversation, recalling the moment he'd found them: *I knelt down between their beds in the middle of that desperate fucking flat, their mam dead in the next room, every atom of innocence ripped from them, and I remember the forensic team left briefly, and I was alone with those girls, and I just* . . . He'd never finished what he was about to say, but as my eyes strayed to the seventeenth floor of Searle House, as the snow continued to fall silently around me, I could almost feel my way through to the next part.

He'd knelt down between them, so much anger in him, but so much sadness too, and felt a swell of responsibility. The weight of knowing that – by chance – he'd become their custodian, their conduit. Their avenger. And quietly, as the forensic team re-entered the room, he'd looked at the girls again, their eyes like lumps of chalk – empty, barren – and he'd told them he would find the man who did this.

Except he never did.

All the things that had happened to him since, mistakes he'd made, lies he'd told, every single failure, it had all started in this moment. *Here.*

This was the case that had broken him and cost him his career as a cop. This was what had shattered his family life, driven a wedge between him, his wife and his children.

This was the beginning of the end.

# CHAPTER 4

When I arrived back at the motel, it was virtually empty, the car park deserted, snow piled high in sludgy grey mounds, skeletal trees thrashing left to right as wind whipped in across the river. Healy was in the bar, at the same booth we'd occupied the night before. I apologized for being late, the detour to New Cross and the city's congested roads having made it a slow journey back, but he didn't reply, eyes already on the file I was holding. I handed it to him and got us both a drink.

By the time I returned with two coffees, he was a third of the way through the file, skim-reading pages, reminding himself of the interviews he'd led, and the work completed by the detectives under his command. His face was like stone, apparently unmoved by what he was reading, but it was all an act. I knew him too well, knew too much of his history, to believe he felt nothing as he returned to this open wound. It would have been the first time he'd looked through the file since he was cut loose by the Met, the first time in eighteen months he'd been so close to the family, to their murder, to the scars their deaths had inflicted upon him. Even if he didn't show it in his face, the file had got to him: he'd removed, and set aside, three printouts – each a photograph of one of them, on their own.

Gail Clark.

Abigail.

April.

He didn't want them to be a part of this file any more, associated with the words in it, the clinical descriptions, the suffering, the dead ends. Every so often, as he kept moving through the pages, his left hand would stray to the pictures – clearly unaware he was doing it – and his fingers would settle close to them all.

Eventually, half an hour later, he was done.

He looked up, a troubled expression in his face, and reached for his coffee. It had gone cold. 'Have you read any of this?' he said, placing the mug back down.

'Some.'

'But not all?'

'No. I wanted you to take me through it properly.'

I glanced at the file as another fuzzy colour printout of the family looked out at me. Pausing for a moment, eyes on the faces of the twins, on the face of the woman who had brought them into this world, I saw how much the girls looked like Gail: same colour hair; same slight bend in the nose from bridge to tip; same smile, one side of the mouth lifted a little higher than the other. Gail was plain, thin, her neck scrawny and loose, as if she'd lost too much weight too fast. She had bad skin as well, blotchy in the lines around her mouth, a trail of acne scarring around the cleft of her chin. But, like her, the twins had warm eyes, as perfect as pools of blue ink – and without any of the baggage of age, the girls were beautiful, flawless. As I looked at them, unable to tear my gaze away, something moved in me again.

'What did you make of it?'

I looked up. 'Make of what?'

'What you read.'

As I'd gone through the file, I'd been impressed once more at how tight Healy's police work was: the angles he'd worked and followed up, the theories he'd built and dismantled, how the interviews had been exhaustive but delicately handled. It didn't square with the man I'd come to know over the past two years, but it squared with the one I'd found online. This was the articulate, reasoned man I'd seen in quotes, the hulking figure who'd fronted press conferences, who'd calmly batted back and rebuked salacious tabloid questioning. This was the investigator that the Met had rated so highly, not the man who'd been sacked at the end.

'Raker?'

'It looks like a good case, Healy,' I said.

'But I missed something.'

I shrugged. 'I don't know. That's what we're about to find out.'

Ordering some fresh coffee, we began.

I decided to let Healy talk me through the time-line of the case as I made notes. When I had a question, I'd ask; otherwise I let him talk. As we started, it was clear that he had an uncanny recollection of the details, perhaps bolstered by having just looked at the file again. Occasionally, he would pull the paperwork towards him to double-check a fact – but mostly it was etched into his memory.

'Did you know she was a recovering drug addict?' he asked.

'Who, Gail?'

'We never ended up making it public, because once she became pregnant, she went into rehab and got off them for good. By the time she died, she'd been clean for almost nine years. Even so, we brought in the local dealer, the guy who used to supply her back in the day. He'd been making people's lives a misery down in New Cross for years, so he wasn't hard to find. But he wasn't our man. I also had one of my team call social services, just to make sure we hadn't missed anything – mistreatment of the twins, neglect in the intervening years, whatever – but it all came up clear. I remember chatting to one of her friends a few days after that.' He stopped, finding the relevant page in the file. 'I quote: "Gail was lovely, don't get me wrong, but after all her problems with drugs, I think she basically became scared about history repeating itself. So she stopped coming out. In fact, she hardly came out with us at all once the twins were born, because I guess there was less temptation that way. It made her more insular."'

Healy stopped, eyes flicking to the photograph of Gail.

'On the one hand,' he said, 'that meant we could quickly write off any connection between her drug problems and her death. On the other, the fact she stopped going out meant she never used to share anything with anyone. Most of the interviews we did with her so-called friends were a waste of time.'

'She was studying as well, right?'

'History and Social Science. But it was an Open University course, so – again – she was never around others while she was doing it. It was part-time. Six years, I think. She worked remotely, hadn't met her tutor face-to-face, hadn't even attended lectures with other students, apart from when she'd sat her final exams. She wrote her last paper a week before she was murdered.' He paused, fingers around his coffee mug, eyes down. 'I called the OU a couple of months later,' he said, quieter now, 'to see how she'd done. By then, it had really started to get to me that she had no one left who gave a shit about whether she'd passed or not.'

'Had she?'

A single nod of the head. 'With honours.'

'What about her parents?'

'Dead.'

'No brothers or sisters?'

'No. Best we could come up with was a cousin, Erica Swiddle. She lived up in Liverpool, though, so they rarely saw each other in the flesh. Swiddle told us the two of them used to chat on the phone every couple of months. That was it.'

'And the father?'

'The father of the girls? Kevin Sims. A waste of fucking oxygen. No one had anything good to say about him. Back in February 2001, he and Gail met at a pub in Peckham – he was twenty-four, she was twenty-one – and, five months later, she fell pregnant. We chatted to Sims's mother, who was still alive at the time, and she said he'd never mentioned the girls at all. She didn't even know she was a grandparent. Can you believe that shite?' Healy stopped; a twist of animosity, a shake of the head. 'The only person who could tell us anything in relation to Sims was Swiddle, Gail's cousin. She said Sims cleared off about two seconds after Gail told him she was expecting. The next time anyone heard from him was when he got himself killed six months after the twins were born, doing one hundred and twenty on the M23.'

'He died at the scene?'

'Yeah.'

I finished off some notes and, when I looked up, Healy was staring out of the window, into the car park, mirroring the position he'd been in the day before.

'You all right?' I asked.

31

He glanced at me. 'Yeah, I'm fine.'

'Are you ready to go on?'

He knew what I really meant by that. His recollection of the case, talking about it, leading me through it, seemed to have revived him somehow, bringing a subtle colour to him. But we'd only scratched the surface.

The worst was yet to come.

He took a long breath, then nodded.

'Okay,' I said. 'Tell me about what you found at the flat.'

# CHAPTER 5

'That place,' he said, 'it was pretty pokey.'
In the file, there was a top-down layout of the flat, reinforcing what Healy was saying. A hallway ran from the front door to the living room at the back. On the left were two rooms, both bedrooms, the first belonging to Gail, the second to the girls. On the right was a kitchen and then the bathroom. Whoever had constructed the map had drawn in windows too: in the kitchen and the living room.

But nowhere else.

'There were no windows in the bedrooms?'

He shook his head. 'No. The bedrooms were up against the flat next door. No windows in them; no skylights, obviously. I remember one of the first things I asked when I arrived was for the lights to be put on. But they already *were* on.'

I nodded and waited for him to continue.

'The girls were in their beds,' he said, pausing, clearing his throat. 'They were lying on their backs, dressed in identical pyjamas, and had been completely covered by their duvets. They'd had their throats cut.' He stopped again, for longer this time, and as he did, my eyes dropped to the file, swallowing as I read the sterile description of what had been done to them, unable to get the sour taste out of my mouth. Healy continued: 'As soon as I got there, as soon as I saw them, I thought to myself, "Why the fuck did *I* end up with this? Why not someone else?" I'd been at the Met twenty-four years by then – but anything with kids, it still got to me like it was my first day on the beat. A little bit of you dies and doesn't come back every time kids are involved.'

He had both elbows on the table, his hands locked together in front of his face, his eyes off beyond me. 'When I got home that night, I found Leanne alone in her room, listening to music,' he went on, talking about his own daughter now. She would have been nineteen at the time. 'I just went in, and I grabbed her, and I held her. She didn't understand why – she tried to shrug me off initially – but eventually she went along with it. I don't know . . . I just had to know that my girl was safe.'

A flicker of emotion flashed in his face as he realized the prescience of those last few words: only six months later, Leanne was taken from him, equally cruelly.

Another case, another killer.

Another lost life.

'Anyway,' he said, clearing his throat again and taking down a mouthful of coffee, 'Gail was in the living room. She was slumped sideways on the sofa, half pressed up against the wall, in a night-dress and dressing gown. It seemed pretty obvious that all three of them had been murdered late evening, and that Gail had known the prick who did it. There was no sign of a break-in at the flat, no sign of a struggle either – and none of her neighbours heard screams or raised voices.'

'So she wasn't frightened of him.'

'The opposite. I think she happily invited him in. She didn't bother getting changed, which meant she was either comfortable around this guy or she didn't expect him to stay long. Lividity put her where she was found, so given the lack of a struggle, no defensive wounds, no signs of sexual assault, I think – when he came at her – she was relaxed.' He stopped, eyes dropping to the black-and-white descriptions of Gail's death. They weren't black and white to Healy. 'He stabbed her nine times in the chest.'

'Sounds pretty frenzied.'

'It wasn't. The wounds were all close together, almost on top of one another, like he'd chosen a spot and was making sure. I think he was a professional.'

I looked at him. 'What do you mean, "professional"?'

'I mean, he'd killed before. There was no worth-while DNA under her fingernails, no evidence she'd had the chance to fight back – scratched, fought, got in a strike of her own. You don't stab someone nine times without them getting even as

35

much as a retaliatory hit in, unless you're *really* good at it.'

'What about DNA elsewhere?'

'Worthless.'

'Nothing at all?'

'We found DNA from other people on Gail's dressing gown, and under her fingernails, but it wasn't semen or saliva, it was hairs and flakes of skin from the family, and from other, unidentified individuals. They could have belonged to the killer – or they could have belonged to friends, passing through the flat over the course of months. If the DNA *did* belong to our man, he wasn't in the database.'

Suddenly, my phone started ringing, buzzing across the table towards me. It was my daughter. I turned it to silent. 'It's just Annabel,' I said to Healy. 'I'll call her back when we're done here.'

I flipped back in my notes to some I'd made while watching the video of Healy at the press conference a couple of nights before.

'You said someone had been seen with Gail and the girls in the months leading up to their murder?'

He nodded. 'Mal.'

'Mal?'

'M-A-L, as in Malcolm.'

'That was his name?'

Healy shrugged. 'Who knows? Basically, her neighbour on the right side was this woman called Sandra Westerwood. Proper busybody in her late sixties, but quite sweet, and she really loved that family. She was the one that called the police because she hadn't heard Gail or the girls in a while.'

He flicked forward in the file, found what he was after, then swivelled it around to face me. It was a transcript from his interview with Westerwood.

WESTERWOOD: I could hear those girls next door, every day, singing their songs, playing their games . . . all the sorts of things kids do at that age, you know? But then it stopped. I thought it was weird, because those bloody flats, they've got walls like paper, and the only time that building goes silent is in the middle of the night when everyone's finally asleep. I thought to myself, 'Maybe they're on holiday.' But they hadn't mentioned anything about going away, and Gail often talked about being short of money.

HEALY: When was the last time you heard them?

WESTERWOOD: Sunday, maybe Monday.

HEALY: Today's Friday 16 July. So you stopped hearing from them on Sunday 11 July or Monday 12 July, correct?

WESTERWOOD: Yeah.

HEALY: When we spoke at your flat yesterday,

you said you'd been around to see Gail on Saturday 10 July.

WESTERWOOD: Right. I ran out of sugar. I wanted a cup of tea but the elevator was bust, and I didn't want to have to walk down seventeen flights of stairs, and then half a mile to the bloody Co-op. So I asked Gail if she could spare some.

HEALY: She seemed okay?

WESTERWOOD: She seemed fine. I could see the girls from the door, watching TV. Gail and me, we spoke for a while.

HEALY: About what?

WESTERWOOD: I don't know. The weather or whatever. But she was fine. Laughing and smiling, you know?

HEALY: That was the last time you saw her?

WESTERWOOD: Last time. Everything went quiet after that. I went round to check on them on Tuesday, cos I thought that would be the right thing to do, and there was no answer. I tried again Wednesday morning, and then Wednesday evening. Yesterday was when I called you lot.

I looked up at Healy, unsure exactly of how this was relevant. It filled out some of the background, particularly with regard to how the police ended up at Searle House in the first place, but there was no mention of the man the family had been seen with in the months before their deaths; the man Healy had talked about at the press conference in the days after, and had told me was called 'Mal'.

As if reading my mind, he moved forward a couple of pages in the interview transcript, then tapped a line halfway down. 'Once we got confirmation that the family were killed on Sunday 11 July,' he said, 'rather than on the Monday, we started zeroing in on what she said to us here.'

WESTERWOOD: I simply can't imagine who would want to do that to them. I mean, they were such a lovely family. Do you think it might have been her boyfriend?

HEALY: Boyfriend?

WESTERWOOD: Oh, I thought she was dating someone.

HEALY: Did she say she was?

WESTERWOOD: No. I just saw her and the girls with a man in the months before they were killed, so I guessed he was . . . you know . . . someone she was seeing.

HEALY: Where did you see him?

WESTERWOOD: There's a play park and a football pitch on one side of Searle House.

The park's got some swings, a climbing frame, some slides, that sort of thing. I definitely remember seeing him there with the girls a few times.

HEALY: How many times?

WESTERWOOD: Oh, quite a few.

HEALY: When was the first time, do you remember?

WESTERWOOD: I guess it must have been about February, because my sister's birthday is the twentieth, and I remember heading down to the Tube at New Cross Gate to go and see her, and they were all out there. I thought to myself that it would be nice if Gail could find someone.

HEALY: So Gail and this guy could have been dating from February, all the way through to July? That's five months.

WESTERWOOD: Yes.

HEALY: Did she tell you his name?

WESTERWOOD: No, but . . .

HEALY: What?

WESTERWOOD: I remember hearing the girls one day, when they were outside playing with him, and they called him something. I think it was 'Mal'.

HEALY: As in Malcolm?

WESTERWOOD: Yeah, I think so.

HEALY: When else did you see the family with him?

WESTERWOOD: Oh, I don't know. Um . . . lots of times, but generally when they were all at the park.

HEALY: You ever get up close to him?

WESTERWOOD: No.

HEALY: So you didn't ever speak to him?

WESTERWOOD: No. But I often wondered whether he might have been some sort of delivery driver.

HEALY: What makes you say that?

WESTERWOOD: He was wearing this olive-green shirt one time, beneath his jacket, and I remember thinking it looked like the sort of shirt a delivery man might wear.

HEALY: Did you ever see him wearing that shirt again?

WESTERWOOD: I can't remember.

HEALY: I really need you to think hard, Sandra.

WESTERWOOD: No. I don't think so.

41

HEALY: So it might just have been an olive-green shirt, not a shirt associated with a particular delivery company?

WESTERWOOD: I suppose so, yeah.

HEALY: Did Gail seem concerned by his presence?

WESTERWOOD: Oh no, definitely not. She seemed happy. She and the girls seemed to be comfortable with him.

At the end of the interview with Westerwood, she'd given a description of the man, but the results were vague: white, five-ten to six feet tall, black hair, mid-to-late thirties, medium build. That was never likely to take investigators very far.

'The Malcolm thing was just one big blind alley,' Healy said, rubbing together the fingers and thumb of his right hand. The coarseness of his skin made a crackling noise. 'My team came back with a list of over eleven thousand men with the first name Malcolm in the Greater London area alone. And what if it *wasn't* Malcolm? What if it was Malachi or something else? What if he wasn't even *from* London? We didn't have the resources to cope with that level of search. The only thing that really went our way was that, according to Westerwood, this guy was Caucasian – that meant we could, at least, discount names like Malik and Jamal.'

'She said he might have been a delivery driver.'

He shook his head.

'That didn't lead anywhere either?'

'Conjecture. We didn't have any other witness statements to back her up, and although people told us they *might* have seen delivery vans in and around the estate in the weeks and months leading up to the murders, no one could say for sure whether they'd seen the *same* van returning over and over. We looked for businesses using olive-green uniforms, we doorstepped delivery companies all over the city, and we got nothing.'

The size of the task facing Healy's team had been formidable: taking a list of 11,236 men called Malcolm, narrowing it down to those in their thirties with black hair and a medium build, then trying to narrow it down further by focusing on those who may have been employed as delivery drivers. That was even assuming Westerwood had heard the man's name correctly, and the green shirt *had* in fact been his uniform. Healy, clearly, remained doubtful.

'So that line of inquiry stalled?'

'Yeah.' He stopped, sniffed, shrugged. 'We found delivery drivers called Malcolm who didn't match the physical description Westerwood had provided, and men called Malcolm who weren't delivery drivers, but matched the physical description. We didn't find a single person who fit convincingly into both camps.'

'What about CCTV footage?'

He looked at me. 'That should have been our best lead.'

'But it was another dead end?'

'The council didn't give a shit about the estate, so nothing worked there. We had three cameras that could have got us something half-decent. One was at the tenth-floor stairwell, but it was bust. It had been vandalized back in February, and no one had been round to repair it. Then there were two cameras on the outside of the building: one faced Cork Hill Lane, which is the only way in and out by car – that's where you must have parked earlier on.'

I nodded. 'And the other?'

'The other camera faced down towards the play park. That's where you'd approach if you were coming from the Tube station.'

'So what happened?'

'The one facing the play park had wiring problems, which meant the feed repeatedly cut out.' He shook his head, chewing on his frustration. 'The further back in time we went, the less pronounced the problems got, so on 26 March we actually found something: an unidentified man, at the swings, with the Clark family. The man matched the description of "Mal" from what we could tell, but they were too far away to make out much detail, and eventually they headed towards the Tube. It was the only time that we caught all four of them on film.'

'What about *before* the camera on the tenth floor packed up?'

'You mean, was there any video of him with the

family prior to February? No. Maybe that was because he and Gail only officially started dating in the March, or maybe it just meant he was clever enough to stay out of shot – at least until he made a mistake on 26 March, and we got him on film at the play park. Either way, it never made much difference. Even when we *did* get him, he was just a blur.'

'So only one camera was working the night they were killed.'

'Yeah.'

'Did you get anything from it?'

He was rubbing his fingers harder now, his muscles and tendons trying to find the cigarette that wasn't there, even while his thoughts remained tethered to the case and its maze of dead ends. Eventually, he reached into his pocket and removed a lighter – placing it next to his coffee on the table – and then a packet of cigarettes. The movement pulled him from his daze, and he glanced at the file.

'Healy?'

'It was all just a load of shite,' he said quietly.

'What was?'

'Everything. If the case had been a dog, you'd have put the fucking thing down. No motive, no DNA, vague witnesses, eleven thousand men with a name that might not even be relevant.' He paused, shifting the cigarette packet around in front of him, opening and closing the lid. Eventually, he picked up the file and began to riffle through its pages again, flipping forward to another witness statement.

When he found it, he returned the file to me.

'What's this?' I said.

'About the only thing worth a damn.'

But I never got the chance to read it.

# CHAPTER 6

A second later, my phone began buzzing again.

It was Annabel for a second time. I glanced at Healy, then back to the phone. We were right in the middle of something, and I could see he expected me to let the call go to voicemail – but it was rare for Annabel to phone out of the blue, even rarer for her to press the issue like this. She was twenty-five, independent, completely self-sufficient, and because she worked with kids, in schools, in clubs, she was a big believer in routine and structure. If she was calling me, and she hadn't mentioned that she would call me, something was up.

'I'm going to have to take this,' I said to him.

He frowned. 'Can't it wait?'

'It's Annabel.'

'So?'

'So, I need to take it.'

'Just phone her back when we're done.'

'I'm taking the call, Healy.'

His eyes flicked between the file – open on the page he'd selected for me – to the phone in my hand. 'This is bullshit,' he whispered, but loud enough for me to hear, and then started to slide out of the booth, propping a cigarette between his lips. Without another word, he headed for the exit. Outside, snow was falling like clumps of wet paper, hard and fast; a man from the motel – hood on, zip up to his chin – was desperately trying to grit the car park as wind ripped off the river. Healy emerged from the front, cigarette already lit, a pissed-off expression on his face.

I pressed Answer.

'Hey sweetheart.'

'Hey,' Annabel said quietly.

'Are you okay?'

'It's Olivia.'

I felt a moment of panic.

Olivia was her nine-year-old sister. Annabel and I had only discovered the truth about our relationship fourteen months ago – and while, biologically, Olivia wasn't mine, the minute Annabel entered my life, they both entered my life.

'What about her? Is she okay?'

'I'm in Torquay,' she said, her words a little smudged. It was clear she'd been crying. 'At the hospital. We've had loads of snow here, and she went out on the sledge with one of her friends – just down to the field at the end of our road.' Annabel burst into tears. 'She hit a tree. She's in surgery at the moment. I just . . .' She faded out.

'Okay,' I said, trying to sound calm. 'It's okay.'

'She's got internal bleeding.'

My heart sank. *Shit.*

'I'm sorry,' she said. 'I didn't know who else to call.'

'Don't apologize,' I said to her, my mind already shifting forward. 'You did the right thing calling me.'

I paused, looking out of the window at Healy. He was halfway through his cigarette, its molten orange glow winking in the snow as he took another drag.

'What have the doctors said?'

'Nothing.'

'They haven't explained her injuries?'

'I'm not sure they know yet.' She stopped, sniffed, obviously trying to regain her composure. 'They just said she had internal injuries and they had to get her straight into surgery. I don't know what to do. What am I going to do if . . .' She started crying again.

I tried to clear my head. There was just no way I could leave her in that hospital alone.

'I'm setting off now,' I said to her.

'You don't have to—'

'I want to.' I glanced out of the window. Healy was in the same spot, his gaze fixed on the man from the motel as he dragged a big bag of grit back towards the entrance. 'It's going to take me four hours, maybe longer, especially in the snow. But I want you to keep me up to date, okay? Phone me any time. If you can't get answers from the doctors, you give me their name, and I'll speak to them.'

'Thank you.'

'All right. I'll speak to you in a sec.'

I ended the call, pocketed my phone and glanced at the file, open on the table in front of me. Healy had been directing my attention to another statement, this time from a witness called Joban Kehal. I grabbed a pen from my jacket and starred the page so I knew where to come back to, then I collected up the three pictures of the family that Healy had set aside and returned them to the case file. Taking the file and my phone, I headed out of the bar and into the narrow foyer.

Healy was already back inside.

'I've got to go,' I said to him.

He stopped, frowning. 'What?'

'I'll take this with me and read it when I'm down there.'

'Down where?'

'I need to see Annabel.'

'You're going down to *Devon*?'

'Olivia's been in an accident.'

The next part of his response had already been on his lips – *What the hell are you going to Devon for when we're right in the middle of something?* – but, at the mention of Olivia's accident, he stopped himself. His lips flattened, almost as if he were trying to hold the words in, and I could see his brain kicking into gear.

'Is she going to be okay?'

I shrugged. 'I don't know.'

'What happened?'

'She was out on her sledge and hit a tree.'

He nodded. 'I'm sure she'll be fine.'

'Yeah, well, I need to make sure.'

He glanced at the file. 'You taking that?'

'I'm going to read over it.'

'While you're driving?'

He said it flatly, but that didn't mask the acidity.

'She's on an operating table with internal bleeding,' I said. 'Shall I just ignore that and sit here for another hour, or two, or three, talking about this file?'

'You don't think it's important. I get it.'

'Don't twist my words. Are you actually listening to what I'm saying?'

I looked at him, waiting for a comeback.

I got nothing in return.

'Whatever,' I said. 'I'm going. I'll call you tomorrow.'

As I headed out, he said, 'Leave the file.'

I turned. 'I'm going to *look* at it, okay?'

He shook his head, something shifting in his expression, and I understood. He wasn't suggesting I leave it because I already had enough to think about. He wanted me to leave it because he was going to go off and work the case himself.

'No,' I said.

'I already know everything in there, anyway.'

'So why are you asking for it back?'

He eyed me. 'Just give me the fucking file.'

'Look,' I said, biting my tongue, trying hard to keep the frustration out of my voice. 'You've got

51

that interview at the builders' merchants first thing in the morning. Maybe concentrate on that for now, and then I'll give you a call at lunch tomorrow and we can pick up where we left off with the file—'

'I'm not going.'

'What?'

'I'm not going to that interview.'

'What are you talking about?'

'Exactly what I just said. I'm not going.'

I took a step towards him. 'It's a decent job.'

'It's store security.'

'The money's really good.'

He shrugged.

I rubbed at my forehead, trying to suppress my anger. 'Can you just do me this one favour? Please. I need you to go to this interview tomorrow because I know the guy who runs the company and he's the major reason you've made the short-list. I talked him into giving you a shot. He pulled strings to get you this interview. So if you don't turn up tomorrow morning, it makes me look like a—'

'I don't care.'

'I *organized* this for you, Healy.'

'Then unorganize it – because I'm not going.'

I moved even closer to him. 'What the hell's the matter with you?'

'Nothing's the matter with—'

'I *told* you I would help you with this case.' I held up the file in front of him. 'I've just *said* I will look

52

at it. *I'll look at it*. Okay? How much clearer can I make it for you? But I need you to be in Deptford tomorrow for this interview. This job, you will have to *seriously* screw it up not to be in with a chance of getting it. Do you understand me? All you need to do is turn up there and say the right things.'

Over Healy's shoulder, one of the motel staff was watching us from the counter, a disapproving look on her face, and I realized how loud I'd become.

I took a long breath. 'I've got to go.'

Healy glanced at the file again and then opened both his hands out in a *Do what you want* gesture. It annoyed me, but this time I refused to rise to the bait.

'I need you to be at that interview tomorrow,' I said.

Before he could reply, I headed for the exit.

# CHAPTER 7

When my wife, Derryn, died of breast cancer in 2009, I gave up all hope of becoming a parent. But one moment of immaturity a quarter of a century ago, with a girlfriend I'd had at school, had eventually returned to the surface and changed my life.

For Annabel and I, the first six months of our relationship had been hard: there was a will to know one another better on both sides, but she was mourning the loss of people she thought had been her parents, and I was trying to come to terms with not only being a father, but being a father to a woman more than half my age. But as soon as I saw her in the hospital waiting room, I felt an indelible pull towards her, an obligation, a certainty that being here with her, and dropping everything at the motel, was the only choice I could have made. This was what a father did for his daughter.

Healy, of all people, should have known that.

It was hard to see Olivia in such a state, her tiny, nine-year-old body wired up to breathing apparatus, an ECG, a drip, bandages at her breastbone and

54

along her right side. The staff were good enough to let Annabel and me stay and, overnight, we sat with Olivia on rotation: while one of us perched at her bedside, the other tried to get some rest in a faded blue nursing chair on the other side of the room. Fortunately, she held steady, and when we talked to the doctor in the morning, he said things were looking positive but there was a long way to go.

At lunchtime, I went to get us both some food and coffee, and when I returned, I found Annabel sobbing, the events of the previous day, and a long night of fitful sleep, finally getting on top of her. In fourteen months, I hadn't seen her cry much, and not only because she lived two hundred and fifteen miles from me. The lies of her past, the loss of the people she'd thought of – and loved – as her mum and dad, a sister who had basically become like a daughter – those things had slowly set like concrete, and although she was never difficult or remote with me, she'd become phlegmatic, perhaps inevitably.

'Sorry,' she said after a while.

'Why are you apologizing?'

'I'm a mess.'

I touched a hand to her shoulder, and she took it in hers, using her other hand to dab at her eyes with a tissue. When she was done, I handed her a coffee and placed a pre-packaged sandwich on the edge of the bed.

'Did I pull you away from something?' she said.

I looked down at her. 'What do you mean?'

'A case. It's just, you look tired.'

'Do I?'

'And I don't mean from trying to sleep upright in a hospital all night.' She smiled and I didn't reply, hoping that would be the end of it. 'Are you on a case?'

'I've just finished one.'

'Was it tough?'

'No, it was pretty straightforward.'

*It's the last seven days with Healy that have been tough.*

She started opening her sandwich packet. 'I don't mean to pry,' she said. 'Sorry if it seems that way. You just look like you might need a break from it all.'

'Maybe we could all do with a break.'

She nodded, but I got the sense that this line of questioning hadn't been put to bed yet. And I understood the reasons why: a few months before, she'd been dragged into a case I'd worked, and although neither she nor Olivia had been in any danger, it hadn't seemed like it at the time. I felt a pang of guilt for that, for the fact it was still playing on her mind, and for what lay behind her asking: her need to be reassured that I wasn't going to put them at risk again.

'Everything's quiet at the moment,' I said.

I called Healy from the front of the hospital.

It was cold, snow thick on roofs and sills, on a patch of grass in the middle of a turning circle directly in front of me. I found his number in my address book and then paused for a moment, taking a breath, stealing myself for a fight. But I needn't have bothered: after eleven unanswered rings, his voicemail kicked in.

'Healy, it's me. Give me a call when you get this.'

I hung up and headed back inside – but then the phone started buzzing in my hand again. On the display was a central London number I didn't recognize.

I answered it. 'David Raker.'

'David, it's Simon Quinn.'

Quinn ran the builders' merchants in Deptford where Healy was supposed to have gone for an interview that morning. I'd met him five years ago at a charity golf tournament organized by a friend of mine, and we'd kept in touch – on and off – ever since.

'Simon. How's things?'

'Yeah, okay,' he said, but as soon as I heard the hum of annoyance in his voice, I knew what was coming: 'I thought you'd want to know about your friend.'

'Let me guess: he didn't turn up.'

'No,' Quinn said, 'Colm turned up.'

'So what was the problem?'

Quinn paused. 'The problem was that he was drunk.'

# CHAPTER 8

Healy finally called me at seven o'clock. I was in the hospital foyer checking my emails, and as I looked at the display, at the number of the mobile phone I'd bought for Healy, I paused, trying to douse my anger. I'd been calling him all afternoon, had texted him, left more messages, spent ten minutes apologizing to Simon Quinn for wasting his time, and another ten defending Healy to him. It had become such an involuntary action, something I did so often, it was almost like a reflex kicking in.

'It's me,' he said after I answered.

'How is it possible to be drunk at nine in the morning?'

He didn't respond.

'Healy?'

'I told you last night that I wasn't going—'

'You *embarrassed* me.' A few people glanced in my direction, so I moved to a quieter corner. 'Why couldn't you just turn up and answer their questions?'

'I did.'

'Sober.'

'Look, I went to that interview today like you asked, and I answered all their stupid fucking questions, and then one of them accused me of lying to her.'

'About what?'

He sighed, the noise crackling down the phone line. It sounded like he might still be drunk, the edges of his words soft, his exasperation amplified.

'About *what*, Healy?'

'"Why haven't you included anyone from the Met as a reference?"'

'That's what she asked you?'

'Yep. So, I made up some story about it being a mistake on the CV, and she saw through it. She actually sat there googling me during the interview, and then steamrollers me with all the details she found online about the day I got sacked.'

'I told you to include Melanie Craw's name on there.'

'*Craw?* Is that a *joke?*'

'She's a DCI at the Met. She's prepared to give you a reference.'

'Craw was the one that *fired* me.'

'Listen. I've spoken to her. I told you a week ago to put her name on your CV. I've told you *every bloody day this week*. Why won't you just listen to—'

'Don't you get it? All these interviews, these morons I've got to pretend to be nice to – and for what? For some two-bit job in a builders' merchants?'

59

'Healy—'

'We should be finding out who killed that family.'

That stopped me. The file was still in the back of my car, untouched from the day before. 'I promised I'd help you, and that we'd find out what happened to that family. And I will. I'll do that, Healy. But I also asked you to do two things for me in return. One of them was to let me help you get a job, and the other was—'

'I bet you haven't even looked at it.'

'And the *other* was you had to stay off the booze.'

'I bet you haven't even *looked* at that file.'

I sighed. 'Come on, Healy. My daughter is—'

'*Your* daughter, *your* daughter – what about *my* fucking daughter? She's in the cemetery now because some piece of shit took her from me. What about the daughters of Gail Clark? What about them? The arsehole who cut their throats is still out there somewhere, walking around without a care in the world.'

'I told you: we'll find him.'

'Yeah? When are we going to do that?'

'When I get back.'

'Which is when?'

I tried to clear my head.

'Which is *when*?' he repeated.

'I don't know yet—'

'*Exactly*. You don't know yet. You're sitting around in hospital with a girl that doesn't belong to you, and another you didn't even realize was yours until a year ago. I had to *bury* my daughter.

I was there when she was born, I was there when she died, and I remember everything from the twenty years in between. You're there because you *think* you should be there. You're not there because you *feel* it. How can you? You don't even know them. They're strangers.'

'That's enough, Healy,' I said, trying to sound calm.

'Don't patronize me. I know what—'

'You were living in a homeless shelter seven days ago – are you capable of thinking back that far? I'm helping you find a job. I'm putting petrol in your car so you can get to interviews. I'm paying for a motel while you organize somewhere else to stay. Do you know what that means? Have you got even the faintest *idea*?'

'No,' he said. 'What does it mean?'

'It means I'm the only person you've got left.'

No reply.

'Call me back when you've sobered up.'

'You think I'm a charity case, is that it?'

'Just call me back tomorrow, Healy.'

'How about I don't?'

This time I said nothing, not wanting this conversation to spiral any further out of control – but my lack of reply only seemed to make him angrier.

'How about I *don't*?'

'I'm ending this call before you say something you *really* regret.'

'You don't know what it's like to mourn *anything*.

Not properly. You'd barely even buried your wife before you were balls-deep in your next-door neighbour. You probably couldn't wait to get your missus in the fucking ground.'

'*What?*'

'Were you glad she got cancer?'

'What the fuck did you just say?'

'You heard what I said.'

I was so angry I could feel it tremoring through my chest, clawing at my throat, the heat like a fog in my head. 'Don't ever speak about her like that,' I said, barely able to force the words out. 'You haven't got a clue what it was—'

'You and me, Raker . . .'

'What, Healy? You and me *what?*'

He paused for a long time. 'You and me are done.'

The words pulsed along the line.

'Well,' I said, 'at least you've finally got something right.'

I hung up.

I wouldn't see him again for nine months.

# PART II

# 2 OCTOBER 2014

# CHAPTER 9

The restaurant was in a converted textile factory, west of Walthamstow Marshes. Perched right on the banks of the River Lea, it was a red-brick, single-storey building with a series of identical windows, each one framed under individual gables. At the nearest end to the car park was the entrance, an ornate, wood-carved doorway with a blackboard leaning against one of its walls, and a faux-Victorian welcome sign. Two lines of six tables were on the gravel outside, matching umbrellas standing sentry at each one.

Two days into October, and with summer showing no signs of waning, the restaurant was packed, people at every table, more on the banks of the river watching boats glide past. At first I couldn't see her among the crowds, and wondered whether she was inside. But then she came into view at the furthest table away from me, staring into space, hand clamped around a glass of water.

'Afternoon,' I said as I reached her.

DCI Melanie Craw turned, removing her sunglasses. She looked out at the crowds around her, at the people queuing up for a table, and then her gaze returned to me. 'Afternoon,' she replied, the merest hint of a smile on her lips.

'There are some paparazzi watching us from the boats.'

She rolled her eyes and put her sunglasses back on.

I sat down. 'What are you doing out in this neck of the woods?'

'Waltham Forest has got a suspect I might be interested in.' She looked at her watch, then out at the crowds again. 'Weaselly piece of shit. You'd like him.'

It was my turn to smile this time.

Craw was forty-four, slim, understated, immaculately dressed in a grey trouser-suit. Ten months ago, she'd asked me to find her missing father. In coming to me, she'd not only gone against protocol, she'd employed someone whom the Met viewed with deep suspicion. I didn't seek out the running battles I'd had with them – far from it – but the conflict was a consequence of my work. Most of the time, when families came to me, it was in the months after the official trail had gone cold.

The irony was, she'd probably harboured more doubts about employing me than anyone. Before I'd agreed to help her, we'd had a series of bitter confrontations during my search for another missing person. But, after I finally brought her answers about her father, perhaps when she'd seen more closely what my cases meant to me and why I never relinquished my grip on them, things changed. She was still a little nervous in public, but in private her defences had lowered.

We'd been to dinner a few times, met in public parks where we'd watch her girls play. Nothing had happened, and perhaps it never would. Yet I liked her company, and as difficult as she was to break down, it was clear the same was true for her. She was so different from Derryn, and from Liz, my former neighbour, who had come after – more guarded, more stoic. Despite that, I identified with her, particularly with the person she tried to hide in her professional life, where she was running a Murder Investigation Team of twenty-eight, twenty-six of whom were men. At the end – when I'd found out what had happened to her father – I saw that hidden side of her clearly: fiercely intelligent, conflicted, vulnerable just like everyone else.

'So why make me come all the way over here?' I asked.

'I wanted to talk to you.'

'About?'

She checked her watch again. It was just before one. When she looked up, she gestured for the waiter to come over. 'Do you want something to eat?'

'Is the Met paying?'

She smiled again. 'You're a funny man, Raker.'

I ordered a steak, salad and coffee; Craw went for a chicken sandwich and another glass of mineral water. When the waiter was gone, she glanced off, past the edges of the restaurant, to where a conga line of kids was racing towards a rust-speckled iron bridge, its feet straddling the river. On the other side were the marshes, mown trails criss-crossing through sun-scorched, knee-high grass.

'Craw?'

She turned back to me. We hadn't quite manoeuvred ourselves away from using surnames yet. Old habits died hard, but there was something else to it too: I could see it brought her a level of comfort, anchoring her to a more familiar time – one when she was more confined and had to give less of herself away.

'Colm Healy,' she said.

His name stopped me dead. 'What about him?'

'When was the last time you talked to him?'

I knew straight away when the last time was, but I paused for a moment, trying to figure out why it would be of interest to Craw. 'It was 16 January. Why?'

'What happened?'

*He insulted me, my daughter, my relationship with her.*

*The memory of my wife.*

'Raker?'

'I'd met up with him a week before that, on 8 January. He'd wanted to get together, so we went to a café in Hammersmith. Then, on the sixteenth, we . . .'

'What?'

'We had a disagreement.'

'What does that mean?'

'He said some things that I couldn't let pass.'

Craw knew what that meant. She'd once put her entire reputation on the line by backing Healy's reintegration into the Met. At the time, he'd just come out of a two-month suspension. She'd vouched for him because she'd seen something good in him, the instincts of a gifted investigator, the humility of a damaged man, and for a while it had worked. But then Healy had self-destructed. That was what he did. That was what made him so frustrating. He was scarred by rooted, painful wounds, but behind the barricades, the aggression, the ire, was a different man; a better, quieter one. It was just hard to imagine it sometimes; even harder when I cast my mind back to what he'd said to me on the phone about my wife's death.

'Why are you asking about Healy?'

She shifted forward in her seat, and some of the opacity left her sunglasses. I could see her eyes on the crowds again, looking out for anyone she might know, for anyone that might be able to place the two of us here, right now, together.

'So you parted on bad terms?' she said.

'He'd been drinking earlier in the day. I told him to call me back when he was sober.'

'And he didn't?'

'Well, I haven't heard from him since.'

'Do you think he's still drunk?'

It was a half-joke, but neither of us was smiling.

69

I leaned back in my seat, and watched a boat crawl along the water. 'Look, before January I hadn't seen him in the flesh for over a year. He just went AWOL. The only contact I had with him during that time was a phone call in December, when I was looking for your old man, as the two of them used to work together. I didn't expect to hear from him after that – but first week of January he suddenly calls me up and wants to meet. So I met him on the eighth, near Hammersmith Bridge.'

'And what happened?'

I shrugged. 'As soon as I got there, it was clear something was rubbing at him. He was agitated. He'd basically . . .' I stopped. *He'd basically hit rock bottom.*

'He'd basically what?'

'He was living in a homeless hostel.'

She frowned. '*What?*'

When she saw I was serious, neither of us said anything for a while. In a way, before she'd hired me to find her father, before Craw and I had begun whatever this was between us, Healy had been the only thing we'd had in common: our shared irritation at him, our regret, our sorrow at the way he'd allowed his life to cave in. 'Anyway,' I continued, 'he said he wanted my help.'

'To do what?'

'To find out who killed the twins – that family.'

She started shaking her head and only stopped when the waiter arrived with our drinks. After he was gone, she leaned forward. 'What did you say to that?'

'I said I'd help him.'

She sighed. 'That's an open case, Raker.'

'It's over four years old.'

'That's irrelevant.'

'It's dead in the water, and we both know it.'

'So you're working murders as well as missing people now?'

'Don't be like that.'

'Like what?'

I studied her for a moment. 'When I met him, he was in a state.'

'He's always in a state.'

'Not like this.'

'So what else did he say?'

'Why are you so interested in him?'

She smirked. 'What else did he say?'

The sun had moved around in the sky, light escaping in under the lip of the umbrella, heat nipping at my arm. I shifted sideways so that I was back in the shade, and watched her. Over the past ten months, Craw hadn't just changed emotionally. She leaned back and tucked her blonde hair behind her ears, shoulder-length now rather than short, and began playing with a thin gold chain at her throat. I'd never seen her wear any jewellery while working, and the chain was only a small concession, but small changes spoke of a greater shift: she didn't want to be the same person as she'd been when she'd first hired me, for reasons she'd laid to rest alongside the memory of her father. And yet there were still moments, almost a year on, when it was much harder to see the change in her. As she watched me through mirrored shades – able to see me, unable to be seen back now – I caught clear flashes of who she'd been before, her face like an echo: unreadable, blank.

I shook my head. 'Are we really still doing this dance?'

She swallowed, said nothing.

'Craw?'

She pushed her half-finished glass of water aside. As she pulled the fresh one towards her, fingers smearing the condensation, she took off her glasses. The silence between us was filled with the excited screams of kids on the bridge, by the chug of narrowboats on the river.

Eventually, she looked up, a mix of steel and regret in her eyes. 'You ever meet Healy's ex-wife?'

'Gemma. Yeah, once. Why?'

'Six weeks ago, she filed a missing persons report.'

'What – for *Healy*?'

She nodded. 'I think you may have been the last person to see him alive.'

# CHAPTER 10

My mind was racing, returning to that first meeting Healy and I had had in the café, to the ones we'd had in the motel bar, to that last call. *Were you glad she got cancer?* I'd cut him loose without even pausing for thought. When I'd returned to London the next day, I'd written *You're on your own* on the front of the murder file, and told the receptionist at the motel to give it to him when he next staggered back.

'His sons haven't heard from him since the week before you last saw him,' Craw said, 'and although apparently he wasn't ever good at keeping in touch, nine months isn't normal.' She leaned forward in her seat. 'What did you two discuss?'

My head was buzzing with noise. 'There wasn't a lot of discussion. I offered to help him get back on his feet and said he could sleep on my sofa. But I'm not sure either of us really wanted that. So, I was helping him find a job, paying for his petrol to get to interviews, and I also fronted up the cash for a motel. He told me he'd pay me back once he got himself together again.'

She nodded, sinking into her seat, a strand of blonde hair escaping past her face. She swiped it away, eyes on the gentle sway of the marshes. 'I didn't even know he was missing until yesterday. One of my team mentioned it to me.'

'How did they find out?'

'He knows someone who works for CID up in Barnet. Some guy called Fifield. Anyway, the two of them – Fifield and my guy, Sampson – used to work with Healy way back when. Fifield told Sampson he'd just got back to the station one day late August, and he passed Gemma coming the other way. They'd never spoken before, but Fifield recognized her from pictures Healy had kept on his desk for years. Fifield went back in and asked around, and ended up speaking to the PC who'd filed the report.' She paused, rolling her chain between her thumb and forefinger. 'The PC confirmed to Fifield that the woman had been Gemma.'

'What else did Sampson say?'

'Just that he'd had a short phone conversation with Fifield two days ago – the first they'd had in four months – and Fifield had mentioned that Healy had been reported missing.'

'That's it?'

Her eyes narrowed, recognizing the subtext. Why hadn't she asked Sampson more questions? Or found out more herself? 'Look,' she said, steely, curt, 'when I had to fire Healy, it wasn't only my life that he screwed up. Sampson had worked on

Healy's last case too. Hell, they were supposed to be *friends*. Because of Healy, all of us spent days in meetings with Professional Standards. Healy contaminated that whole investigation – and everyone on it.'

There was a flicker of something in her face. She'd fired Healy because he'd lied to her, his deceit jeopardizing one of the biggest manhunts in Met history. Yet that didn't stop her feeling a pang of guilt. Despite everything, she'd always been like me. She saw something in him.

Something worth saving.

I sat there, mind ticking over. I couldn't forgive him for what he'd said to me, even now, even nine months on, but the idea of him missing, of him being a victim, it bothered me. It was an itch I had to scratch. Was it because somewhere, deep down, his plight still saddened me, the sharp trajectory of his fall? Or was it gravity at work: him, once again, without even being here, manoeuvring his way back into my life; me, inextricably being pulled towards him? The more I thought about it, the more conflicted I felt, the less able I was to see straight. My life was simpler without him – and yet I'd never been able to abandon him before.

'He's probably not even missing,' I said.

'His ex-wife says different.'

'His ex-wife doesn't know him.'

'And you do?'

I pulled my mug towards me, steam coiling off

the surface. 'Maybe I don't,' I said, 'maybe no one does. But he was living in a homeless shelter before I offered to help him. If he returned to that life after our last phone call, who would know whether he's missing or not? He could have spent the last nine months moving around the city, one hostel to the next. He could be living on the streets for all we know.' I stopped, remembering something Craw had said: *His sons haven't heard from him since the week before you last saw him.* That *was* unusual for Healy – even during the darkest times in his life, he'd maintained some sort of contact with his kids – but a lack of contact still didn't guarantee he was genuinely missing. If he was back on the streets, he'd have no money, no phone, just the clothes on his back. He'd have his pride too. He'd go silent before he showed the world what he'd become.

'What's the name of the PC that Gemma spoke to?' I asked.

Craw shook her head. 'I can't get involved.'

'You haven't even looked at the report?'

She came forward, a flash of resentment in her eyes, that echo of her old self I'd seen earlier. But then she stopped before a single word had escaped: her jaw loosened, her muscles relaxed, she breathed in and sat back.

'You know I can't,' she said quietly. 'You know all the reasons I can't get involved in this, even if I wanted to.'

I nodded, realizing how quickly things had changed

between us. In our old lives, she'd have let that flash of resentment turn to anger, and she'd have ripped into me. I wouldn't have backed down, it would have escalated, and then it would have festered. These were the moments when it felt like there was something between us, even if neither of us knew what it was.

My thoughts turned back to Healy.

'What's the matter?' she said.

'It bugs me.'

'What?'

'Why would Gemma report him missing?'

Craw shrugged. 'I imagine because he hasn't picked up the phone to their sons for the past nine months. Or maybe because she was once his wife.'

'They've hardly spoken in three years.'

'So?'

'So why would she assume he's missing and not just in another spiral? Healy kept in touch with his boys, but he was hardly Dad of the Year. Sometimes he could go weeks between calls to them, especially recently.'

'Yeah, but it's not been weeks. It's been nine months.'

'It's longer than usual, obviously, but it's not unprecedented. Healy went over a year without speaking to me, and I've probably been as close to him as anyone since he and Gemma split up. So you can bet he's been the same with her. You can bet he's been the same with his boys too, especially if things have gone *seriously* south. He wouldn't want them to see him like that. The way he was back in January . . .' I paused, looked at her. 'He was in a bad place, even after I'd bailed him out. Who knows how much worse it got afterwards?'

'Maybe he failed to pay Gemma child support.'

'His sons are both adults.'

'Maybe he owes her money.'

Her eyes returned to me, and we could both see what had gone unspoken: the only reason she could think of for Gemma reporting him missing was Healy owing money. Yet I knew, unequivocally, that wouldn't be the reason. Healy was many things – by the end he was destitute – but he wouldn't run because of a debt.

I leaned back, watching cattle grazing in the distance, moving through the marshland like ships on a sea of grass. 'So, are you asking me to find him?'

'I'm not asking you anything,' she said.

Except we both knew that wasn't true.

He'd gone more than a year without picking up the phone to me until he'd called in January. When our paths had crossed before that, in the search for the man who'd killed his daughter, there'd been no contact from him for the following seven months. This was his MO, his pattern. If I was apathetic to him, or perhaps realistic about the way he was programmed, I'd have given Craw a prediction: days, weeks, months from now – when things got *really* desperate – Healy would finally ring me, because he'd run out of options. And yet, intuitively, there was something I couldn't shake, a bad feeling.

*Why would Gemma report him missing?*

'You want me to speak to her?' I asked.

'Gemma? I think that would be a good idea.'

'You're not even going to source his missing persons report for me?'

She shook her head. 'I can't. I'm sorry.'

I saw something in her face: frustration at not being able to help me, but a little relief too. This way, she didn't disturb any ghosts from her past, but she got to find out first-hand what had happened to a man she'd once rated so highly.

'So Gemma filed the report in Barnet,' I said to her, 'which probably means she's not living in the house she shared with Healy in St Albans any more.'

Craw nodded once, reached into the pocket of her trousers and brought out a slip of paper. 'This is the address listed on her driver's licence.'

'What happened to you not getting involved?'

'Yeah, well, this is where it begins and ends. She's using her maiden name again now: Doherty.' She paused, eyeing me. It was clear she thought she saw something else in my expression. 'This was a sixty-second PNC search.'

I didn't say anything.

But she wasn't done: 'Searching the computer for Gemma's street address isn't going to raise any flags. Accessing a missing persons report on a disgraced cop that sold me down the river and almost burned an entire case to the ground – that's completely different.'

'Okay.'

'I'm glad we're clear, then.'

'We're clear,' I said, opening up the piece of paper.

The address was Bells Hill, on the western fringes of Barnet.

'You can use me as a sounding board if you want,' Craw said quietly, and when I looked up, she was glancing left and right, as if someone might have heard her offering to help. When her eyes pinged back to me, there was a focus to her; resolute, unwilling to negotiate. 'I'm happy to discuss things with you.'

'But?'

She let out a long breath, one that spoke of so much painful history. 'But I can't be audited and logged looking for him in the database. I can't get burned by Healy again.'

I didn't particularly want to get burned by him either. But maybe, quietly, Craw was acknowledging what I'd always tried to hide from myself: that in the end, when I believed in a cause, getting burned wouldn't ever be enough to stop me.

The streets shimmered with a mix of heat and exhaust fumes as I made my way back to the car. Summer should have been long gone by now;

instead, every air-conditioning unit on every building was humming, doors were wide open, kids were covered in sunblock. On some of them it was smeared like war paint, yet to be rubbed in properly, and as that thought came to me, so did another: two other children, long gone, and their mother, all three of them slaughtered and cast aside; and the cop who had become their vessel. For most people at the Met, that family were memories from another time, words on a page in a file.

But not for Colm Healy.

I was still chewing on that when I finally reached the car. It was a creaking eighteen-year-old BMW, and as I pulled the driver's door open, it wheezed like an old man and the heat of the interior crashed against me like a wave. I got in and fired it up, trying to clear my head, but Craw's words were on a loop.

*You may have been the last person to see him alive.*

Grabbing my phone, I dialled the last number I had for Healy, a mobile I'd bought him from a supermarket back in January. It rang continually for twenty seconds and then hit the generic network voicemail message. 'Healy, it's Raker,' I said, after the tone. 'People are concerned about you. You need to call me back.'

Next, I logged into the email account I'd set up for him at the motel. He'd had another one before that, which I didn't have the username or password for, but he'd stopped using it as things began unravelling in his personal life. The new account had been an attempt to motivate him, to focus him on the process of applying for jobs. It was cheap psychology, and we both knew it, but it meant I now had access to it. Except there was nothing to find: the inbox had been in stasis since January, and the last Sent messages and deleted emails were for job applications before 16 January. After our argument, he'd washed his hands of it all.

Phoning Directory Enquiries, I got the landline number for Gemma's new address in Barnet and asked to be connected. It rang for thirty seconds until an answerphone kicked in. I listened to her voice, her Irish accent subdued after living in London for so long. The last time I'd spoken to her was at the funeral of their daughter, Leanne, in November 2011, so I wasn't sure if she'd remember me or not. Given that, it was going to be better to meet her in person: to look her in the face and reassure her; to discover her reasons for reporting him missing. That was key. When we'd met in January, Healy had still been wearing his wedding ring. Three years on from their split, I doubted Gemma would be doing the same. Yet something had compelled her to go to the police.

Something had drawn her back to him.

'Gemma,' I said, after the tone had chimed, 'it's David Raker. I'm not sure if you remember me, but I've just heard about Colm, and I'd really like the opportunity to talk to you. Maybe I might be able to help in some way.'

I left her my number and hung up.

# CHAPTER 11

Stuck in traffic on the way home, I hunted down the details of Healy's sons Ciaran and Liam.

The eldest, Ciaran, was straightforward to find: he worked in Enfield, at a small insurance firm, his photo included on their website. Liam was even easier: he was a second-year Art History student at the University of Essex, and seemed to have catalogued his student life in pictures on an unprotected Facebook page.

I punched Ciaran's work number into my phone, my thumb hovering over the Call button. But then I backed out again. Talking to him at work about his missing father wasn't the right approach, plus I hadn't even had the opportunity to speak to Gemma yet. What if she didn't want me getting involved in the search for Healy? What if she had someone else looking for him?

The idea gave me pause. Could I just step back without finding out the truth about him? Could I accept not knowing? Could I let Gail, April and Abigail Clark continue to rot on a hard drive at the Met, without knowing everything about their case? Returning to my phone's address book, I realized I'd already made my mind up.

I couldn't.

The person I was looking for was Ewan Tasker. He was a semi-retired ex-police officer who'd worked for the National Criminal Intelligence Service, its successor SOCA, and was now an advisor to its current incarnation, the National Crime Agency. Back when I was a journalist, our relationship had begun as a marriage of convenience – he'd fed me stories he wanted out in the open, I'd broken them first – but, over time, we'd become good friends. He'd been the one who had got me a copy of the Clark family murder file back in January, but that was gone now, left on a reception desk for a man I thought I probably wouldn't see again.

'Raker,' he said when he picked up.

'How you doing, Task?'

He paused briefly, and the sound of background conversation faded. He'd moved somewhere private. 'Yeah, all good, old friend. So what can I do for you?'

'A couple of quick things, neither of which should be too difficult. The first is a missing persons report. It was opened back in August at Barnet. The name of the person who filed it is a Gemma Doherty – G for Gemma, no c in Doherty.'

'Got it. Who's missing?'

'His name's Colm Healy. C-O-L-M.'

A brief pause. 'Healy. Wasn't he a pal of yours?'

'Something like that.'

'He was on the Snatcher task force, right?'

'There's nothing wrong with your memory, old man.'

'I heard that was his last gig.'

'Yeah, he got fired from the task force. It's a long story.'

'One for another time maybe,' Task said, but didn't probe any further. That was what I liked about him. 'Okay. No problem. What's the second thing?'

'I don't know if you remember, but back in January you sent me a file for a triple murder down in New Cross. This would have been July 2010. A mother and her two daughters. No arrest was ever made. The family name was Clark.'

'Vaguely.'

'It doesn't matter. I need another copy of it.'

'Okay. Is that Clark without an e?'

'That's right.'

'Okay, I'm on it.'

'I appreciate that. Thanks, Task.'

As I sat there, I thought of Healy, picturing him coming back to the motel in the days after our argument and being given the murder file at reception. I'd already called them to see if they still had a record of his stay, which they didn't. But when I brought up the subject of the case file, and whether it had been passed on to him as I'd requested, the woman I spoke to said that rang a bell with her, and that she was certain that it had.

86

It also helped to spark off a memory of when Healy might have officially checked out. 'I'm sure it was shortly afer I gave him that file,' she said. 'Maybe one or two days.'

If he'd continued to carry the casework with him over the past nine months, there was simply no way he'd have allowed it to gather dust. He was going to work it again. For Healy, the murder of April and Abigail Clark, the death of their mother, was a broken levee – so maybe the file would be the most effective lead in finding him, because it was all that mattered to him. Everything that washed through afterwards started in a single moment: the moment that killer got away with it. Every cop had a case that had stalled on them, leads that had fizzled out, suspects they couldn't put at the scene. Healy had those things too – and all that followed.

All his broken promises.

All his lies.

All his failures.

# EVERYTHING YOU LOVE

## 74 days, 12 hours, 33 minutes *before*

They came across the grass in front of the flats, the dog running on ahead, the girls either side of him, hands in his, telling him about a vegetable patch they'd planted at school. He listened to them without interrupting, loving the excitement in their voices, the way they made everything sound so new, as if they were the first people in the world to have ever planted a potato. Sometimes, when he was alone with them like this, he became quite emotional, glimpsing a point in time – perhaps only two or three years away – when the girls would no longer take to him so quickly and innocently, when the purity of childhood became the fickleness and cynicism of the teenage years. In the months after he'd met Gail, he'd been surprised at how fast the girls had accepted him as part of the family, and he didn't want that to change. The idea of being alone again scared him. He loved this sense of belonging.

He loved being a part of their lives.

Putting an arm around each of their shoulders and

bringing them into him, he said to them, 'You two will never understand how special you are to me.'

They didn't say anything in return, but that was okay: sometimes kids forgot to say those things, or didn't realize their importance, never imagining the weight similar words could carry when they came from a child. Instead they wrestled free of his bear hug, first April, then Abigail, and tore off across the grass, in the vague direction of the dog and the looming shadow of Searle House.

He broke out into a run himself and chased them across the grass, then – once they were all inside – up the stairwell. The dog ran on ahead, the girls half a flight further back, screaming with delight as his best evil laugh echoed off the walls. 'I'm coming for you!' he joked, and they moved even faster, both of them trying to be first, one sister attempting to get in front of the other. Twelve floors up, they started to flag, so as he finally caught up with them, he told them to pause and catch their breath, and they walked the rest of the way together. After a while, the girls started singing a song they'd learned in choir.

When they reached the flat, he let them both in, and the smell immediately hit them. 'Fajitas!' April squealed with delight, shedding her coat, leaving it on the hallway floor and running through to the kitchen where her mother was cooking dinner. Abigail shrugged hers off too, equally excited, but in a quieter, steadier way: the girls were identical twins, born within minutes of one another according to Gail, but he'd already noticed there were differences between the two of them; small, barely perceptible differences, but differences he'd begun to know so well.

Once Abigail had hung her coat on the end of a peg, she looked back at him. 'Do you think Mum remembered the sour cream, Mal?'

'I'm sure she did, honey.'

He hung up his own coat, took the dog off its leash and let it escape through to the living room. Then he followed Abigail into their tiny box kitchen, where Gail was frying some pieces of chicken. April was sitting on the window ledge to her right, back pressed against the glass, the London skyline ashen and hazy in the distance behind her. He leaned in and kissed Gail on the cheek.

'The girls told me they don't want fajitas tonight, Mummy,' he said, winking. 'They'd much rather have a big plate of vegetables.'

'We didn't say that!' April shouted.

He broke out into a laugh. 'Oh, I must have misheard you.'

'Did you remember the sour cream?' Abigail asked.

'Of course I did,' Gail replied, pointing to the fridge. 'You only reminded me about seven thousand times, Abs.' One hand swishing the chicken around the pan, Gail reached out to Abigail with the other and pulled her in. 'Why don't you and your sister go and watch TV for ten minutes? Mal will set the table and call you when it's ready – and then we can all tuck in.'

After the girls were gone, he took April's place at the window and he and Gail started talking about their days. Gail worked three mornings a week at a library just down the road from them and was studying for an Open University degree in the evenings. He worked five days a week as a delivery driver but always finished early on a Friday, so he'd come home and take the girls out with the dog, and Gail would cook something special. Fridays were treat night in their flat, and this week the girls had chosen fajitas.

'I'm going to get changed,' he said.

'Be quick. I'm almost done here.'

He kissed her on the cheek again, then headed across the hallway to their bedroom. Like every other room in the flat, it was small and slightly shabby, but they'd been good enough to accept him here, and he was used to this place now: living on top of one another, the smell of damp in the kitchen, the lack of natural light in the rooms. It was all they could afford for now, and until either he or Gail landed better jobs, or maybe won the lottery, he knew they'd make the best of it.

As he was taking off his trousers, his mobile started buzzing in the pocket. He pulled it out, dumped his trousers on the bed and looked at the display. An unknown number. Pressing Answer, he wedged the phone between his ear and shoulder, and began looking through the wardrobe for his tracksuit trousers.

'Hello?'

Silence on the line.

'Hello?' he said again.

'What are you doing?'

He stopped, pausing in front of the open wardrobe.

'Uh, who is this, please?'

'What are you doing?' the voice said for a second time: same flat tone, exactly the same pronunciation, like a recording on a loop. There was a slight buzz on the line; an echo, as if the call had come a great distance. 'What are you doing with that family?'

'I beg your pardon?'

'What are you doing with that family?'

A coolness slithered down his spine. 'Who is this?'

'This must be stopped.'

'What? Who is this?'

'This must be stopped now.'

'Who the hell is this?'

The line glitched, buzzed.

'Everything you love must be taken away.'

# CHAPTER 12

I didn't get home until almost six-thirty, the sky a vast, markless sweep of mauve, the sun too low to be seen beyond the roofs of the city. I pulled into my driveway and got out, and as I removed my laptop and some files from the boot, I glimpsed my neighbours, both of them on their knees and tending to the same flower bed.

They were a couple in their thirties, Andrew and Nicola, and six months after they'd first moved in, we'd barely spoken. In their first week, I'd introduced myself, found out he worked for an Aston Martin dealership on Park Lane, while she had some kind of marketing job in the City. And that was it. In half a year, that was all I'd managed to get out of them. We'd talked a few times in between, but it was bland, vacuous stuff: the house, the weather, the London property market.

Most of the time, it didn't bother me. I lived alone, I spent my working life the same way. But occasionally, I felt regret – even a sort of mourning – for the woman who'd lived there before. That had been Liz, the first person I'd fallen in love with after the death of my wife, and a woman I'd eventually had to let go.

I closed the boot, its dull thud not disturbing either of them from their gardening. Even as I made my way up the drive, they didn't turn around, and by the time I saw Andrew glance across the fence, my front door had long since closed and I was inside the kitchen, looking out from the darkness of the house.

Opening it up – the windows, the rear doors – I started preparing some dinner, and once it was ready, I took my plate through to the back garden and sat on the decking with a bottle of beer, watching the sky burn out until it was black.

An hour later, the doorbell rang.

To begin with, I thought I was hearing things. I rarely got visitors at home – an indictment of my social life, of who I'd allowed myself to become – and as I turned in my chair on the back deck, a third empty beer bottle beside me, all I could hear was birdsong and the gentle crackle of a ceramic wood burner I'd bought the previous spring. Thinking I must have misheard, I watched the logs gently shift inside the burner, fire licking at them, embers spitting up and out of the chimney.

Then the doorbell sounded again.

I made my way through the house, turning on the interior lights, and opened up. The security lamp bathed the driveway in a lake of stark white light, washing out to where a Yaris was parked up, a woman about to get back inside.

'Can I help you?'

She looked back at me, surprised.

It was Gemma.

I almost didn't recognize her. At her daughter's funeral three years before, she'd been dark-haired and thin, her green eyes revealing so much about her – her strength, her instinct for survival – even in the hours after Leanne's casket had been lowered into the ground. Yet all that had changed. This version of her was flabby, inflated, the lines of her face hidden behind thick, black-rimmed glasses and untidy strands of brown hair. She swiped some of it away, her black roots spidering out, and took a couple of steps closer. I remembered her being three years older than Healy, which put her in her early fifties, and she now seemed to carry so much of that half-century. As I came down the front steps, she pulled her hair back from her eyes again and I saw how marbled they were, how blotchy and irritated her skin was, how recently she'd been crying.

'Gemma.'

She pushed the door of the car shut. 'David,' she said, her voice quiet, eyes on the house. 'When you didn't answer, I figured you weren't home.'

'Sorry. I was in the back garden.'

She nodded.

'Do you want to come in?'

A black handbag was wedged between her breast and the inside of her arm, and as she looked from me to the house and then back again, she seemed to press it closer to her. 'Yes,' she said, nodding for a second time. 'Thank you.'

I led her inside, the ghost-white glare from the security lamp replaced by the semi-darkness of the hallway. 'Would you like some tea or coffee?'

'Tea would be fine.'

I filled the kettle and set it boiling.

For a moment, we stood opposite one another in the kitchen, awkwardly, her hovering in the doorway uncertainly, me half perched on one of the stools.

'I take it you got my message?' I asked.

'Yes,' she said. 'I did.'

'I didn't want you to have to drive all the way down here.'

'It's fine,' she said, eyes drifting to where steam was chugging out of the kettle and into the spaces above us. 'I wanted to . . .' Her eyes narrowed, as if she was first trying to form what she needed to say in her head. 'I'd been thinking about calling you. I know this is kind of your . . . well, I guess this is what you do.'

'I'm glad you came,' I said.

A small smile: fleeting, fatigued.

I didn't ask her anything else. Instead, I made her tea and led her through the house to the back deck. Gesturing for Gemma to take one of the chairs, we sat down either side of the burner, the brief silence filled with the pop of the wood. She laid her handbag on the floor, and then reached over to her tea, fingers lacing together around it.

'How did you hear about Colm?' she asked.

'I know a few people at the Met.'

'In Barnet?'

'Not specifically, but I heard on the grapevine that you'd been there at the end of August. I'm conscious of stepping on any toes. But I wanted to call you.'

She nodded. 'I'm really pleased you did.'

That was a good start. I wasn't exactly sure how Gemma would view me, especially through the prism of the press – or perhaps through Healy himself. If she'd spoken to him on the phone in the moments after the two of us had fallen out, Healy would have ensured I'd come out looking second best. But Gemma was nothing if not battle-hardened: she'd been married to him for over twenty years, and that was a long time to get to know someone's faults.

'I don't have any . . .' She paused, looking down into her mug. 'I don't have much money, David. The boys are grown up, Colm's gone. I don't know how I—'

'Don't worry about that.'

'You can't do this for free.'

I smiled. 'I'm not even sure what "this" is.'

She swallowed, put her tea down and went to her bag. After a few seconds, she brought out an envelope. It was creased, a little marked, a trace of a coffee stain on its edge. Taking it from her, I saw it was addressed to her in an untidy, wavering hand. It had been postmarked 21 August.

'What's this?' I asked.

Her eyes lingered on it, on the frayed corners of the envelope. It was clear she'd looked at it many times; taken it out and put it back. The flap was incapable of sticking any more, the adhesive long since worn out. 'I think it might be . . .'

I waited, not interrupting.

'I think it might be Colm's suicide note.'

# CHAPTER 13

Something began to churn in the pit of my stomach as I opened the envelope and removed the letter. It was an ivory-coloured sheet of A4, thin stock, folded in half. On the side facing me, Healy had written *GEMMA* in uneven capital letters.

I glanced at her. She was leaning forward in her seat now, and I saw a flash in her eyes, the glow of the wood burner painting one side of her face. A second later, a tear welled, forming along the ridge of her lashes, and she lifted her glasses to wipe it away; but then another came in its place and this time she let it fall, a trail tracing the contours of her cheek. I wondered what could reduce her to this, a woman Healy had driven away, whom he'd wronged, hurt and betrayed, who no longer wore a wedding ring and was three years past caring what he did with his life.

But then I opened the letter.

It was in black ballpoint pen and barely legible in places. Halfway in, I couldn't understand what he had written, and had to retreat back to the previous line to try to get a sense of his meaning. But even if his words weren't always clear, his intention was obvious: this was Healy at his most vulnerable, his most lucid. This was a man who could feel the walls closing in.

*Dear Gemma,*

*This letter is long overdue. I have had a lot of time to think over the past months about how I treated people, particularly you and the boys. I did what I thought was best for you all, for Leanne too, our precious daughter, our baby, our beautiful girl, when she was alive. I miss her so much, some days it's like I can't breathe. I couldn't get to her in time – another failure to add to all my others – but I've often wondered what things would be like if I had.*

*Do you think maybe if I'd saved her, that would have made it right with her? With Ciaran and Liam? With you? All the arguments we had, all the stupid, petty fights I instigated with you four, do you think maybe we could have all gone on together as a family if I'd been a different, better person? I suppose it's impossible to answer, what's done is done, but when I lie awake in this place at night, it's all I can think about. Because I had my time again, and I screwed it up the same as before.*

*Still, at least here at the end, I can do something*

*right. I'm sorry for everything, Gem. Tell the boys I love them.*

*Colm*
*x*

I looked at Gemma, her face marked by tears, mascara smudged, her body small again, as if she'd suddenly lost all the weight she'd gained. I closed my eyes, trying to get my own head straight – because I could see what she'd meant now.

I understood.

It was a suicide note.

Trying to focus, I put the letter down, drew my notepad towards me and picked up my pen. But then reality kicked in: what was I going to write down?

What was there to say?

'Do you think he's dead?' she asked.

I glanced at the letter, then at Gemma, her eyes flickering in the light from the burner. A faint breeze picked up and sent the envelope drifting across the table, like a boat being carried away in a storm. I stopped it and pulled it back to me, trying to figure out what the best response was. I had no idea if he was dead.

But, in this moment, it felt like it.

'What does he mean here?' I said, pointing to the end of the second paragraph. '"Because I had my time again, and I screwed it up the same as before." Did you two get back together at some point – was that what he meant by that?'

She shook her head. 'No.'

'So do you know what he means there?'

She was still shaking her head, dabbing a finger to her eye. 'No. Do you think maybe he's talking about his work? You know, before he was fired. About being given that second chance, after his suspension, and how he messed it up.'

I reread that same passage again. 'But he's talking about you, the boys and Leanne. He's talking about family here. This whole letter is about you four.'

'I know.'

'I don't think he's referring to his time at the Met.'

She shrugged. 'I don't know, then.'

*Because I had my time again, and I screwed it up the same as before.* My eyes moved to the previous clause: *when I lie awake in this place at night, it's all I can think about.* What place? A homeless shelter? A hostel? Emergency housing? It was unlikely he'd have been referring to a place he might be renting. Nothing in what he'd written suggested that. Back in January he was desperate, basically penniless, years away from being able to take money from his pension, his savings all but wiped out, whatever cash he'd had from the sale of his home in St Albans gone on child support, on university fees for the boys, on rent, on petrol, on booze. It seemed impossible he would have been back on his feet by the time he mailed the message to Gemma in August. This letter, these words, they were the endgame; they didn't even sound like they were written by the same person I'd given up on at the end. There was an unexpected eloquence to them. No anger, just stark self-reflection; a glimpse of the ghosts that lay inside him, the ones Craw and I had continually tried to coax out.

'What about this?' I said to Gemma, placing a finger near the bottom of the note. '"Still, at least here at the end, I can do something right." What was he doing that was right – do you know?'

There was a sudden change in her expression, and she seemed to recover some of her poise. Wiping her eyes again, she took a sip from her tea, as if gathering her thoughts. 'We've only talked once, David, you and I. But do you remember what we talked about that day at Leanne's funeral?'

I eyed her. 'We talked about Healy.'

She nodded. 'On the day of my daughter's funeral, we talked about her father. It feels like I spent the last ten years of my marriage talking about him. Not about the kids, about what they needed from us, the things we *should* have been worrying about as parents – but about him. Our entire lives were dictated by him. His anger, his stupidity, his selfishness.'

Her voice was still quiet, but her tone had solidified. I got the sense she knew exactly what Healy had meant in that line near the bottom, and it might not paint her in the best light – so she was going to make damn sure I understood her reasons.

'In the early days it was different,' she continued. 'We all meant the world to him. The kids . . . they were *everything* to him. I know that sounds like an obvious thing to say, but he was so good with them. *So* good.' She paused, turning her cup, the china chiming gently against the surface of the table. 'But he found their teenage years much harder. The minute they became capable of doing their own thing, of having their own opinions, of answering back, it was like he began to drift away from them. The older they got, the worse it got. He preferred it when they were small. I think in a lot of ways, despite everything, Colm just needed to feel like he was wanted. Like he belonged to something. When they were small, they needed him, they couldn't survive without him. As they got older, he couldn't cope with the way they changed. I think he became lonely.'

Off the back of that, I thought I could see where this was going, and what Healy was referring to at the end of the letter – but I kept quiet, watching her.

'Things began to change in the year before Leanne was killed,' she said. 'As he became more distant from the kids, he started doing longer hours. He'd sink himself into his work – and then he got that case. The twins. He *really* changed after that. That case got to him so quickly, and he just became more and more insular. He hardly talked to me, he never talked to the kids. I asked him to discuss it with me, because I could see him bottling it up, and I knew from bitter experience that the more he bottled something up, the worse the meltdown would be. But he didn't. He became uncommunicative. He was like a stranger. It got so bad, I couldn't think what to say to him. A man I'd spent twenty-six years with.'

I nodded. 'He didn't just send the letter to you, did he?'

She glanced at me, surprised that I'd been able to see where it was going. But it wasn't so hard, and as her eyes lingered on me, tears welled in them again. I imagined these weren't out of grief this time, but out of a sense of guilt, out of the responsibility she felt for what I held in my hands.

'No,' she said, pulling her fringe back from her face. 'A year and a half ago, I went to see a solicitor about making things official.'

'You mean getting a divorce?'

'Yes,' she said, looking at me like she expected me to say something. When I didn't, she continued: 'Colm and I . . . there was nothing left. There was too much water under the bridge by then. After we separated, we hardly even spoke. His work became everything to him. That case he had – the twins, their mother – it ruined him. At the time . . .' A snaking strand of hair fell forward again but she didn't bother addressing it. 'Just before the start of that case, I . . . I stupidly started seeing someone else, someone to fill the gap he'd left behind at home . . .'

She paused again, looking at me, as if waiting for me to pass judgement. But I knew this part of her history already: how she'd drifted into the arms of another man – and how Healy had responded when he'd found out.

'And a month into that case, he discovered what was going on,' she said, 'and that was when he *really* lost control.'

He'd only ever mentioned that incident to me once, right back when we'd first been drawn together. We'd been nursing drinks in a place near East India Dock Road, rain lashing against the window, and he'd asked me if I'd ever done anything I regretted. I hardly knew him back then, but he began to admit to what he'd done anyway, as if he needed it out in the open, even in front of a stranger. *If I'd found out she was seeing someone else any other time, I would have thrown some furniture around. Put my foot through a door. I know I've got a temper. It's who I am. I'm too old to change. But I found out when I was up to my neck with photographs of those twin girls. So when she told me . . . I totally lost it.*

He'd hit her.

He'd hit her so hard, he'd put her in a neck brace for eight weeks. It was an unforgivable act, with nothing to justify it and no way to ever take it back. But I'd seen the remorse in his face enough times to know he hated himself for it, every single day, even if he'd found it hard – until this final letter – to articulate an apology.

106

'My solicitor sent him divorce papers,' she said, looking out on the gathering darkness, where even the birdsong seemed to have faded. 'But he refused to sign them. July through to October last year, I tried again and again, explaining to him why it was for the best. But then, towards the end of last year, it became harder and harder to get hold of him, and eventually – in November – my solicitor found out he wasn't even renting a place any more. We couldn't trace him. He wasn't using his mobile phone. Every time I called him, it just went to voicemail.'

'He was living in a homeless shelter.'

She studied me like she was waiting for the punchline.

'What?'

'He called me in January and asked for my help. I tried to get him back on his feet, loaned him some cash, put him up in a place just off the motorway, and then a week later he phoned me up drunk and we haven't spoken since.' I ran a hand across my face, finding the story painful to recount now, given everything I'd just read. 'So, when he said in the letter he was doing something right by you, he meant he'd finally signed the divorce papers and sent them with the letter?'

'Yes,' she said, faintly. 'Yes, that's right.'

It was obvious that, in the letter, Gemma glimpsed the re-emergence of the man she'd married, the man who had always been so good, and so close, to her and the kids. That was what was getting at her: doubt over whether she'd been too hard on him; guilt over her brief, failed affair with another man; anger that Healy would only reveal this side of him again when things had reached the end of the line, when it was too late for her to do anything about it.

When, perhaps, all that was left of him was a husk.

A memory. A ghost.

A body.

# CHAPTER 14

'What date did you report him missing?' I asked.

We were in the living room now, Gemma more determined. She'd been to the bathroom and cleaned herself up, wiped the mascara away and tied her hair up into a bun. I'd spent time alone trying to recover some fortitude of my own.

'I went to the police on Friday 22 August,' she said.

'The day after you received the letter and the divorce papers from him?'

'Yes.'

'What was the name of the cop you spoke to?'

'PC Miriam Davis.'

I wrote both things down and pushed on. 'Okay, so you decided to report him missing based on what he'd written in the letter – nothing else?'

She shook her head. 'I didn't initially report him missing. I just wanted to tell someone about the letter, about what I thought it might mean.' She paused, a grimace on her face, but she was definitely in control now, seeing the importance of these moments: I needed her clear-headed, honest, decisive. 'PC Davis seemed reluctant to do anything about it to start with,' she went on. 'When I told her our history, I think she saw it as some kind of . . . I don't know, domestic. Something that would blow over. I told her I hadn't seen him for a year, hadn't spoken to him *at all* since October 2013, and that the only contact we'd had between then and now was the letter. But she said she couldn't report him missing if all he was doing was choosing not to keep in touch with me.'

'So what changed?'

'I told her it was a suicide note.' She paused, disturbed again by those last two words. 'I told her that none of us – not me, not even Ciaran or Liam, who he always tried to stay in contact with – had heard from him, and if she chose not to look into it, his death was going to be on her. She seemed so young, skittish – like she hadn't been in the job very long – so I suppose I took advantage of that, and I made a bit of a scene.' Gemma stopped again, this time for longer. 'It was worth it. By the time I was finished, Colm had been officially registered missing.'

'What happened after that?'

'PC Davis asked if she could come to the house to get a DNA sample from Colm's toothbrush, but I told her, "I haven't lived with him for three years. There *is* no toothbrush. I don't own a single thing that belongs to him." So she said she'd organize something through the employment records they had on file for Colm.'

I frowned. 'Meaning what?'

'I guess, meaning they'd get a DNA sample that way.'

She was clearly being palmed off by Davis: police officers didn't give DNA samples as part of the job, and scrapings couldn't be taken from the work-station Healy had used because, by the time Gemma reported him missing, he'd been out of the force for two years. His desk was occupied by someone else, if anyone at the Met even remembered which desk he'd once sat at. Things got even more compli-cated when you factored in his status as homeless. In fact, the only thing he'd kept through all of it was his car, a rusting red Vauxhall, which wasn't taxed or insured until I'd paid for both of those things in January. But perhaps he'd finally got rid of that too in the months leading up to August. Davis could have found out through the Police National Computer. The fact that Healy hadn't been located suggested that it was no longer regis-tered to him – or, more cynically, she remained so unconvinced about Healy actually being missing, she hadn't bothered looking in the first place.

'Has PC Davis been in touch since?' I asked.

'Once,' Gemma replied, pushing her glasses back to the bridge of her nose. 'A month ago, the first week of September, she called to say that she'd passed all of Colm's information on to the Missing Persons Bureau.'

She studied me, to see if that meant anything.

The MPB worked with police, trying to attach the names of missing people to unidentified bodies. They wouldn't have a DNA sample for Healy, but they'd have his physical description, and could access his medical and dental records. If any match had been found on the system, it would have been found quickly – and Gemma would have received a call. Yet, a month on, the phone hadn't rung.

Dead or alive, Healy was still out there somewhere.

I looked at Gemma again, trying to decide where to go next. Normally at this stage, the families were giving me detailed descriptions of their loved ones, their last movements, state of mind, routines, hang-ups, addictions, reasons for leaving. Here, I had none of that. I had the kindness of a woman who could easily have abandoned her ex-husband, especially after everything he'd done to her – but one who'd gone even longer than me without seeing him. Apart from what she'd read in the letter, she had no real idea who Healy was any more: she didn't know how he thought now, or where he'd been in the three years since they split.

She didn't have his recent history.

I didn't have much of it either. I had year-long gaps in my knowledge, where I had no idea what he was doing or where he'd been. A lot of the time, he'd remained a mystery to me, even when – briefly – we'd been living under the same roof.

But I had eight days in January, and soon I'd have the Clark family murder file.

That gave me something.

I walked Gemma to her car and told her I'd keep her up to date with what I managed to find out. She spoke again about money, but I told her not to worry. I was less concerned about being paid, and more concerned about the anxiety that was starting to pick at me. Could he really be dead? And, if he was, how much blame lay at my door?

The things he'd said to me were like a residual ache, even if their impact had dulled over time, but the choices I'd made – to walk away from him, to leave him to fend for himself – seemed, at best, impetuous now, at worst misjudged and irresponsible. I should have had the capacity to look past the words and see the man underneath. I should have had enough control not to just abandon him.

Heading back inside, I grabbed my pad and started to construct a timeline of Healy's movements over the last two years, starting with him leaving the Met.

*JUNE 2012 – Fired from police.*
*JANUARY–MARCH 2013 – Starts and finishes short-term, two-month security job at building society in Kennington.*
*APRIL–DECEMBER 2013 – No other work, then homeless.*
*7 JANUARY 2014 – Calls me (from phone box), wants meeting.*

113

I stopped. The phone box had been close to the hostel he was staying in at the time. Going back through my notes, I found an entry I'd made on 8 January, during the meeting I'd had with Healy at the café: *Hostel on Goldhawk Road.* If he'd been staying there before 8 January, maybe he returned there after checking out of the motel in Kew. I located the number of the hostel and tried calling them.

It was a dead line.

Doing another web search, I soon found out why: the George Lyon Shelter on Goldhawk Road had closed four months ago, at the beginning of June, citing a lack of funds. I tried not to let the disappointment get to me, and returned to the timeline, adding in more dates, beginning with that January meeting.

*8 JANUARY 2014 – Meet at Hammersmith café.*
*8–16 JANUARY – Stays at motel.*
*17/18 JANUARY – Checks out of motel on one of these days.*
*17/18 JANUARY–20 AUGUST – ???????*
*21 AUGUST – Sends letter and divorce papers to Gemma.*
*22 AUGUST–2 OCTOBER – ???????*

I circled the final three entries.

He'd spent months unaccounted for since our argument on 16 January – but had he gone completely off grid? It was hard to do that. In fact, it was almost impossible.

Picking up my phone again, I dug around in the S's for Spike, a Russian hacker living anonymously in London on an expired student visa. I didn't know his real name, and had never asked, but while Ewan Tasker was my man on the inside at the Met, Spike was my skeleton key for everything else. I'd made my peace long ago with the fact that what he did for me was illegal, and I cared even less about it now. The files from Task would be arriving in tomorrow's post – the missing persons report, the triple murder. What I needed now was Healy's life.

'Laundromat,' Spike said, when he answered.

'Spike, it's David Raker.'

'David! How are you?' His accent was a composite: the sternness of Eastern Europe, an American twang, a hint of south London.

I gave him as much as I knew about Healy: his employment history, his former address in St Albans, the address of the place he rented when he returned to the Met after suspension, all the mobile numbers I'd ever had for him and the registration of his car. When I was done, I said to Spike, 'I need everything.'

'Everything?'

'Literally everything you can find on this guy from June 2012 on. That was the month he got the push from the Met. From then to today is what I need.'

'It's a big job,' he said. 'Might take me twenty-four hours, a little less, hopefully not too much more. Depends how much of a footprint your guy's left.'

Now all I could do was wait.

# CHAPTER 15

A little while later, I called Annabel on Skype. After a couple of rings, she answered my call, dressed in a blue training top and sitting in the living room, the blinds pulled shut behind her. She looked like she'd just been exercising, her hair up in a ponytail, a sheen of sweat still visible at her hairline.

'How are you doing, sweetheart?'

'Good. A bit knackered.'

'You been on the running machine?'

'Six miles,' she said, and then collapsed backwards on to the sofa. She came up smiling. 'Plus, I chased around after six- and seven-year-olds this afternoon.'

Her career teaching dance and drama to kids didn't pay much, but she loved it, and with Olivia in a good school, and the mortgage paid off on a beautiful house on the edges of Dartmoor, I understood the reasons she didn't want to relocate closer to me. We began talking about her schedule for the rest of the week, her other classes and their plans for the weekend, and then, eventually, she asked about my day.

At the start, I'd made a promise never to lie to her about my work, but it was a promise I'd already failed to keep many times over. She knew about Healy, because we'd talked on and off about the cases I'd worked, including the ones I'd worked with him, but I didn't want to get into a discussion about him – or the murder of a family. It would be too close to home for Annabel.

'So when are you coming to visit us?' she asked afterwards.

Before I could answer, Olivia leaped into shot, arms around her sister's neck. She was a beautiful girl, her Asian heritage visible in the curves of her face and the dark sweep of her hair. 'Hi David!' she squealed, the speaker distorting.

'Hey Liv. How are you?'

'Good.'

'Good, *thank you*,' Annabel corrected.

'Good, thank you,' Olivia repeated, and then instantly became distracted by something on TV. After about twenty seconds of Annabel trying to get Olivia to tell me about what she'd done at school today, she disappeared out of shot.

'The last of the great conversationalists,' Annabel joked.

'How's she doing?'

'Yeah, she's good. We went to see the doctor yesterday for a check-up, and he said he was really pleased with everything and there were no signs of any setbacks. Her hip's still giving her a bit of gyp, but he says it'll come right.'

'That's great news.'

'Yeah, I'm really pleased,' Annabel replied, and then I caught her looking at me, eyes narrowing slightly, as if she'd picked up on something.

'I'll be down the weekend after this one,' I said, trying to head her off, but there was no response this time, and I realized it was too late.

'You look troubled,' she said with a half-smile, trying to make her concern seem less intense.

'No, I'm good.'

'Are you sure?'

I glanced at the bottom right of the window, to where my face looked out. Did I look weary? Distressed? Emotional? Or had I just become that easy to read?

'All good,' I lied.

'Okay,' she said, 'if you're sure. Is it still all right if you put us both up at the end of October? Liv's got half-term and I thought we could show her London.'

'I can't wait.'

'Thanks,' she said, and then there was a minor hesitation, as if she wanted to add to what she'd said – but she didn't and I didn't raise it.

Yet I knew what it was.

My concerns in getting to know Annabel were few. Sometimes, quietly, she reminded me of lost years, and of lost people; of Derryn's cancer and how it had stopped me from ever sharing the joy of building a family with my wife.

Sometimes I worried that my work would

eventually drive an irreparable wedge between us, just like it had done with my neighbour Liz, and I became fearful – in the quiet of early morning, in the moments when I was on my own – that knowing Annabel might force me to give up on my search for the missing. My connection to the lost, and to their families, had been my constant, a map that had led me through the shadows, as I'd buried my wife, mourned her loss and struggled to come out the other side.

I didn't want to lose that.

But mostly it was something much smaller and more personal: it was the fact that, even after almost two years, she still didn't call me anything. I didn't expect her to call me Dad because, for most of her life, someone else had been that person to her. But she didn't even call me David. We were caught somewhere in between the memories of her surrogate family and the reality of who I was to her now.

I was her father.

Just one without a name.

I went to bed straight after, exhausted, worn down, and lay on top of the duvet, looking out at the shadows in the corners of the room. Moonlight escaped in through the open window, casting a pale glow across the ceiling, the air in the room hot and still, the world beyond the house as quiet as a tomb. I sweated so much, the bed became damp, but it wasn't the unseasonable heat that was doing it, it was what was filling my head: Healy, where he might be, the words he'd written in the letter, that last conversation we'd had.

I didn't sleep all night.

Things only got worse from there.

# CHAPTER 16

At 6 a.m., I got up and went for a run, beginning in darkness and ending in bright sunlight, and then sat at the counter in the kitchen as my neighbours went off to work together. At eight, I re-watched the video of Healy at the press conference, and at nine, the postman finally came up my drive, holding a brown A4 envelope.

The murder file.

The missing persons report.

I took them through to the decking at the back, along with my third coffee of the morning. There was no note from Tasker inside, no hint as to who'd sent me the printouts, but that was pretty standard. Normally he'd send a separate email to ensure I'd received what I'd asked for, keeping his language ambiguous.

I'd check for that later.

I started with the missing persons report, an official police photograph of Healy on the first page. He was in uniform, the insignia of an inspector on his shoulder, making the photo at least five years old. He looked marginally younger, but not much: a little more hair, more colour in his cheeks. He was carrying plenty of bulk, and there were traces of a shaving rash above his shirt collar. I recalled he'd had a similar rash, in a similar place, one night at the motel bar.

I knew most of his personal details already, so skipped past those, on to the next page where the report had been filed with PC Miriam Davis at Barnet.

Gemma's statement began with a brief history of their marriage. She was pretty kind to Healy to start with: they got married in 1986, when they were both in their early twenties, and had bought a house in St Albans – 'a total wreck, but Colm worked so hard on it for us' – and then Ciaran was born two years later. Eighteen months after that, Leanne came along, and then two years later, Liam. But as the statement went on, the tone of it slowly began to change, and the turbulent later days of their marriage cast a pall across Gemma's descriptions of Healy.

Her account of how he had changed, especially in the days and weeks after he found April and Abigail, echoed much of what she'd told me the night before, and after they separated in 2011, she said they could go months without speaking to each other face-to-face, communicating only via email and text.

PC DAVIS: Why was that?

GEMMA: I couldn't bear to look at him.

PC DAVIS: Why?

GEMMA: I think, after Leanne died, something got lost between us. I had nothing to say any more. But it wasn't just that. He'd ruined our marriage way before then. That case with the twins, that completely messed him up. I mean, I understood why it got to him. They were eight years old. Them, their mother, it was all so senseless. But Colm worked cases like that every day of his life, and they'd never got to him like that before.

PC DAVIS: So why did this one?

GEMMA: I think they reminded him of our kids at that age. And I think they reminded him of a time in his life when he understood them – and they understood him back.

Finally, in July 2013, after giving it some prolonged thought, she said she decided it was time to officially file for divorce, and went and saw her solicitor.

Gemma told Davis that the papers were mailed to a shared house Healy was renting a room in, on the Isle of Dogs, on 23 July 2013, and she followed up with a call a couple of days later, trying to tell him why it was for the best. Over the next three months, she repeatedly tried, again and again, to get him to sign them – 'I was basically sending him texts, begging him to sign, for both our sakes' – telling PC Davis she had always intended to keep things as congenial as possible.

But then, in October, Healy fell off the map.

GEMMA: My solicitor did a little digging and found out that in November Colm wasn't living on the Isle of Dogs any more.

PC DAVIS: So where was he living?

GEMMA: I don't know.

PC DAVIS: You couldn't find him?

GEMMA: No. He stopped responding to my texts, my emails, didn't call the boys again until January. He was just gone.

But he wasn't gone.

He was homeless.

He was too embarrassed to tell his family the truth, to let Gemma and the boys know that, by November 2013, the money had run out.

He had nothing.

Except for a phone call to his sons in January – when he was staying at the motel – as far as the rest of the world was concerned, November was the point at which Healy had vanished, at least until the letter and the divorce papers were sent to Gemma on 21 August 2014. But I'd been with him for eight days from 8 January to 15 January. It meant Craw was probably right when she'd said I was the last person to see him alive, and it meant

I had *some* knowledge of his movements after everyone else lost his trail.

Some, but not much.

And, after that last phone call on 16 January, nothing at all.

That was where Davis's police work should have taken up some of the slack. The Met should have been trying to track Healy's movements from November 2013, through the next ten months to 21 August 2014 – when they knew he was definitely still alive – and into early September, when things became less certain. Instead, apart from the case being referred to the Missing Persons Bureau, things had barely progressed.

As I went through the report, I couldn't find a single useful lead. There were no interviews, apart from the one with Gemma, and Davis had failed to locate Healy's whereabouts, at any point, between November and the date the letter was posted. She had no witnesses, there were no bank statements or phone records attached, no evidence of emails either. Did that mean she couldn't find a single trace of him anywhere between those dates? That the only time he came up for air in that entire period was the eight days he spent in the motel?

I'd find out for sure once Spike had got back to me, but it seemed unlikely: the Healy I knew wouldn't have had the discipline for that, especially if he was in the middle of another spiral. Yet Davis was at more of a disadvantage than I was: she

126

didn't know he'd become homeless, because –
when she reported him missing – Gemma had no
idea either. As a result, Davis wouldn't have
thought to try to find him in hostels or emergency
housing.

His reappearance in January would have gone
undetected, because I was the one who had paid
for his accommodation, lent him money and
organized a new phone. If he'd gone back to
the streets after that, haunting the shadows of the
city, the anonymity of doorways and shelters,
he'd have taken the mobile I'd given him, leaving
Davis trying to track him via the phone he had
*before* that.

So, in theory at least, because the Met weren't
aware of his new number from January, Healy
could easily have drifted uncharted for months.
But, in order to do that, he would have had to
rein in *every* aspect of his life. Because it was
hard to disappear without a trace, perhaps impossible, and I doubted Healy's ability to do that,
even at his most focused. He might not have
used credit cards, had an address, paid rent or
run a car, but I was willing to bet he'd left a
footprint.

I just had to find out where.

In the end, the best Davis had managed to do
was confirm that the letter had come via the
Mount Pleasant Mail Centre in Clerkenwell,
which was futile. It was one of the largest sorting
offices in the world, with millions of items being

processed every day. Trying to track a signed-for package would be hard, but Healy's letter had been sent first class. That made it basically untraceable.

Returning to the timeline I'd begun constructing the night before, I started adding more of Healy's known movements, combining them into one long list:

*23 JULY 2013 – Solicitor mails divorce papers to Healy. He's renting a room in a shared house on the Isle of Dogs. (Where?)*
*23 JULY–OCTOBER – Gemma tries to get Healy to sign papers.*
*OCTOBER – Healy harder to get hold of. (Is this when the money runs out? When does he leave the shared house?)*
*NOVEMBER – Healy disappears completely. (Homeless)*
*7 JANUARY 2014 – Calls me, wants meeting.*
*8 JANUARY – Meet at Hammersmith café.*
*8–16 JANUARY – Stays at motel.*
*17/18 JANUARY – Checks out of motel on one of these days.*
*17/18 JANUARY–20 AUGUST – Where is he during this time? What is he doing?*
*21 AUGUST – Sends letter and divorce papers to Gemma.*
*22 AUGUST – Gemma reports him missing.*
*23 AUGUST–2 OCTOBER – Where is he during this time? What is he doing?*

The seven months between 17 or 18 January and 20 August felt like the centre of the case. I'd paid for ten days at the motel to start with, which meant he would have checked out on 18 January at the latest. I'd also loaned him enough cash to see him through another couple of weeks of expenses – perhaps to the start of February – but, after that, he'd have had nothing else to draw on. Yet he'd survived almost another seven months, apparently without either a job or a room to call his own, before sending Gemma the letter, entirely out of the blue. So what prompted him to do that? What had changed? Where did he go during that time?

What seemed certain was that he was alive just six weeks ago, and at the end of the file there was a log, listing all updates in the case since it was opened on 22 August, which confirmed it – to a point. The last recorded activity was nearly two weeks into the case, 2 September, when Davis got confirmation from the MPB that none of the unidentified bodies they'd recovered in the period up to, and including, 31 August matched Healy's physical description or dental records.

That left two possibilities: that Healy was out there somewhere, and still alive; or that at the time the MPB conducted their search – 31 August – his body hadn't yet been found.

I didn't linger too long on the second prospect and instead refocused my attention on the file in front of me. Except there was nothing else for me to see.

It was done.

Six weeks after Gemma had turned up at Barnet station and reported him missing, the police investigation into Healy's disappearance was effectively over.

# CHAPTER 17

I opened the murder file.

The Clark family looked out at me, April and Abigail standing either side of their mother, Gail in the centre, kneeling, her arms around their waists. In the background I could see foil party banners and balloons, for the girls' birthday.

It wasn't the same photo I'd looked at nine months ago, but as I traced the lines of their faces, their light hair braided, their skin unblemished, it had the same effect on me: I felt a part of me take flight. I'd tried to steel myself for this moment, had been dreading it, and as I gazed into their eyes, I wavered. Any ideas I'd had about remaining impassive, ideas of control and containment, were gone; when I looked at them, I felt anger burning a hole in the centre of my chest, an animal instinct kicking in. In a strange way, it moved me closer to Healy too; this family, this crime, it was worth more than the words we'd exchanged at the end. None of what he'd said to me mattered now. It was just this.

I started turning the pages.

A lot of it I remembered from what Healy and I had discussed in January, but I reread the same sections again, bringing myself up to speed: how the girls were found, covered with their duvets, and then their mother, on the sofa in the next room, stabbed nine times; the way Gail had cleaned up her life, and her absolute dedication to her daughters after that; her Open University course in History and Social Science, her part-time job at the library, the way her children and her coursework usurped a social life and close friends.

I went back through the testimony of her next-door neighbour Sandra Westerwood, who'd been the first to raise the alarm and who claimed to have seen the family with an unidentified man in his mid-to-late thirties – dark hair, medium build – in the months leading up to their deaths. Then there were the dead ends – the name 'Mal' or 'Malcolm', the delivery driver in the olive-green shirt, the lack of usable DNA evidence, the broken CCTV cameras in and around Searle House. Witnesses – or, at least, witnesses that might help push the case forward – were relatively few, but as I got to the point which Healy and I had reached in January, just before Annabel had called about Olivia, a name leaped off the page.

Joban Kehal.

*If the case had been a dog, you'd have put the fucking thing down*, Healy had said to me. *No motive, no DNA, vague witnesses, eleven thousand men with a name that might not even be relevant.* But then he'd taken the file, riffled through the pages and shown me a statement from another witness. I'd asked him what it was.

*About the only thing worth a damn.*

Kehal's name was the last thing I read in the file before everything went south, and as I looked again nine months on, turning the pages, I realized there were actually *two* further witness statements, aside from Sandra Westerwood's. One was from Kehal, who lived five doors along, in the flat closest to the stairwell on the seventeenth floor; the second was from a woman called Bridgette Koekver, who lived on the fourth floor. She'd been arriving back at Searle House on the Sunday night after going to a party.

I started with Kehal's statement.

The layout of his flat – which he shared with his wife and two children – was exactly the same as the Clarks', and he told police that on Sunday 11 July at around 10.30 p.m. he'd been coming out of the kitchen – the room closest to the front door – when he'd heard someone walking back and forth outside his flat.

As Healy pressed him, Kehal described how, at first, he thought he was hearing one person walking past and another coming the other way, but then it happened a second time, and a third, so Kehal stepped up to the front door and used the peep-hole. Outside, he could see a man off to his right, at the entrance to the seventeenth-floor stairwell. He was now standing there, with his back to Kehal.

HEALY: Standing there doing what?

KEHAL: Nothing.

HEALY: Just standing there?

KEHAL: Standing still. Not moving. Like he was waiting.

The file included pictures of the stairwell. There was no separation between stairwell and flats, and there was an open balcony too, which ran opposite the endless rows of uniform blue doors. On a top-down diagram of the stairwell, the corridor and Kehal's flat, the man's location had been marked with a cross. He'd been about fifteen feet away.

Unfortunately, Kehal's English was only passable, so the interview started fraying around the edges when Healy began trying to drill down into the detail.

The distance from Kehal's door to the stairwell didn't help, but as Healy tried to get a sense of what the man may have been doing, Kehal just repeated the same thing: that the man was standing still, with his back turned, as if he was waiting for something. *Or psyching himself up*, I thought, and then saw that one of Healy's team had speculated the same thing, writing: *Nervous? Having doubts?*

So was this 'Mal'?

Thinking that Kehal's recollection might be improved if he were able to communicate in the language he'd spent most of his life speaking, Healy

134

brought in a Punjabi interpreter, and interviewed again. Kehal articulated himself better, but failed to add much texture. One thing that caught my attention, though, was when Healy pressed him on whether the man had looked nervous or scared.

KEHAL: No.

HEALY: He'd been pacing up and down the corridor before that. It sounds to me like he was nervous.

KEHAL: I don't think so.

HEALY: What makes you so sure?

KEHAL: He seemed . . . I don't know, he just seemed relaxed. He kept checking his watch to see what time it was.

HEALY: He kept checking the time?

KEHAL: I didn't stand there and look at him for long, but he checked his watch at least twice. Maybe three times.

HEALY: So it was like he was working to a schedule?

KEHAL: Working to a schedule, yes.

Using the interpreter again, Healy concentrated on a physical description of the man. He'd had his back to Kehal the entire time, and Kehal estimated that – in total – he'd spent no more than forty seconds watching through the peep-hole. Nonetheless, he was able to describe the man as being in his mid forties, with blond hair tied into a short ponytail, and about six to six-two in height. It didn't appear to be the same man Sandra Westerwood had described seeing with Gail and the girls, but, with this second suspect, Kehal gave Healy more to work with: he was wearing jeans, a short, dark blue raincoat and a white T-shirt.

Nevertheless, the interview with Kehal and the pinpointing of the man on the stairwell made for slim pickings. With the man not moving from his position – or showing his face – it was impossible to connect him directly to the Clarks. If it wasn't Mal, who was it? Their killer? Or just a man in a block of flats that housed six hundred and eighty other people, waiting for someone to meet him?

I moved on to the interview with Bridgette Koekver.

Koekver was a 25-year-old legal secretary, origin-ally from Hoorn in Holland, who worked for a firm of solicitors on Marsh Wall, south of Canary Wharf. On Sunday 11 July she'd been doing over-time, as part of a big case the firm had coming up that week. She'd left work at 7 p.m., and had then gone to a colleague's house-warming party at an apartment overlooking Blackwall Basin. At 10.15 p.m., she got the Tube back from Canary Wharf, changed at Canada Water and walked home from New Cross Gate station. At around

10.45 p.m. – fifteen minutes after Kehal said he saw someone with their back to him, on the stairs of the seventeenth floor – Koekver described passing the same man as he left the building's ground-floor entrance.

Again, the scene had been sketched out via a top-down diagram, showing Koekver's position in relation to the man, their approximate routes in and out of the building added as a series of dotted lines. They'd passed within feet of one another, Koekver approaching the doors from the left, the man veering off to the right. He'd headed in the opposite direction to the way she'd come, down towards Cork Hill Lane, the road that led into Searle House and its two sister buildings. I remembered driving along it back in January, so I could take a look at the flats.

What made Koekver's statement compelling wasn't just the fact that the person she described seeing – mid forties, blond with a ponytail, jeans, a dark blue raincoat, a white shirt – chimed exactly with the one Kehal had seen on the stairwell, it was that the man had been sprinting as he'd left the building.

And something else too.

He'd had blood on his hands.

HEALY: How much blood?

KOEKVER: Not a lot . . . but . . . like, dots, you know?

137

HEALY: Spatter?

KOEKVER: I'm not sure what that means.

HEALY: Lots of dots?

KOEKVER: Not lots. But some.

HEALY: Enough for you to notice?

KOEKVER: Definitely enough, yes.

HEALY: And you're sure it was blood?

KOEKVER: Now I know what happened to that family, I'm sure. But when I saw him, it was dark – not much light, you know? – so I wasn't completely sure.

HEALY: Which was why you didn't report it at the time?

KOEKVER: Yes.

This was where CCTV footage should have helped.

Except two of the cameras that night were on the blink, which meant the investigating team had to rely on the only one that worked: the camera that faced out towards Cork Hill Lane, the solitary road in and out of the estate.

At this point, it looked like they may finally have caught a break.

In a series of black-and-white stills from the night of the murders, the blond man with the ponytail was caught on camera leaving Searle House and heading to where a row of cars was parked on Cork Hill Lane. The clearest shot of his face was right at the start, as he exited: a side-on freeze-frame, his jacket covering a part of his chin, his ponytail obscuring an ear and cheek as it swung from behind him, swaying to the movement of his run.

He had a blond beard, the same colour as his hair, unsculpted and untidy. I wondered briefly whether it may have been deliberate, an effort to disguise himself: if it had been a conscious decision, it had been a clever one. The quality of the camera wasn't good enough to differentiate clearly between the lines of his face – the angle of his jaw, the point of his chin, the crescent of his upper lip – so the lower half of his face became a blur of blond, like a bleach stain on the film.

Above that, things were more distinct.

His nose was short, a little compacted, and looked as if it may have been broken a couple of times, without ever being properly reset. He was overweight too: not much, but enough. He didn't overtly carry it on his body – he looked tall, well built, powerful – but I could see his cheeks were a little puffy, his eyes too.

*His eyes.*

They were the part that didn't quite fit.

There was an odd dichotomy to them, as if they should have belonged on someone else's face. The colourless printouts didn't help, reducing their subtlety to opaque black discs, but even if their actual hue was brown, hazel or bottle green, they looked out of place alongside his blond hair and fair skin.

That was the clearest picture the police had of him.

A second shot showed him halfway down towards the line of cars, his coat billowing behind him.

A third showed him reaching the pavement.

But then I got to the fourth.

I'd expected him to keep going, heading off in the direction of New Cross Road, but instead the fourth picture showed him reaching forward and opening one of the cars parked against the pavement. It was a dark-coloured Mondeo.

He was getting into the passenger side.

In the fifth, he was already inside the vehicle, pulling the door closed, but with the interior light on I could – for the first time – see something else.

*There's a second man.*

He was on the driver's side, gloved hands on the wheel, indistinct face turned slightly towards his accomplice. The man at the wheel had a very similar black or blue raincoat on, and appeared to be wearing a dark baseball cap. In the sixth and final picture, the door was shut, and the Mondeo was pulling out.

The registration number was clearly visible.

I turned the page and found the line of inquiry on the vehicle: it had been found three weeks later in the Long Stay car park at Heathrow Terminal 4.

As soon as it was found at Heathrow, Healy's team sourced footage from the car park, in order to get a clearer shot of the men, and traced the ownership of the car. But the car was stolen from an estate in Charlton on Friday 9 July.

And, as one avenue closed, so did another.

The Heathrow footage was worthless. The men appeared to have planned ahead: the car was parked two hundred and fifty feet from the nearest camera, in a corner of the lot that had the least amount of coverage, and when they left the vehicle, they'd changed clothes: black beanies, black coats with high collars. The fact that they'd dropped the car off in darkness, at 1.57 a.m., only helped them.

Afterwards, Healy's team had gone through the footage from the Cork Hill Lane camera, trying to see if the blond man had been there *prior* to the family being murdered – watching them, scoping out their location and routines. But he never appeared again. Yet it seemed unlikely it would have been his first time there, especially if Gail let him in willingly. The conclusion the team reached was the obvious one: if he'd been to Searle House before, he'd approached from the direction of the Tube. Had he just got lucky, inadvertently using the failing CCTV on that side of the building to his advantage? Or had he known the camera was out of service? The second option was the more worrying: it spoke of someone in control of every step, aware of his surroundings. It was cold-blooded planning.

I returned to the stills of the man leaving Searle House.

The first shot of him – the best the investigation had – was borderline unusable, which explained again why no physical description, or picture, was ever released to the public in the aftermath of the family's death. It was blurred, over-saturated, even after going through forensics, and the public would have to work hard to make sense of it. His nose was an identifying characteristic – the fact it looked like it had been broken in a couple of places – but something about his eyes, the way they were at odds with the rest of him, didn't sit right with me.

Maybe it hadn't sat right with Healy either.

I traced the man's face with my finger, trying to get to the bottom of what was bugging me – and then, suddenly, the murmur of an idea formed and grew.

His hair. His beard.

*They don't belong with his eyes.*

Because his hair and beard were dyed.

Instantly, it made sense: Healy hadn't released the photograph because he knew he'd be asking the public, the media, to find the wrong man. That was why the beard was so unkempt – *because the man had never planned on keeping it.* And as I thought of that, I thought of something else: the 'Mal' that Sandra Westerwood had described seeing the family with, at the play park, in the months leading up to the murders – five-ten to six feet tall, black hair, medium build.

*Were they the same person?*

Apart from the difference in hair colour, they were certainly in the same ballpark physically, and it would explain why the blond-haired man was seen so close to the Clark's flat that night. It might explain too why Gail had let him in, willingly, at night – even though he'd dyed his hair and changed his appearance – and why there was no sign of a struggle. No shouting. No noise.

Because she trusted him.

So, who was the second man – the driver?

I flipped forward in the file, to the fifth picture taken from the security camera at the front of Searle House. The blond man was inside the Mondeo, hand on the door, pulling it closed. The front light cast a dull glow across him and the person in the seat next to him. The driver's face was a smooth, undefined mass, his eye sockets reduced to shadows, his cheeks just smooth, grey sweeps. Again, I took in the raincoat he was wearing, and the dark baseball cap, but there were no recognizable name brands on them – not helped by the quality of the footage.

I felt a knot of irritation form, imagining again how much worse it must have been for Healy at the time, sitting and looking at this succession of murky pictures, obscured by shadows and bad angles, overexposed, achromatic.

But then, off the back of that, I felt something

stir, out on the periphery of my thoughts. As I failed to grasp it, my eyes returned to the shot of the two of them – but specifically to the driver, both his hands on the wheel, black gloves on, body half turned in the direction of his passenger. There were two versions of the shot in the file: the original, taken from the CCTV feed; a second, magnified by forensic techs, cleaned up, its noise reduced, but with far less definition. The bigger the shot had become, the less sharp, its edges tapering off.

*There's something I'm not seeing.*

I compared and contrasted them both, hoping it would come to me, but the only thing I spotted this time was what must have been a mark on the CCTV camera lens itself: a crack, a hair, a fibre, something. From the angle of the shot, it made it seem as if the left-hand side of the driver's face had cracked, giving him an even stranger quality than he had already: the neutral, emotionless lines of his face; the black discs of his eyes; the lack of definition around his mouth and nose.

I leaned back and looked out at the garden, the truth hitting home: Healy hadn't been able to find either of the men because – through luck, but more probably, through good planning – they'd both made themselves untraceable.

One had changed his appearance.

The other appeared to have no face at all.

# THE MAN IN THE RAINCOAT

**22 days, 3 hours, 24 minutes** *before*

He woke suddenly, heart hammering in his chest, T-shirt and shorts soaked through. The moment he opened his eyes he instantly forgot what the dream had been about, but he knew it had been bad: his clothes, his pillowcase, the sheets he'd been cocooned in were all doused in sweat; and even as the thud of his heart receded, there was a residual sense of something, as if the dream had left a scar.

He sat up, flipping back the covers.

There was no window in the bedroom, but faint light washed in through the open doorway, cast by the moon as it angled down into the kitchen across the hall. He shifted, looking back over his shoulder. Beside him, Gail slept, her breathing soft and steady, and – as he watched her – he felt a swell of relief that whatever he'd dreamed about remained buried deep in his head. He was thankful to be back in reality.

Back with Gail. Back with the girls.

Peeling off his wet T-shirt, he grabbed his dressing gown, slipped it on and left Gail sleeping. He peered in at the room next to theirs, where the girls lay. They were sleeping soundly in adjacent beds, their night light plugged into the wall, a pale glow rinsing across their faces. They both went to bed with comforters, April a tatty cotton blanket, Abigail a brown-and-white puppy. There wasn't a window in their room either, so he'd helped paint them a mural on the wall: a floor-to-ceiling view of a sun-kissed beach. They'd quickly added all sorts of things to it, including aliens, lorries and castles, and their room had also become home to the dog, who loved curling up next to the mural because that was where the bedroom's radiator was.

Smiling to himself, he left them and padded through to the kitchen, filling the kettle. On the oven it read 03.42. As he stood there, he looked out of the window, into the night. The grass in front of Searle House was almost black, the other two buildings – identical to this one – like huge, beached ships around the same dark sea. There was no light in the sky now, the moon submerged behind banks of twisted cloud, so the only relief came from the orange glow of the street lights, one of them – close to the play park – blinking on and off, like a lighthouse.

Light. Dark.

Light. Dark.

Briefly, a breeze moved through the branches of a tree below – the only one this close to the building, its canopy five storeys beneath him, level with the twelfth floor – and as the wind died away again, he could see a figure emerge from the darkness on the far side of the park, arms in the pockets of a blue raincoat, baseball cap pulled down, eyes fixed on the ground. The figure was holding something.

A memory started to come back to him – some distant recollection – and as he stepped closer to the windows, he pulled the dressing gown a little tighter around him and a coolness began sliding beneath his ribcage. Below, the figure was crossing the grass in front of the flats, eyes still down, passing in and out of pools of light. Mal tried to grasp at the memory, but it was too indistinct. Did he know this person from somewhere? Was it the way they were dressed? Was it what they were holding? He tried to zero in on what the figure was carrying in their right hand, but it was small, being held close to their leg, and disguised by the darkness.

Slowly, as the kettle reached boiling point, the window began to steam up, and by the time he'd cleared it the figure was passing directly beneath him. He leaned right against the glass, trying to follow the figure for as far as he could.

'Are you okay, Mal?'

He started. Gail was standing in the doorway, dressing gown on. He glanced out of the window, but the figure was gone. 'I'm fine,' he said. 'Just couldn't sleep.'

'Bad dreams again?'

He frowned. 'Again?'

She came in, slid her arms around him, and they stood there for a moment, comfortable in the silence. 'You just seem to be having a lot of them lately.'

'Do I?'

She broke off, grabbed two mugs from the cupboard and started making them both some tea. 'Don't forget, you need to take the girls to school . . .' She looked at her watch and smiled. 'In four hours' time. I've got to be up early to get the bus.'

'The bus?'

'I've got my first exam paper today.'

'Ah,' he said. He'd forgotten. One of the most important days of her life, and he'd totally forgotten. He smiled at her, trying to pretend he hadn't. 'Your exams.'

'Did you forget?'

'No.'

That playful smile again. 'Okay. I believe you. Today could be the start of something good for us. I could be Gail Clark BA (Hons) in a few months.'

'You deserve it, honey.'

She went to the fridge to get some milk.

While her back was turned, he looked out of the window again, down seventeen floors to the area in front of Searle House; to the route the figure had taken, past the rows of wheelie bins.

'Mal?'

He turned back to her.

'Are you sure you're okay?' she said. 'I've come in here a couple of times and found you like this, looking out of that window. When I ask you what the matter is, you say you've had a strange dream. How often are you getting them?'

'On and off.'

'Are you going to be all right to go away?'

'Away?'

'Next weekend.'

He remembered then: he was supposed to be going off with some mates for the weekend. It had been in their diaries for a year. 'Yeah,' he said. 'I'll be fine.'

'You're not going to be much use to them if you're falling asleep.'

He smiled. 'But I'll be a cheap drunk.'

Gail returned the smile and, as she finished off the tea, he looked out to the darkness that surrounded the block of flats.

'What do I say I've dreamed about?'

She handed him a mug. 'Huh?'

For the first time she was studying him, as if she wasn't quite sure what was going on in his head. He smiled at her, trying to allay her fears, and rephrased the question. 'Do I ever mention what my dreams are about?' he said matter-of-factly.

'You don't remember?'

He shrugged; smiled again. 'All I know is I sweat a lot.'

'You've told me you've dreamed about a man.' She backed up against one of the kitchen counters, watching him. 'You say he's always wearing the same dark blue raincoat – and he's always carrying something in his hands.'

# CHAPTER 18

The day seemed to grow hotter as I went through the murder file again, making notes, posing questions to myself about possible new angles. I called Ciaran Healy and spoke to him for twenty minutes, asking him questions about his father, but things meandered once I got definite confirmation that neither he nor his brother had spoken to Healy since the turn of the year. At times there was a cynicism in his descriptions of his father, an acidity in the way he blamed him for the destruction of his parents' marriage, and I realized Gemma hadn't shown him Healy's last letter yet. If she had, I doubted he'd have been talking the same way.

After that, I made a series of calls, retracing Healy's original path through the investigation: the school the twins had gone to; the library Gail had worked at; friends of hers listed in the police file and neighbours at Searle House. It got me nowhere. I spent a while staring out at the garden, trying to gather my thoughts, trying to gain a clear line of sight – and then my phone started buzzing again.

It was Spike.

'David,' he said. 'How are you doing?'

'I'm good. Have you got something for me?'

'Everything you asked for, basically. This is the complete picture on this guy Healy, starting 1 June 2012 and going all the way through to yesterday, 2 October 2014. Finances, phone records, bank account, car, rent – it's all there. To be honest, when I started, I thought, "Shit, this is going to take me *days*." But after November 2013, he scales right the way back. Like, *really* scales back. He shuts up shop and vanishes. He stops paying for anything, stops making phone calls.'

That tallied with what Gemma had told me: July through to October 2013, after she'd sent him the divorce papers, she'd frequently been in touch, trying to get Healy to sign them. Then he became harder to get hold of, then she couldn't reach him at all. Two months after that, in January, he called me up and we met in the café – and the reasons why Gemma couldn't reach him became clearer.

'Anyway,' Spike continued, 'I'll email this through to you now. I've dug out the names and addresses of every incoming and outgoing caller on his phone records too. Otherwise, it's exactly as you asked for. I'll text you through the details about where to drop my money off.'

'I appreciate it, Spike.'

I hung up and then returned to my laptop, accessing the PDF files that Spike had emailed through. It was after five o'clock, and despite the heat of the day and the emptiness of the sky, some of the light had begun to drift.

I'd already been through the email account I'd set up for Healy, but Spike had got me the username and password for the one Healy had maintained before that, in the years after he'd been fired from the Met. It was similarly fruitless: the last message he'd received was from Gemma, almost a year ago, on 28 October 2013: *I've tried to be cordial about this*, she wrote, *but it doesn't have to be this way. Please, Colm, sign those divorce papers so we can all move on with our lives.*

He had no mortgage, no insurance policies, only a small amount of money left from the sale of the house in St Albans, no online subscriptions or pay TV. There was documentation for his pension, which looked pretty healthy, but it was like a pot of gold at the end of the rainbow: despite twenty-six years of service, he'd forfeited four years of pension contributions under the terms of his dismissal, and was unable to access his retirement pot until he turned fifty-five.

That was another six years away.

In the end, what the PDF basically amounted to was two distinct sections: Healy's finances across twenty-eight months, and then his itemized phone bills.

I started with his finances.

Through his bank statements, it was possible to subdivide his life into three further stages: June 2012 to March 2013; April 2013 to October 2013;

and then November 2013 to October 2014. Each stage illustrated a gradual decline.

Between June 2012 and March 2013, even after he was sacked by the Met, his account remained relatively buoyant. A month after he was fired, I offered him the spare room at my parents' old place down in Devon, so between July and November he stayed there, not having to worry about rent. In the November, he'd decided to return to London, and started paying out for a double bedroom in a shared house on the Isle of Dogs, presumably seeing that as a springboard to finding work. Spike had included the tenancy agreement as part of the document, which he'd got hold of through an estate agency. From there, it became possible to track some of the weekly routines via food shops and visits to petrol stations. Healy also took out direct debits to pay for his mobile, and insurance on his car.

In December 2012, his account was bolstered by ten thousand pounds' worth of savings from a second, separate account which he'd closed, cleared out and brought across. It was the last of the money from the property in St Albans. After that, things got even better before they got worse: in January 2013, he was offered the two-month security job at the building society, which paid him a total of £3,205 after tax, and that cash carried him through until the end of March.

That was when the decline started. It began as a slow drip of money going out, but not coming in. Throughout April and May, I could see evidence of him applying for jobs: filling up his car at petrol stations on opposite sides of the city; cash withdrawals from ATMs which, with the help of Google and job sites, I saw were situated close to places that had been advertising for security positions. By June, he swallowed his pride and applied for Job Seeker's Allowance – just shy of three hundred pounds per month – paid on a Friday, in weekly instalments.

Throughout June, he'd continued looking for work, but by July 2013 the routine began to wane. The money from his stint at the building society was long gone, and now he'd begun eating into his ten grand. As a result, he'd started to scale back his job applications, his travel, even his direct debits, cancelling the insurance on his car. When I zipped through to the back of the document, I found a copy of a SORN application. Healy had put his car into cold storage, securing it off-road somewhere. It made sense, as he wouldn't have to pay anything on it. It wasn't until the following January, after our meeting in Hammersmith, that I'd loaned him enough money to tax and insure the car, and get it back on the road.

What the financials hid was what else happened in July 2013: Healy had received the divorce papers from Gemma's solicitors. I wondered if that might have been a part of the reason why he scaled back his job search. He would have been affected by that: knocked off balance, probably surprised, definitely angry.

By September 2013, a lot of the ten grand was gone, on running costs and bills. He was down to his last thousand pounds. He'd already moved out of the house on the Isle of Dogs, cancelling the tenancy agreement midway through a second six-month term. As a result, he had to absorb one month's worth of rent.

Now came the systematic closing down of the account, dismantled piece by piece. By October, all direct debits had been cancelled, and he'd switched his mobile number to Pay As You Go. There was no evidence of where he was living – definitely no other tenancy agreements, no payments to B&Bs or motels via his account – so at this point he'd either found someone's floor to sleep on, which seemed unlikely given how few friends he had left, or he'd already become homeless.

I felt another pinch of sadness for him.

By the end of October, just seven months had passed since his contract finished at the building society. That was only seven months of unemployment, plus his JSA – as small as it was – was still being paid in, every Friday. Millions of other people had gone far longer without being able to find work – but millions of other people didn't have Healy's history. All the time he couldn't find a job, his boys continued drifting away, his wife filed for divorce, his daughter remained a harrowing memory, and he was haunted by his failures as a cop. His career, the only job he'd ever wanted, was long gone, and the attritional process of applying for work he didn't care about only accelerated his decline. In truth, he'd started along this road a long, long time ago, not just in the aftermath of his short-term contract ending in March. Even when he'd been staying with me in Devon, even when his account had still been healthy, he was a mess – resentful, grieving, self-destructive. Eventually it became hard to carry that burden, however well you disguised it. Eventually, you broke.

Healy broke in November.

Between November 2013 and February 2014, there was still *some* movement of funds – including, in January, the paying in of a small amount of money I'd loaned him, to go alongside the motel room, petrol money and Oyster card – but, from the end of February, he basically vanished from the page. In effect, the account became dormant. Even payments of his unemployment benefit, so consistent throughout the previous eight months, were halted in the third week of February, presumably because he'd stopped turning up for his interviews at the Job Centre.

From March, there was nothing.

*Literally nothing.*

From 1 March until 2 October there were no card payments or cash withdrawals at all. This left his balance at two hundred and fifty in the red, because of an overdraft limit that basically locked down his account until more money was deposited into it. If I'd been hoping that his financial picture might give me a steer on what he'd done and where he'd gone in the months after we last spoke, I quickly realized that hope was forlorn.

*Or maybe not.*

As I went to close the file, something small caught my eye.

# CHAPTER 19

In the five weeks between 16 January, the day of our phone call, and 22 February, the date the last JSA payment entered his account, Healy developed a short-lived but noticeable routine. Every Saturday, after the Job Seeker's Allowance was paid in on the Friday, he'd go to a cashpoint and take it out in its entirety. Different times on the Saturday, but always the same process.

*And always the same cashpoint.*

It was a Barclays ATM, identified on his statement with the abbreviation ELECA. ELECA would be its geographical location. Off the top of my head, I could think of only two possibilities – Electric Avenue, or the Elephant and Castle – but I spent a couple of minutes making sure, using another web search to try to locate any other London streets that might match, and then seeing where 'Eleca London' took me. It basically took me nowhere – to classified ads for guitars, and companies dealing with electricals – so I returned to my original two addresses.

This, I realized, was where I had an advantage. What the Met didn't know, because Gemma didn't know it at the time, was that when Healy posted the letter and the divorce papers in August, he'd been homeless since the previous November – except for ten days in a Kew motel in January. That meant that, even if the Met applied the same method I had, and used the abbreviation as a way to get a handle on his movements after November 2013, they'd have been looking in the wrong place. They'd have probably gone looking for tenancy agreements he'd made at the time, evidence of him possibly renting a place near Brixton, or close to the Elephant and Castle. It would have been a pointless search, because he wasn't renting anywhere.

But it didn't mean he hadn't been close by.

I spent the next ten minutes locating hostels and homeless shelters within a two-mile radius of both locations. The nearest to Electric Avenue was 2.1 miles away, and when I checked ATMs in the immediate area, I found two branches of Barclays within half a mile – but, crucially, no ATMs on Electric Avenue itself.

Would the bank still use an ELECA abbreviation if its branch wasn't on the road itself? It seemed unlikely, and when I began looking into ATMs in and around the Elephant and Castle, I discounted Electric Avenue entirely: there was a Barclays next to the northern entrance to the Elephant and Castle Tube station.

*This is where he was.*

What made it more compelling was that there

were two hostels within a half-mile of the ATM, one – at the top of New Kent Road – barely any distance at all. Both were run by the same people, a charity called Christopher Gee Housing.

Dragging my phone towards me, I tried the one nearest to the ATM first. It went unanswered, then to voicemail. I decided against leaving a message, and tried the second one. It was in the other direction, west along St George's Road.

This time someone picked up.

'CGH.'

'Hi,' I said, pulling my notepad in closer. 'My name's David Raker, and I'm trying to find an old friend of mine. We lost contact back in January, but I think he might have sought shelter with you shortly before and after; possibly between November 2013 and February 2014. I'm not sure if you keep records of who comes and goes, but—'

'We do, but those details aren't something I can give out over the phone.' It was a woman, softly spoken with a hint of a continental accent. 'I'm sorry. We operate a privacy policy here, so for us to release that information you'll either have to apply in person – with documentation to prove you're a relative or guardian – or you might be able to find what you need by contacting social services directly.'

'A relative or guardian?'

'Correct.'

'What about if he hasn't got either?'

'I'm sorry?'

160

'What if he doesn't have any family left?' I said. I kept my voice even and friendly, but made it clear that the rules weren't going to get us very far. 'He's a 49-year-old man. His parents are dead, his wife's long gone, his kids too.'

'Have you contacted social services?'

'No, I thought it would be better to get in touch with you guys first. I'm pretty sure he was there, or perhaps in your sister shelter on New Kent Road. Either way, I've got reason to believe he might be in danger. I need to find him.'

'Danger?'

I looked out at the garden, making her wait. It was an old technique, one I hoped she wasn't savvy enough to read. She sounded young, but that didn't mean she wasn't smart. Even if she saw right through it, I hadn't lost anything.

Out of the corner of my eye, I saw movement next door. Nicola, in shorts and a vest, was watering the pot plants along the edge of our shared fence.

'I'm sorry,' she said. 'I'm not allowed to—'

'Okay. What was your name again?'

'My name? Ingrid.'

'Okay. Thanks, Ingrid.'

I hung up, and immediately tried the other shelter again. It rang for about thirty seconds, then someone finally picked up. A man with a Scottish accent.

'CGH.'

'Hi, my name's Alan Schaefer, from Southwark

Social Services. I think we spoke last week? Anyway, I've just talked to Ingrid, and she told me to call you.'

'Okay.'

'I'm trying to trace the whereabouts of a man called . . . uh . . .' I paused as I checked paperwork I didn't have. 'Colm Healy. That's Colm spelt C-O-L-M. I think he stayed at your place on New Kent Road, but Ingrid couldn't find his records. Anyway, I was in the process of dealing with his emergency housing application but he's failed to turn up, and – given his recent history – I'm concerned for his well-being. I was wondering if you might be able to help with a couple of things.'

'What things?'

'He was with you between November last year and February this year, correct?'

A pause. 'What was his name again?'

'Colm Healy.'

'Fine. Give me a sec.'

'Okay, thanks.'

As he put me on hold, I felt a charge of adrenalin. If they had anything on Healy, I couldn't get it mailed to me now – if they were even inclined to do it in the first place – because I'd lied about who I was. But if they had something, and this *was* the right place, that was a start. I could work around it. I wasn't sure exactly what I hoped to find, or how this would progress any search for him, but it was better than a set of bank statements that presented everything after 1 March this year as a blank.

The man came back on. 'Right.'

I could hear pages being turned.

'Colm Healy. According to this, he came to us on 18 January and stayed for nearly six weeks. He wasn't with us in November or December, so if he was in accommodation it was at another shelter.'

*The now-defunct one on Goldhawk Road*, I thought.

'Okay. When did he leave you?'

'His last recorded day with us was on Thursday 27 February. We didn't see him after that.' Another pause. 'Someone made a note here, saying he left his stuff behind. Clothes, personal belongings, all that kind of thing. Any idea why?'

'No,' I said. 'No idea.'

But in reality my mind was moving fast. The fact that he'd left his things behind suggested he hadn't been expecting 27 February to be his last day at the hostel. Five days before, on the twenty-second, was the last time he withdrew his unemployment benefit from the ATM at the Tube station. So when he'd taken the £71 out on that Saturday, had he already known he was going to drop everything – clothes, belongings, what constituted his life – just five days later? If so, why?

What would motivate a decision like that?

I thought about the alternative, that whatever happened on 27 February, happened without him ever seeing it coming – but reasons for that seemed even less clear. He was still alive in August, because

163

he sent the letter to Gemma, so it seemed unlikely he'd come to any physical harm. So had he left because he hated the hostel? The people there? Even if he had, that still didn't explain why he would purge so much of his life that day. After all, why leave his *clothes* behind?

'Has this got anything to do with 18 August?' the man asked.

I tuned back in. 'Sorry?'

'I've got a note here that says he returned on 18 August.'

'Mr Healy did?'

'Yes.'

*Three days before he sent the letter to Gemma.*

'Did he stay with you again?'

'No. I'm just reading my colleague's notes here.' A brief pause. 'Okay. She's written down here that she asked him if he needed a bed, and he said he didn't. When she asked him where he was staying, he was a little evasive, but in the end she managed to persuade him to tell her – and he said he was at The Meadows.'

I wrote it down. 'Is that another shelter?'

'No. Well, certainly not one I've heard of. Not one my colleague had heard of either, as she's put a question mark here, next to the entry for it.'

'Did he say anything else?'

'He asked if we'd kept any of his things.'

'The things he'd left behind on 27 February?'

'Right. His backpack. The clothes in it.'

'Had you?'

'Apparently, after a month, with no sign of him coming back, we boxed up his clothes and sent the best ones to charity. However, we did keep some of his personal belongings, in case. He had a phone, some photographs, some paperwork.'

*Paperwork.*

That had to be the divorce papers.

'Do you know what the photographs were of?'

'My colleague has put here that they were of his family.'

'What happened with those?'

'He said we could dump them.'

'All of them?'

'Everything except his paperwork. It looks like he took that with him.'

A silence settled between us: him, perhaps wondering why a man would choose to dispose of photographs of his family; me, caught between two ideas.

On the one hand, that it wasn't Healy who had returned.

It was someone else.

On the other, that it was, and in the hours before he wrote that letter to Gemma, he'd set his mind to doing one final, noble thing for her: signing the papers. In a way, the second idea was even worse, because it clearly spelt it out.

By then, it was over.

Clothes didn't matter to him.

Neither did photographs.

Healy was finished.

# CHAPTER 20

There were no organizations, shelters or homeless hostels in London that went by the name of The Meadows. The search term was too vague to get me anything through Google either. And an hour later, as darkness clawed its way in, I was done with Healy's phone records as well. Calls had tapered off from the middle of 2013, coinciding with the point at which Gemma had first sent him the divorce papers, and he'd stopped applying for jobs. At points in the months that followed, he could go a fortnight without making a single call to anyone. From November, calls became the exception rather than the rule, and by March – the same time he disappeared from the pages of his financial records – his phone fell silent too.

I felt hollow.

The idea of how he'd spent his last few days rubbed at me, an emptiness settling in the pit of my stomach. I didn't understand why he would go six months before returning to the shelter, or why he would leave without any of his things in the first place. I had no idea where The Meadows was, or if he'd even been telling the woman at the shelter the truth. Basically, despite whatever advantage I had over the police in knowing some of Healy's movements after November, I wasn't that far on from where the official search for him had ground to a halt. I'd doubted the intensity of their investigation, seen apathy in the file, but maybe, when it came down to it, the Met had gone as far as they could.

I went inside and began making myself some dinner, but halfway in I just perched on the stool at the kitchen counter – meat lying raw on the chopping board, vegetables half prepared – and realized I wasn't even hungry.

In every missing persons case I'd ever worked, there had always been the same routes in: financial statements and phone bills were like fingerprints, a trail formed of addresses and locations that propelled me forward, returning me to the moments before the victim became lost in the shadows. When they failed me, there were always the families: husbands and wives, parents, brothers and sisters, all able to paint a clear picture of the person they loved, and the ways in which they might have changed in the months before they disappeared. They gained me access to the parts of their loved one's lives that no one else had ever glimpsed.

With Healy, there was none of that.

The traditional platform on which to build a search – his money situation, his phone calls – faded to grey from the moment he became homeless. He may have come up for air in January, but it was brief, and it had led nowhere. His family didn't know him, even – arguably – when he was a part of their lives, and all that was left behind was a shell.

A lonely, drifting soul, unattached to anything.

Two hours later, I got a call.

I was in the living room, lights off, silent, a beer bottle resting on my chest, when my phone began buzzing across the sofa towards me. It was Melanie Craw.

'Hey,' I said, picking up.

'You all right?'

It sounded like she was calling me from her car: there was the hum of an engine in the background, as well as a song on the radio. 'Yeah,' I said. 'I'm fine.'

'You sure?'

'Just a long day. Where are you?'

'On my way back from the office.'

I looked at my watch.

*Nine-forty.*

'How's that thing going?' she asked.

She meant Healy. 'It isn't.'

'What do you mean?'

I paused, thoughts returning to the day I'd spent out back on the decking, the pages I'd pored over, the data I'd tried to make sense of, the reality I'd had to face by the end. 'I can't find him,' I said. 'After 1 March this year, he vanishes into thin air for nearly six months and doesn't leave a trace. I mean, literally no trace at all. He doesn't access his bank account, he doesn't make any phone calls. He's gone.'

'So what's different?'

'What do you mean?'

'What's different from every other case you work?'

'In the others, financial history and itemized phone bills aren't my starting point. The families are. They notice changes in routine, in patterns, the way the person they love is behaving. I know where they disappeared from, the date, the location, who else was around. Even the official police report normally gives me something. An idea, a spark, *something* to run with. The best I can muster with Healy is the likelihood that he was still alive on 21 August, because he sent his ex-wife a letter in which he tells her he's going to do one, final thing for her.'

'Which was?'

'Sign their divorce papers.'

Silence on the other end of the line.

Eventually, she said, 'Do you think he really killed himself?'

'I think he was suicidal.'

'Yeah, but do you think he's dead?'

'I don't know. Normally I can read him, or at least read him enough. But this time . . .' I took down a mouthful of beer. 'Do you know he upped and left a homeless shelter on 27 February without

169

taking anything with him? He had a backpack, clothes, belongings he kept there with him – and he just left them all.'

'All of it?'

'Everything. And then he vanished into the ether for six clear months. In the middle of August, he returns, picks up the divorce papers and tells the people at the shelter to dump the rest – even the pictures he had of his kids.'

I watched the wood burner begin to fade outside on the decking, its fire reduced to dying embers, its colours washing in across the living-room carpet.

'You don't have *anything*?' she said.

'Just some place he told the people at the shelter he was headed. It's not another hostel. Knowing Healy, he was probably just palming them off.'

'What was the place?'

'He called it The Meadows.'

She didn't reply.

'Craw?'

'The Meadows?' she said.

'Yeah. Have you heard of it?'

A pause. 'Yeah. Yeah, I know where that is.'

# VOICES

## 8 days, 9 hours, 58 minutes *before*

As he was heading out with his friends at the weekend for two days of drinking, he promised the girls he'd take them to school on the Tube that morning, instead of walking. It was only two stops, but they were excited about the change of routine and ready in plenty of time. At the station, he led them through the gateline and down the steps to the platform, and then they all sat on a metal bench playing 'I Spy'. April always cheated, defaulting to the 'I Spy with My X-Ray Eyes' version of the game, but never telling her sister until Abigail had repeatedly failed to guess correctly. Eventually the girls started bickering, so he suggested they stop the game and talk about what they were going to do at the weekend instead.

They emerged from the Tube station ten minutes later and he walked them along the street to school. Kissing them both at the gate, he watched them amble side by side up the driveway, dressed identically, with the same satchels and the same hair, plaited in the same way. Their classroom was at the front of the building – an old, red-brick Victorian structure – and Gail told him that she always liked to wait at the gate until they appeared in the window of the building to show her they were inside. He did the same. After a minute, first April, then Abigail, came to the glass and waved at him. He blew them both kisses and pretended to catch theirs in return, then – once they'd retreated from view – he made his way back to the Tube.

Just as he was about to head down into the belly of the station, his phone started buzzing. He stopped, returned to street level and looked at the display.

An unknown number.

'Hello?'

Static, like a bad reception.

'Hello?' he said again.

More static but then, briefly, another sound. Was it a voice? It played out, over and over in the background, beyond the buzz of the interference, like a recorded message on repeat. He cupped a free hand to his other ear.

'Hello?'

'. . . them.'

'What? Who is this?' He heard a high-pitched squeal, like the whine of a fax. 'I can't understand what you're saying!' he shouted.

'. . . a chance to save them.'

The line cleared instantly.

'Hello?'

'Don't let him take them from you.'

He felt his heart shift. 'What?'

'Look at what he's carrying.'

'What?'

'Look at what he's carrying in his hands.'

'Who is this, please?'

Another high-pitched squeal.

'He'll have it when he comes for them.'

Mal lurched awake, body swaying to the beat of the Tube train. For a moment, he was disorientated, still cast adrift by the echoes of the dream; then he looked up at the route, fixed to the carriage above him, and realized he was seven stations past his stop and one station from the end of the line. Sitting forward, he pulled his phone out of his pocket and looked at his Recent Calls list: the last one made to his phone had been from Gail, the day before. He remembered it: she'd asked him to stop and get some milk on the way home, and he'd forgotten.

He ran a hand down his face.

He'd been having trouble sleeping for a few weeks now, and it was starting to get to him. Dropping off on the Tube was just his latest concern. He'd been forgetting stuff, been so tired some days he was even starting to hear things – voices calling his name, conversations between people who weren't there. And then there were the dreams when he finally did get off to sleep: so vivid that at points he struggled to remember what was real and what was imagined. In fact, in his quietest moments, he'd started to worry that he might eventually get to the stage where he wouldn't even be able to tell the difference.

As the train squealed to a stop, he got off, exited

the platform and made his way over to the south-bound track. There was a series of empty benches.

He collapsed on to one.

Maybe you really are losing it, he thought, and his mind returned to a night about a week before: as he lay awake in bed, he swore he could hear whispers coming from inside the flat. He'd got up to investigate and found Gail and the girls fast asleep, the TV off, and silence from the adjacent apartments.

After a while, the voices had stopped.

In the days after, he'd started smoking again, even though Gail had told him she didn't like it. He'd got into a routine of sitting at the window in the kitchen – 2 a.m., 3 a.m., 4 a.m. – looking out across the grass at the front of the tower block. Sometimes all he'd see were trees swaying in the night breeze, or rain hitting the uneven, pockmarked concrete in the Searle House car park. But sometimes he'd see other things: movement in the branches; shadows among the tree trunks; figures at the very corners of his field of vision, running between pools of light and then disappearing again. And then there was someone who never attempted to hide.

The man in the dark blue raincoat.

He felt a chill pass through him, a ghost of a memory, as he recalled the man: how he always kept to the same path – emerging from beyond the tree-line, passing rhythmically under street lights all the way down, moving to the front of the block of flats, then disappearing into the darkness at its side – and how the man was always dressed the same way. That same raincoat. That same dark baseball cap. Jeans. Black boots. The man never looked up, just kept one hand in his pocket, the other at his side, holding something, head lowered, eyes on the floor. Mal had no idea why the man had got to him; why – when he saw the man out on the path – all that filled his chest was dread, an instinctive need to protect Gail and the girls. The man had even infected his dreams, returning again and again, a figure crawling out of the shadows inside his head.

Except somewhere, buried deep down, he could hear a voice that he couldn't switch off; a whisper, on repeat, massaged by all the doubt, the exhaustion, the insomnia. A voice that kept saying to him, Are you actually dreaming when you see that man – or are you awake? What happens if that man is real – or not real?

What if you're slowly losing your mind?

What if the greatest danger to Gail and the girls is you?

# CHAPTER 21

Early the next morning, with the sun yet to rise, I sat in the darkness of the BMW and waited for Craw. The car park was small and surrounded by high banks of fir on three sides, as perfectly smooth as plasterboard. An arched doorway had been carved into one section of it, a black iron gate inside that, but the other side was still murky and indistinct, The Meadows disguised by the smoggy grey of dawn.

She arrived a couple of minutes later, steering her Mini into a parking bay two spaces down from me, even though there wasn't anyone else around at this time. I got out and closed the BMW, then watched as she emerged from the darkness of her own car, the subdued morning light painting her skin a pallid grey, her black trouser-suit merging with the shadows as she came towards me.

Out through the entrance to the car park behind her, I saw traffic passing on Dog Kennel Hill, a road that curved south-east through Southwark, towards Peckham Rye Common. But the high walls did a good job of suppressing any sound, the thick firs reducing engine noise and car horns to a hum and replacing them with the trickle of water from a stone plinth on the other side of the gate.

'Morning,' Craw said, as she got to me.

'Morning.'

'You all right?'

I nodded. 'This is a remembrance garden.'

She looked past me. 'Yeah.'

'For who?'

'Come and have a look.'

She moved past me and lifted the lock on the gate. It squeaked on its hinge and then fanned out into the half-light of the garden. Over her shoulder, I now had a much clearer view of the sandstone plinth, carved into the shape of a crucifix and sitting on an island in a square of shallow water. It was possible to gauge the size of the garden for the first time: maybe only ten feet across, but about twice that in length, hemmed in by high hedges, except for a slab of marble that was embedded in the fir behind the plinth. As I followed Craw inside, I saw that the marble was engraved, the top half with a line from Elizabeth Barrett Browning's 'Sonnets from the Portuguese': *I shall but love thee better after death*. Beneath was a series of dates that felt familiar to me – 4 January, 12 January, 17 January, 25 January, 31 January, all five suffixed with the same year, 1988 – and, under that, six equally familiar names.

Four men. Two women.

'You ever heard of Ian Arnold?' Craw said.

At the mention of his name, I knew straight away why I recognized the dates. In January 1988, I was just seventeen years of age, still living in Devon, months short of moving to London, but I'd watched the news reports about him at the time, seen his face in the papers, and had continually heard him referenced by journalists I'd worked with in the years after. Some of them had covered the events of the time. Some were still affected by it. I didn't know there had been a garden of remembrance built, didn't know they'd named it The Meadows – but I knew what had happened on those days, because everyone remembered Ian Arnold.

'I never realized they'd built this,' I said to her.

Her gaze was on the marble wall. 'Arnold's case was way before my time, but Dad was drafted in on it towards the end. Just another warm body, I guess.'

She paused at the mention of her father, a man who'd spent thirty-five years at the Met. Since I'd worked his case, since she'd laid his memory to rest, she never talked about him; only ever in passing.

'I've spent twenty years on the force, and every day I hope I don't land a case like this one,' she went on, and then stopped a second time, as if gathering her composure. 'I remember Dad saying the guy never even broke a sweat. He said Arnold was interviewed for two solid days and he barely batted an eyelid.'

My attention returned to the six names on the wall, to the four men and two women. Except I knew now that they'd never been men and women at all.

They'd been children.

The Highdale housing estate, a sprawling maze of five-storey flats only two minutes' walk from The Meadows, was Arnold's stalking ground. It was half demolished now, in the process of being rebuilt as something more modern and efficient, following infamous estates like Heygate and Havelock into oblivion. But when Arnold had lived there, it had been different, a labyrinth of doorways and walkways, ugly and broken, zigzagging across the spaces between Dog Kennel Hill and Grove Park. Ultimately, its anonymity had been exactly what Arnold had needed: he'd kidnapped and murdered six children – all aged between eight and twelve – in a short but devastating twenty-seven-day spell. He'd snatched two of them on the same night, 31 January 1988, and was only caught a week and a half later – on 9 February – because his seventh victim managed to escape his grasp and run screaming along a fifth-floor corridor he and his mother had lived on.

With the promise of newer, better housing to come, many argued that Highdale's worst days were behind it – yet the truth was they were never going to be far enough away to repair its reputation entirely. I'd been down here many times as a journalist, as politician after politician cynically used it as a backdrop to try to launch campaigns about social inequality, about child poverty, about drugs and gangs and knife crime. But the reality was, shadows as long as Highdale's would always weigh heavy, even if its façade was a little newer, its doorways a little less dark.

And there was no shadow longer than Ian Arnold's.

I kept my eyes on the wall, on the names of the children whose lives had been taken so cruelly from them; then to the plinth, water gently cascading from the top of the crucifix and tumbling past its right angles to the pool below.

As I tried to imagine why Healy would tell the people at the shelter he was coming here, why he might choose this place as the termination of his journey, I kept coming back to the same idea: *It's to do with the fact that they were children.* The kids at Highdale had suffered the same loss of innocence as the twins. They'd left this life at the hands of someone equally callous, someone equally abhorrent.

I saw that.

I understood his reasons.

*But where did he go from here?*

As the sky brightened further, the first hint of crimson staining the wide-open spaces above our heads, the crest of what was left of the old Highdale – its trademark turrets, like the last bastion of a crumbling castle – emerged from the gloom. I couldn't see anything else, not above the thickness of the high firs, but it was enough for an idea to form: the estate was divided into two, one half being rebuilt before the second half was demolished. People remained in the older half, yet to be rehoused – but a lot had been moved out to temporary accommodation.

That left a lot of empty flats.

'Raker?' Craw said.

I turned to her, and saw she'd taken a step closer, hair clipped away from her face, eyes fixed on me, studying me. As she moved closer still, the heels of her court shoes clicked against the flagstone path that had carried us into this place.

'Did you hear what I said?'

I realized then that, as I'd been thinking about Healy's next move, about him possibly having holed up in Highdale, Craw had been telling me something.

'Sorry,' I said. 'I was miles away.'

'You know why Healy came here?'

I looked across the tops of the hedges to where the turrets continued to emerge from the dark. 'I think he recognized something in the murders,' I said.

She nodded. 'I think you might be right.'

'You sound like you know something I don't.'

She looked at her watch, then sank both hands back into the pockets of her coat. 'After his suspension, when I tried to reintegrate him back into the force in 2012, I remember reading through his history at the Met. I mean, it was a big risk giving him a second chance, and I wanted to make sure that my instincts were correct. I was well aware that, if it went wrong, I'd be getting my arse handed to me.' She paused at that last sentence – because, in the end, that was exactly what had happened. 'Anyway,' she went on, 'I'd got to know Healy's CV pretty well by the time he finally joined my team.'

I saw a glimpse of what was coming.

Craw took a step closer, seeing the recognition in my face, and started to nod. 'He joined the Met in April 1986 as a uniform in Southwark. I remember sitting down with him in 2012 and telling him he needed to rediscover the reasons why he wanted to be a policeman in the first place.'

'You're saying he worked on the Arnold murders?'

She shook her head. 'No. He was just a constable at the time, but he told me he was at the scene, right at the start, when detectives began to interview the seventh kid – the one that escaped. He said *that* was the reason he wanted to become a murder cop. That was the moment that started it all. What it came down to was he didn't ever want to see that fear in another kid's face.'

I looked at her, silence settling between us.

But it felt like we were both thinking the same thing: these names on the wall, this collapsing housing estate, this was just another ghost to be exorcized.

He'd rid himself of one by writing Gemma an apology, committing words to paper that he'd never had the courage to speak aloud. He'd done it again by signing the divorce papers, unshackling her, giving her the freedom that she'd long wanted. And here he'd done it a third time, perhaps for the final time, returning to his first few years of being a cop, to a case that, two decades on, would be mirrored by the murder of the twins and their mother.

He'd have seen the similarities between the two cases: the age of the victims, the brutality of their killers, the two crumbling housing estates against which the crimes took place. And, despite there being over twenty years between them, perhaps a part of him may even have seen the parallels as some kind of sign, as his inevitable fate. Years ago, he'd watched from the back of the room. In 2010, he'd watched as a killer slipped away.

Both times, he'd been powerless.

The beginning was the same as the end.

# CHAPTER 22

I left the car where it was, and walked up Dog Kennel Hill to Helton Way. Craw passed me as I did and beeped once. It wasn't a greeting, it was a reminder: she'd asked me to call her with an update later if I found anything at Highdale. I acknowledged her, watching as her Mini disappeared over the brow of the hill.

Helton Way was the road that bisected Highdale, although the estate – half a mile from corner to corner – was actually subdivided into quarters, each part as huge as a cruise ship, its balconies lined with endless doorways, its walls dotted with satellite dishes. Every window on the side of the estate still standing was made of frosted glass, milky like cataracts after years of neglect; but on the other side of Helton, Highdale was reduced to memories and rubble.

Trucks and diggers were parked on mounds of dry mud, a crane with a wrecking ball too, vehicles and building-site Portakabins secured behind endless mesh fencing. I stopped and took in what lay beyond the fence: one quarter of the estate was gone entirely, nothing left of it but its concrete base; another had been reduced to half a building, roof gone, walls torn away, interiors revealed. I could see dangling electrical wires and crumbling plasterboard, floral wallpaper, half-rooms with walls dotted in mould. Another few weeks, and both quarters would be consigned to history. I turned back to the half that remained.

It seemed to loom over me, even though it was only five storeys high. A single walkway – suspended at the fifth floor – connected one quarter to the other; otherwise it could just as easily have been one vast structure, two back-to-back L-shaped buildings designed to be perfect mirror images of one another.

Highdale was built on a slight slope, and this half sat higher than the part already in the process of being demolished. That meant the tiny car park I was standing in, enclosed on three sides by hundreds of flats, was below the level of the ground floor. I took a flight of concrete steps up from the car park, where the main entrances to each block faced a patch of scorched grass. This early on, with the sun only just up, the place was quiet: I could hear a car engine somewhere close by, the throatier sound of the traffic on Dog Kennel Hill, birdsong, but not a lot else.

I started with the building on my left.

It had no name of its own, no identity to speak of, and inside it was like a photocopy, duplicated and stuck together, over and over. Unlike the building that Healy had found the twins in, Highdale was all enclosed, its corridors long and windowless, smelling of industrial cleaner and damp. The flats here looked like they were still occupied: as I passed them, I could hear sounds from inside.

On the second floor, things were exactly the same, except it looked like the council had colour-coded the doors. The ground floors had been red; these were blue. On the third floor they were green, on the fourth yellow, and by the time I got to the fifth it was back to red, but one marginally darker than before.

At the end of the fifth-floor corridor, a set of double doors opened up on to the walkway I'd glimpsed from outside. I headed out, into the freshness of the morning, and was met by the same sounds as before, except with better views: I could see the building site to the north more clearly, workers starting to arrive.

I headed inside the other building.

Despite the same layout and colours, a sheet of paper had been attached to each of the doors on the fifth floor. I moved closer and looked at the first one.

It was an eviction notice.

The same printout had been taped to every door, all the way along, and as I headed further in, towards the stairwell that would take me down to the floors below, I started to realize that this corner of the estate *was* different from the last. There was no sound.

No music. No televisions.

186

No voices.

This was the next part of the site to go, its occupants already departed, its life mapped out now in days not weeks. There were no internal lights on, and there was no stench of cleaner or polish, no suggestion anyone had been inside for weeks. I began trying doors straight away. They had no handles on the outside, just a single Yale lock; I pushed at them, seeing if any of them were ajar. They weren't. I got to the stairwell at the end and headed down to the fourth floor.

It was the same here, except it was darker, unlit by the daylight from a walkway. The same notices were pinned up. I continued to try the doors, and on the third floor too. But just as I was starting to think that the entire building had been cleared, I got to the second floor and found a few people in the process of moving, their doors open, household items under their arms as they carried them out to their cars. No one paid me much attention as I passed, or as I paused on the stairwell and listened to one of the residents telling a guy in the blue uniform of a removals company that they had to be out of here before Monday.

That was two days' time.

I headed down to the first floor, where the scene was exactly the same – a few open doorways, people starting to move out – and then a small foyer, just inside the main entrance, with views out across the car park I'd started in twenty minutes before.

Outside, I stood there in the space between the two buildings, the sun up but still hidden behind the turreted roofs of Highdale. There was more noise now: the chug of diggers; the whine of cranes, cars and lorries out on the main road; birds squawking from the balconies above my head. I heard the rattle of a skateboard and watched a kid pass, headphones on.

*Where now?*

As disappointment fizzed in my guts, I headed into the space between the two buildings, under the fifth-floor walkway I'd crossed not long before. At the back was another car park, boxed in by ugly grey walls and a series of air-conditioning units growing out of the buildings like a line of blisters. They were all off, soundless, none of the fans turning inside their white metal casings.

Under them, something caught my eye.

At ground level, adjacent to one of the units, a grate had been removed. It was about two feet high and six feet long, and should have been screwed to the wall. Instead it was propped against the space it was supposed to be covering.

I moved across to it.

Dropping to my haunches, I tried to angle my head to get a better view of what lay inside; but it was hard to see anything, so I got down on to my belly.

Directly inside, level with the top frame of the grate, was the underside of a metal ventilation shaft. Beneath that, the space dropped down six feet – maybe more – into a cramped space, bricked on all sides with white concrete blocks.

There was a mattress inside.

As my eyes adjusted to the lack of light, I was able to make out even more. Next to the mattress was a cardboard box, turned upside down and being used as a table. There was a tin cup and a book on it. Beyond that, partially set in shadow, were the edges of a black-and-yellow backpack, tatty and stained, the zip broken. Spilling out of it was a red T-shirt with something printed on it.

A flash of familiarity formed.

*Was it something about the T-shirt?*

I started to edge closer on my stomach, shuffling across loose stones and gravel until my head was all of the way inside the shaft.

Then I stopped.

A body lay face down in the corner.

The smell hit me a second after I saw him. It crept up the walls, drawn into the daylight, gluey and ripe like meat left to rot in the sun. I swallowed once, again, again, trying to rid myself of its grasp, but it kept coming, forcing its way into my throat until I had to wriggle my way out and suck in gulps of fresh air.

As dread gripped the well of my stomach, I returned, took a deep breath and headed in with the phone out in front of me, its light casting a grey pall across the walls. Once my head crossed the lip of the shaft, into the darkness, the smell hit me a second time, but I pushed on all the same, moving as far in as I could get and directing the light down, into the corners of the space.

Now I could make out what was printed on the T-shirt, and knew why I recognized it: I'd seen it before, on 14 January, when I'd met Healy at the motel.

*Boys on Tour – Dublin 07.*

He'd been wearing it.

# CHAPTER 23

I put my phone in my pocket, turned myself all the way around and, gripping the ventilation shaft with both hands, shuffled along on my back, gradually dropping into the space below feet-first. I started to feel nauseous, and not just because the smell seemed worse than ever.

I didn't want to go any further.

I didn't want to see him like this.

When I hit the floor, the darkness seemed to waken: something scurried away, the scrabble of claws on concrete, and then there was a low, soft buzz.

*Flies.*

They bumped against my face, against my arms, and when I removed my phone again, directing its light out to where the body was, I realized it wasn't flies, it was wasps: they drifted endlessly in the shadows, like black snowflakes.

*The body's too old.*

*The flies have already gone.*

Putting a hand to my mouth, I inched forward.

He had a bright blue beanie on, his head turned to the right – away from me – his right arm caught under him, and facing off in the same direction as his left. He was wearing a thick woollen sweater, which had ridden up, exposing the dirty white T-shirt he had on underneath, and the small of his back, which had become ashen. He'd flattened in death, sinking against the skeleton as he'd dried out. I stopped, four feet from his legs, keeping my hand pressed against my face, overwhelmed by what I was seeing. It was hard to recognize him as the man I'd known, the skin on his face thin and papery, and clinging to the curves of his cheekbones and eye sockets. I'd seen enough death to know for sure now he wasn't fresh. Maybe twenty days.

*Maybe five weeks.*

Five weeks ago would have been the end of August, days after he'd sent Gemma the letter; days after he'd been back to The Meadows, returning to those moments when he'd sat at the back of a flat on the fifth floor of Highdale, as the mother of Ian Arnold's seventh, surviving victim told detectives what had happened. He'd spent his last hours connecting the cases that began and ended his career.

And then, after that, he'd come here to die.

If I had any doubts it was him, if I retained any hope that his life hadn't ended here, in this hidden part of a decaying building, they disappeared as I directed the light out past him, to the spaces beyond his emaciated fingertips.

Because there – its battery disconnected and cast

aside – was the mobile phone I'd bought him from a supermarket in January. Next to that was a box of Zoplicone sleeping tablets, an entire tray consumed, the foil in every pocket punctured, the pills long since gone. Beyond both, open, pages spilling out of it, was the Clark family murder file, *You're on your own* scrawled across the front page of the file in my handwriting. And then, finally, tacked to the wall, were three photographs.

Gail.

April.

Abigail.

# PART III

# 31 OCTOBER 2014

## FUNERAL FOR COP FOUND DEAD IN DEMOLISHED HOUSING ESTATE

The funeral of former Metropolitan Police detective Colm Healy will take place at Bells Hill Burial Ground in Barnet today. Mr Healy's body was found in a maintenance room under notorious south London sink estate Highdale on 4 October. He'd committed suicide.

Healy had been a detective inspector at the Met before his dismissal in 2012, which was down to 'investigative decisions not in the public interest' and 'insubordination', according to a spokesman. However, one of his former commanding officers, Detective Chief Inspector Melanie Craw, said ex-colleagues on the force were still 'extremely upset at the passing of a man who served with great distinction until the regrettable decisions of his final few months'. She also confirmed that a contingent from Scotland Yard would be present at the funeral.

# CHAPTER 24

The day of the funeral it rained. The late summer was long gone, replaced by the grey of autumn, cloud knitted together, the temperature down to single figures.

I was surprised at the number of people who turned up to say goodbye to Healy, and while I felt nothing for him but sadness, his last months haunted by ghosts he'd never been able to control, a part of me was strangely relieved. As I'd driven to the cemetery that morning, I'd been worried the only other people at his graveside would be Gemma, her sons, Craw, and maybe a few former cops who felt sorry for him. Instead, despite all that he'd done, all his history with the force, forty-six travelled up from the Met, joining some former neighbours from his time in St Albans, and some cousins of his who'd flown over from Ireland.

He was buried a two-minute walk from Gemma's house. It was difficult to know where else we could lay him to rest: at the end, he'd had no home, no anchor to anywhere, so I suggested Bells Hill to Gemma, and she went along with it. In the days after I'd found him, she'd gone along with most things.

It had been a long time since she'd thought of Healy as her husband, but that didn't mean, in some small way, she hadn't still loved him. In that first week, as we waited for DNA results, for definite confirmation it was him, she was dazed, a little punch-drunk, so I offered to take care of all the arrangements.

She didn't cry at any point in the run-up to his burial. Instead, she'd sit there, staring into the middle distance, telling me she trusted my judgement, that the coffin I'd chosen was fine, that the flowers were lovely, that the hymns were perfect. For a month, she was like a dam groaning under the weight of water.

I watched his sons during the service, having only met them once in the flesh, at their sister's funeral three years before. Ciaran, whom I'd chatted to on the phone briefly in the days before I found Healy, was thinner, physically similar to his mother, and showed nothing, staring at the coffin throughout, hands in front of him, suit dotted with rain. His brother, Liam, was the opposite: bulky like his father, red-haired, intense, emotional. He began welling up as the coffin was lowered into the ground, gripping his mother's arm as if trying to prevent himself from falling in after it. Gemma, immaculately turned out, held out for an hour, first in the church and then out at the graveside, but on the walk back to the car park I saw her stumble a little, like her legs had given way.

Then, finally, she cried.

★　★　★

The wake was held at a golf club on the northern fringes of the town. Although Craw was there, she never spoke to me, her doubts about being seen with me in public keeping us on opposite sides of the room. Instead, as I stood on my own at the windows of the clubhouse, looking out at the greens, I saw a reflection shift in the glass to my left, and when I turned I realized I'd been approached by a couple of CID cops I'd crossed swords with before. One, a softly spoken Scotsman in his early forties called Phillips, had been the senior investigating officer on the case that had led Healy and me to the body – and the killer – of Leanne; the other was a pudgy, aggressive detective sergeant in his fifties called Davidson. Davidson had worked alongside Healy on the Snatcher task force in 2012, but the two of them had loathed one another.

'David,' Phillips said.

I nodded at him, and we shook hands.

Davidson didn't offer me his hand, just looked me up and down.

The three of us stood there in an uncomfortable silence for a moment, then Phillips said, 'I understand from what I've read that you were the one that found Colm.' It wasn't a question, so I just nodded again and let him continue. 'Still running around trying to save the world, I see.' He stopped, this time for longer. During my dealings with him, I'd never liked Phillips as a person, although I'd come to admire his abilities as an investigator – but it was clear he didn't feel the same way about me either personally or professionally. 'It seems that every time I pick up a newspaper these days, I find your name plastered all over it. Why can't you just let us get on with our jobs?'

'I didn't realize I was stopping you.'

'You're damaging cases, David.'

'You don't believe that.'

'Don't I?'

'I'm searching for people no one else cares about.'

'So it's a public service?'

I shrugged. 'It's whatever you want it to be.'

He smiled but didn't say anything.

Next to Phillips, Davidson had edged around so he was almost side-on to me, and through the gap that had opened up between them, I could see a crowd of other detectives looking on, Craw among them. They were obviously all in on whatever this was. Briefly, my eyes met Craw's, but she showed nothing in her face, and then a guy leaned in and whispered something to her, his eyes on me, and she broke out into a smile. I felt a spear of anger.

'We first met in 2011, didn't we?' Phillips asked.

'I try not to remember,' I replied.

'Three years on and we're still chasing around after you, trying to clean up all the messes you make. I feel sorry for Colm – of course I do. His life was tragic. None of us wanted this for him' – he glanced at Davidson, as if to assure me that even he felt the same way – 'and, if I'm honest,

David, I don't think we'd be here now, and I don't think he would have had this ending, if he hadn't met you.'

I frowned. 'How do you figure that?'

'You corrupted him.'

'That's bullshit,' I said, and took a step closer to him. 'Healy was already well down the road by the time I met him, and you can look a bit closer to home for the reasons why.'

'Really?'

'When Leanne went missing, no one at the Met cared.'

'That's not true.'

'It's why he went off on his own, trying to find her. She'd been missing for ten months when he and I finally discovered she was dead – and you lot spent the entire time sitting on your arse doing nothing.'

'You're rewriting history, David.'

I shrugged. 'Whatever helps you sleep at night.'

'You've still got all the answers, haven't you?'

Davidson this time. He had a thick East End accent.

'Why are you even here?' I said to him. 'Healy hated you.'

'You don't know anything about me – *or* Healy. He was a good man before he met you.' He looked out at the rest of the room, over to where the group of detectives was: every face was on us now. It seemed to spur Davidson on: 'If you had a shred of fucking decency, *you'd* be the one who stayed away today. We're burying the poor bastard, we're leaving his sons fatherless, because you got inside his head. You're the reason he's dead.'

I swallowed my anger again but this time it didn't disappear as easily, and as Davidson glanced off at the crowd, starting to find his feet, I noticed that Craw was the only one among the group who wasn't looking at me now. She'd turned away, pretending that something else had got her attention, unable to face me.

'Well, it's been great catching up,' I said, and before they had the chance to come at me again, I barged between them and made my way out across the room to where Ciaran and Liam were standing together, talking to one of their relatives.

Behind me I heard the cops erupt into laughter as Phillips and Davidson returned – swaggering, triumphant – but I didn't look at them. Instead, I said goodbye to the boys, sought out Gemma and told her that I would catch up with her at some point over the coming days – and then I made a break for my car.

Twenty minutes later, as I headed south on the A1, rain spitting against the windscreen, traffic heavy as rush hour crept closer, my phone started going.

It was Craw.

'I didn't realize you'd gone already,' she said.

'Didn't you?'

'You should have told me you were leaving.'

I laughed a little at that, but there was no humour

in it. 'Yeah, I'm sure you would have appreciated me coming over to say goodbye to you in front of everyone you work with.'

Silence on the line.

'Look, Raker—'

'It doesn't matter.'

'I can't be . . .' She stopped herself, the rest of the sentence hanging there in the space between us: *I can't be seen with you.* 'It's difficult. There are people—'

'Just forget it.'

'. . . who will try to take advantage—'

'It doesn't matter, Craw. I get it.'

As I joined the North Circular, everything ground to a halt and I came to a stop next to a Holiday Inn that looked more like a grain silo. To start with, neither of us made an effort to resume the conversation, the line filling with a soft buzz.

Then, finally, she said, 'What's the matter with you?'

'What do you think's the matter?'

'We're all upset—'

'It's not about Healy.'

I looked over the roofs of the cars in front of me, the road rising to a ridge beyond which I could see nothing. The rain got heavier.

'What do you want me to do?' she said.

Except, because I understood her, I knew she wasn't offering to help me, she was confirming our situation. She meant: *What do you want me to do about the fact that I'm a senior detective in the Met – and you're a man the Met loathes?*

'I don't know,' I said. 'I don't know *what* to do, or *what* to say, but I guess I'm just tired of taking lessons from people whose jobs I end up doing for them.'

'What the hell's that supposed to mean?'

'It means I'm sick of being treated like a leper.'

It was out of my mouth before I'd even given thought to it, a rare lapse of control on my part, but I was surprised at how little regret I felt. Maybe on this day, of all days, having buried a man whose brutal honesty had often cut deeper than any knife, it was time to make her understand exactly what I was feeling.

'Are you saying you regret finding him?'

'No,' I said, 'that's *not* what I'm saying. But that's my point: *I* found him, just like you wanted me to – just like you *asked* me to – and yet I had to stand there today while two arseholes with warrant cards took potshots at me and told me to my face that I'm the reason Healy is dead.'

'What did you expect?'

'What did I *expect*?'

'You pick up the pieces on cases they can't close. Of *course* they're hostile. You're finding out what happened to their victims. You're showing them up.'

'"Them".'

'What does that mean?'

'That's you, Craw.'

'No—'

'This "them" – that's *you*.'

'No, I don't speak to you—'

'What's the difference between having to eat shit from a half-cop like Davidson, an hour after I buried someone I care about, and you standing across the other side of that room today, nodding in agreement as all your friends on the force formed a huddle and took turns to lay into me?'

'That wasn't what—'

'Don't tell me that wasn't what was happening.'

She didn't reply. The lull was filled with the chatter of rain, with the hum of cars moving inch by inch towards the city. I looked at the phone in its hands-free cradle, the mobile's display showing her exactly as our relationship had defined us: no first name, just Craw.

'Is this going anywhere?' I said to her.

'Raker, look—'

'It makes no difference to me whether anyone sees me sitting at the same table as you, so I'm fine about it. I'm prepared to run with whatever this is. And you know what? I don't even really care that I had to watch you pretend not to like me today, just so no one would find out that we've had dinner together. I mean, you *do* like me, right? This isn't just some elaborate trick you're playing?'

'Of course not.'

'Good. So, what I need to know is this: am I going to be standing across the room from you in three months, in six months, in a year, in five, while you still treat me like an outcast? Frankly, I couldn't give a shit about the rest of them in there today, what they say or what they think – but I care about what you think.'

Another long silence.

'Craw?'

'Look, Raker, I like you. I think you're a good man.'

'But?'

'It's complicated. My situation is complicated.'

Something collapsed in me, not anger now, something deeper and more painful. And then reality hit home: I was saying goodbye to two people today.

'So this is what we are?' I said to her, calmly, quietly.

'Raker, you need to understand—'

'I don't think I need to understand anything.'

And when no further reply came, when there was no attempt from Craw to salvage the wreckage of our conversation, I hung up.

# CHAPTER 25

The day I found Healy's body, I left the scene immediately. I didn't go through his backpack, his clothes, I didn't check the shadows for something that might help progress my search, I just climbed back out and dialled 999. The search was over. Healy was the full stop. I couldn't bear to spend one more second alone in that room with his body, with the memory of who he'd become, with the insects feeding on him and the reality of his final moments.

I knew at the time that everything in that room would be processed and released, and I'd get my turn with his possessions. Ten days later that was exactly what happened: after DNA tests confirmed it was him, and his body was released, Gemma called and said the police had asked her to collect Healy's things – his backpack, clothes, cup, the book he'd had on him, his mobile phone.

The only thing they didn't release back to Gemma was the Clark family murder file. I called Ewan Tasker to let him know that someone at the Met might try to find out how the file had ended up in Healy's possession, but he didn't seem perturbed, and in the days after, something else began gnawing at me instead: what if I'd never left the file at reception for Healy? Would things still have ended up the same way? Or were my actions what had reduced him to this?

I went with Gemma to collect his effects, waiting outside the police station in Peckham, and when she came out, she was holding a transparent plastic bag in one hand – the empty backpack inside – and another pressed between her arm and ribcage, with all his other belongings in it, as well as three photographs.

Gail, April and Abigail Clark.

As I drove her back home to Barnet, north through the city's clogged arteries, she turned to me, bone white, no tears in her eyes, and said, 'Why didn't he have any photographs of Ciaran, Liam and Leanne? *They* were his kids. He should have had pictures of *them* at the end.' She looked down at the three photographs in the bag. 'Why only these?'

I tried to think of an answer that would help her.

Eventually, I realized I had nothing.

'I don't know,' I said.

Yet I knew what the answer was the moment she asked. They were the three photos in the murder file, the same three printouts he'd laid out on the table of the motel bar nine months ago. He'd been attached to the shots back then, his fingers straying towards them without even realizing he was doing it, and he'd remained attached to them right up until the end. Because in a way, however difficult it was to grasp – even for me, who knew him so well – in his final days those pictures were his entire world. Gail, April and Abigail were the only family he had left.

When I got home from the funeral, I showered and changed, grabbed a beer from the fridge and sat at the half-light of the living-room windows. I hadn't slept well for a month, not since I began the search for Healy, and as I listened to the rain peppering the glass, I knew immediately that tonight would be the same again.

On the living-room table was the plastic bag Gemma had taken possession of, Healy's belongings still inside. She'd told me to keep it, that it would be of more use to me, but that wasn't entirely the truth. I think mostly she was unsure of what to do with his things, with his tatty clothes, marked with the grime of the homeless, including the red T-shirt he'd been wearing the day before our argument; with a tin cup that reeked of alcohol, of the whisky he'd used to wash down ten Zoplicone; and with a phone he'd barely used since I'd first given it to him back in January, its battery long dead, its Call List empty.

I didn't blame her for not taking ownership of the book he'd had on him either, but of all the things he'd left behind, that was the item I found hardest to square off. Entitled *A Seaside in the*

*City: The History of Wapping Grand Pier*, its presence in the space beneath Highdale bugged me. It was a crumb left on the table; a lone, dangling thread. Old, faded and coffee-stained, it seemed bereft of relevance, of a reason for being there – and that was why I couldn't let it go. I'd skim-read the book three or four times in the last two weeks, trying to understand why he might have kept a copy of it. He'd never expressed any interest in the narrative of the city; in fact, I'd never once seen him read a book in the entire time we'd known each other. Yet I had to accept that in his last days and weeks, in the grave he'd made for himself at the end, he'd chosen *this* book as a keepsake. The question was why.

I finished my beer, headed to the kitchen and grabbed another, then removed the book from its bag on the way back. At one time it must have belonged to a library: it had a stamp on the inside front cover, faded and difficult to read.

The front cover was a black-and-white photograph of a pleasure pier, a Ferris wheel at the end of a slatted wooden promenade. The shot looked like it had been taken at the southern edges of Wapping. In the background was a London skyline that no longer existed: warehouses and wharfs lined the Thames all the way to Tower Bridge. There was no Shard, no Fenchurch Street 'Walkie-Talkie', no 'Cheesegrater'. This was the city before skyscrapers, before glass and steel.

The front-cover image was bleached, discoloured

by age, but I could still make out the top half clearly – *A Seaside in the City* – and the rest of it, *The History of Wapping Grand Pier*, well enough. The author was a woman called Carla Stourcroft, and when I'd googled her name in the days after receiving Healy's things from Gemma, I found out that she was a journalist and lecturer who had written a series of books, all centred on London. Her most well known was an acclaimed biography of Eldon Simmons, the notorious 'Invisible Ripper' who raped and murdered five men in run-down west London hotels in the early 1950s, but the rest of her output was much drier and had virtually no commercial impact at all.

She was hard to find on the web because of that: a few interviews off the back of *Invisible Ripper*, which was how I discovered she'd been a lecturer, but not much else. Her previous books were all released through small presses, or – in a couple of cases – self-financed and self-published, and without a website of her own and no social media presence, her footprint was absolutely tiny. Buried on the second page of my Google search, though, I did find one thing: a very short obituary that had run in a local newspaper. Stourcroft had died aged forty-six. It didn't specify what her illness had been, but it said she'd passed away with her family around her.

I knew little of Wapping Grand Pier myself, other than that it had been a brave Victorian experiment to transplant the experience of a seaside pier to the capital. But over the course of the past few weeks the book had helped fill in some gaps in my knowledge. As I opened it up again, it fell open naturally to an eight-page section in the middle, stitched in on glossier paper, featuring a series of photos. It was a chronology of the pier, from the time the first support struts were driven into the bed of the Thames in 1888, to its total destruction during the German bombing of Wapping in the Second World War, and on to its gradual reconstruction in 1948. In 1967 the site was bought by an American businessman called Arnold Goldman, who modelled it on the pier at Weston-super-Mare, where his English wife was from, and – according to Stourcroft – the 1970s were the pier's most successful period, making Goldman as much as eight million pounds.

The key to Goldman's success, it seemed, was to give Londoners a taste of Victoriana. Shops selling ice creams, candyfloss and popcorn were made out of mahogany and cast iron, and finished off with period typography, mirroring the places that had lined the pier when it had first opened in 1889. In fact, Goldman gave it a theme-park feel all over: everyone who worked there had to dress in costume, while a brass band was employed full-time to occupy the bandstand he'd built beyond the pavilion. He also opened a hall of mirrors, and a penny arcade inside the pavilion itself, where visitors traded in the currency of the time for copies of Victorian coins, to spend on period arcade machines: bagatelles, an early arcade equivalent of pinball; steerable ball games; laughing sailors; coin-operated fortune tellers; strength and true-love tests. Goldman kept it running at a profit all the way through the 1980s, but the fallout from the recession of 1990 was hard and fast, and Wapping Grand Pier never really recovered. In 1993, one hundred and four years after it had first opened, Goldman reluctantly closed it down.

The last photograph in the middle section of the book was one of only four in colour, taken in 1996, three years after the pier had shut its doors to the public. It was a shot from Waterside Gardens, looking east along the Thames, the towers of Canary Wharf in the distance. The pale pavilion looked like the carcass of a dying animal, marooned on the boardwalk, the whole pier built on stilts lathered with seaweed. The Ferris wheel had gone by then, dismantled and shipped north to a pier on the east coast, but the skeleton of the bandstand remained.

The book was published in 2002 and, in a caption under that last picture, Stourcroft predicted it would be too expensive to refurbish the pier, suggesting that because of this its future might be bleak. Yet it was still standing twelve years on, a crumbling hulk reaching out into one of the busiest rivers in the world. According to its Wikipedia page, a company called Rook's Head now owned it.

I closed the book, studying the cover image for

what could have been the tenth, the twelfth, the twentieth time.

I'd thought frequently about it, but I still couldn't imagine what power these pages had held over Healy in his last days. Why this book? Why this subject? I'd searched its pages for handwritten notes, for evidence he'd connected with something in it, a word, a paragraph, but there was no trace of him at all: nothing written on the covers, no scribbles in the margins. I knew he was a man on the precipice at the end, fractured and confused. I knew those things and yet I couldn't quell the belief that he'd had the book for a reason.

He'd seen something in it.

And so while I could forget the T-shirt and the tin cup, the mobile phone and the backpack, I couldn't forget the book. The book kept playing on my mind.

The book was the reason I still couldn't sleep.

# CHAPTER 26

At 1 a.m., unable to drop off, I padded through to the living room, picked up the book again, grabbed my notepad and pen, and returned to bed. For the very first time, I began reading the book properly. As rain stopped and started again, as the moon first broke through the clouds and then returned to darkness, I slowly moved through the history of Wapping Grand Pier. By 3 a.m., 101 pages into the 284, I could feel myself losing concentration, tiredness kicking in, so I set it down.

I woke again at six, tired, drained.

Making my way through to the kitchen, I put on some coffee and watched as, next door, Andrew and Nicola left their house, armed with suitcases for a weekend away, and then I headed back into the bedroom.

Picking up where I'd left off the night before, I reread the account of how Arnold Goldman bought Wapping Grand Pier in 1967. Carla Stourcroft's narrative was ultra-dry, but I tried to keep focused as she talked about the expansion of the Goldman empire – to Las Vegas,

Australia's Gold Coast, even to a casino on Brompton Road in London – and then returned to the subject of the pier. After an hour, I glanced at my notepad, saw it was empty, and moved to the living room – a few brave shafts of sunlight puncturing the glass on the living-room windows – hoping a change of position might give me a fresh perspective. But, as I kept on turning the pages, getting further and further into the book, I found nothing of use in the long, rambling accounts of the pier's last years on the river. In the Epilogue, it talked about the sale of the Ferris wheel to a Norfolk pier, and the 'Spectacular Mirror Maze' and Victorian penny arcade being sold to Rook's Head, the same company that had then bought the entire site from Goldman in 2001, eight years after it had closed. Shortly after that, the book ended.

My pad empty, my major questions still hanging, I sat there staring at the cover again and a part of me began to rebel. *The book was irrelevant. It was random. It meant nothing to Healy. It was an artifact from whoever had occupied the space beneath Highdale before him.* Yet, though I could give voice to all those things, though I looked at my pad and worried that I'd found nothing – even on a detailed read-through – I couldn't let go of the idea that the book represented something more. Its being there, next to the body of a man who rarely read, or showed any interest in history, didn't sit right with me.

I went and grabbed my laptop.

Feeling like I knew everything there was to know about Arnold Goldman, I instead put in a search for Rook's Head. A little surprisingly, it didn't have an official corporate website, but its name brought up several related articles.

One was an interview on the website Business UK with a man called Gary Cabot, who I found out was the founder of Rook's Head. The other was a link to the site for Wapping Wonderland and Museum, a place I'd never heard of, but which seemed to be a hybrid of amusement arcade and historical repository, built inside an old paper mill that lay on the banks of the Thames, directly behind the Grand Pier itself.

The design of the site was pretty clunky, a little ugly – and when I clicked on a picture gallery, I realized it was fairly reflective of the museum itself.

Like Goldman's original Wapping Pier, Cabot's Wonderland had taken its theme as Victorian and Edwardian Britain, the interior of the mill dominated by old signage, its staff dressed in slightly amateurish costumes, the corridors lined with stalls set under period typography; but the effect was rather spoilt by what they were selling: cans of fizzy drinks, disposable cameras, a raft of cheap plastic that normally cluttered up claw machines in modern arcades. Under one picture in the gallery section, a caption confirmed that Wonderland's penny arcade was 'the biggest Victorian amusement arcade in the UK, including seventy-two machines rescued and restored from the original Wapping Grand Pier'.

There was a café and a museum – where black-and-white photos formed a timeline across walls, detailing the history of Wapping Grand Pier, the paper mill, and the opening of Wapping Wonderland – and a shop as well. But the truth was, while the paper mill had a beautiful English baroque exterior, and the location was interesting, inside Cabot was running something scruffy and low rent.

I backed out and went to the profile piece on him in Business UK. It was a year old. At the top was a photograph of Cabot, taken next to the main entrance of the mill, WONDERLAND in bright red lettering behind him, alongside a ladder of four signs, each one promising something different: *Journey back to the 19th century! Spend old money in the UK's largest penny arcade! Lose your mind in the Spectacular Mirror Maze! Read the incredible history of Wapping Grand Pier!* Around that, the walls were adorned with reproductions of old Victorian adverts for tonics and powders, soaps, cocoa and cigarettes.

Cabot himself was in his early sixties, had thin, greying hair, and thick arms resting on a paunch. He had the slightly dishevelled look of a man for whom success still came as a surprise: his beard was ragged along the jaw, even patchy in places, his shirt too big for him, his hands marked by grease. He was the antithesis of a figurehead, a self-made success story that had never wanted to make the leap from shop floor to boardroom, and – given his age now – probably never would. Beneath the picture, a caption read: *Cabot was described as a 'shabby Richard Branson' by one national newspaper, but he takes it all in his stride: 'I started off life repairing things and I still do, so why should I change just because I have more money?'*

About halfway down was a brief history of Rook's Head. It described how Cabot had left school in 1967 to train as a mechanic at the garage his father, Joseph, owned while, at the same time, beginning a lifelong obsession for the penny arcade games on Wapping Grand Pier. Because of that, and 'being in the right place at the right time', Cabot also started a side line, repairing broken arcade machines for Arnold Goldman.

'Penny arcades were all but gone by the late 1970s,' Cabot says. 'It was all this soulless electronic stuff. But Mr Goldman had seventy-two machines on Wapping Pier, some from as far back as the 1880s, so I was still doing that for him until it closed in 1993 – oiling them, polishing them, staining them, ensuring mechanisms worked as they should. When the pier closed, he offered the entire stock to me for an excellent price, and later I took the mirror maze too. In 2001, the year I opened Wonderland in the paper mill next to the pier, Mr

Goldman offered me the original pier itself. I bit his hand off. I planned to reopen it once I got Wonderland off the ground, but the costs have always been prohibitive. So, for now, I keep it as a piece of history; one that no one else can touch as long as I'm the one that owns it.'

It was getting harder than ever to see what connection Healy could have made to any of this. Was this *really* what had mattered to him at the end? The story of an American billionaire, who built, closed and then sold a pier – and the local boy done good, who took it on from him and opened a bargain-basement museum in an adjacent paper mill? I sat there, eyes on the picture of Cabot, and knew I had to dig out some sort of answer, however insignificant it turned out to be. If I didn't, the incongruity of the book, and the disconnection between the museum and Healy, would continue to play on my mind. It would eat away at me. I worried that it might stop me from sleeping properly – and not just in the coming days.

For weeks, for months.

For years.

But, even deeper down, something else worried me more than all of this: that without knowing what Healy had found within the pages of the book, I might not ever be able to shake an uncertainty that had been shadowing me since the funeral – that there might be an element of truth in what Phillips and Davidson had said to me.

That I *was* the reason Healy had killed himself. That all of this was my fault.

# CHAPTER 27

As I headed past Ealing Common in the car, rain in the air, traffic slow along Gunnersbury Avenue, my phone started buzzing across the passenger seat. I thought about not answering, my head full of static, already focused on the museum at Wapping and my plan once I got there – but then I saw who it was.

Annabel.

I hit Answer. 'Hey sweetheart.'

'Hi,' she replied. 'How are you?'

'Pretty good. I thought you had your weekend workshop today.'

'Just finished.'

'Ah, right. How did it go?'

'Good. The Saturday morning kids are my favourite bunch.'

I looked out at the northern fringes of the Common, oak and horse chestnut trees swaying gently in the breeze. On the other end of the line there was a brief silence, as if Annabel wanted to say something but wasn't sure how to articulate it.

'Is everything all right?' I asked.

'I just . . .' A pause. 'I just wanted to make sure you were okay.'

It took me a couple of seconds to catch up, and then I realized what she was talking about: Healy. His death. His funeral. I felt a swell of emotion for her then at this small act of kindness, and with it, a flicker of recognition of what it was like to have someone looking out for you. It was the sort of call Derryn would have made to me, my parents before that. And while what I felt for Annabel was different from both – more protective; in its own way, more daunting – I liked how it returned me to the points in my history when I'd been at my happiest.

'I'm doing okay,' I said to her.

'How did the funeral go?'

I thought of the service, of being cornered by Phillips and Davidson, of my argument with Craw, and said, 'As well as can be expected, I guess.'

'I'm sorry I couldn't make it.'

'I didn't expect you to.'

'I know. I wanted to be there to support you. You've told me about Healy before. I know you two weren't close exactly, but that doesn't make it easier.'

'That's really good of you, Belle.'

Finally, the heavens opened, rain hammering against the windscreen and roof. The signal faded in and out a little, and when Annabel returned, it was halfway through a sentence: '. . . you working on next?'

'What was that?'

'What case are you working on next?'

I went to answer and then stopped myself.

What *was* I working on?

I wasn't sure what the answer was, perhaps because I didn't recognize the DNA of what I was doing: since I'd sat down with Healy in a Hammersmith café nearly ten months ago, no one else had asked for my help in finding the man who murdered the Clarks, no fee had been agreed, there had been no interviews with relatives, no recollections, no time spent in the rooms of their house. If this was a missing persons case, it was unique, one where I already knew how the pursuit ended. No one was coming home alive. Everyone was dead. There was no happy ending.

The only mystery was the motive.

*And who did it.*

Perhaps that was it. Perhaps that was the thing that was lost in all of this. Why that family? Why would anyone kill two innocent children in their beds?

Reason was what was missing.

*The killer was what was missing.*

Ten minutes later, as the traffic began to break up and I headed east towards Wapping, I was still thinking about that, the hum of the car helping me gather myself. The more I learned, the more anger I felt at the death of the family, the death of a cop unable to extricate himself from their suffering, and the impact that had resonated through to countless other lives: the family's neighbours at the flats, the parents at the girls' school, the kids the twins had sat alongside in lessons, Gemma, her two sons, even Craw. It was a ripple on a lake, moving across the surface of the water, all the way to shore. Some were more affected than others, but death was nothing if not seismic: it crazed and ruptured, and then the innocent fell through the cracks.

By the time I got to Wapping, my resolve had hardened even further. This wasn't the type of case I specialized in, but I was going to get answers all the same. I was going to bring home the reasons like I brought home the missing. And I was going to do it for everyone who had fallen along the way.

Gail Clark.

April and Abigail.

Healy.

# TOM

## 1 day, 23 hours, 11 minutes *before*

The pub was on the river. There were eighteen of them, tucked into a dingy corner, music playing from speakers directly above their heads. He didn't know everybody, but he knew enough of them: they were all men, all part of the way to being drunk – or already there. One of them was telling a story he'd heard – or, perhaps, made up – about one of the girls at work being bisexual, while a conversation was being held in parallel, at the other end of the table, about the brand-new football season.

Mal sat there in silence, drifting between both conversations but not really taking part, and after finishing his drink told a couple of them he was heading out for a cigarette. It was a Saturday night, so the pub was packed, and he had to negotiate his way through countless clumps of people to get to the exit. By the time he finally hit the street, the night clear and warm, he was hot, tired and on edge.

The cigarette calmed him down, and as he watched people pass on his side of the road, on the other side of the river, he thought of Gail and the girls, of how they'd probably all be asleep now. The girls went to bed at seven-thirty every night, like clockwork. Gail was a big believer in routine. She tended to follow on at about ten, half past, sometimes earlier. She was much more of a morning person than him. He'd always liked the night, felt more alive then, but since his insomnia, his bad dreams, he'd started to find the darkness less appealing. These days, as he watched Gail doze off on the sofa in the middle of a film, or listened to the soft purr of her breathing while a football match was on, he just wanted to be able to do the same.

'Too busy for you in there, Mal?'

He turned. It was one of the men from the group, a guy called Tom Ruddy. He'd known Tom for a long time, their histories entwined, first through work and then through a moment, three years before, when they'd both been at the same family charity event and one of Tom's kids had almost drowned in a lake. Mal had been the one who had pulled Tom's boy out of the water that day, dragged him up on to the shore, given him CPR, breathed air into his lungs. He'd saved the kid's life, and understandably it had never been forgotten by Tom, his wife or their family.

He'd never regretted saving the boy, not for one second, but sometimes he'd regretted the echoes it had left: Tom became different after that day, retentive, clingy, his gratitude manifesting as a need to be close, to be complimentary, to buy the first round of drinks, to offer to help even if help wasn't needed or wanted. And slowly, over three years, it had begun to annoy Mal, to niggle at him. It had got to the stage where he would honestly have rather gone back to the bad old days before the incident, when Tom used to be just like the other guys in the pub: bawdy and masculine, full of moronic stories about things that probably weren't true.

'Those stories always sound better after six pints,' Tom said.

Mal grunted a response and continued smoking. He would have offered Tom a cigarette, but he didn't smoke. Tom wasn't out here because he was dying for a fag, he was out here because his son had been pulled out of a lake, lungs full of water.

'How are things going with Gail?'

He looked at Tom. 'Good.'

'The girls okay?'

'They're good, yeah.'

They stood in silence for a moment, watching the crowds. After a while, he started to feel guilty about not asking after Tom's family, after his wife and boys, but he knew – whatever approach he made, however he phrased the question – it would lead back to that day at the lake, and then he'd feel the suffocation of Tom's gratitude again. Tom would start thanking him, and that would aggravate him.

'How's work?' Tom asked.

'Pretty good.'

'Busy?'

He shrugged. 'Usual.'

'You still working at the same place?'

Same place as every other time you've asked over

the past three years, Mal thought to himself. Out loud, he said: 'Yeah. The life of a delivery driver isn't very exciting, I'm afraid, so if you're looking for juicy stories, I'm not really your man.'

'Delivery driver?'

He frowned. 'Yeah.'

Tom pursed his lips, as if puzzled.

'Is there a problem?'

Tom started shaking his head, the frown falling away. 'No,' he said. 'It's good that you're busy. It's important to have full days, I think, otherwise work starts to drag. We've just taken on three people at our place, which was definitely needed. I guess the thing with what I do is that people always die, so we always have work.'

He looked at Tom: there was a half-smile on his face, which quickly faded as he realized the irony in his off-the-cuff remark. Three years ago, his son had almost died too. Three years ago, Tom could have been perched on a stool at his desk, filling out paperwork for his own boy.

'I guess I was just lucky,' Tom said.

Here it comes, Mal thought.

'That you were there for Jonah.'

He nodded at Tom.

'We're all just so grateful, every day, that you—'

'You don't have to thank me again, Tom,' he said, holding up a hand. 'I did what I did, I would do it again, but you don't have to thank me any more. It's done.'

★　★　★

They landed back at Heathrow late the next day, all of them a little worse for wear. The weekend had been short, but the drinking felt like it had gone on for weeks. Now it was time to return to their responsibilities: wives, kids, work, mortgages.

'You got much on this week?'

He'd sat next to Tom on the flight back. As they waited for the doors of the plane to open, he looked out at the darkness, lights blinking next to the runway, the glow from the terminal building revealing people working in the shadows beneath.

'I've got tomorrow off.'

Tom rolled his eyes. 'Lucky bastard.'

'I've got to pick the girls up from school.'

'I'll trade your day for mine.'

He smiled. 'Yeah. They're not exactly a bind.'

As the passengers started to file off, Tom held out his hand. 'It was good to see you again,' he said. 'If you ever need anything . . . you know . . . just call me, okay?'

They shook.

'Anything at all,' Tom added.

'Okay.'

'I hope the, uh . . .' Tom paused, eyes narrowing a little, as if he were trying to avoid causing offence. 'I hope the delivery business keeps on going well for you.'

He watched Tom go, suddenly disquieted for reasons he couldn't quite place – and then he got up from his seat and grabbed his bag from the overhead lockers.

\* \* \*

Kids spilled out of the main doors of the school, satchels hanging off them, across their chests, on their shoulders, some dragging theirs behind them like a cart.

He stood on a grass bank to the left of the doors, waiting for April and Abigail. He'd brought them back a treat from his weekend away, picking up two giant bottles of bubbles at the airport. The girls loved bubbles, seeing how big they could get them, seeing how far the bubbles would float before they finally popped. A couple of times he'd taken them up to the top floor of Searle House and watched as they'd sent bubbles out over the balcony, twenty storeys up.

A wind briefly stirred, moving the branches of the trees at the front of the school. He watched the way warm summer light winked through the foliage and cast an orange glow across the faces of the kids close by – and then his eye was drawn to the entrance of the school again. It was darker now. Children had suddenly stopped flowing out and a gloom had taken hold beyond the main doors.

He looked around him.

Most of the rest of the parents were leaving, their kids next to them, big arms around small shoulders. Others were standing at the main gates, or out at the edges of the school boundaries, children playing while the adults chatted together.

But he was still waiting.

When he turned back to the main entrance, he saw a flash of movement inside. A blur of colour against the darkness. He took a step forward, the first tremor of concern taking hold. Where were the girls? A second step, a third, and then he felt a weird kind of resistance, and it took everything he had to move again, to take another step closer to the doors. Finally, as he did, he saw someone shift against the dark of the corridor.

His heart dropped.

He tried to say something, but no words came out. When he tried again, he felt his voice catch, like there was dust in his throat, and he began coughing. He turned to the other parents, calling for their help, but there was no one left at the school. Not a single person. No kids. No parents. All the cars were gone from the car park, all the windows were shut, all the doors locked.

He was alone.

He turned back to the main entrance. The doors were closed now, chained and padlocked from the inside. He began to panic, began to scream the girls' names, looking out at the main road, trying to get the attention of passing cars, pedestrians, cyclists, anyone. But as he finally found his voice, the wind whipped in and took his words away, and he felt himself slowly, magnetically, pulled back in the direction of the school. On the other side of the glass, obscured by shadow, a man was standing still, looking downwards.

A dark blue raincoat on.

A baseball cap covering his face.

'No!' Mal screamed. 'No! No, don't hurt th—'

Instantly, he woke, dizzy and confused, his clothes

soaked through with sweat. It took a second for him to establish where he was: in the living room of the flat, the TV playing on silent, the dog curled up at his feet.

He let out a breath.

It had been another dream.

He got up and hurried through to the girls' bedroom. They were both asleep, their night light on, its pale glow revealing the gentle rise and fall of their chests. April lay in the foetal position, her comforter – a tatty cotton blanket – close to her face; Abigail was on her front, one hand clutching her brown-and-white puppy, the rest of her cocooned in a pink-and-white duvet. He felt the tension ebb away as he watched them, the colours from the mural above their bed – the sun-kissed beach, the outline of houses, the random aliens – adding a red tinge to their skin.

Pulling their door to, he made his way through to the kitchen. The digital display on the oven said it was 3.40 a.m. He set the kettle going and sat at the table, and after a while clocked movement out in the hallway. He watched as Gail passed from their bedroom into the toilet, bleary-eyed and exhausted. She'd been up late, studying for her second exam paper.

It's okay, he said to himself.

Everything is fine.

Everything is normal.

There's no need to worry.

# CHAPTER 28

Temporarily the sky cleared, late autumn sun weakly punching past the frayed edges of the clouds. It wasn't warm, but it was better than being pelted by rain.

The old paper mill which housed Wapping Wonderland and Museum was on the high street, directly adjacent to Waterside Gardens, a small park on the fringes of the Thames. It was a brown-brick, three-storey building, its huge second- and third-floor windows perched on iron platforms, alongside a wooden treadmill crane attached to the wall, all of which spoke of the building's previous life. Before Wapping had been redeveloped, before the luxury flats had moved in, the windows had been doors, used for unloading goods that had been shipped in on the river.

I'd called ahead, trying to get Gary Cabot on the phone, and had eventually been redirected to his PA, who told me he was in Dubai for a few days, at an auction. In his absence, and after some persuasion, she'd given me the name Calvin East, the museum's curator.

The museum closed at six, and I wanted to wait

until last entry at five for a reason. Cabot's PA had said Calvin East would be tied up with tours of the penny arcade and the museum until five-thirty, and I needed to make sure I got a run at him without hordes of tourists vying for his attention at the same time.

As it was only half-four, I headed along a thin, cobbled street at the side of the museum, wedged between the mill and Waterside Gardens. Part of the way down, out in the grey of the Thames, the pier began to drift into view.

I saw its blackened legs first, and then the remnants of the bandstand, clinging to the limits of the pier like a limpet. The further I went, the more of the pier slid into sight: first, furthest out, the pavilion, old, discoloured, huge broken letters spelling out GRAND PIER above its doors; then the wooden, three-hundred-foot promenade, echoes of Arnold Goldman's theme park still evident in the blistered, boarded-up Victorian shopfronts that dotted its edges; and then, at last, the entrance, a huge white arch built on a slab of paved land at the back of the mill, with a turret on either side in which flags had once flown. Inside the arch were fifteen-foot metal gates topped with electric fencing, preventing anyone from getting on to the promenade.

Despite its location on the Thames, despite the boats drifting along the water barely feet from where it concluded, there was a strange sense of isolation here; a loneliness to the pier that was difficult to explain. I'd been to many places like this, inside structures that were nothing but skeletons, along corridors that were vessels for memories, for the nightmares that had taken place in them. I'd even started to believe, somehow, that I might be drawn to them, that my years of trying to track the missing had awoken something in me; a sort of magnetic pull. Maybe my own heartache had marked me. Maybe these places sought me out now.

A noise snapped me out of my thoughts, and I turned to see the rear doors of the mill opening up, a group of middle-aged American tourists filing out on to the paved area and gathering at a rusty ticket booth, waiting further instruction. At the back of the group was a tour guide. He was in his early forties, studious, serious, wearing a pair of red-rimmed glasses that were too bright for his face and too big for his eyes. He adjusted them and came forward again, the costume he was wearing – a tailed coat, a waistcoat, a white shirt with a winged collar, a top hat – ill-fitting and unsuited to his flabby frame. He had the wispy hint of a beard, and bristles of black hair escaped from under his hat.

On his lapel was a name badge.

Calvin East.

'Okay, ladies and gents,' he said in a soft London accent he'd worked hard to iron out, and began on the history of the pier. I stuck around for a while and then left, heading back around to the front and paying the admission fee.

Immediately inside the museum was a section

marked *Journey through Time*, which turned out to be the room full of pictures I'd seen on the web. I passed through it, casting my eye across a photographic history of the pier and the mill, and then lingered on a last shot of Cabot, taken under the pier's arched entrance in 2001, after he'd purchased the site. It was clearly a shot that had run in local newspapers, Cabot with his arms above him, like he'd just won the lottery.

At the edge of the shot was Calvin East.

Thinner. Younger. Skittish.

I exited, and headed up the stairs.

On the first floor was the start of the penny arcade. It was fenced in by a pavilion-style façade, funnelling people through to the room beyond, which had been done out like the inside of a pier: slatted floors, wooden walls, windows with amateur-looking paintings in them, replicating the view out to sea.

Clearly the machines were the museum's highlight.

They swept across the space in five perfect rows, like gravestones in a field. They were mostly pinball precursors, though there were a couple of early 'pushers' too, machines with sliding trays moving back and forth, coins tumbling from one tray to another, and – with any luck – into the slot that paid out at the bottom. At the other end of the room was a spiral staircase, directing people to the next floor, with the promise of more machines, the mirror maze and a shop.

I headed up.

The place was virtually empty. At the top of the stairs was a fortune teller called the Oracle, a dial on its front handing you your fate. But with no plug to power it, it sat dormant and mute, just like the strength testers, kinetoscopes and early fruit machines that surrounded it. A little while later, off to my left, I heard a laughing sailor, his voice ringing out, and then the jangle of Amberolas – coin-operated phonographs. Mostly, though, the room was as silent as a mausoleum.

I imagined Healy walking this floor, these rows – a ghost among the gravestones – carrying his copy of the Stourcroft book. Had he found anything?

Each of the machines had a brassplate screwed to its side, with the date it was built, and – in some cases – where it originated from. While all seventy-two of Wapping Grand Pier's machines were here, even without counting them it was clear there were way more than that, Cabot continuing his rescue work by salvaging old machines from lost piers all across the UK: St Leonard's, Plymouth Hoe, Morecambe Central, Shanklin. The piers were demolished, their wooden frames scattered like bones in the sea – but while they were gone, the machines survived.

The thought put an unexpected pause in my stride – and then I suddenly realized I was alone, the other visitors having drifted quietly out of the room without me even noticing. As I stood there, archaic machinery for as far as the eye could see, I felt a bristle of unease. I couldn't place the feeling to start with, couldn't understand where it had come from. But then, as I continued on, passing through the middle of the room, surrounded by dark walnut cases, by the slowly rusting metal grooves of century-old pinball machines, I paused.

I felt like I was being watched.

'Mr Raker?'

A voice startled me and, when I turned, Calvin East was standing right at my shoulder, dressed in the same costume I'd seen him in earlier. I looked past him, expecting to find a tour group, but he was on his own. Behind me, next to the shop – manned by a disinterested girl in her late teens – was the entrance to the mirror maze. As if on cue, a burst of maniacal laughter came from a tannoy above it, and then a voice straight out of a 1950s B-movie said, 'You'll lose your mind in our mirror maze!'

'I didn't mean to surprise you,' he said. 'Kathy, Mr Cabot's PA, mentioned that you would be dropping by at some point, so I've been keeping an eye out all day for anyone that didn't look like they belonged to a tour group.' He stopped, rocking his head gently from side to side, a guilty expression on his face. 'Although I admit I may have given myself a *slight* head start by googling you.'

Which meant he knew all about me.

'You're an investigator,' he said. 'You find missing people.'

I nodded, dug around in my pocket and removed a business card. He took it from me, studied it.

'Are you free now, Mr East?'

'Calvin. Yes, I am. Actually, now is a very good time because no one turned up for the 5 p.m. tour, and I was due to speak to Mr Cabot on Skype at half past.'

'Would he be available to speak to me?'

'Yes, I'm sure he would.'

'So is there somewhere we can chat?'

'You mean you don't want to have to listen to an animatronic sailor laugh loudly every one hundred and ten seconds?' He smiled, loosening his collar, and pushed his red-rimmed glasses up the bridge of his nose. 'Please, follow me.'

# CHAPTER 29

He led me back down to the first floor, through the canyons of machines, to a door on the far side marked STAFF. Next to it was a number pad. As he input his code, the door buzzed away from the frame and opened into a short corridor with three doors on the left, what looked like a staffroom at the end, and two huge sash windows on the right. The view, partly obscured by the brickwork of the building next door, was of the Thames, all the way down to Tower Bridge.

'This way,' East said.

All three rooms on the left were offices, the first two small and cluttered. In the third, a big glass panel looked through to what I assumed was Gary Cabot's working space when he was in the country. His office was bigger, the furniture nicer, more modern, the mill's brickwork complementing the design. There was more light too. A window opened up on to a perfect view of the pier, perched on the river like an insect. Behind the desk, in a studded, antique leather chair, was a man in his late eighties, grey, stooped, eyes staring off into space. As we got closer, I realized he was talking to himself.

'You work them hard here,' I said.

East looked from me to the old man and smiled. 'Oh no, that's just Mr Cabot's father, Joseph. *Joe.* He likes to come in a couple of times a week and soak in the atmosphere out there. Joe's the reason Mr Cabot fell in love with the pier. Without him taking Mr Cabot to the pier, we'd all have very different lives.'

Beyond the door, I could hear the tinny sound of what must have been Gary Cabot, his voice coming through the computer speakers as he described the hotel he was staying in. He had a strong local accent, and he sounded upbeat and excited about being in Dubai. His father – clearly, I now realized, talking via Skype rather than to himself – seemed to be enjoying hearing about it too. His reaction reminded me of my grandparents, who always found the idea of foreign travel incredibly exotic, even when everyone in the world was doing it.

'When Mr Cabot's away, he likes me to look after Joe,' East said, pausing outside the office door. 'I've got to drop him back at the nursing home after this.'

As the door squeaked open wider, the old man looked up, but not directly at us. His gaze was askew, somewhere off to my left, milky eyes like a couple of pearls.

He was blind.

'Joe, it's Calvin.'

'Calvin, my boy,' the old man said, his accent similar to his son's. One of his hands was gripping the head of a walking stick, the other was reaching out into space, fingers grasping at air as he searched for East's hand. 'Come and say hello to Gary. He says he's staying on an island that's the shape of a palm.'

East moved around to face the computer, taking Joseph Cabot's hand, pale and liver-spotted, in his. 'Hello, Gary,' he said to the screen. 'How was the auction?'

'All right, Calvin?' the reply came. 'Yeah, good. Some interesting pieces, but nothing that floated my boat. I've got a last-minute appointment, so instead of talking after this, we'll just catch up when I'm back. That okay?'

'Of course,' he said. 'That's fine. I've got someone here, though. His name is David Raker. He's an investigator. He wanted to ask you some questions.'

'An investigator?'

'Yeah.'

'What have you been doing, Calvin?'

Both Cabots laughed.

East only smiled. I couldn't decide if it was because he didn't like being the butt of the joke – or whether it was because Cabot had hit on something a little too close to home. I filed it away for later.

East waved me towards him. 'Mr Raker?'

Next to him, Joseph Cabot searched the room for me, presumably trying to listen for a voice, for a sound I might make that would help him better pinpoint my position. He was thin, his skin like a yellowing bed-sheet, and he kept one hand on his knee, rubbing at it as if it were sore. But, beyond the evidence of his age – the jowls, the intricate network of wrinkles, the hairless dome of his head, the creaky knees – it was possible to see the man he may once have been: tall, probably quite handsome, with the kind of physique a runner would have had.

I reached out and took his hand. 'Pleasure to meet you, Mr Cabot.'

'Oh, please. Joe.' He shook my hand, his grip a little soft, then smiled. 'A pleasure to meet you too, Mr Raker. I hope Gary hasn't been up to no good.'

'No, nothing like that, sir.' I came into view of the computer's camera and saw Gary Cabot on-screen, the picture a little pixelated, but clean enough. 'Hello, Mr Cabot,' I said to him.

Physically, he looked exactly the same as he had done in the photograph of him I'd seen online, except he was dressed in shorts and a T-shirt, the latter a little snug for him. Behind him was an opulent-looking hotel room, with a sliver of window off to his left, Dubai at night reduced to a series of shimmering lights.

'Mr Raker,' he said, 'what is it I can do for you?'

I looked from him to his father, to East standing

off to my left. This wasn't exactly an ideal set-up for an interview, via Skype and surrounded by onlookers. Luckily, Cabot Jr seemed to pick up on it, even from three thousand miles away.

'Tell you what,' he said, looking at his watch, 'my flight back to London is at 2 a.m. Don't ask me why Emirates have to keep such unsociable hours, but that's the flight time.' He shrugged, smiled. 'I'll be back at 6 a.m. London time, so should be around tomorrow afternoon. I'd be happy to catch up then – as long as you can put up with me being a little tired. I don't tend to relax much on planes.'

'That sounds fantastic,' I said.

'Good. Get Calvin to give you my numbers.'

'I will do. I'll call you tomorrow afternoon.'

'Perfect. All right, I'd better go.'

'Travel safely, son,' Joseph Cabot said.

'I will do, Dad. I love you.'

'I love you too, my boy.'

I stepped away from the conversation, out beyond the computer, feeling like I was intruding on this moment. There was a clear bond between father and son, one that made me think of my own father, a man for whom words didn't come as easily, or outpourings of emotion – but one I'd loved nonetheless.

A second later, East had helped Joe Cabot sign off.

'Modern technology,' Cabot said. 'The irony of me being able to see my son halfway around the world, but *not* be able to see him, definitely isn't lost on me. So, do you work for the police, Mr Raker?'

'David. No, I work for myself.'

'Oh, how exciting,' Cabot said. 'Like Philip Marlowe?'

I smiled. 'Something like that, sir, yes.'

'Sometimes I think I should have been more ambitious,' Cabot went on, but then seemed to lose the trail of his thoughts, fingers scratching at a dry patch on his right hand. 'I spent most of my life under cars, trying to wash engine oil out of my hands, and thought that was a good career. But when I hear about my boy jetting off to Dubai, and listen to people like you, with these fascinating jobs, I think, "Joe, you *really* missed a trick." But, alas, it's a little too late for me now.'

He paused and looked down at himself, an instinctive movement that spoke of the fact that he hadn't always been blind, but then it seemed to click that he couldn't do that any more; that he was even incapable of being able to examine the shell he now called a body. He rubbed at his right knee again, and I heard a pop as he tried to straighten it out. When he looked up, his eyes were that same milk-white, but there was a sadness to them now.

'Anyway,' he said quietly, 'I'll let you two get on.'

I glanced at East, who leaned down to the old

man. 'I'll call someone to come up and take you to my car, Joe. Will that be okay with you?'

'Just get them to call me a taxi, son.'

'I shouldn't think we'll be *that* long, will we, Mr Raker?'

East looked at me like he was attempting to catch me out, as if I might feel obliged to keep our conversation short because the old man was waiting for him.

'I couldn't say for sure,' I said.

The smile fell from his face, but not from Joe Cabot's, who appeared amused by my comeback. I'd warmed to him instantly. 'Just call me a taxi,' he said.

I took his hand again. 'Nice to meet you, Mr Cabot.'

'And you, son,' he said.

# CHAPTER 30

Unlike Cabot's office, Calvin East's was a mess.

The desk was in the middle, in front of a small window, and around it, filling every space, were books, vertically, horizontally, in towers on the floors, spilling off shelves. Next to a pitching skyscraper of encyclopedias was a metal filing cabinet, but that and East's computer were the exception; the rest was a cascade of paper.

East grabbed a chair for me from the staffroom, brought it back and set it down, then returned next door when one of the museum staff arrived for Joseph Cabot. As they helped the old man out, I realized how quiet the building was, the noise from the Thames and the streets below reduced to a low hum. All I could hear was East's computer, purring softly, and the gentle snap of paper as pages in a book, high up on one of the shelves, were caught in the breeze from an air-conditioning grille.

When East was done, he offered me a coffee, but I told him I'd pass, keen to get going. I watched him come around and push aside a reference book with *London 1600–1699* on the front.

'So what can I help with?' he asked, sinking into the leather chair on his side of the desk. It wheezed as it took his weight, and he began turning from left to right, its mechanism making a tiny squeak every time he changed direction.

'You've got a lot of books here.'

He smiled, looking around the room. 'London has about four thousand years of history, give or take, going all the way back to the Bronze Age. So when I'm telling people about the story of this place, about this amazing city we live in, I like to know what I'm talking about. Plus, I'm a hoarder – and I'm a collector.'

'What do you collect?'

'Books, paintings, antiquities. I'm fascinated by London, I've lived here my whole life, so my collection is centred here. Are you a fan of history, Mr Raker?'

'As long as we learn from it.'

'Very wise,' he said, smiling. 'I have no formal education, which is why I would never be considered as a curator at any other museum. Everything I've learned has come from these.' He gestured at the books around his office. 'Gary Cabot was good enough to let me be a part of this, to help shape the tours here.'

I said nothing, taking out my notepad and pen.

He studied me, as if he'd noted something in my expression; something he didn't necessarily like. 'You know, a lot of people look down on us here. They say this isn't a proper museum, that

251

we're a seafront arcade, just one that happens to come with a big city tax band. But this place . . .' He paused. 'Do you know how many other non-coastal pleasure piers there are in this country, Mr Raker?'

'David,' I said, and shook my head.

'Zero. None. Do you know how many there are *in the world*?'

'No.'

'None. Wapping Grand Pier is unique. Utterly unique. That thing out there, it's a one-off. Whatever people's opinion, there'll never be another one of those.' East seemed to glaze over for a second, eyes on the pier, thoughts somewhere else. 'Ever since it was first built, it's been divisive. When it went up in 1888, some said it would be a white elephant, that the money would be better spent on Wapping's flagging maritime industry. Others said it was in completely the wrong place, the wrong part of London, that no one would come down to *Wapping*, this place full of growling sailors and salt-blanched warehouses. But they came. They came in their hundreds of thousands, right up until Hitler flattened it in 1940. And then they came again when Arnold Goldman finally resurrected it in 1967 – because people can see it for what it is.'

'Unique.'

He nodded. 'Correct.'

'Is Gary Cabot ever going to reopen it?'

'The pier?' East shrugged. 'I'm not sure. You'd

have to ask him. I know he would like to, but it's Grade II listed, which complicates things. You have all sorts of hoops to jump through – rightly, I should add – before you can make structural changes to a listed building, and that only adds to the cost. Plus it's in a general state of disrepair, hence the warning signs at the front. For now, I think he's just happy that it's his name on the ownership documents, because it means *he* gets to make the decisions about it. After all, history does nothing if not repeat itself.'

'With regard to what?'

He ran a hand through his hair, one side of it matted to his scalp where the rim of his top hat had pressed it flat. 'I mean, there are people out there who wouldn't be disappointed if the pier got knocked down tomorrow. Some think it's an eyesore on the river. Some, like the police marine unit next door, say it gets in their way and stops them doing their job. Even the mayor's on record as saying he's not a fan of it, that it's located too far out for tourists, and too far from a convenient Tube stop.' He held out his hands in a *What are you going to do?* gesture. 'People had problems with the pier a century ago, they've got problems with it now. But they can complain all they like – it's not going anywhere.'

I picked up my pen.

His eyes flicked to my pad. 'Anyway, I'm rambling. Sorry. It just constantly amazes me that people can be so negative about the pier, because *look* at it. It's *history*. It's part of the city's DNA, its biography. We even have our own ghost!'

'Is that right?'

East smiled. 'The Devil of Wapping.'

Unexpectedly, he got up from his seat and looked out of the window behind his desk. He beckoned me over.

'That bit down there,' he said, pointing a pudgy finger at the paved area in front of the pier entrance, 'was where they found one of his victims. The Devil had a taste for old women. He killed nine in all, and the one he left here was the oldest. Eighty-three. Anyway, when they finally caught Samuel Brown, aka "The Devil", they hanged him here in 1674 – right where the paving slabs are now – and they say his ghost haunts this part of the river, and possibly the pier too.' He turned to me, eyes wide, as if he'd mistaken our conversation for another part of his tour. 'A cleaner on the pier in the '70s said she thought she saw someone walking through the pavilion, dressed in a coat, breeches and stockings. Whoever it was had a noose around his neck.'

'Maybe he was on a stag night.'

East smiled politely but looked hurt, as if I'd spoilt the mood, or the tour, or whatever this was. I returned to my seat and waited for him to do the same.

'So,' I said, 'I was looking for some information.'

I dug around in my jacket pocket and took out

a picture of Healy, setting it down on the desk in front of East. The picture was about eight years old, taken by Gemma in the garden of their house in St Albans. *Different time, different life.*

'I wondered if you recognized this man?' I asked him.

East picked up the photograph.

It was harder to see his expression now, his head slightly bowed, his eyes hidden behind the rim of the glasses. He began shaking his head. 'No. Should I?'

'He might have come here himself, back at the start of the year.'

'He's missing now?'

'Yes,' I said, unsure exactly why I was lying.

He looked up, Healy's photo pinched between his thumb and forefinger, and returned his glasses to the bridge of his nose – a habit he repeated at least once every sixty seconds – his eyes fixed on me, his expression neutral. He'd crossed his legs under the desk, which tilted his body slightly to the left, and I could see one of his shirt tails had escaped the beltline on his trousers, revealing a shelf of pale white fat at his waist. I recalled, then, the photograph of him I'd seen downstairs, caught on the edges of the picture of Gary Cabot the day he had bought the pier from Arnold Goldman. Calvin East had been at least two stone lighter in 2001, but in the thirteen years since, clearly that hadn't been the only change. That one picture of him, out there on the periphery of a celebration

– nervous, intimidated – had captured something true about his personality at the time,
something about his nature that was impossible to
articulate, but very clearly on show. Yet here, in
his early forties, that wasn't who he was any
more. Now he watched me from behind those
big lenses, quiet, suddenly a little aloof, as if he
was trying to do the same to me as I was doing
to him: figure me out.

'What's this man got to do with the museum
and the pier?' he asked.

Briefly, there was a flash of something else in his
face – *panic?* – there and then gone, and I thought
again about how the years might have changed
him.

*Or maybe they haven't changed him at all.*

*Maybe he's just become better at disguising who he is.*

'I found a book among his belongings,' I said.
'*A Seaside in the City: The History of Wapping Grand
Pier*, by Carla Stourcroft. Are you familiar with
it?'

'Yes. I've read it.'

'He made some notes in the back of it.'

*Another lie.*

He came forward in his seat, shrugging off his
jacket and unbuttoning his waistcoat. 'Interesting.
I wonder why he would be looking into the pier.'

'That's what I'd like to find out.'

'I see.' His gaze lingered on me for a second. 'We
always get people in here asking questions about
historical items of interest – the pier itself, Victorian

and Edwardian Britain. I mean, last week I was filling someone in on quack remedies, for example – specifically the ones that had cocaine in them.' He laughed a little too hard. 'Most of those remedies were outlawed by the early twentieth century, certainly by the start of the First World War.'

'So you don't recognize him?'

'This man?'

'He wasn't one of the people you described?'

'Described?'

'The people you just talked about – coming in here and wanting to know about the history of this place, and of the pier.'

'No,' he said. 'No, definitely not.'

I glanced at my notes. I'd written nothing down.

When I looked up again, East was out of his seat. 'Are you sure I can't get you a coffee? I think I'm going to make myself some fruit tea.'

'I'm fine, thank you.'

He headed out.

I went back over the last ten minutes. There wasn't much to go on. Scraps. Maybe not even scraps. What bugged me more than that was why I'd felt compelled to lie to him. Was it that second of panic I'd seen in his face? That brief glimpse of the cowering boy inside him, the one I was positive I saw in the picture of him downstairs?

A noise out in the corridor.

I looked over my shoulder and then got up, walking to the door of East's office. I looked left, down towards the staffroom.

'Mr East?'

When there was no response, I headed towards it, pausing in the doorway. It was small. A table, four chairs. A counter with a microwave, a kettle and a toaster.

No exits.

Turning, I looked back to the other end of the corridor, to the door I'd first come in. I could hear noise from the other side: a laughing sailor, the tinny sound of Amberolas, the tannoy from the maze on the next floor above.

*Because the door's ajar.*

East had made a break for it.

# CHAPTER 31

I headed out into the first-floor arcade.

It was five minutes to closing time and completely empty. I looked across the tops of the machines, along the canyons of cabinets, a familiar feeling passing through me. I'd felt it out front, at the gates to the pier; I'd felt it as I'd stood here earlier, alone, surrounded by the wooden skeletons of long-forgotten machinery. *A mechanical graveyard.*

Movement on my left.

Feet on the stairs, heading up.

I followed, taking two steps at a time. As soon as I hit the second floor, I stopped again, looking around, trying to spot him. On the other side, the shop wasn't manned, the girl I'd seen earlier no longer behind the counter. I could see a wall lined with T-shirts, a different Victorian advert on each. Elsewhere there were pens, erasers, plastic beakers, replica coins, doorstops, mill photographs, old maps, countless junk.

More movement.

In the mirror maze this time: in one of its panels, reflecting a point much further in, I'd seen something – a man, dark clothes – there and then gone again.

It was East.

*Or was it?*

My eyes darted to the shop, to the vacant till, and then out at the room behind me, the machines as perfectly aligned and as silent as rows of corn. And then, out of nowhere, I started to feel unsteady on my feet, unsure of whether I'd actually seen anyone at all, my head thumping, a fuzz forming behind my eyes.

*What the hell's the matter with me?*

Suppressing a ripple of alarm, I headed into the maze, under the warped, bleached sign, my reflection emerging on one of the panels in front of me. Ten paces in, the maze dog-legged right, although it was difficult to tell, identical panels under identical coving making it seem as if the maze went on for ever. My reflection appeared on a panel next to me, then on one in front, then on both at the same time. I stopped just short of mistaking a solid glass wall for the next part of the maze, my face inches from making an impact. At another time, I might have seen the humour in my situation, the absurdity of all of this.

But not this time.

*More movement.*

Ahead of me: a flash, a shadow.

I upped my pace, hands out, unsure until I was almost upon it what was a reflection and what was the next turn. I glimpsed the exit somewhere in front, then realized it wasn't in front at all, it was behind me, and I was looking at another pane of glass. I stopped, rounded the corner, double-backing on myself, a sense of panic starting to grip me. The worse it got, the more the walls seemed to close in. Suddenly, my breathing stuttered, my knees giving out from under me.

And, like someone hitting a switch, I blacked out.

The noise of my phone brought me around.

I'd fallen forward, cracking my head against a glass panel, the ripple still passing along adjacent panes as I started to wake up. I watched the impact go on for ever, repeated over and over, as the maze reflected ahead, into infinity. The more lucid I became, the louder my phone seemed to get, still ringing on the floor next to me. I looked down at the display. It was Craw.

I ignored it.

'Hello?'

A female voice from somewhere else.

I felt saliva spill from my lips. When I'd hit the mirror, I'd punctured something on my face, and now my blood was warm and slick against my skin.

'Hello? Is everything okay in there?'

I tried rolling on to my back, and as I did, I thought I saw a brief, blurred impression of someone in a glass panel to my left. East. Maybe someone else. But then it was gone again.

I lay there, alone, at the centre of the maze, until

the girl from the shop found me a couple of seconds later. It was her voice I'd heard. She knelt down, trying to help, telling me she'd popped to the toilet while the place was quiet, which is why it had been unmanned, and returned to hear a crash from here.

I was slumped against one of the glass walls, blood running from a cut on my right cheek. She fired a series of questions at me – *What happened? Are you all right? Do you want me to call a doctor for you?* – and then something seemed to click and she began trying to negotiate instead, pleading with me not to tell her boss that she'd left her station unattended. I told her she didn't need to worry and tuned her out, trying to regain my composure. But as my nerves settled and the blood began to clot, I realized something: I was dazed, in pain, disconcerted.

And I was scared.

*What the hell had just happened?*

I shuffled out of the maze and straight to the toilets, cleaning myself up. At my hip, I could feel a lump forming, tender and bruised. The cut on my cheek was small and manageable, but my head throbbed, a pounding bassline that made me feel woozy.

When I got back down to the ground floor of the building, there were a couple of staff milling around, one cashing up in the restaurant, one sweeping.

'Uh, sir, it's past closing time now,' the older of the two said.

'I know. Is Calvin around?'

'He's already gone home.'

'You saw him leave?'

She looked at the cut on my face. 'Yes.'

My hip was agony now, my face throbbing. Touching a finger to my cheek, I noticed the cut had opened again, a trail of blood worming towards my chin.

Dabbing at it with the sleeve of my jacket, I felt a subtle change in the spaces around me, as if the air had shifted. Looking out to the entrance, back the way I'd come, I became aware of one of the staff asking me if I was all right.

I headed for the entrance, stumbling, nauseous. Was this what exhaustion felt like? What a month of broken sleep did to you? Or was it the blow I'd taken when I'd blacked out? Was I in danger?

Was I dying?

At the bottom of the steps, I backed up against the wall of the paper mill and closed my eyes.

*Calm down.*

I regulated my breathing, relaxed my muscles and turned my thoughts away from my body, back to East; to where he may have gone, to how I was going to pick up his trail – and why he might run in the first place. By the time I opened my eyes again, I felt better, clearer, back in control of myself.

*Forget it. Move on.*

*Healy's all that matters now.*

# WHAT REMAINS

## 0 days, 0 hours, 4 minutes *before*

It was late on Friday night, with Gail and the girls already in bed, when Tom Ruddy called Mal. He'd been dozing in front of the TV when his mobile erupted into life and started travelling across the sofa towards him. He looked down at the display, saw it was Ruddy and thought about not answering: the last time he'd seen Tom was five months ago, when they'd both ended up on the same stag weekend, and the conversation had inevitably returned to that day at the lake, when he'd rescued Tom's son from the water.

He let it go to voicemail, picked up the remote control and started flicking through the channels. Sixty seconds later, his phone beeped again and the display revealed that Tom had left a message. He picked it up, dialling into his voicemail.

'Hey, it's Tom.' It sounded like he was in a pub somewhere. 'Sorry to call so late. Haven't seen you for a few months, so thought I'd check in. Just, you know . . . seeing how things are. Uh, anyway, give me a call back sometime.'

Mal deleted the message, dropping the phone back on to the sofa.

Maybe another time, Tom.

Three hours later, he stirred, not having realized he'd dropped off to sleep in the first place. On the TV, the channel he'd been watching was now replaced by a title card telling him its programmes would return at six the next morning. When he checked his watch, he saw that it was after 3 a.m. He edged forward on the sofa, head throbbing, hands slick with sweat. He felt a little disorientated, fuzzy-headed, as if he'd woken up somewhere he didn't know and wasn't familiar with.

You're tired, he thought.

Getting up, he shuffled through to the kitchen, filling up the kettle. Out of the window, on the edges of the darkness that ringed Searle House, he saw something shift in the shadows and realized it was a tree – most of which he couldn't make out – its branches moving like the arms of a conductor as wind passed across the grass. He watched it for a while, mesmerized, its graceful actions almost keeping him pinned there, his breath fogging up the glass.

Someone was standing next to it.

Obscured by shadows.

'Are you okay, honey?'

He jumped, turning to find Gail at the door to the kitchen, in her nightdress. She looked from him to the window, then came across to where he was standing, one arm snaking around his waist, her eyes on the view. She squeezed him and asked again if he was all right, and he reluctantly looked out to where the tree was.

But there was nothing now.

No figure.

Just the tree.

'I'm fine,' he said.

She took a couple of steps away from him, returning to the door, a mixture of concern and fatigue in her face. He wondered for a moment whether she looked tired because of the hour or because she was becoming frustrated with him. She'd urged him to go to the doctor months ago, after weeks of sleeplessness, after he continued to wake up – time after time – from sweat-soaked dreams about the man in the raincoat. He'd told her about the dreams to start with, but couldn't communicate the sense of fear they brought, of foreshadowing, like a premonition playing out over and over. So he'd stopped telling her. Basically, he'd lied to her for the first time in their relationship. He told her the dreams had stopped coming, and he was feeling better, and he was sure regular sleep would return. But the truth was, he couldn't go to a doctor – because he couldn't explain what he felt.

'You go to bed, sweetheart,' he said to her.

She didn't seem disappointed at the offer. As well as his insomnia, the twins had had colds the previous week, and they'd been up and down for five nights. Gail was short of rest just like him. The only difference was that she'd had five nights of broken sleep.

He'd had five months. Maybe six. Maybe even more than that.

He couldn't remember any more.

After she was gone, he poured himself a cup of tea and fished his cigarettes out of the drawer. Then he opened the kitchen window and lit up, looking down across the trees and pathways seventeen floors below, at the play park off to the left. His eyes drifted back to the tree, out there on its own like a lighthouse without a lamp, wind coming through its leaves again, branches shifting and rocking. He watched for movement on the pathway running parallel to it.

The man isn't real, he thought. It's just my insomnia.

Then, suddenly, he became aware of a noise.

A scratching sound.

He stubbed the half-smoked cigarette out in the ashtray and moved to the door of the kitchen. Silence. He checked again on the girls, and then on Gail.

She wasn't asleep yet, and clocked his movement. 'Are you okay?'

There was no noise now.

He smiled; a sense of relief. 'I'm fine.'

'Why don't you come to bed, Mal?'

'I will. I'll just finish my tea.'

She returned the smile, and he felt a sudden, overwhelming love for her, for the girls too.

'I love you, Gail,' he said to her, and heard the tremor in his voice.

She seemed touched. 'I love you too, baby.'

'I love you all so much.'

And then he heard the scratching again.

He turned away from the bedroom, looking both ways along the hall. The noise came a second time. He waited for it again, unsure of which direction it had come from. In the bedroom, Gail was calling his name now, concern in her voice, but he didn't reply, instead trying to pinpoint the origin of the sound. In the silence of the flat, all he could hear was the hum of the television on mute, and the fridge.

Then it came again.

He turned.

It was coming from the other side of the front door.

Moving quickly, he unlatched it, turned the key in the lock and opened up. There was nothing on the other side, just the seventeenth-floor walkway, enclosed inside a monolithic tunnel of concrete. Something dripped close by, and a bulb was on the blink further down, way out of his line of sight, repainting the walkway a muted cream. He turned back, facing into the flat, and saw Gail come to the doorway of the bedroom. She had tears in her eyes. He tried to find the right words, words that would bring her comfort, reassurance that everything was okay – that he wasn't losing it here, right in front of her eyes – but then he made a move towards her and she crossed her arms, squeezing them tight around her, protecting herself, and he realized something: she was frightened of him.

'What the hell is wrong with me?' he said.

She backed away from him.

'Gail?'

A tear fell from her right eye, tracing the outline

of her cheekbone, but when he tried to make another move towards her, arms out in front of him, desperately trying to bring her into him, she swivelled and headed back into the bedroom. The instant she passed the door, swallowed by shadows, a smell hit him: an awful, tangy stench, one he couldn't place but somehow recognized. As he said Gail's name again, the odour hit him a second time, even more powerfully than the first, filling his nose and mouth, crawling its way down his throat. A second later, he started coughing, reaching out for the nearest wall, barely able to support himself, barely able to get to Gail, the smell getting stronger and stronger as he gasped for air.

He doubled over, phlegm sticking to his throat like tar, and as he did, he noticed something: a thick trail of blood running out of Gail's bedroom and into the hallway. As horror bloomed in his chest, the coughing subsided, and two more blood trails emerged beyond that, from the twins' room now, moving in parallel.

'No,' he said. 'No, no, no.'

'That's their death you can smell.'

He started, turning.

A man stood in the doorway now, blue raincoat buttoned up, dark baseball cap on, knife in his hand. He was looking down at himself, at his legs, his face obscured beneath the peak. There was blood all over his trousers, caked to the legs.

Then, finally, he looked up.

He was wearing a grey mask.

It was smooth and featureless, plain, and had a

crack on the left-hand side, like a splinter in a pane of glass. Mal looked at the man in the mask, at the eye sockets, but there was nothing except black.

Only black.

'No!' he said again. 'Please don't hurt them. Don't hurt my family.'

'They're not your family,' a voice behind the mask said.

'They're my girls!'

'Your girl is dead.'

Tears started to choke his words. 'That's my wife.'

'Your wife left you.'

'Don't hurt them. Please don't hurt them.'

'You're nothing to them.'

'Please . . .'

'You're nothing to anyone, Healy.'

# CHAPTER 32

After calling Spike for a second time, I managed to find out that Calvin East lived in Bermondsey, in a tight network of new-build houses west of Southwark Park. His was a sand-coloured end terrace, an unremarkable two-up, two-down with white fascia boards and slate-coloured roof tiles. At the bottom of his road was a bricked-up former railway arch, with a studded iron bridge on top, its panels painted a bruise-coloured mauve. I drove past his house, getting a feel for the road – watching as a train moved along the bridge, the smell of diesel following in its wake – then pulled a U-turn and found a space fifty feet away.

The rain had gone, the early evening bright and clear. I inched the window down, letting air drift in, and found myself thinking of the last time I'd felt sun on my bones, of how I'd sat by a Walthamstow canal, had lunch with Craw, then agreed to look into what had happened to Healy. What if I'd said no to her that day? Would not knowing be better – or worse?

I turned my attention back to the house.

The curtains were drawn on the first floor, but not on the ground, and there were no lights on inside – or, at least, none I could see – making it hard to tell whether he was home or not. In the row of houses opposite, an old man was putting some rubbish out. Next door to East's place, a mother was collapsing a buggy while her young son looked on. Other people came and went. The road wasn't busy exactly, but if I had any ideas about getting out of the car and having a sniff around, it wasn't as quiet as I needed it to be.

All I could do was wait.

An hour later, a green Citroën estate pulled into the driveway of East's house. It was ten years old, dirty, the wheels coated in mud, the underside of the chassis plagued by rust. It stopped and then started again, inching further up the tarmac. At the end of the driveway was a garage I'd seen when I'd first arrived in the road, set back, level with the rear garden. A few seconds later, the driver switched off the engine and the interior light came on.

There was a man at the wheel, no passengers. He was balding at the crown of his skull and wearing a bright red Adidas training top. His head was slightly bowed, the soft glow of a mobile phone shining in the skin at his throat. Half a minute later, he got out of the car and locked up.

I had a better view of him now: wispy, untidy hair, presumably because he was in denial about the fact that he was balding; mid forties, tall and skinny except for a paunch poking through his dull green T-shirt. He wore a pair of oversized blue combat trousers too, the colours clashing so badly he looked almost comical.

Almost, but not quite.

As he glanced out into the road, I sank into my seat, disguised by the advancing darkness, and saw the truth: that despite the bad hair and the worse dress sense, this wasn't a man to be laughed at. His eyes were small, set back into his skull like craters, his nose wide and flat, the contours of his face slightly misshapen – odd, awkward, a little off – like an artist's impression gone wrong.

I'd never seen him, and I didn't know him.

But I already didn't like him.

He walked to the front door of East's house and rang the doorbell. As he waited he looked out into the street again, eyes moving from window to window, from one vehicle to the next. I shifted further down into my seat, so my eyeline was level with the dashboard, watching as his gaze moved from the car in front to mine, lingering for a fraction of a second before moving on to the one behind.

Had he seen me?

A second later, the door opened.

*East.*

He'd changed out of his period costume and was dressed in a pair of tracksuit trousers and a plain white T-shirt, too small for him so it emphasized the fat he carried around his middle. He looked out into the street briefly, then back to the man at his doorstep. They said something to one another, East nodding and pushing his glasses up to the bridge of his nose, and then the man seemed to surprise East by stepping past him, into the house.

The door closed again.

A few moments later, I watched another light come on in the living room, both men appearing briefly at the window before East stepped up to it, looked out into the street a second time and pulled the curtains shut.

Ten minutes. Twenty.

Thirty.

Forty minutes later, the front door reopened and the two men emerged again, East following as they headed down to the garage, out of sight.

I picked up my phone, took a photograph of the Citroën, another of the licence plate – both shots aided by the glare of East's security light – and then sent the two pictures through to Ewan Tasker with the message:

PNC check on this car? Thanks, D.

When I looked up, the two men had reappeared, each carrying something from behind the house and heading towards the car. In East's hand was a slab of wood. In the other guy's, a wooden box. A few moments later, as the boot popped open and they began loading the objects in, I realized exactly what they were: the box was a penny arcade machine, three sides of it intact, the fourth open, as if repair work was being done on its interior; the slab of wood was its back panel.

After they were done, the man stepped away from the car, said something to East, then whipped the boot shut. East just nodded, a timidity to him. *He's scared.* The man's eyes lingered on East, and then he looked out into the street again, studying the homes opposite, the cars parked at pavements, the footpaths that bisected properties and joined one road with another. I slid down into my seat as his gaze passed my car, and then watched his small eyes come back again, along the same path they'd already travelled – me, my car, other vehicles, other houses – like a pendulum. Finally, he returned his attention to East at the door. He said something: soft, inaudible.

East nodded diffidently.

Quietly, I wound down my window further, to about halfway, to see if I could pick anything up. East asked something, but with his back turned, it was impossible to make it out. Yet, as the man in the training top moved around from the boot of the car to the driver's side, I heard him say to East, 'Stay here and lock the doors. If you see or hear from this Raker guy, you phone me, okay?'

He had an accent: Eastern European.

East just looked at him.

'*Okay?*'

A small nod of the head.

The man paused there – one hand on the roof of the Citroën, the other on the open door – and eyed East for a long time, as if unsure whether to trust him. Then, finally, he got in at the wheel and fired up the car. Reversing out of the drive, he switched his lights on and immediately accelerated away, heading north through the residential streets that would take him out on to Jamaica Road.

East closed the front door.

I waited another five minutes – and then I headed for the house.

# CHAPTER 33

The driveway was tarmacked, eroded at the edges like an old carpet, and East's garden was plain and undistinguished, the grass about half a foot high, one solitary flowerpot sitting guard outside the front door, with nothing inside but soil.

There was no gate to the driveway itself, just a space between identical brick walls where one might have sat. On the side of the house, there was an old piece of wooden trellising, a vine snaking through its gaps, and a big metal dustbin. Beyond that was the garage, detached from the house, but bricked in the same style. It had a roof which funnelled to a point, and a light brown roller door.

I paused at the top of the driveway – checking up and down the street for cars, for people, for curtains twitching – then headed along it, as fast as I could.

The security lamp sprang into life.

There was no way to avoid it, the driveway too narrow to veer out of its range, so I picked up my pace, all the way down to the garage, and slipped into a space at its side, between its right-hand wall and the fence which surrounded the property. Halfway along, the shadows began to close around me and I stopped.

At the house, the side door opened.

I watched as East's head emerged, looking up and down the driveway for any sign of life. I doubted, until he'd decided to make a run for it at the museum, that he'd ever been worried about the reasons his security light was going off.

But he was worried about it now.

He came down, on to the first step, eyes in my direction, squinting slightly. He was checking whether the gate through to the back garden – just ahead of me, in the space between the garage and the rear of the house – was ajar. When he saw it was locked, he looked the other way, up towards the silence of his street.

He lingered there a moment more and then retreated back inside, followed by the audible click of a key being turned.

Coming out from beside the garage, I paused in front of its door, making sure that the security light's range didn't extend this far, and then started picking the locks. Lockpicking was fiddly, frustrating work – but garage doors were easier. After a couple of minutes, I felt something pop.

Double-checking that East hadn't returned to the side door, I turned the handle on the lock and the roller door juddered upwards on its runners, turning in on itself, its hinges moaning gently.

I slipped inside, pulled the door back down and flicked my torch on.

The garage was small.

On the back wall was a tool board, with hammers, chisels, screwdrivers, drill bits, spanners and more, all hanging from hooks, all organized impeccably. Beneath that was a workbench, stretching wall to wall, a vice screwed to it and a series of shelves underneath, packed with old pieces of metal and wood. On top of the workbench, its back panel removed, was another penny arcade machine.

I turned it gently, silently.

It was a bagatelle, the penny arcade equivalent of a pinball machine, encased in iron rather than wood. It looked almost like a medicine cabinet. Inside the glass front panel were eight holes, big enough for a ball the size of a marble to drop through, six of the holes marked with numbers – 100, 200, 500, 1,000, 2,000 and 5,000 – the other two with 'Scratch'. The launcher for the ball sat on the underside of the cabinet, although East had removed it, so all that was left was a square, and a view of the interior. I turned it back around to see what he was doing inside, and could smell Brasso. When I looked back at the rest of the garage, running the light along every shelf – top to bottom – I couldn't find anything else of note. Was this *really* what the two men were doing? Discussing penny arcade machines? It seemed so insignificant, so mundane.

I exited the garage, closing it behind me.

At the rear of the house was his kitchen, the light still on. Through a door into the living room, I could see a sofa, a lamp, books. There was a television too, but it was off. To start with, there was no sign of East, but then I took a couple of steps closer and saw that he *was* there: he was on his side, head propped on a cushion, looking up at the ceiling.

*What's he doing?*

But then I realized.

He was crying.

His chest moved up and down, heaving as tears escaped along his cheeks, their trails glistening in the half-light of the living room. He wiped them away, and then again, and after a while pressed the thumb and forefinger of his right hand to either eye, as if plugging a dam. A minute later, maybe more, he began to gather himself, sitting up, perching on the edge of the sofa, elbows on his knees.

I returned to the car.

# CHAPTER 34

O nce I was back inside the BMW, I picked up my phone and saw that I'd missed a text. It was from Craw. I remembered then that I'd ignored a call from her as I'd been swimming back to consciousness in the mirror maze. She'd kept the message short:

**Call me.**

I tried to imagine what she might want. I had enough on my mind – Healy, his interest in the pier, whatever the hell had happened to me at the museum, Calvin East, the man he was working with – without being drawn into another argument. Craw had never been big on apologies, so I doubted she was calling to say sorry, and when I tried to think of another reason for her to get in touch, I came up with nothing. I texted her back, keeping mine brief too:

**Busy at the moment.**

Thirty seconds later, my phone erupted into life, her name flashing up on the display. It was going to be hard to pretend I wasn't around to answer it now. Finger hovering over the button, I glanced out along the road to East's place. The living-room light was off, and now an upstairs light was on.

I pushed Answer.

'Raker?'

'Yeah. I'm right in the middle of something.'

A pause on the line. 'What's the matter?'

'I'm fine.'

'You sound groggy.'

'I'm fine.'

'Does this have to do with Healy?'

I looked across at East's house. 'Healy's dead.'

'But his case lives on,' she said.

She meant the Clark family. She meant the man who killed them was still out there, unaccounted for, and without Healy, there was only one person who was going to pick up the baton and finish what Healy started – and that was me.

'I haven't got time for this now,' I said.

'That is an active case, Raker,' came the weary reply. 'It doesn't matter if it's one or five or ten years old, it's unsolved, so it's still on the books.'

'Whose books?'

'The Met's books.'

'The Met couldn't pick that family's faces out in a line-up. The three of them are history. They're consigned to a drawer in the basement.'

'You know how much you're starting to sound like him?'

'I'm not sounding like anyone.'

'This is the stuff Healy was saying,' she said, clearly trying to contain her frustration. 'However much you dispute it, you and him are alike. You're smarter than him, better with people; kinder, with a clearer sense of right and wrong. But you're still two sides of the same coin. You're an obsessive, so was he. You're both dangerous, destructive obsessives. And one day soon – maybe not with this case, but sometime soon – you're going to become so fanatical, so unable to detach yourself from this connection you think you have with the missing, that you're going to destroy yourself. You're going to lie down in the dark, and you're going to eat the same pills Healy did.'

*Or I'm going to black out and not wake up.*

'Raker?'

'I get it,' I said to her.

'Do you?'

She took a long, audible breath and I pictured her tucking her hair behind her ears, a habit she had picked up since she'd grown it longer, her slight frame – muscular, fit – shifting on whatever chair she was sitting on. Slate-grey eyes, like unpolished stones. Fingers pinching the chain sitting at the base of her throat.

'I need to go,' I said.

'The search for Healy became too personal,' she continued, as if she hadn't even heard me, 'and I

283

should never have asked you to get involved. But this search you're on . . . Look, if you think you've got something we can use, that's good. I can get a guy from my team to call you, and you can share what you've—'

'Share? This is my case.'

'It's not your case. It's a *police* case.'

'It was Healy's.'

'Healy's dead.'

'Is this *really* what you wanted to call me about, Craw?' I said, exasperated, frustrated, trying to close off the conversation.

The upstairs light in East's house was still on.

'Craw?'

Silence on the line.

'*Craw?*'

'I don't know what it is about you, Raker,' she said, but there was no aggression in her voice. In fact, almost the opposite. 'I've been stewing on what you said to me at the funeral yesterday for twenty-four hours. No one's ever made me feel like this before. No one's ever got to me like this.'

I wasn't sure what to say.

'This fixation you have with Healy's case, it's going to make you sick, if it hasn't already. It's all wrong. The way you work, it's all wrong. If I had any sense, I'd be running in the other direction.' She stopped, and a long breath crackled down the line. 'And yet here I am.'

'What are you talking about?'

A pause. 'I might have found some information for you.'

'About what?'

'About Healy.'

She'd hooked me and she knew it. 'What about him?'

'Have you been able to pin down his movements before he died?'

I thought of my notes, of the gaps in his timeline, between the ten days in January and the moment I found his body under Highdale a month ago.

'No,' I said. 'Why?'

'I think I might know what happened to him.'

# SEVENTY-FOUR DAYS

0 days, 0 hours, 1 minute *after*

Nearly six months ago, at 5.37 a.m. on Monday 12 May, Inoka Gunasekara – a senior nurse in Cardiology at King's Cross General – was checking the blood pressure of one of her patients when she noticed movement in his face. She removed the cuff immediately, set the monitor aside and studied him. He'd been in a coma for seventy-four days and hadn't shown any muscle motility in his face until now. After a couple of minutes, with no further movement, she returned to her station where one of the registrars was seated, preparing forms for the day's surgeries.

'I think he just winced.'

The registrar looked up. 'Who?'

'Patient A.'

His eyes lingered on the nurse. 'Really?'

He studied her like she was trying to catch him out. The patient had become known as 'A' because, as of yet, they'd been unable to find out his real name. He'd had no ID on him, no one had claimed him, and – because there was a cost attached – a request to try to ID him through police records was still being passed through layers of government bureaucracy. During his seventy-four-day coma, he'd shown some response to stimuli in his fingers and toes, in his calves too, as well as through an increased heart rate, but no facial motility, nothing in his upper arms or shoulders. When it was clear Nurse Gunasekara was serious, the registrar followed her to the room.

The patient lay on the bed in exactly the same position he'd been in since he'd suffered his heart attack. That had been almost eleven weeks ago. Against the soft chirp of the ECG, the registrar leaned into the patient and watched him. Removing a penlight from the pocket of his coat, he lifted both eyelids, working either side of the oxygen mask, of the feeding tube, checking for pupil dilation.

'Where was the movement?'

'The left corner of his mouth.'

He placed the penlight back into his pocket, checked the printouts from the ECG, then removed the medical records from a slot at the end of the bed.

'Just keep an eye on him,' the registrar said.

He went to leave – but then stopped again.

The nurse, who'd been reading the medical records over the registrar's shoulder, glanced at the doctor, saw his gaze fixed on the patient, and followed his line of sight. The patient was still in the same position, unmoved, silent.

But something subtle had taken hold.

His breathing had changed, become quicker.

'Hmm,' the registrar said. 'Something is definitely—'

Suddenly, a pained expression gripped the patient's face, at the corners of his mouth, in the lines of his forehead. They both watched as one of his cheeks twitched, his face seeming to shiver as a ripple passed through his chest and legs.

'Has this ever happened to him before?'

'No,' the nurse replied. 'Never.'

The patient's eyes squeezed shut.

'Do you think he's okay?' the nurse asked.

The registrar's eyes were on the ECG.

Then a series of sounds. Gurgles.

The nurse frowned. 'Did he just try to say something?'

The registrar didn't reply but stepped in towards the bed again, turning his head so his ear was right next to the patient's mouth. Five seconds. Ten. Then another noise, this one from deep down in the throat: the words were inelegant, smudged by the feeding tube. But they were words. They were definitely words.

'What did he say?' the nurse asked.

The registrar glanced at her, surprise in his face. He'd seen people wake up from comas many times – but not like this. The patient rocked from side to side, slowly at first and then more forcefully, the bed squeaking on its locked wheels.

Then his eyes opened.

The registrar and the nurse watched as the patient struggled to focus.

'Can you hear me?' the registrar asked quietly.

The patient looked at him.

'Sir, can you hear me?'

The patient blinked.

This time Nurse Gunasekara came closer, placing a hand on the patient's arm. 'Sir,' she said, almost whispering it. 'Can you hear what I'm saying to . . .'

She stopped.

Tears had started to form in the patient's eyes.

'Sir,' the registrar said.

The patient opened his mouth, said something.

'What did he just say?' the nurse asked the registrar.

The registrar stepped away from the bed, eyes on the patient, watching as silence settled inside the room. 'He said, "Don't let him hurt my family."'

# CHAPTER 35

To start with, it was hard to even process what Craw was telling me: the idea seemed so alien, so irrational. But then, slowly, the concept of Healy being in a coma began to take grip and I realized that it made complete sense. It explained how he'd suddenly vanished in February, leaving everything he owned at the homeless shelter in south London.

'How did you find out?' I said to her.

'I did everything I told you I wasn't going to do: I got involved.'

'Why?'

'Why do you think?' she said sharply. *I don't know what it is about you, Raker. No one's ever made me feel like this before. No one's ever got to me like this.* 'I didn't tag him by name,' she went on, softer and more sombre, as if she were mourning some lost part of herself. 'I'm not that suicidal. Not yet, anyway. But I put in a database search for a 49-year-old man, about six feet tall, sixteen to seventeen stone, with red hair. And I found something.'

'What?'

'A request from King's Cross General hospital. A senior nurse who works there . . .' She paused, checking the name. 'Inoka Gunasekara. She wanted help IDing a guy they'd had in there for eleven weeks – fingerprinting, DNA, dental, whatever we could organize. He had red hair, was forty-five to fifty years of age, 1.8 metres tall and 100 kilograms. That's six feet tall and sixteen stone in old money.'

I tried to remain calm, realistic. 'It's the right ballpark, but that doesn't necessarily mean it was Healy.'

'The request took three months to sign off at our end because the government is full of idiots with calculators who only care about their bottom line. So by the time we were ready to get in there with our fingerprint kit, he'd already woken from a coma and discharged himself.'

'What dates are we talking?'

'He was brought in on Thursday 27 February, and woke on Monday 12 May. He walked out of the hospital five days later, on Saturday 17 May.'

The date he was admitted fitted the timeline.

'I remember a story you told me once,' Craw continued, 'about when you and Healy first got together, when you were trying to find Leanne.'

'So?'

'He got stabbed, right?'

'Yeah, in the chest.'

'This so-called "Patient A" had old scarring on his chest.'

I felt a charge of electricity.

'He suffered a heart attack,' Craw said.

I recalled sitting across from him at the motel, ten months ago, his fingers straying to the centre of his ribcage, as if in discomfort. Had it been bothering him back then?

'When he woke up, Gunasekara and a registrar called Richard Anawale described him as "unresponsive" to questions about who he was, with neither able to get even as much as a confirmed name out of him. According to Anawale, it wasn't because the patient was incapable of communicating, it was because he chose not to tell them. However, Gunasekara said he spoke in an "Irish accent".'

*Healy.*

'It says here, he was referred to a psychologist.'

'A hospital psychologist?'

'On Friday 16 May. Dr Meredith Blaine.'

Blaine's notes were obviously never going to be a part of the ID request the police had received, so I couldn't say for sure whether she'd been any more successful, but it was hard to see Healy bowing to the gentle pressure a psychologist might apply. He'd have hated being analysed like that. I added her name to my notes.

'What else?' I said.

'Gunasekara relayed an account of the day paramedics were called to the scene of Healy's heart attack. She said a civilian, a former army sergeant, had been close by and performed CPR, and then the paramedics had applied their own procedures as they'd arrived.'

'Where was this?'

'Stables Market in Camden.'

*What the hell was he doing there?*

He didn't have any money, so it wasn't going to be a shopping trip. It was also six miles away from the homeless shelter he'd been staying in near the Old Kent Road, which made it inconvenient to get to. Yet he'd gone nonetheless. Why? What had he found out?

As I tried to align my thoughts, something Calvin East had said returned to me: *I'm a hoarder, a collector. Books, paintings, antiquities. I'm fascinated by London, I've lived here my whole life, so my collection is centred here.* Stables Market was home to countless antiques shops.

Had Healy followed East there?

'They found some items on him,' Craw said. 'A book – and three photographs.'

I didn't need more than that. The book would be *A Seaside in the City* by Carla Stourcroft. The photographs would be Gail, April and Abigail.

Everything else had been left at the homeless shelter.

I looked down at the passenger seat, Healy's copy of *A Seaside in the City* lying creased, dog-eared, and then thought about what may have happened after he discharged himself on 17 May. The next time anyone saw him was on 18 August, when he returned to the homeless shelter to retrieve the divorce papers. That left three months still unaccounted for.

Notepad in my lap, phone to my ear, I realized that I'd become distracted. I was supposed to be watching the house.

As I looked up, Calvin East walked out of his driveway.

# CHAPTER 36

He paused at the gates, winter coat on, collar up, and looked either way along the street. Then he was off, heading away from me, north towards Jamaica Road.

'Raker?'

I'd almost forgotten I was still on the line to Craw. 'I have to go,' I told her, 'but thank you. Thank you for doing this.'

She didn't reply immediately. 'You and me, I'm not sure what the answer is. I love my job. It's full of bullshit and politics and frustration, but I love it. And the minute people at the Met find out about us, about what I've just done for you . . .' She paused, obviously conflicted. 'Just be careful, okay?'

'Okay,' I said. 'Thank you again.'

I hung up.

Ten minutes later, I was inside East's kitchen.

I'd thought, briefly, about following him, to see where he was going, why he had been in such a state, then realized I might not get another chance like this to have a look around. East, and whoever he was associated with, knew who I was, and knew the kind of questions I'd been asking: about Healy, about the pier. The more time passed, the more they were going to circle the wagons.

I moved through the darkness of the interior, keeping my torch off. There was enough light – from street lamps, from digital displays on electronics, from a luminous wall clock in the living room – to navigate my way, room to room.

The house was like the garage: small, packed, but well organized. In the kitchen, he'd left his dinner plate in the sink, and the ripped packaging from a microwave lasagne on the counter, but otherwise it was clean. The living room was a lounge-diner, one long room that ran front to back. He had a small table at one end, next to the patio doors, and two sofas at the other, in an L-shape around a TV cabinet. A floor-to-ceiling bookcase dominated the space, six long shelves groaning under the weight of hundreds of books. These had been treated with more care than the ones in his office, many preserved in transparent sleeves.

Beyond the living room was a hallway, the front door to the right, stairs to the left. I headed up. At the top were three further doors: the first led into a tiny bathroom, tiled white with a wicker cabinet full of toiletries on the wall; the other two opened into bedrooms. One was clearly where he slept: clean, plain walls, a single bed with a pale blue duvet, and two stand-alone pine wardrobes.

The other room was full of antiques.

On its ceiling, he'd replaced the light fixture with three long fluorescent tubes, each covered in a UV filter. At the window was a thick blind, perfectly cut to fit inside the window space and prevent any light coming in from outside. As I moved further into the room, I could see he'd arranged his antiques in a vague S-shape, creating a path through them, that took you into the room and back out.

There were more books, again plastic-wrapped, but this time inside a revolving oak bookcase. Next to that was a polished mahogany bureau, perched on spindly legs, a lock on each of its drawers. I tried them. They were all empty.

I passed a striking walnut dresser, built low to the ground, a sheet of felt placed on top of it, a selection of plates, silver and sculptures on top of that. Then there were two ash dining chairs, and an art deco office chair, built on wheels, in green studded leather. Finally, there was a tortoiseshell writing box on the floor. I opened it up but there was nothing in it, just like the bureau.

Moving through to his bedroom, I looked in the pine wardrobes. One had five versions of the same outfit he wore to work, an additional top hat placed on a shelf above. His other clothes were the unremarkable attire of a middle-aged man. At the bottom he kept his shoes, all the same black boots, highly polished, except for a pair of light brown brogues.

The other wardrobe was full of junk.

He'd used it as a dumping ground for clothes he no longer wanted, for old photo albums, for more books, for a wristwatch that had stopped working and a phone without a back or a battery. There were Christmas cards, unwritten and unsent, the remains of an old stereo system, even an old typewriter. There were DVDs too. *A Touch of Evil. The Godfather. 12 Angry Men. Casablanca.*

On the spine of the *Casablanca* box, an X had been added in red marker.

Removing it from the pile, I opened it up. Inside were two discs. One was the movie itself; another was a blank DVD, nothing written on it. I checked the other films, but they just contained the discs they were supposed to. It was only this one that was different.

I felt a flicker of unease.

Clipping the official disc back into the *Casablanca* box, I returned it to the shelf, pocketed the blank disc and went through the remainder of the wardrobe.

After a while I found a scrapbook, a beach scene on the cover. East had written *World Tour* at the top. I opened it up and saw what it was: a chronicle of a gap year he'd had in his early twenties, photographs, ticket stubs and faded receipts from all across Asia, Australasia, Fiji and the US west coast.

A few pages in, something fell out.

It was a newspaper cutting.

It had been inserted loose inside, towards the back, and had nothing to do with his trip. When

I unfolded it, I saw it was a story from a newspaper called the *North London Gazette*. I wasn't familiar with it, and was pretty sure the paper wasn't even in circulation any more – but that wasn't what grabbed my attention.

It was the fact it *wasn't* a story.

It was an obituary.

7 August 2010

## CARLA STOURCROFT

Carla Stourcroft, a lecturer and local author, was perhaps best known for her last book, *Invisible Ripper* (2009), the acclaimed biography of serial killer Eldon Simmons, who raped and murdered five men in the 1950s. But she was also the author of four other books, all based around her love of London history: *From Richmond to Regent: London's Parks from A to Z* (1996); *Metropolitan: The First Underground Line* (1998), which she wrote under her married name of Carla Davis; *A Seaside in the City: The History of Wapping Grand Pier* (2002); and *South of the River* (2006). As well as her career as a writer, she lectured in history at the University of East London. With her deep love of the area, and keen support for the local community, Ms Stourcroft's tragic death at the age

299

The obituary had been torn off at the bottom.

My mind shifted back to when I'd first started reading *A Seaside in the City* at home. I'd found a similar obituary online when I'd googled Stourcroft, but not much else. Her career as a writer – except for her last book – had gone unnoticed, and even *Invisible Ripper*, although acclaimed by critics, only charted for a week. That made her hard to find on the web, especially given her lack of a website or social media presence. But one thing I was certain the other obituary *hadn't* referred to were the circumstances of her death. Why was it referred to as tragic here?

And why had East made a special effort to find her obituary in one of the few media outlets that seemed to have covered her passing in any detail?

It *had* to have something to do with *A Seaside in the City* – except I'd read that book cover to cover, and there was nothing in it. There were no secrets, nothing that pointed to anyone or anything. It was clear East was hiding *something*. He'd made a break for it after I'd shown him Healy's photograph at the museum. But if the answers were in Stourcroft's book, they were so well hidden behind the dry, prosaic text that I doubted they'd ever be found.

I went back to the obituary and read it a second time. A third, a fourth. On the fifth, something stopped me.

*. . . Metropolitan: The First Underground Line* (1998), which she wrote under her married name of Carla Davis . . .

*Her married name.* The first time I'd read the obituary, it hadn't even occurred to me. But it did now. Taking out my phone, I went to the web and, instead of searching for Carla Stourcroft, I went looking for 'Carla Davis'.

My heart dropped.

Carla Davis hadn't left much of an online footprint either – but she'd left enough. The first four links were for stories in the nationals – the *Sun*, *Guardian*, *Telegraph*, *Mail* – but when I clicked through to them, each of the reports was tiny; news in briefs forgotten as quickly as they'd been printed.

## 7 August 2010

## POLICE CALL FOR WITNESSES IN 'ROBBERY GONE WRONG'

Police have appealed for witnesses to come forward after a woman died from injuries sustained in what detectives are describing as a 'bungled robbery'.

Carla Davis, 46, was attacked after reportedly trying to fight off a thief who'd attempted to snatch her handbag. Police said CCTV footage showed Mrs Davis refusing to let go of her bag, before her attacker produced a knife and stabbed her once in the stomach. 'Although doctors initially managed to stabilize her,' said Detective Inspector Oliver Cowley, 'Mrs Davis later died from her injuries. We don't believe that her attacker intended to kill her, but clearly this is now a murder investigation.'

Mrs Davis, a writer and lecturer, lived on Chalk Farm Road and had only been back in the country twenty-four hours after spending a month with her sister in Australia. According to police, her attacker confronted her as she was leaving Stables Market . . .

I stopped reading.
*Stables Market.*
She'd died in the same place Healy had had his heart attack.

# CHAPTER 37

As soon as I was back at the car, I grabbed my phone and searched for Stables Market. In a former life, as its name suggested, it had been a stables and horse hospital, its intricate design unravelling through a series of passages, stairwells and viaducts, alleys criss-crossing like veins, its spaces now occupied by both single-trader stalls and businesses big enough to fill the site's converted railway arches.

I quickly found a list of four hundred proprietors at the market, a column of names I felt certain hid the reason Carla Stourcroft, and then Healy, had been drawn there. They'd gone separately, years apart, but in the end they'd suffered the same fate, Stourcroft losing her life in an apparent robbery – just outside the market walls – in August 2010; Healy suffering a heart attack three and a half years later, which he'd survived – but only physically. Seven months after that, I'd found him under the foundations at Highdale – a man alone, a man who'd given up his fight long ago. Increasingly, I was starting to wonder how much of the blame lay here.

In this list.

In these names.

What had drawn Stourcroft and Healy to the market? Was it Calvin East? Someone else? Whichever it was, the long list of antiques shops seemed like a good place to start. I worked my way through them, cross-checking the name of the business and the proprietor with my notes. There was nothing. I moved on to antique furniture shops, businesses dealing in clothing and jewellery, in homeware, even toy shops and shoe shops, and still got nothing. When I returned to the antiques shops for a second time, to ensure I hadn't missed anything, I was more methodical: I used the name of the business as a jumping-off point, and went searching beyond the trading name, using Google in the worst way possible, to trawl social media for the accounts of the men and women who rented space there; their Facebook, Twitter and LinkedIn profiles.

But it was the same as before.

A dead end.

Copying and pasting the list of business names and proprietors into an email, I sent it to myself, so I'd have easy access to it, checked it had come through, and then backed out of my inbox. Almost immediately, the phone started buzzing in my hand again.

It was Ewan Tasker.

I remembered then that I'd messaged him pictures of the Citroën belonging to the man I'd seen earlier at the house, removing one of East's penny arcade machines. I'd asked Task to put the car reg and the owner through the Police National Computer.

'How you doing, Task?'

'Good,' he said. 'Is it too late for you?'

'No. Your timing's perfect. How did you get on?'

'That Citroën,' he said, 'is registered to a Victor Grankin.'

'Okay,' I said, grabbing my notepad. 'Who is he?'

'Born 25 January 1967 in Pärnu, Estonia. His parents emigrated to the UK in 1974, but were killed in a car accident in April 1975, so he grew up in care. No information on him as a minor, and certainly no record – *if* there even was one. Until 2006, police weren't obliged to keep juvenile records on the system, so a lot of guys Grankin's age who might have history as a minor won't raise any flags.'

'What about as an adult?'

'No, he's clean.'

'Has he got a home address?'

'Yeah. 3 Poland Gardens, Whitehall Woods.'

'I don't even know where that is.'

'I think it's up near the Essex county line. He's been there since October 2010. Before that, he lived in a flat down in Beckton, near the airport. He runs a company called VG Security and Protection Ltd from his home address, but he's the only employee. I dug around a bit for you and it looks like he hires security grunts from an agency on an ad hoc basis, as and when he needs them. Anyway, VGSP's been going since January 2001. It's some sort of private security firm.'

'Okay. What about known associates?'

'No.'

'No black spots in his history at all?'

'Only thing I could find was an incident four years back, when Grankin was wheeled into the station at Bethnal Green after being accused of stealing.'

'Stealing from who?'

'Someone called, uh . . . Gary Cabot.'

That stopped me. 'Really? What did he steal?'

'Uh . . . "a thirty-six-tin box of Hoberman's".'

'Which is?'

'Wood varnish.'

'Honestly?'

'That's what it says down here. "Thirty-six 250ml tins".'

'Wood varnish?'

Task sighed. 'Crime's clearly not what it used to be.'

'What else have you got there?'

'Hold on,' Task replied, and I could hear him muttering under his breath, as he read back the paperwork. 'The entry's vague because no charges were ever brought, but it looks like this Cabot guy ran some sort of tourist attraction in Wapping – "Wapping Wonderland and Museum" – and he claims that during a summer fair they had there, Grankin stole these pots of varnish. Part of the

306

reason Cabot was so upset was probably because this Hoberman's stuff is expensive.'

'How expensive?'

'It's about forty-five quid per tin, so sixteen hundred quid in total for a box, plus the cost of transporting it down to London. It's made by some company up in Blackpool.'

'So the investigation never went anywhere?'

'Cabot said he hired Grankin in 2002 to look after security at the museum, and never had any problems with him until 2010, when Cabot says he went into Grankin's office at the museum, the day after the summer fair, and found traces of this varnish on the floor, next to Grankin's desk. Cabot went to wherever they stored these tins of Hoberman's at the museum – and there was a box missing.'

'So why were no charges brought?'

'The police looked into it, interviewed Grankin but never found the tins. They narrowed down the theft to the evening of Sunday 11 July.'

'Wait, what was the date?'

'Sunday 11 July 2010.'

*The night the Clark family were murdered.*

I felt myself tense.

'Anyway,' Task went on, 'Grankin had hired four guys from a recruitment agency to help cover the fair, and the time slot of the theft – 8 p.m. to 10 p.m. – immediately put all four in the clear. Long story short: most of the museum was shut off to the general public, including where these tins of varnish were stored, and a whole bunch of eyewitnesses saw these four blokes outside at the fair, on and off, all night. The police were more interested in this Grankin guy – but he had an alibi. He'd popped out for a few hours to meet another potential client at a pub on St Katharine Docks, about seven forty-five. When interviewed, this client confirmed that they'd met in the pub that night, and footage pulled from a CCTV camera on the docks showed Grankin heading in that direction just after eight o'clock.'

'Was he caught on film returning to the fair?'

'No.'

'So no one saw him come back that night?'

'One of Cabot's employees said he saw Grankin return at about half past ten. No footage to back that up, just the word of this guy. Uh . . . Calvin East.'

*East.* He was Grankin's alibi.

I grabbed my pad and flicked back to the notes I'd made from the official casework on the Clark murders. It took me a couple of moments to find it: *Murders carried out between approx. 10 p.m. and 11 p.m. Sunday 11 July 2010.*

'Who was the client Grankin met at the pub?'

'Uh . . . some guy called Paul Korman.'

'Korman?'

'K-O-R-M-A-N. Police interviewed him and he vouched for Grankin being with him, at the pub, between approximately eight o'clock and quarter past ten.'

I started to align my thoughts. Grankin was running security at the museum fair on Sunday 11 July. In the evening, he left to meet a client at 7.45 p.m. According to East, Grankin then returned at 10.30 p.m. At the same time, four miles south, a family were slain in a New Cross tower block.

The only person who could vouch for Grankin still being at the pub on St Katharine Docks, at 10.15 p.m., was whoever Paul Korman was. The only person who could vouch for his return to the fair was Calvin East. Police had two clean alibis from two separate people, enough to cast doubt on Gary Cabot's suspicions about Grankin stealing that varnish. But what if both men were lying to police?

What if Grankin was actually in New Cross?

*What if Korman was too?*

I thought of the CCTV stills I'd studied from the night of the murders.

Grankin wasn't the blond man, I knew that for sure. That man had been too well built, too different from Grankin's skinny physique; he had distinctive features too: the dark eyes, the damaged nose. But Grankin could have been the driver.

Sitting, watching, waiting.

'Is there an address for this Korman guy?' I asked.

'Back then?' A pause. 'Paul Benjamin Korman, 145 Bell Park Road. He told police he was renting it, which he was. But he hasn't lived there since

April 2011, and I can't find another address for him anywhere.'

I felt my stomach tighten. 'No photo or physical description, right?'

'No.'

I thanked Task and hung up. I was starting to think I had found the man who drove the car to the family's flat that night.

Now I was wondering whether I had found the man who murdered them too.

# THERAPY

4 days, 3 hours, 40 minutes *after*

'*D*on't *hurt them. Please don't hurt them.*'
    '*You're nothing to them.*'
    '*Please . . .*'
'*You're nothing to anyone, Healy.*'

He woke.

For a moment, he was disorientated, unsure of where he was, sweat in his eyes, twisted bed-sheets pinning him down like the roots of a tree. Then, slowly, things started shifting back into focus: the bleached white of the hospital room; a saline drip swinging gently from the UV stand; nurses out in the corridor, doctors in coats, patients passing in wheelchairs. He rolled his head across the pillow, in the direction of the window. All he could see from here was a square of daylight.

There was no detail outside.

No shapes. No definition.

Just sky.

The view, these dreams, waking up soaked through and out of breath, this was his life now. In the days before his heart stopped, he'd stared

311

at the walls of the hostel he'd been staying in, at his possessions – paltry and unimportant – in a backpack next to his bunk, and he remembered thinking he'd hit rock bottom.

But that wasn't rock bottom.

Healy knew that now.

There was still much further to fall.

He was sent to the psychologist at lunchtime on Friday 16 May. It had been four days since he'd woken up, and a succession of staff had tried to get him to talk.

Now someone else was going to have a go.

The nurses hauled him out of bed and into a wheelchair, his bones aching, creaking, like the hull of a wooden ship. As he shuffled his toes across the foot plates of the chair, he watched them wheel the UV stand around behind him and check his drip and catheter were still attached. His chest felt bruised, his breath catching in his throat, but he didn't say anything. Healy cared more about the fact that his gown was open, his penis on show.

'It's fine,' he said, his words slurred.

One of the nurses looked up. 'We're just making sure.'

He didn't say anything. Maybe he would have done once, but he couldn't summon the energy now. The nurse covered him up, put a dressing gown on him and asked him if he was ready. He shrugged, and the nurse wheeled him out.

The psychologist was on the third floor of the

hospital, in an office at the far end of a long corridor of closed doors. Hers was partly open. On a name plate halfway up, it said CLINICAL PSYCHOLOGY. Beneath that was a small whiteboard, the remains of other names – wiped away, but not entirely – at its edges.

Written there now was MEREDITH BLAINE.

The room was compact, airless, and had a single vertical window that looked out over the car park. She was seated at a small desk, with a computer on it and a desk tidy. There was an in tray, but there was no paper in it. Next to it was a red sofa, worn along the seams. The nurse wheeled Healy inside, then hauled him out of the chair and on to the sofa. Once the UV stand was in place, the nurse left the room, closing the door behind him.

'My name's Meredith Blaine,' the psychologist said.

Healy just looked at her.

'What can I call you?' she asked.

She was in her early forties, dark-haired, small and bookish, but she was confident and unyielding. He tried staring her out, but she faced him down and eventually he had to look away, out to the car park, where the sun was shining.

'You suffered a serious heart attack,' she went on. 'You were in a coma for a long time. There are unique psychological pressures associated with that, with coming out of it like you did. But there's a medical issue too. Without you telling us who you are, we have no history, and we can't prescribe the best treatment.'

Again, he said nothing.

She didn't seem perturbed about the lack of response. Instead, she turned to the computer, tabbed through some options, and a record of his treatment – since the heart attack – appeared on screen. The room was so cramped, he could read it all clearly. He could see they had no idea who he was. No idea what his story was. Where his name should have been, there was just a hospital number.

'Why won't you tell us your name?'

He shrugged.

'Are you in trouble?'

That made him smile.

'Something funny?'

'I just spent eleven weeks in a coma,' he said, and then stopped. He hated the sound of his voice now, edgeless and soft, like he was drunk. 'I'm pissing through a tube. I've forgotten how to walk. I'd say I'm in trouble, wouldn't you?'

'I meant, have you broken the law?'

'Ever?'

It was her turn to smile this time, but – as that faded – a withering look emerged. 'We're waiting for the police to come in and take your fingerprints for us, but I'm pretty sure they're not currently looking for you. I do some consultation work at the Met and have a few friends there. They checked for me. No one matching your description has raised any flags recently. No family or friends have come forward to tell us who you are. What I'm saying is, if you broke the law before your heart attack, if that's why you won't tell us your name, the police don't know about it – at least until our request gets signed off.'

On the desk beside her was a water carafe.

'Would you like something to drink?' she asked.

He looked from the carafe to her, and nodded.

She poured him a glass of water and placed it down beside him. 'You were found in Stables Market,' she said, and as she sat back down again, he caught a whiff of her perfume. 'I spoke to one of the paramedics yesterday who treated you at the scene, in preparation for this meeting. He told me that a retired army sergeant called Gregory Finn pretty much saved your life; that without the CPR Finn gave you at the scene, you'd probably be dead. You're actually very lucky.'

'How do you figure that?'

'CPR alone won't save your life – but, until the ambulance crew arrives, it gives you a fighting chance. If Finn hadn't been there, you'd be dead now.'

He shrugged.

'Would you rather be dead?'

*Maybe.*

She paused for a moment, eyeing him. 'Finn also told the paramedics that, in the seconds before your heart attack, he saw your collapse.' She stopped again – but this time Healy caught a glimpse of what was coming. 'Finn said that you appeared to be running after someone, and that – when he opened up your shirt to administer CPR – he found there was already bruising on your chest.' She used a finger to indicate the centre of her own chest. 'Why did you have that bruising?'

He didn't reply.

'Who were you running after?'

He turned and looked out at the car park.

'Had they taken something from you?'

When he eventually faced her again, she was studying him, unmoved, seemingly unaffected by this one-way conversation. A couple of seconds later, a flicker of something passed her lips, and then her eyes. Some knowledge of him.

Instantly, he realized what.

'The paramedics found some items on you,' she said.

A pause, as she looked for a reaction.

Healy felt a tightness in his stomach as he thought of the photographs, of the book. The photos were the only permanent thing he'd kept on him before the heart attack. The book had just happened to be with him that day. He'd wanted it for reference. He thought he might need it at the market. Blaine moved, shaking him from his thoughts, and he watched as she placed four pieces of paper down on the table in front of him. Photocopies of the three pictures; one of the book's cover.

'*A Seaside in the City*,' Blaine said. 'I've heard of

Wapping Pier. I've never been down there. What interests you about that place?'

He could feel her eyes on him.

Again, he remained silent.

'What about these pictures?' she asked.

He looked at them.

'Are they your family?'

A tremor passed through the centre of his chest, up into his throat. Tilting his head so she couldn't see his face, he repeatedly swallowed until he felt like he'd regained his composure. He looked up – stoic, stable – and said nothing.

'Is that your wife?' Blaine asked.

He glanced at the picture of Gail.

'Are those your daughters?'

He looked at April and Abigail.

'Can we call them for you?'

*Please don't hurt them.*

*Don't hurt my family.*

'No,' he said quietly. 'You can't call them.'

The words were out of his mouth before he could pull them back in, as if some primal part of him was desperate to give voice to what he'd been through, what he felt. How they'd been alive in his head. How he'd been there with them.

Spoken to them.

Loved them.

He glanced at her, and she must have seen the panic in his face, because she came forward in her seat, hand up. She was telling him everything was okay.

'Is this your family?'

He looked at her for a long time, breathing slowly, composing himself. He wasn't going to tell her. She wouldn't understand. He wasn't sure *he* understood. He'd been Healy, but not Healy; Mal, but not Mal. He'd been living in their flat with them, taken the girls to school, put them to bed at night. He'd walked the dog with them – except the family had never owned a dog. The dog in the dream was Charlie, Healy's dog; the dog Leanne, Ciaran and Liam had grown up with, not the girls. In his head, he'd gone on the same stag weekend to Dublin that he'd organized when he'd been at the Met in 2007. It had been him, but someone else.

It had been a dream.

But for eleven weeks, it had been his reality.

'Is this your family?' Blaine asked again.

She was leaning all the way forward in her seat now, one long finger pressed against the picture of April. She watched him, waiting for a response.

Then something happened.

Suddenly, uncontrollably, he started crying. He tried to wipe his tears away, embarrassed, unnerved, but he was unable to stop them.

Blaine edged closer. 'It's okay,' she whispered. 'They're your family, aren't they?'

He shook his head.

*They were mine*, he thought.

*But only for a while.*

# CHAPTER 38

I looked out into the night, trying to figure out my next move, thinking of Craw, of the conversation we'd had an hour ago. East needed to be found – and Grankin and Korman may have been the men at Searle House that night. That made one of them a killer and the other, at best, an accessory, at worst someone equally capable of taking a life. I knew that I was on the edges of something, circling the drain, being drawn deeper and deeper into whoever they were and whatever they'd done.

Was I ready for this again?

I thought of when I'd blacked out in the museum, the crushing sense of panic, and began wondering what it might feel like to call Craw up and pass on the entirety of the case, to protect myself for once, to relinquish control of an investigation before I'd brought it to its conclusion, before I had answers, reasons, a sense of closure. I'd never done it before, because the idea felt like a betrayal. I promised the families of the missing that, somehow, in whatever form, I'd bring their loved ones home, whatever it took – and that's what I always did.

But this case was different.

I'd already found my missing person. I'd watched him being buried. I'd brought a skewed sense of conclusion to the family he'd left behind.

*So what am I doing here?*

As that question lingered, my attention moved to the passenger seat, to Healy's copy of *A Seaside in the City*, to my laptop on the floor in the foot-well, and the blank DVD I'd taken from Calvin East's house, lying on top of it. There was no writing on it. No label. No marking of any kind. It could just as easily have been new and completely empty. Except, as I picked it up, I got that same sense of unease I'd had when I'd been in East's house, standing in front of those wardrobe doors, finding it for the first time. Did the unease come from instinct, from a history of dealing with liars, knowing how they thought and tried to cover their tracks? Or had I now become so weary – and such a paranoiac – that I suspected everyone of everything?

I grabbed my laptop, powered it on and slipped the disc into the drive. A couple of seconds later, I watched as the DVD function kicked into life and footage of East popped on to the screen. It was an uneven, shaky video of him filming himself – and six other men in their early twenties – as they tried to skim pebbles on a beautiful, mountain-lined lake. He panned around and I saw a sign on a jetty close by: Queenstown Boats. They were in New Zealand.

*It's just footage from his travels.*

I fast-forwarded it, doubts kicking in.

Ten minutes passed. Twenty.

After thirty, he'd switched countries – to Australia, and the Barrier Reef – and, as I watched him filming the same friends, each of them laughing riotously at a joke one of them had told, I grabbed my phone. This was innocent. There was nothing here. I was tired, sore; my instincts were off.

Craw was right.

*It's time to call her.*

But then, immediately, the footage switched again. And, as it did, I realized something: this wasn't footage from his travels.

This was something much worse.

# CHAPTER 39

The last scene before the switch was of the six men East had been travelling with, sitting in a bar in Sydney, the Harbour Bridge just about visible through tinted glass behind them. They were laughing again – a different joke in a different place – empty bottles of beer scattered like debris on the table in front of them.

I could hear East laughing too, although not as wildly, as if laughter didn't come as easily to him. His voice distorted the microphone as he asked the men to look towards him, to give the camera a thumbs up, but most of them didn't even hear him – or ignored him. Eventually, he turned the camera around to face him, and for a few brief seconds I caught a glimpse of a younger, slimmer version of him; the boy I'd seen on the edges of the photograph in the museum. Callow. Uncomfortable.

Always on the periphery.

Then the footage cut to somewhere else.

An anonymous park.

Except it wasn't: I watched the camera pan, could see grass and a concrete path. Edging further left, a climbing frame came into view, a mixture of ladders and circles. Then a swing, and another. A roundabout.

*Searle House.*

As the camera kept going, the north side of the tower block drifted in and then back out of view. When East returned his attention to the play park itself, he began zooming in on the swings. Both of them were occupied.

On the left was Abigail.

On the right, April.

Instantly, my mind shifted back to the witness statements I'd read over and over again, to what Sandra Westerwood – the family's neighbour – had said to Healy about seeing a man with them all in the months before they died: *The park next to Searle House has got some swings, a climbing frame, some slides, that sort of thing. I definitely remember seeing him there with the girls a few times.*

This was him.

The man was East.

Another cut, and he was suddenly right next to them, the girls laughing at something he must have said seconds before he started filming. April looked at the camera and began singing a song that had been big in 2010. It was hard listening to her – a knot forming in my throat – not because she was out of tune, or had the words wrong, but because she sang so freely. She was unencumbered by the rules of adulthood. She sang so loudly, so inno-cently, I felt the knot in my throat harden and my composure drift. I thought of Annabel, and of Olivia, a girl the same age as April and Abigail, but a girl I'd been able to protect. There was no protecting the twins. They were gone.

They only existed now in film.

As one of my eyes blurred, Abigail appeared on-screen: shy, quiet, more contemplative than her sister. 'Are you going to sing too, Abs?' East asked, and as his voice broke the spell – the attachment I'd built with the girls through the eye of the lens – I felt my grief subside and a rage take hold. It was so strong it frightened me.

'No,' Abigail said. 'I don't want to sing.'

'But you've got a beautiful voice.'

'No, I haven't.'

'You have.'

On-screen, Abigail looked from her sister back to the camera, and then off to the side of the shot. East swung the camera around, following the direction she was focused on: Gail Clark was approaching from Searle House.

'Tell her, Mummy!' East shouted.

'Tell her what?' came the response.

'Tell Abs she's got a beautiful voice.'

'You know you have, Abs,' her mother said to her as she reached the park. On the swing, Abigail shrugged, but was smiling. 'Cal wouldn't lie to you, hun.'

*Cal.*

They called him Cal.

Westerwood thought she'd heard the family call

the man 'Mal'. A whole line of inquiry had been built on the idea the suspect had been called Malcolm.

But it wasn't Malcolm she'd heard.

It never had been.

As the footage jerked quickly from side to side, I realized East was giving the camera to Gail. She took it from him and started filming him with the girls.

He was wearing an olive-green shirt.

Again, I saw how another key pillar of Healy's investigation had crumbled to dust. Westerwood had told him in her interview that the suspect was wearing the kind of shirt a delivery man might wear. She was right. It *did* look like that.

But it wasn't a delivery company he worked for.

Back in 2010, the shirt must have been what museum employees wore when they weren't in Victorian costume. Or maybe, for a while, Gary Cabot had given them the choice between the two. I could see a Ferris wheel was stitched into the breast pocket, the words *Wapping Wonderland and Museum* below that, too small to be seen from where Sandra Westerwood would have passed. Clearly, soon after this, things had begun to change at the museum, because I hadn't seen a single person with a shirt like this anywhere in the building. Cabot must have realized the period costumes were part of the attraction for tourists – so the shirts were binned.

I watched as East started pushing the girls on

the swings. He was more of a familiar shape now: tubby, a hint of beard growth, thinning black hair parted at the side. He wore the same style of glasses too, the lenses a little big for his eyes, but they were less conspicuous, the rims a muted grey.

The girls started laughing, asking him to push harder, and he did, saying something – disguised by a breeze in the microphone – that made them laugh. He started making a *whoosh* sound every time he gave them a shove, a process that went on for a minute, maybe more. The longer it went on, the more I started to see something take shape in his face, his eyes, in the way he was laughing with them.

*This isn't an act.*

He wasn't trying to dupe them. He liked being here.

The screen went black.

It was back a couple of seconds later; this time, he was inside the Clarks' flat. He was behind the camera again, filming Gail and the two girls playing Scrabble in the living room. Around them was the story of their lives – the photo frames, the DVD boxes, books, clothes cast aside, a table set for dinner – that I'd never seen in the crime-scene photography. That version of the flat had been a graveyard, a monument full of memories that looked like it should never be occupied again.

This was alive, vivid.

This was home.

With a bump, East placed the camera down on to a nearby coffee table, and went across the room to join them in the game. I watched them all, unable to take my eyes off the footage, mesmerized by this hidden chronicle of their life.

'Wait a second,' he said, looking down at his letters. He broke out into a smile. 'I reckon there have been some busy fingers, swapping out my vowels.'

April descended into giggles, unable to maintain the lie.

East began laughing.

After a couple more minutes of them playing, East got up again and came across to the table, the camera rocking slightly as he pushed the on/off button.

Blackness.

It stayed like that for a short time and then snapped back a decade to when East had been travelling. He was in South East Asia somewhere, filming from a high window. Below, car horns blared in a crammed street full of vehicles and people, massive neon signs attached to buildings like barnacles.

I fast-forwarded it, all the way through his tour of Asia, through China, Hong Kong and Thailand. The last shot was from the airport terminal in Bangkok, out across the brightly lit tarmac to where a Boeing 747 waited to take him home.

Then there was nothing.

No more footage.

No answers.

I tore my eyes away from the screen, my vision

momentarily adjusting to the darkness outside the car, and snapped the lid of the laptop shut. I needed to find East. I needed his reasons. I needed to understand why this had happened.

I could break him.

*I could make him pay.*

Closing my eyes, I tried to settle my nerves, tried to force the tension out. It felt like I had a migraine coming, a drumbeat thumping at the side of my head.

Did he keep this as a way to remember them? He'd put the footage in the middle of a DVD of his travels, presumably so it wouldn't be found. Because he was keeping it back from Grankin? From Korman?

Taking a series of long breaths, I forced myself to calm down. It was after eleven. I'd been up for seventeen hours. I was exhausted, bruised, emotional.

I opened my eyes again.

Across the road, the security light had sparked into life at East's house. In the brief seconds between closing and opening my eyes, something had set it off.

I watched, waited, gaze fixed on the entrances to the house. After a couple of minutes, the light flicked off and a semi-darkness settled around the property. A street light cast an orange glow across the garden and the front of the house.

And then I saw movement.

Someone was in the living room.

# CHAPTER 40

Ducking on to East's driveway, I hurried towards the living-room windows and dropped in beside them. My back to the wall, I looked out into the street. It was quiet. In the houses opposite and adjacent, curtains were pulled and blinds closed. It was after 11 p.m., and most of his neighbours had turned in for the night.

I stole a look at the living room.

It was dark, lit only by the lights from adjoining properties at the rear, and – this side, at the front – the orange glow from the street. The room looked no different from the way it had been when I was inside earlier. Nothing had been moved or disturbed. I took a breath and checked the road. It was clear.

I peered inside a second time.

At the back of the property, the sliding doors were slightly ajar. Not much, but enough. Had I mistakenly left them like that? I'd come in that way, picking the locks on that same door, identifying them as the easiest way in.

Had I got sloppy and forgotten to close them?

A noise made me start, out on the street: the

sound of gravel being kicked along the pavement. When I looked, it was a cat, tracing the fence at the front of East's property, eyes peering through the slats at me: there, gone, there, gone. I watched it all the way, as it first stopped at the mouth of the driveway, staring in at me, its eyes glinting in the half-light; and then as it disappeared out of sight.

*Thump.* The sound of a door closing inside.

I looked again.

This time I saw someone.

A man was in the doorway connecting the living room to the kitchen. He had one gloved hand on the frame, almost leaning against it, and another at his side, and was looking out of the rear windows of the house. His back was to me, making it hard to get a sense of who he was, the hood up on a knee-length green raincoat. It was almost like a fisherman's jacket, its plastic sheen catching the light as he adjusted position, a fractional movement from left to right that saw him glance across the living room. I edged back, even though he hadn't seen me: the drawstring on the hood had been pulled tight, so all I could make out was the vaguest hint of a face. He was tall, skinny, and wearing dark combat trousers.

*Grankin.*

What would he be doing back here? Why return without the car? Over one shoulder was a brown leather bag – like a satchel – its buckles unclasped, and below the lip of the raincoat, a pair of black boots. I watched as he turned away from me again to face the sliding doors, and stepped further into the living room. And then, as he scanned the room – eyes darting from one piece of furniture to the next – I realized he was holding something at his side: a four-inch kitchen knife.

I felt a flutter of alarm.

*He's come back for East.*

Except East wasn't here.

He moved towards me, heading in the direction of the hallway. I whipped back out of sight, breath catching in my chest, and waited. Thirty seconds later, I peeked into the living room again. He'd left the lights off, but I could see the blink of a torch from upstairs. He was looking around the bedrooms.

I headed back to the car and waited.

Five minutes later, Grankin emerged from the side of the house, hood still up on his coat, torch and knife back inside his satchel. At the top of the driveway he paused, looking up and down the road, and then he headed towards the railway bridge behind me. I slid gently down into my seat, watching him pass on the other side of the road, and then grabbed my coat and my phone.

There was a footpath running under the bridge, adjacent to one of the arches. As soon as he disappeared through it, I got out of the car, locked it and went after him.

'Are you ready to go?' I said.

He nodded.

'I need to walk back to East's place and get my car, so you sit tight here – I shouldn't be longer than forty-five minutes.'

'And when you get back – what then? What are we going to do with East?'

In my hands was Healy's roll of duct tape.

'We're going to take him with us.'

# CHAPTER 41

He headed east, through a maze of side roads and alleyways, until he finally got to Southwark Park. I kept about eighty feet between us, sometimes more, and as we crossed the park I dropped even further back as the number of people began to thin out and cover became harder to find. Once we emerged into civilization again, I closed the gap, getting a sense for the rhythm of his movement, the pace he maintained, the way he'd look to his left and right, but rarely behind him. Every time his satchel slipped around to his back, he'd place a hand flat to it – grey and bony in the lack of light – and return it to the front. And, every time he did that, I noticed a kink in his step, as if he were carrying some minor injury.

Once he got to Lower Road, he emerged into a crowd of people gathered outside a pub, stopped and then crossed the street. I kept to the same pavement, watching him from the other side until he veered right on to Surrey Quays Road. Two minutes later, as the huge, inverted pyramid of Canada Water Library came into view on the right, I finally realized where we were heading.

The Tube station.

I hung back, letting him get ahead, wondering why he hadn't just got on to the Tube at Bermondsey. There wasn't much in it, but Canada Water was marginally further. *He must be getting the Overground.* Once we were inside and beyond the gateline, I saw I was right: he found a seat on the platform, hood still up, satchel on his lap. I got confirmation of where he was, and then backed out, hovering in the concourse area. It was eleven-fifty, and the station was virtually deserted.

I didn't want to get caught out now.

Three minutes later, the train pulled in.

I watched as he boarded, then did the same much further down. As the doors slid shut, I started to wonder where he was headed. The train was going via Peckham and terminated at Clapham High Street, which meant the choices were limited. Surrey Quays. Queens Road Peckham. Peckham Rye. Denmark Hill. Clapham.

Thirteen minutes later, I got my answer.

At Denmark Hill, just as I'd done at the previous three stations, I edged out of the open doors and looked along the train. This time, Grankin got off. I waited until he'd disappeared into the concourse, and then exited the carriage.

Out of the station, he made a beeline for Denmark Hill itself. He kept on readjusting the satchel, bringing it back from behind him, as well as the hood of his coat, which he continually checked was still in place. As we moved on to Camberwell Road, a breeze suddenly picked up, ripping down towards us.

Grankin barely broke stride, pressing forward at the same pace, with the same pattern of movement: his satchel, his hood, the hint of an injury. Eventually, at the corner of Burgess Park, he took a left, leading me through a series of side streets and then into a cul-de-sac surrounded by low-rise blocks of flats. Someone had forgotten to take their washing in from a third-floor balcony; on a telephone wire above us, a pair of trainers hung by the laces. Otherwise it was quiet, lifeless, and it wasn't until we were right at the end of the road that I saw what else lay ahead, sitting there in the shadow of the flats, almost forgotten about: a row of six terraced homes, hidden from view unless you were looking for them. All six were boarded up.

Two had been gutted by fire. On another, the roof had collapsed, its tiles falling away to reveal the support beams underneath. On the one next to that, the rendering had cracked, jagging up the middle of the house in a rift as wide as a hand. Others were being attacked by weeds, fusing themselves to drainpipes, doors and windowsills.

I stopped in a nearby doorway, watching.

In front of the row of houses, he paused, looking back in my direction, and then at the windows and doors around him. Once he seemed content that the coast was clear, Grankin started moving again, towards the last of the houses, on to a small, dark path that presumably led to the rear gardens.

I followed, crossing the space as quickly and silently as I could, and then paused at the entrance to the path. Briefly, I caught the green flash of his raincoat and then he was gone again. Once I got to the back of the house, I saw him coming around in an arc, beyond the fences that still marked the boundaries of the properties, broken and warped. The lawns were dumping grounds, the shrunken, rotten bones of old prams and chairs, refrigerators and tyres, sitting among waist-high grass, weeds and dense brambles. Each of the houses was identical: a set of patio doors, a kitchen window, a back door. Every possible way in to the properties had been boarded up, and every space covered with graffiti.

I wondered where exactly Grankin was headed, but then he came to a half-collapsed fence panel at the foot of the garden belonging to the third house along – one of the two that had been burned from the inside out by fire – stepped through it, and started down towards the building. He went slowly across the garden, but knew exactly where to tread. At the back door he stopped, looked either way along the terrace, then placed his thin fingers at the edge of the panel. It swung against the wall, like the blade of a windmill, one of its screws, on the top left side, still pinning it to the brickwork. Beyond the panel, the blackness of the interior revealed itself.

He disappeared inside.

Once the panel rocked back into place, I followed his path towards the house, stopping at the top of the garden. *What now?* Grankin was dangerous. I didn't need to see the knife he'd been holding earlier to know that: I'd seen as much in his face. Pull back the panel – and then what? I didn't know the layout of the house at all. I had no idea what it was like in there.

But what if he *was* the driver that night? What if it *was* him waiting in the car outside Searle House, sitting there, knowing what was going on inside? Could I just walk away from this moment with one of the men responsible *here*, on the other side of a broken panel, just feet away from me? Could I walk away without getting answers for that family? For Healy?

Steeling myself, I headed down to the house, grabbed hold of the panel and inched it aside. There was hardly any light. Somewhere, something fluttered – like a candle – but it seemed far off. I waited, letting my eyes adjust to the depth of the darkness, and then I heard a noise: the gentle moan of a floorboard.

He was upstairs.

I slipped through the gap, set the panel back in place and waited a second time. As my eyes adjusted further, I realized the light I'd seen from outside *was* a candle, its flickering glow coming from the next room, but painting the edges and right angles of the one I was in. This was a kitchen, the worktops long gone, the units stripped down to melted, twisted bones. On the only flat surface that remained, Grankin had stacked canned fruit and tins of processed meat. The room smelled of the fire that had gutted it, but also of decay, dust and mould.

I passed out of the kitchen, into a narrow hallway.

A bathroom was on the right, ravaged like the kitchen, and on the left were stairs, the steps broken and misshaped. Beyond the bathroom was the dining room, nothing in it except a tatty foam mattress and a sleeping bag. Via a connecting archway was the living room, a table in the centre with a chair pushed under it. There was a stack of papers on one side, and a set of three candles next to that. Only one of them was lit, but I could see others dotted around the sides, on the floor, in coves, or on shelves that still remained.

Then: a noise from above me.

Another floorboard.

*He's moving around.*

I double-backed to the kitchen and searched for something I could use to protect myself. Sitting among the cans were a tin opener, a fork, a spoon and a serrated bread knife. Grabbing the knife, I returned to the bottom of the stairs.

Looked up, listened.

No more sound, no sign of Grankin.

My brain fired a caution, warning me that I had no idea what lay at the top, but by then I was already moving, the steps bending beneath my weight. The further up I got, the worse the damage became, walls charred and burned, paint peeling and blistered, plasterboard and cavities exposed. The fire damage seemed to deaden any noise, and when I was almost at the apex of the stairs, I could see he'd lit another candle, this one burning in the furthest room to my left – what I guessed was a bedroom. There were three doors: the one with the light, the one in the middle – another bedroom – and one directly in front of me, a bathroom.

I stopped, listening again, eyes on the room with the light. Another creak, this time in tune with a sudden gust of wind, the house moaning and shifting before settling again. Then I became aware of something else: a new sound.

Whimpering.

Gripping the knife, I checked the bathroom was clear and stopped at the doorway to the first, unlit bedroom. In the dark, it was hard to get any real sense of the size of the room, and it was only recognizable as a bedroom because a metal bed frame stood against one of the walls, blackened by the fire.

It was empty.

Eyes on the second bedroom, I started to move again, knife out in front of me, being pulled towards something I wasn't sure I wanted to see. Through the door jamb, half lit, I glimpsed a figure, obscured by shadows. He was crouching.

No, not crouching.

*Doubled over.*

As I edged around the door, I saw him clearly, one of his shirtsleeves torn, his trousers dotted with blood. He was tied to a chair at the back of the room.

Bound. Gagged.

Calvin East.

Suddenly, he seemed to sense he wasn't alone and looked up – eyes wide, full of tears – and, through the gag, he started to plead for my help, shifting on the chair, his words indistinct and unrecognizable. I put a finger to my lips and used my other hand to tell him to calm down. It wasn't Grankin I had heard up here.

It was East.

Which meant Grankin was somewhere else.

I turned just as he came up the stairs. Instinct kicked in, and I jabbed the knife in his direction – but something odd happened. He didn't come for me. He just stood there, hood pulled tight, most of his face hidden among its shadows.

He was unarmed.

He stared at me, one of his eyes catching the remnants of the candlelight, glinting like a distant shore. And then he began to loosen the knot holding the hood in place, his movements slow and laboured, unable to muster the precision.

Eventually, it fell away.

His face was skeletal and colourless like a death mask; the curve of his eye sockets sunken and dark, as if they'd been sketched out with a stick of charcoal. His head was completely hairless – not a hint of growth anywhere – and his chin poked through his skin like a balled fist, jaw covered in a scattering of stubble. He coughed once, and again, the second time a thick, congealed sound like he was hacking up big globs of syrup.

'No,' I heard myself saying. 'No way.'

He nodded – a movement that said so much.

*You're not seeing things.*

*I'm not a ghost.*

*I'm here. I'm alive.*

It wasn't Grankin I'd been following. It never had been.

It was Healy.

# ALONE

'How are you feeling today?'

Healy looked across the room at Meredith Blaine. She was dressed more smartly than the day before. Blue skirt. White blouse. Heels. Her hair was up in a bun and she had a gold necklace with some sort of pendant on it, half disguised by her top button. He wondered whether she was due at a meeting later. Maybe she'd get asked questions about him; who he was. Or maybe she hadn't dressed like this for work at all. Maybe she was heading out afterwards to meet someone.

A partner. A husband.

Her family.

The room was warm, stuffy, sun pouring through slatted blinds in a series of horizontal sheets. He shifted on the sofa. The drip was still attached to him, its metal stand rigid in the space beside him, like a guard standing to attention. The catheter had been removed, though, which he was relieved about. He had bigger problems than feeling embarrassed about pissing through a tube but it had got to him all the same. It made him feel feeble.

Blaine shuffled forward in her seat. Her photocopies of the book cover, of the photos he'd carried, weren't out on the table today. They were probably in a file somewhere, hidden in her desk. She'd found out more about him in those few minutes than the medical staff on the ward had found out in four days. When Healy had looked at the family, he'd relived every moment he'd spent with them.

'How are you feeling today?' Blaine asked again.

He shrugged.

He hadn't wanted to be wheeled up here by the nurse, didn't want to have to sit in a chair, be seen like this, be judged. But he'd had no choice. His legs were weak, machines he had to awaken again through physio, through repetition. He hated it; hated feeling like this. Even as he sat in the chair, immobile and useless, pain still gripped his body, his bones, his muscles. And the physical pain wasn't even the worst bit. The worst bit was catching a glimpse of himself in the windows of the third floor, the creamy glass reflecting back the man he had become.

Old. A failure. A drunk.

*Don't hurt them. Don't hurt my family.*

A fantasist.

'Can I call you something?' Blaine said.

Healy looked at her.

'If you won't tell me your real name, maybe there's something else I can call you.' She opened her notebook on the desk. 'I feel you should have a name.'

'Why?'

'It makes it hard to have a conversation otherwise.'

He drew his dressing gown tighter around him, a starched white robe, cleaned endlessly, worn so many times by patients the seams had started to inch apart. It smelled of washing powder and antiseptic.

'So what can I call you?' she said.

*Malcolm.*

He knew, even if he chose to say it aloud, he'd be unable to make the *col* sound properly. When he spoke, there was a soft, humiliating slur to his words. But why *would* he say it aloud? That wasn't even his name.

It wasn't *anyone's* name.

Back in this failing body, he was just Healy again, his history scattered behind him, the debris of his marriage, his daughter's death, his lost sons. Perhaps this was fate, him being like this. Perhaps this was the perfect vessel for who he was: a physical reflection of his life, of its impotence and failure.

But why did the traces of *them* have to linger? Why did he still have to feel the girls' tiny hands inside his? Why could he still smell Gail's perfume? Why did he still hear the conversations they'd all had inside that flat like they were being spoken now, here, in this moment? He knew, vivid as they were, they were only dreams, hallucinations, maybe some sort of madness. But what he'd felt for them all . . .

'It was so real.'

Blaine shifted. 'Pardon?'

He looked at her, struck into silence. Where had that come from? Why had he spoken? He was unshakeable, grounded, stony. *That's* who he was, who he'd always been his whole life. Now he was talking without even realizing it. He was confused and he was ill. Maybe this *was* madness. Or maybe, somewhere deeper down, the coma had stripped him back, broken his defences, left him a shell.

Lonely.

Alone.

'What was so real?' she asked.

He dropped his head, hands in his lap, the palms open and facing up to the ceiling, as if he were praying. 'Do people ever . . .' He stopped. He hated the way he sounded now, the deformity in his words. 'How many people like me are there?'

'People who've been in comas?'

He nodded.

She brought her notebook from the desk to her lap and removed the lid of her pen. 'A great many. Circumstances vary, of course. Some people are in a coma for a few days, others can be comatose for years, although the length of time will not have

345

a direct effect on the speed or success of any recovery.' She paused, pen hovering above her notes, studying him. 'Everyone's different. Some patients recover very, very quickly and return to their lives largely unaltered. Some patients suffer severe physical and psychological difficulties and never recover.'

He cleared his throat. 'What about dreams?'

'In what regard?'

'While in a coma.'

She'd been writing something down – but now stopped. Carefully, she placed the notebook and the pen back on to the desk, and said, 'Did you dream?'

He didn't look at her, staring off into the corner of the room, thinking of those moments at the end, in the flat, as the man in the raincoat had come to the door. *The mask he wore.* He was a composite, Healy could see that now. He was the blond man and the driver – everything Healy had memorized about the two suspects, right down to their choice of clothes. Two men, in the same body.

'What did you dream about?'

He sat back, his bones creaking.

'I dreamed I had a family again.'

'"Again"?' Blaine said.

'I had a family once,' he replied softly, eyes on the space between them. 'I lost them. I let them drift away. I became consumed by my job, by what I thought needed to be done, and was important. And then I turned around one day and . . .'

346

'What?'

'They'd forgotten me.'

He wiped some saliva away from his lips. This was the most he'd spoken in almost three months. The effort of it throbbed in his throat.

'So did you dream about having your family back?'

'No.'

She frowned. 'Then I'm not sure I follow.'

'It doesn't matter,' he said.

A brief moment of alarm in Blaine's face, as if she could see this opening – this first real opportunity – slipping away from her. 'A lot of coma patients talk about not experiencing anything while they're unconscious,' she said, keeping her voice steady. 'They say, being in a coma was like blinking. I've read accounts of people being admitted on Christmas Day, and waking up two months later and asking their family what time the turkey's being carved. But I've also read accounts of patients having dreams that felt *utterly* real. Sometimes these dreams featured the actual doctors and nurses attending to the patient: the patient is fully aware of who he is and who's around him, but isn't able to wake up and communicate.'

He said nothing.

'Was that like your dream?' she asked.

'No.'

'What happened in yours?'

He didn't answer. He could still feel them on his skin, smell the shampoo in their hair. He could taste the meals Gail had cooked him, the joy and the ease every time he sat across the dinner table from them, every time he took the girls to the park, or tucked them into bed at night. He could see them when he blinked, lying there in their beds, with their comforters, under the mural he'd helped them paint.

Except he'd never painted a mural, and he'd never taken them to the park. He'd never had dinner with them. He'd never lived in that flat.

He was nothing to them.

Nothing to anyone.

'I'm alone,' he said.

That evening, two hours after he left Blaine's office, he wheeled himself down to the hospital foyer, telling the nurses on the ward that he needed some air. He had no mobile, and no money, but he headed to a bank of phones against the far wall.

Underneath one of them was a phone book. He yanked it out, laid it on his lap and leafed through until he found R. It took him a couple of minutes to get to the number he wanted, but once he did, he picked up the handset, dialled 0800 Reverse, punched in the phone number from the book and spoke his name.

The line connected.

Eventually, someone picked up.

A message kicked in, asking the receiver if they were prepared to accept the call and the charges.

*Please*, Healy thought. *Please accept it. Please accept it.*

A click.

'Colm?' Tom Ruddy said.

'Tom,' Healy replied. 'Tom, thank you for accepting the call.'

He thought of their history, of how that history had leaked into his dream. Healy had been someone else during the coma – himself, but not himself – and Tom had been the only one to recognize it. In the dream, he'd told Tom he was a delivery driver, and Tom had looked at him oddly, as if to say, *But you're not.*

*You're a cop.*

Because that was how they'd known each other.

In the real world, that was how they'd met.

Back in 2004, Healy had saved Tom's nine-year-old son from drowning in a lake at a Met charity event, and their relationship had changed for ever.

It had mutated into something different.

Tom – once one of Healy's regular drinking buddies, a borderline alcoholic, a serial cheater – changed overnight. His son's brush with death altered his DNA, made him re-evaluate himself: he sobered up, he became serious. Worse than that, every time he looked at Healy, he saw that day at the lake – he saw a different moment, when his son didn't come back to shore alive – and Tom's suffocating debt to Healy returned, silent, stifling. Healy hadn't talked to Tom for years, not since before Healy was given the boot from the Met. In truth, he hadn't foreseen a day when he would *ever* need to talk to Tom.

But he needed to talk to him today.

'Tom,' he said quietly. 'I need your help.'

# PART IV

# CHAPTER 42

I had a million questions.

But I didn't even know where to start.

Healy shrugged off his coat – letting it drop to the floor, its bulk gathering around his feet like a punctured inflatable – and then looked beyond me, his face pale and unmoved, to where he'd been keeping Calvin East, bound and gagged.

'I went to his house to try and find a laptop or computer,' he said, speaking to me like our last conversation had been an hour ago, as if ten months hadn't passed since I'd hung up on him. *As if he wasn't supposed to be dead.* 'He brought his phone with him, so I've got his numbers. I can see who calls him. But he doesn't email from it. He doesn't use the Internet on it. Who doesn't use email and the Internet on their phone these days? So he's wiping it clean. He's hiding something.' He tore his eyes away from East and they settled on me. 'But if he's got a laptop, it must be at work.'

As I watched him, everything seemed to shift into focus, like a light passing across shadows. *It's really him. It's really him standing here.*

*He's alive.*

'I just . . .' I stopped. 'Healy, I just . . .'

I was struck again by the change in him. It was hard to reconcile the man I knew with the one who was looking at me now. I'd only known him as heavy, a man whose shirts strained at the waist, whose face bulged and hung, who had to use gel to keep his thick red hair back from his face. Now his jumper hung off him like a smock, his neck scrawny and taut, muscles and cartilage showing through skin as slight as tracing paper. As he leaned forward, hands on his knees, I saw blobs of light form on his hairless head; a shrunken cap that didn't fit properly.

'I didn't know if you would understand,' he said.

'Understand what? That you're still *alive*?'

'No, not that.'

'Then what?'

He came forward, off the last step of the staircase.

But he said nothing.

'What don't I understand, Healy? Have you got any idea what you've put your family through over the past month? They *buried* you yesterday. If it hadn't been for Gemma—'

'They're better off without me.'

His voice was soft, crackling like fat in a pan. He had phlegm caught in his throat, and when he tried to cough it out, his body spasmed in pain. I felt so much in seeing him again – so many emotions – but whatever anger I had, at the way he'd deceived me, fooled his family, whatever his reasons and however he'd done it, I couldn't bring myself to tear into him. A part of me was just elated at seeing him here, alive, in front of me. But it was more than that. I couldn't go for him like this, not this version of him. He was ill, and his sickness cloaked him like a shroud.

'How is this even possible?' I said.

He looked at me for a long time, a blank look in his eyes, then he said softly, 'There's this guy I know. Tom Ruddy.'

He didn't make a move to continue.

'Healy?'

'His brother was a cop I used to work with. This guy used to drink like a fish, but Tom was like the next level up from that. We'd go out on the lash, and he'd have us under the table. When we were flat out on the floor, he'd be across the other side of the pub, still stone-cold sober, with his hand up some woman's blouse. I don't remember us letting anyone outside the Met into our little drinking group, *ever* – but Tom was different. He fitted in with the rest of us.'

'So?' I said, unable to see the relevance. 'So what?'

'You asked me how this is possible.'

'And you're telling me some story about—'

'We were at this family charity day the Met organized at Hampstead Heath back in 2004,' he said, cutting me off, 'and Tom's kid wandered into one of the bathing ponds. I was hammered, and had gone off into the trees to take a piss. As I was coming back, I saw him out there, thrashing around. I don't know how the hell he got that far from the group, but Tom's wife wasn't there, and Tom was too busy necking his tenth beer to notice his boy wasn't playing with the other kids. So I went in after him. I swam out there, I grabbed him, and I brought him back in.

'He was fine.' He paused for a moment, taking a long, rasping breath. 'But Tom changed. I mean, proper, Road to Damascus change. Gave up booze, stopped banging around with anything in a skirt, concentrated on his work, spent every waking moment with his family. That was fine. It bothered some of the lads, but not me. What bothered me was that he became so fucking *clingy*. He'd always bring up what I'd done – *always*, every time – just telling me how grateful he was. Every conversation we had was about that day, about how he owed me so much, that he'd always be in my debt. "I owe you, I owe you, I owe you." This went on for three years, until we all went to Dublin for his brother's stag do in 2007.'

He looked up at me, cleared his throat.

'You probably remember the T-shirt,' he said.

I nodded. *Boys on Tour – Dublin 07.*

'Anyway, we're there and he started on it again, and I was pissed, and I just lost it. I said, "Stop fucking *thanking* me! I get it, okay? I wish you'd just have a pint of beer with the rest of us, or go and screw someone and get it out of your system."

Basically, I was an arsehole to him. I belittled him. I took that one small act of kindness – that one good thing that I'd done for someone – and I ruined it.'

Silence.

Seeing Healy, hearing him talk like this, had almost hypnotized me – but then, in the quiet of the house, I was suddenly back in the moment: East was tied up in the next room.

'What are you planning to do to him?' I said.

'Tom worked for—'

'*Healy*. What are you planning to do to East—'

'Do you want to hear this or not?' he said, and looked down at his feet, where his coat was gathered, as he shifted from left to right. His left leg was giving him problems. 'After that, I didn't speak to Tom for years. Not until a few months back. After I woke up from my coma . . .' He faded out, looking across the room at me, one of his eyes moist. Just then something showed in his face: an awful, pained expression. 'I was in a coma,' he went on. 'I'm not sure how much you know, but I was in a coma for seventy-four days, and when I woke up, my life . . .'

He shook his head, as if unable to articulate himself.

After a long pause, he said, 'I called Tom up.'

'Why?'

'I wasn't exactly sure at the time – not entirely. I just knew that – sooner or later – I was going to need him. I had to apologize to him, square things off.'

'*Why*, Healy?'

He paused, rubbing his fingers together, his system clamouring for a cigarette – and suddenly I was back in the motel bar months ago, watching him doing exactly the same thing.

'Even before they shut the Forensic Science Service,' he went on, 'the Met was outsourcing a lot of lab work to private companies. When I worked murders in Southwark, we used this company up in Harlow, and another one out west, in Staines. All the murders went to Harlow, everything else went through this company in Staines.'

Immediately I saw what was coming.

Healy nodded at me, seeing that I understood. 'Tom ran the lab at Staines,' he said. 'When that body you found under Highdale came in, he made sure the police believed it was me.'

# CHAPTER 43

I stood there, stunned.

'He wasn't a scientist, just a desk jockey,' Healy said, his voice even and clear, perhaps for the first time. This was something he'd put so much planning into, a sequence of events he knew so well. 'But he was still the suit in charge there, and all requests went through him. He did it so he could log everything, make sure response times and work quality were up to scratch. As long as he did that, his company kept on getting that juicy government contract.'

'Who did I find down there?'

'Under Highdale?'

The woollen jumper he was wearing was slowly unravelling at the edges. His fingers started playing with some of the loose thread.

'I read how you found the body,' he said. 'I saw it in the newspaper a few days later. I didn't expect *you* to be the one who actually discovered it, but that book – that *was* for you. Specifically, you. I left it there because I hoped – if it all went to plan – the book, and the photos, my T-shirt, that old tin cup, would be passed to Gemma and eventually they'd find their way to you. I hoped you might read the book and start to ask questions about that pier. I didn't give a shit if you spent a single second trying to find out the reasons why I might kill myself, but I cared about those girls. You said you would help me.' He looked off into space, fingers falling away from the threads. 'That family, it's all that matters now.'

'*Who* did the body belong to, Healy?'

His gaze returned to me. 'His name was Stevie.'

'Who was he?'

'After I left hospital, I was . . .'

He stopped.

'Things happened to me in there.'

'Like what?'

He obviously saw something in my face that wasn't there, his expression twisting up, a second of fire, a glimpse of the old Healy. 'You don't *understand*,' he said. 'I wheeled myself out of there five days after I came out of a coma. I was a fucking mess. I'd only stopped pissing into a tube the day before. I couldn't walk, I could hardly form a sentence. I found this place, and I lay here, and I waited to die. I lay here with the smell of piss and shit, and I begged to be taken. *Begged.* You think you know what that's like, Raker? *Do* you? Because it's not like when you got stabbed. Being in that coma, it took my survival instinct away. It took *everything* away. I didn't *want* to live.'

'Okay.' I held up a hand. 'Okay.'

He stared at me, the fire receding.

I struggled to recall a single time I'd ever seen him let down his guard like this. I'd watched him fall apart before, but every time it happened – after Leanne died; after he was sacked from the only job he'd ever loved – I could still see the struggle he was going through, the effort of trying to rein in this side of himself. He used to see it as weakness.

But not now.

'Just tell me who Stevie is,' I said.

He stood there for a moment, unmoved. 'I lay in this place,' he said, so softly it was hard to hear him at first, 'and days became weeks, weeks became months. I don't know when Stevie arrived – maybe July, maybe August – but he came in here, and he lay there in that room downstairs, on the opposite side to me, and we hardly said a word to start with. I could see, though. I could see he was just like me.'

'But you ended up at Highdale?'

'I only moved to Highdale at the end, before Stevie . . .' *Died*. He sniffed. 'Highdale was in Southwark – so I knew that when the body was found, forensics would get sent to Tom's lab.'

'How did Stevie die?'

Healy didn't respond, a distant look in his face.

'Healy?'

'After we'd been together for a while, he asked me to end it.'

'To *kill* him?'

'He said he was too scared to do it himself.'

Healy paused, eyes downcast. 'I tried to talk him out of it, over and over again, but he begged me. We sat here together in this house, and he begged me. He was done. Finished. All he wanted was for someone to physically put the pills in his mouth. That's all he wanted. He said he couldn't do it himself, and when I finally started considering it, thinking about it, when I finally said yes, I realized – after it was done – *he* could help *me*.'

I shook my head. 'Are you *listening* to yourself?'

'I know what I did.'

'Are you sure?'

'I know what I did,' he repeated.

'You *killed* him, and you used him.'

'I helped him.'

'You fed him those pills.'

'*So?* So what? You think giving someone a way out like that is only okay if they're *physically* ill? He was gone behind the eyes. It was over. You don't have a clue what that feels like. You think I would have done it if he hadn't been there, on bended knee, crying, *begging* me, every fucking day for months?'

'What about his family?'

'What about them?'

'Didn't they deserve the chance to—'

'*Deserve?* You don't get it, do you? He had no one left. He was completely and utterly alone. The only difference between me and him, the only reason *I* didn't sit there and neck a bottle of pills

362

myself, was because I still had something I needed to do. But *deserve*? What does that even mean? Deserve means nothing. Deserve is just fantasy. No one gets what they deserve. You think the Clarks *deserved* what they got? You think Stevie *deserved* to be in this rat-filled shithole at the end of his life, asking me to finish him off? You think *I* did?'

He gestured to himself, to the body he carried with him, empty, brittle, and it was hard not to feel sorry for him. His breath seemed to catch in his throat as he calmed down.

'I phoned Tom for a second time and told him I was calling in my debt. Tom said no, straight off the bat. I expected him to. I told him he owed me, that he'd spent years *telling* me he owed me, but he just kept saying no. "This isn't what I meant. This is illegal. This is ridiculous and insulting." So I threatened him. I told him I would call up his wife and tell her about all the women he'd screwed behind her back. I had five, six, seven years of women to draw on. I knew some of them. I could give her names, details, dates. I told him I would ruin his professional life too. I'd make anonymous calls to the authorities and claim impropriety at the lab. Mismanagement. Evidence tampering. He'd never get another government contract again by the time I was finished. He'd be unemployable. I told him he was going to do this thing for me or, with one call, I would tear his life apart.' He stopped, a flash of guilt. 'When he said yes, Stevie and I moved to Highdale.'

'How the hell are you coming back from this?'

'Coming back?'

'Here. *Life.* You're supposed to be dead.'

He looked at me for a long time, and something he'd said moments before returned to the surface. *The only difference between me and him, the only reason I didn't sit there and neck a bottle of pills myself, was because I still had something I needed to do.* I saw it then: once this was done, he *wasn't* coming back.

'What about your boys?' I said.

'Stevie told me this story—'

'Healy, what about your boys?'

'*He told me this story,*' he said, pausing for a moment, eyes fixed on me. 'He told me this story about how, years ago, he got caught stealing nappies, boxes of Calpol, wet wipes, dummies, all from a pharmacist up in Dalston. He said this PC called Blake arrested him. Blake was in his twenties with no family of his own. He had no idea how much Calpol kids got through, or how many times you changed a nappy a day, so he never bothered asking Stevie about his kids, or his reasons for stealing all that stuff. Blake just waited at the pharmacy, caught Stevie in the act and slapped the cuffs on him. He took Stevie back to the station, questioned him, but saw the case for what it was: a few hundred quid's worth of stolen goods. Something that size, it's wasted time and energy, for everyone. So Blake called the chemist and managed to persuade her not to press charges.'

For the first time, I could hear rain on the roof, a chant from somewhere beyond the walls.

'About a year later, Stevie goes back to another chemist and does the same: grabs a shitload of Calpol and wet wipes and nappies, and makes a run for it. Blake hears about it from one of the boys in his station, picks up the case and goes down to the pharmacy. He checks the in-store tape and sees it's Stevie again. The only thing that had changed in the time since the first arrest was that Blake had started a family of his own. He had a young son now, which meant he knew all about Calpol, the cost of nappies, all that other shite. So he drives to Stevie's home, arrests him, takes him back to the station, and he says, "Why the hell did you steal so much, Stevie? Why not take those things in smaller amounts? You steal a bottle of Calpol here, a few nappies there, no one's going to notice. It's less conspicuous. You do it like that and your kids aren't going to be talking to you from the other side of some prison Plexiglas." Stevie said that Blake didn't seem to care that he was stealing. He was just worried for Stevie's kids – and that was when Stevie told him the truth.'

Healy turned to me, a sickly yellow tint pooling in the stretched contours of his face. 'His wife, his baby boy, they were killed in a house fire a decade back. The two of them had been dead for years.' He came forward, shrugged. 'Blake is shocked, obviously, and he says, "So, why the hell are you even stealing this stuff?" and Stevie looks at him and says, "Because when my wife and boy died, my whole life was taken from me – and, sometimes, even though I know it's wrong, it hurts so much, I don't want other people to be able to live theirs.'"

In that moment, something else became clear.

Healy wasn't just ill.

He was mourning.

'My daughter was murdered,' he said, voice cracking, 'both my boys despise me, my wife is repulsed by me . . . and yet, for seventy-four days, I had a family again. Those girls were mine, Gail was mine, that life was *mine*. I breathed the same air as them. I could smell the shampoo in their hair. I could taste Gail on my lips. I was in that flat, tucking them in at night. When they told me they loved me . . .' His words tailed off as tears filled his eyes. 'I could feel it . . . I could feel it.'

He'd dreamed of them all.

Suddenly, I remembered a line from the letter he'd written to Gemma:

*I had my time again, and I screwed it up the same as before.*

He'd been talking about Gail, April and Abigail.

I went towards him, unsure of exactly what I was going to do, but then he stepped away, one hand up in front of me, one desperately wiping tears away.

'Healy . . .'

'Stevie had nothing left,' he said, his words broken and smudged. 'But I have. I've got one last thing I need to do.' Another pause, long and drawn out. 'I'm dead. The police won't come looking for me. How can they? I don't exist. I'm a ghost. I'm nothing. I'm just a name on a piece of granite. So here's what I'm going to do: anyone who was there that night, anyone who had *anything* to do with what happened to that family, I'm going to find them . . .'

'Healy—'

'I'm going to *find* them, and I'm going to kill them.' He gathered himself, wiping tears from his cheek with his sleeve. 'And we're going to start with that prick in there.'

# CHAPTER 44

Healy headed in the direction of the room behind me, the one he was keeping East in, but as he got level with me, I grabbed his arm, preventing him from going any further. I could feel his bones beneath my fingers, the paucity of him.

'Wait a second.'

He frowned, looking down at my grip. 'Get your hands—'

'Calm down,' I said quietly. 'Don't you think it would be better if we compared notes before you go charging in there? I can tell you what I know; you can tell me what you know. If you want to get East to talk, it's going to go a hell of a lot smoother if we don't look like a couple of strangers.'

He swallowed, turning the idea over.

Tentatively, I let go of his arm, but he didn't move. Eventually, he nodded – as much of an acknowledgement as I was going to get – and gestured for us to go into the second bedroom. As I followed him in, I felt floorboards bend like springs beneath my feet and worried, briefly, about the whole structure giving way – but Healy moved with such confidence, as if he were tapped into the heartbeat of this place, that I just carried on in his wake.

'These places have been boarded up for years,' he said. 'I remember one of the murder teams finding a body in here a few months after the original fire gutted it. Some homeless guy. One of his eyes had been removed with a knife. Because of that, the drifters don't like it – bad juju, I guess – which is why I knew it would be empty.' He looked around the room, most of it slathered in shadow. 'I never asked Stevie where he was from. We never talked about stuff like that. But it wasn't from around here. If he was from around here, he would have been like all the others – scared of this place. Some of them, they act like it's haunted.'

He moved across to where the bed frame stood, and leaned against it. Perched there – stooped, small – he looked like an ancient, withered bird, a man half the size of the one I'd known, weightless and shrunken.

'Sometimes I think there really *are* ghosts in here,' he said.

He removed a penlight from his pocket, switched it on and directed it to my right, into the space next to my shoulder, where two cracked wall panels were hidden by the dark. Across them was a series of drawings: a succession of grey masks, in every available space, some overlapping, some more developed, some in pencil, some in pen.

Every single one was a variation on the same design: a regular party mask – coloured in grey chalk – with two eyeholes, pinprick-sized nose holes, but no space at the mouth. In the most detailed ones, the grey mask was cracked on the left-hand side.

'Did you draw these?' I asked.

He nodded.

'Why?'

His eyes lingered on the wall. 'In January, after our phone call . . .' He faded out again, a hint of regret at that last conversation we'd had. 'After I left the motel in Kew, I went to the hostel on the Old Kent Road. That was where I was at night – but during the day I'd be down in New Cross, at Searle House. I told the people at the hostel that I was out, trying to find work, but all I was doing was driving down there and sitting outside that building day in, day out. I did that for a couple of weeks. That became my routine. That was how I first saw him.'

'Saw who?'

He signalled to the room next door. 'East.'

Stopping, he patted a space on his chest where a breast pocket might have been, where he might once have kept cigarettes, but there was no pocket and no cigarettes. It was habit, muscle memory, an echo of a former life.

'The first time I saw him was 1 February,' he continued quietly. 'You know what's significant about that date? It's Gail's birthday. He came all the way up to the children's play park and stood there for ages, just looking up towards the seventeenth floor. Twenty minutes, maybe more. Then he placed these three cardboard crosses in the earth next to the play park.' He ran a hand across his head, tiny bristles of hair making a crackle against the dryness of his palm. 'Three days later, he was back again, standing in exactly the same place as before.'

'That was when you started following him?'

'Yeah. I switched my routine. I followed him, found out he worked at the museum, and began to watch that place instead. I'd sit outside that place for *hours*. It was *all* I did. I'd watch him go to work, and then I'd follow him home. By that time, it must have been towards the end of February. I had no idea what my endgame was, I just knew I had to find out what was going on with East. Those cardboard crosses . . .' He shook his head, clearing his throat. 'The rain had turned them to mush a day later, but I started to think that might have been the point: he didn't want anyone to know about them.'

It was all tallying up now. Healy's Job Seeker's Allowance ceased being paid in around the same time, because he'd stopped signing on. He'd stopped caring about finding work, if he'd ever cared in the first place. He was too busy with East.

Before he started speaking again, he broke out into a gluey coughing fit. When it was finally over, he looked across at me, a resignation in his face that I'd never seen before. 'The money you gave me,' he said, hoarse now, 'it lasted me until the second week of February. I made it last a month, which was a month longer than I thought I would. But when it ran out, things started to get desperate. I'd stopped signing on, so I knew my JSA would end, and – once that ended – I knew I'd have no money for more petrol, no money to put clothes on my back or food in my stomach, no money to even pay for a bed.' A long pause and then a wince: but it wasn't because he was in physical pain. Not this time. 'So I robbed this corner shop in Poplar. This old Indian guy. I scoped it out, saw it didn't have any cameras, and turned it over . . .'

The rest went unspoken. Healy swallowed, his face creasing into a frown, and then he shifted position at the bed. Somehow, he seemed even more frail now.

'He was stubborn. A few days later, I read that he'd needed ten stitches in his head. I took two hundred and ninety pounds, and put an old guy in hospital.'

I tried not to react. 'What happened to your car?'

'I sold it for scrap, no questions asked. The guy who bought it from me didn't fill out any paperwork, so there was no record of it. That suited me fine. I just needed the money.'

He seemed to fold in on himself, leaning forward to his knees, as if trying to support the weight of his body. I gave him a moment. 'And East?'

He shrugged. 'All I could think about was those cardboard crosses he'd planted in the ground. It was like being back at the Met, back on a case. I became obsessed by it again. I started going to the local library, reading up about the pier, about its history, everything I could.'

'That's how you got the book.'

'Right,' he said. 'They had a copy. So I swiped it. I read it while I waited outside the museum, day in, day out. East would come and go, the same routine every time, and I'd follow him. I robbed another store, made off with almost four hundred quid, and I used that money to fund my Tube travel, back and forth to Bermondsey, to Wapping, trying to get a sense of the guy. I thought about approaching him, about grabbing him and beating the truth out of him, but I became terrified of screwing things up like I did when I was at the Met.' He stopped, swallowing. 'I realized there never *was* any "Mal". *This* was my Mal. East. I finally had a decent lead. All those months I spent on the case before, and I never had a single lead as good as this.'

Outside, the rain got harder again, drumming against the roof. For some reason, I thought of Craw then, of the day we'd met at Walthamstow Marshes and she'd first told me that Healy was missing. Only a month had passed since then, but that October day, the heat shimmering off the tarmac, the kids in shorts and summer dresses running down towards the river; the two of us sitting there as I tried to convince her that Healy wasn't missing – it all felt a lifetime away.

I tuned back in as he started talking again: 'The day I had my heart attack, East left work early. That never happened. *Ever*. I'd been watching him almost a month, and he'd never deviated from his routine. So I followed him, but instead of heading west on foot, towards Tower Bridge, like he normally did, he went the other way and got on the Tube. He rode the Overground up to Camden Road.'

'He was going to Stables Market.'

He nodded.

'To do what?'

'He went into an antiques shop there.'

'Do you know which one?'

'Gray Antiques and Collectables.'

I took out my phone and opened up the email I'd sent myself earlier on, with a complete list of the shops at the market, and the names of the proprietors. Halfway down, I found the shop that East had gone into: *Gray Antiques and Collectables. Proprietor: Benjamin Gray.* I felt a memory stir as I remembered the phone call I'd had with Ewan Tasker about Paul Korman, the client Victor Grankin claimed to have met on the night of the murders, and the man – along with Calvin East – who had provided Grankin's alibi for Sunday 11 July.

He'd told police that his name was Paul Benjamin Korman.

Were Korman and Gray the same man?

'What happened after East went into the shop?' I asked.

'I waited and waited, out of sight. The market started to clear out, but East didn't reappear. I just stayed there, not moving, but it was like he'd vanished. After a while, I began to panic. I started to think, "Have I missed something? Have I made a mistake?", so I went into the shop and wandered around, pretending to be a customer, and there's this weird guy behind the counter, just watching me.'

'The owner – Gray?'

'I didn't know who he was back then, but the way he looked at me . . .' He paused, unable to put it into words. 'There was something familiar about him.'

Because, without knowing it, Healy had recognized him.

*The blond man from the CCTV footage.*

Nerves scattered down my back. 'What did he look like?'

'He'd shaved his head – but not because he was losing it. He had this black shadow on the top, where the stubble was showing through. It was thick. It covered his entire head, ear to ear, forehead to neck. He didn't shave his hair because he was losing it – he shaved it because he wanted it that way.'

*It was a way to hide who he was.*

I thought of those dark eyes, the ones that never

fitted with the colour of his hair in the CCTV film. He'd dyed it to disguise himself, let it grow long so he could shave it off in the hours after. He'd grown a beard too, altering himself, changing who he was. He knew he'd be caught on film, so he became someone else.

'Anyway,' Healy went on, 'East wasn't in there.'

'He'd definitely gone in?'

'Definitely.'

He stopped again.

'What happened after that?'

'I'd been having pains in my chest,' he said to me. 'This burning sensation. It had been going on for a while, from way before we met in January. I got into this habit of pressing my fingers to my chest, pushing at it, because that helped a bit. I did it without even realizing. Most people didn't even notice. But this guy did.'

'The guy who ran the store?'

He nodded, distressed. 'I look around and suddenly East is there, as if begging to be followed. So that's what I did. I followed him through the market, through all these alleys and lanes, and he kept picking up the pace, kept going faster and faster, until I was virtually running in order to keep him in sight. And my heart . . . Things started to get bad. It felt like it was being crushed.' He swallowed. 'After that, I lost East altogether. I was angry. I turned – and the guy in the shop, he's . . .'

'He was there?'

'He was *right* there – behind me. I realized, too

late, that I'd been drawn in to a part of the market that was already closed. There was no one else around.'

'He attacked you?'

'He punched me square in the chest, right on my heart, over and over. It was like a fucking jackhammer. I must have been massaging my chest when I was in that shop, wincing, because he knew. He *knew*. And it felt . . . it felt like I'd been hit by a car. I stumbled back and collapsed against a wall, and then he was off again. My vision was blurred. My chest was on fire. I could hardly get to my feet.'

He swallowed again, the noise registering in the silence, and I thought of Carla Stourcroft. She'd been stabbed there three and a half years before Healy, in what looked like a robbery, dying hours later in a hospital bed. It could have been Korman or Gray – or whatever his real name was – who'd wielded the knife that day, or it could have been Grankin, but one or both of them was involved, I felt certain of that. The question was, why did Korman change his method of attack for Healy? Why not stab him too?

Whatever his reasons, something about the attempt on Healy's life got to me, disturbed me, perhaps even more than what had happened to Stourcroft. It painted an even darker, more frightening portrait of Korman, a man capable of picking up the scent of weakness instantly, like an animal. He'd never seen Healy in the flesh before he walked into that shop, but it took Korman only a couple of minutes to spot Healy's vulnerability. The attack was less conspicuous too. Perhaps *that* was the reason Korman changed tack: Stourcroft's death must have been messy, visible – perhaps it had brought the authorities closer to his door than he would have liked. But with Healy, it was just an overweight man in his late forties, a heavy smoker, an even heavier drinker, having a heart attack.

'What happened after that?' I asked.

'I managed to haul myself up,' he said, 'despite everything, and I tried to take off after him. I mean, I could still *see* him. He was looking back at me, baiting me, this *smile* on his face. I'd lost my head by then. I couldn't see straight I was so angry. But I got about fifty feet, back out to where there was a crowd, when my vision went again. And then the pain . . .' His fingers drifted to his chest. 'I've never felt anything like it. It was like my chest was ripping itself apart. All he did was stand among the crowds and watch, that same look on his face. And, there, in that moment, that was when I saw it.'

'Saw what?'

'It was the guy I'd never been able to find. It was *him*. He'd shaved his hair and beard off, had his nose fixed, but it was so clearly him: the same one from the CCTV video I'd watched over and over and over again. I'd finally found the man who'd ruined my entire fucking life – and all I could do was lie there and die.'

# CHAPTER 45

The penlight dropped to his side, its glow skittering over the remains of the carpet, and his face seemed to shrivel in the lack of light, his body shrinking as it was claimed back by shadow. Yet his eyes were the same: moist, sombre.

'So where does this come in?' I said, trying to keep him at it, pointing at the drawings he'd made of the grey mask.

'I had this journalist I used to work with from time to time when I was still at the Met,' he said. 'You used to have your sources at the Met. You know how it is. Anyway, he worked the crime beat for six years in the late 2000s, spent a lot of time covering Scotland Yard, high-profile cases, police politics, all that shite. I pushed a few things his way during that time – scratched his back, he scratched mine. I liked him. He wouldn't screw you over. So, three weeks after I found the family, I met with him. I thought I could use the media to cast the net wider, try and draw those two men – the blond guy and his driver – out into the open. I didn't know how – I mean, there was no plan as such – I just knew I had to do *something*. So I met this source and showed him some of the case.'

'And?'

'And I showed him the picture from the CCTV cameras.'

'Of Korman?'

'Korman? Is that his real name?' He paused, taking in the new information. 'Yeah, him. Korman, Gray, whatever the hell he's called. But I also showed the driver to my source. The driver was even harder to identify.'

'I think his name might be Victor Grankin.'

Healy shrugged. 'I believe you – because what else do I have?'

'What do you mean?'

'I mean, I showed my guy those pictures of the two men, and he looked at them, and he said to me, "How are you ever going to find out who the driver is?" I said, "That's why I'm meeting with you." But he shakes his head.' Healy stopped, wiping an eye with the sleeve of his jumper. 'He says to me, "No, what I mean is, you can't even see his face clearly. The driver may as well be wearing a mask."'

*A mask.*

Instantly, something snapped into focus. Not just the drawings Healy had made, over and over again on the walls, but the CCTV photographs I'd studied from the night of the killings.

*The driver. Both his hands on the wheel, black gloves on, body half turned in the direction of Korman, as Korman got into the car.*

That shot of them had been cleaned up by forensic techs, its noise reduced, but the bigger the shot had become, the less sharp it had got, edges tapering off. I remembered being out on the decking at the back of my house, looking at that photo, seeing a hair or a fibre that must have been on the lens of the CCTV camera, transposed on to the picture. *The neutral, emotionless lines of his face; the black discs of his eyes; the lack of definition around his mouth and nose. The position of the hair on the photo made it seem as if the left-hand side of the driver's face had cracked somehow, giving him an even stranger quality than he had already.* But it wasn't a hair, and it wasn't a fibre. It *was* a crack – on a mask.

Grankin had been wearing one that night.

'Why would Grankin wear a mask, but not Korman?' I said.

'Because that was Grankin's thing.'

'Thing?'

Healy held up a finger, telling me the answer was coming. 'A week after, my source calls me again. We'd agreed to meet a second time, to firm up the details of what he was going to write – but, instead, he started apologizing, telling me he'd been offered a job he'd gone for the month before, and now he had to drop everything and head out to the Middle East. This was August 2010. My plan to use him, to use the media, got flushed down the U-bend with everything else.'

I tried to imagine where this was going, to get

a sense of it from the look in Healy's face. But I couldn't see ahead. I couldn't see where he was taking me.

'Anyway,' he said, playing with the threads of his jumper again, 'I didn't have anyone else in the media, and you know what happened after that.' Another solemn pause. 'Then, back in February this year, after I'd been watching Calvin East for a while, I got hold of that copy of *A Seaside in the City*. I never, for one second, thought about trying to find out who Carla Stourcroft was. It didn't occur to me. I mean, what difference did it make who wrote it? What mattered was the pier, the *story* of the pier. What mattered was East and those cardboard crosses. So I read the book, *kept* reading it, trying to see if there was anything in it that would connect with East – but I never gave Stourcroft a second thought.'

I'd done exactly the same. Her low profile and her lack of sales meant she had left only the tiniest of footprints online. The local newspaper obituary that Calvin East had kept had been torn off at the bottom, before it had got to her cause of death. It was only when I'd looked for her under her married name that I'd found out. The fact that the nationals had hardly covered her murder, and local stories were weighted almost entirely in favour of the writer Carla Stourcroft, not Carla Davis, meant the connection between maiden and married names hadn't come up in web searches. So, while *Invisible Ripper* may have been her biggest success, it wasn't big enough for her to be treated as anything more than a footnote by the national media; a brief mention, a paragraph, a few lines of ink. At the thought of that, I felt deeply sorry for her – and vowed that it wasn't going to happen again.

I looked at Healy. 'So what changed?'

'My heart attack.'

'What about it?'

'I came back to this place, and I lay here for weeks, *months*, and then when I decided . . .' He stopped, glanced at me: a flash of remorse. 'When I said to Stevie I would give serious thought to what he was asking me to do for him, when I had some strength back, I started going out again. I'd go to a library down the road here, and I'd dig around on the Internet. I didn't know what the hell I was looking for, but I was looking for *something*. And that was when I found out about her.'

'About Stourcroft.'

He nodded. 'How she died. It basically went unreported – you know that? She was so small fry, none of the nationals gave a shit about her. The Met calling it a "bungled robbery" – that was a big mistake too. It made the crime seem like an aberration; like an error of judgement. It instantly made it less interesting for the Fleet Street vampires too. Who wants to read about a robbery gone wrong?'

'But you knew it wasn't a robbery.'

'I read an obituary in a local newspaper that said her married name was Davis.'

*The same one I read.* 'Which is when you found out where she died.'

'Yeah,' he said. 'When I saw where she died, I knew it wasn't any "bungled robbery".' He wiped some saliva away from the corners of his mouth. 'She died in the same place I was attacked. Six hundred square miles of city and we both get done at the same market?' He shook his head. 'No,' he muttered. 'No way.'

'And after that?'

'I called her husband.'

I looked at him. 'Stourcroft's husband?'

He nodded again. 'I found his number and called him up, pretending to be with the Met. I said we were reopening the investigation, and I needed to talk.'

A flicker of guilt in his face, presumably at the thought of lying to Stourcroft's husband and playing with his emotions. Four years on, the pain of his wife's death might have subsided a little for him – but, from bitter experience, I knew it would still be there; that it would never be gone entirely. Yet I couldn't judge Healy. After all, what were we doing here if not reanimating an old case?

'What did he say?' I asked.

'He said they never found out who did it, that the Met told him they suspected it was some heroin addict from Barnsbury who had robbed an old lady the month before in the same way. He said . . .' Healy stopped, eyes shimmering in the half-light of the room. 'He said, about a year after she died, he put the house on the market. "It was four walls with bad memories" – that's what he said to me. He didn't want to be there any more. Too many ghosts. Six months after that, he finally sold the house and started to clear it out, getting ready for the move.'

I studied Healy. 'Did he find something?'

'He said he'd gone up into their attic and stumbled across a load of unsorted boxes. He sat there and went through them, and in one of the boxes he finds all the research that Stourcroft had got together for *A Seaside in the City* – including the new notes she'd added for the revised edition.'

'Wait,' I said. '*What* revised edition?'

Healy's eyes moved beyond me, into the darkness, as if searching for something. 'Before her death, Stourcroft had been planning to update the book.'

'Update *A Seaside in the City*?'

He nodded.

'But that book sold nothing.'

'I know.'

'So her big plan in 2010, after coming off *Invisible Ripper*, was to go back to a book that had sunk without trace in 2002? That doesn't make any kind of sense. How was she planning to update it?'

'She had new information.'

'You mean these notes she'd kept in the box?'

'Yeah. In 2008, before she published *Invisible*

*Ripper*, she spoke to this guy, Winston Cowdrey, who lived in Wapping, close to the pier. The reason she wanted to speak to him was because back in the 1950s he was over in west London, living in the same building as Eldon Simmons. You know who he is?'

'The Invisible Ripper.'

'Right. So, Stourcroft interviews Cowdrey about what living in the same building as Eldon Simmons was like, what Simmons himself was like, whatever else she needed for *Invisible Ripper*, and then they finish up and Cowdrey starts asking her about what else she's written. She goes through the list, and when she mentions *A Seaside in the City*, he says he's always maintained a passing interest in the pier, and she says she'll send him a copy of the book, and they start talking about its history, that sort of thing. Then, out of the blue, Cowdrey begins telling Stourcroft about this weird thing that happened on the pier in September 2007.'

'Two thousand and seven?'

'Yeah. Way before the twins, way before Stourcroft was killed. Anyway, Cowdrey's living-room window looks out over the pier, and he tells Stourcroft that he was up – when he couldn't sleep one night – watching television, and he thought he could see movement, down by the water's edge. This is, like, two in the morning. So he goes to the window . . . and there's this guy, out on the pier.'

'What do you mean, "out on it"?'

'I mean, on the other side of the locked gates.'

'On the *promenade*?'

Healy nodded.

'Doing what?'

'He's walking towards the pavilion. Cowdrey watches him all the way up, and then this guy goes *inside* the pavilion. He spends about half an hour in there, before he comes back out again. Cowdrey says the guy's got a hood up on his coat now, because it's started to rain, making it hard to see his face. But he watches this guy return, unlock the gates, relock them, then – about twenty feet from the front of Cowdrey's place – he realizes why it's so hard to see Mystery Man's face.'

'Because he's wearing a mask.'

'Right.'

*Grankin.*

'Stourcroft's husband told you all this?'

Healy started shaking his head. 'No. He'd just looked through some of the notes she'd left in the box. The rest, I read myself.'

'He gave you her research?'

He didn't answer, bringing the torch up from his side, the light changing in the room. Shadows shifted and crawled as he directed the penlight to the wall opposite the sketches of the mask. I turned towards a space about halfway up, where Healy had pinned a series of printouts and bits of paperwork, in two lines of ten. On the top row was the transcript from the interview Stourcroft had done with Winston Cowdrey; on the bottom were seven pages of handwritten notes that she must have made. Then, right at the end of the bottom row, there were photocopies of three newspaper stories, each one featuring the same picture of a couple in their twenties, arm in arm, somewhere tropical.

'What's this?' I said, stepping closer to one of the reports. NEWLY-WEDS MISSING AFTER NIGHT OUT. Beneath that, the sub-headline read: *London couple, Neil and Ana Yost, had only been married two weeks.* Next to that was a second headline, from a different paper: FAMILY CONCERNED FOR 'PICTURE BOOK' COUPLE. Finally, the last was a printout from a tabloid: HONEYMOON HEARTACHE. All the stories were published on the same date: Friday 22 September 2007.

*September 2007.*

The same month that Winston Cowdrey had seen Grankin at the pier.

'Take a look at the tabloid story,' Healy said.

He'd circled one of the paragraphs about midway down. Under the crosshead PARTYGOERS was a description of how the Yosts had attended a fancy-dress charity ball in the West End, the night before their disappearance.

One witness described seeing the couple talking to a man in 'Phantom of the Opera-style' fancy dress. 'Except he was wearing a full grey mask,' the witness told police. Someone else there that night also reportedly told investigators he overheard Neil and Ana talking to the same man, and that the man had a 'foreign accent, possibly Eastern European'.

*Grankin again.*
I looked back at Healy. 'Who are the couple?'
'I don't know.'
'But these stories were in with the transcript?'
'Yeah.'
I moved towards the handwritten notes. 'And these?'
'They're in shorthand. I can't read them.'
I knelt down in front of them. I learned Pitman shorthand back when I'd started as a journalist, and knew a little of Gregg shorthand too, which was more popular in the States. But this was neither. 'It's not shorthand,' I said.
'What is it then?'
I traced the lines of Stourcroft's words with my finger, the paper crackling against my skin in the silence of the house. 'It's something she must have developed,' I said. 'An insurance policy against this – against this falling into the wrong hands.'
It was impenetrable, indecipherable.
I returned to the newspaper stories.
'What would Grankin want with that couple?'
I failed to notice at first that Healy hadn't replied, my thoughts on what Winston Cowdrey had told Carla Stourcroft: that Grankin had been *on* the pier, *inside* the pavilion, years after its closure.

I turned and looked back across my shoulder at him.

'Healy?'

'Maybe it's time we asked our friend next door.'

# CHAPTER 46

East's eyes widened as he saw us enter, and he made a muted sound behind the duct tape: a whimper, followed by a muffled plea for mercy. As Healy's penlight illuminated him, I saw for the first time that there was blood on East's face.

'What did you do to him?' I said.

Healy glanced at me, eyes narrowing. 'If you don't want to be here, you know where the door is.' He gestured with the penlight. 'In case your short-term memory is playing up, he's got that family's blood on his hands.'

East looked at me, wide-eyed, and started shaking his head.

'You saying you *don't*?' Healy frowned, taking a step closer, and it was like there was life in him again. The anger – the resentment he felt for East – was oil, easing his joints. Calvin East continued shaking his head.

'Really?' Healy said. He paused there, a few feet away, East's eyes on him. There were beads of sweat on East's forehead, even though it was cold and damp in the house. 'You're perspiring, you little shite. You nervous about something?'

'How did you get him here?' I said.

'I lied to him.' He flicked a look at East, eyes moving from the sweat to the blood, and then back to me. 'I've spent the past two weeks pretending to be an antiques dealer. I've been chatting to him on the phone, built this whole story about how I had an old chair that my grandfather had given me. When I called him tonight, he dropped this hint that he wasn't supposed to go out – that he'd been told to stay home – and when I thought of the reasons why, I kept coming back to the same thing: you. That was when I realized you had the book, that you'd picked up his trail – even though I didn't know how far behind me you were. So I kept at him, and told him I had another buyer interested – and eventually I lured him down here with the promise of a late-night sale. And when he arrived, I did what I had to do.'

Healy had brought the satchel in with him, and as he said *I did what I had to do*, he opened up the flap and reached inside. He removed a 9mm pistol.

'Where the hell did you get that?'

He shrugged. 'Who cares?'

'It's a *gun*, Healy.'

'I know what it *is*. How else was I going to get him in here?' He signalled to himself, using the gun like a conductor's baton. 'I didn't think I'd be able to overpower him – did you?'

'What are we going to do with him?'

'What do you *think* we're going to do with him?'

'I don't mean now.'

*I mean after he's answered our questions.*

Healy was wheezing, shoulders rising and falling, and – just as his body finally settled again – he broke out into a coughing fit. It started off like the bark of a seal, hard and hoarse, and then became worse, thick and glutinous, bubbles of saliva forming at the corners of his mouth. I took a step towards him, trying to help, but he waved me back, inching away until his heels bumped the wall.

After he'd finished, he stayed where he was, bent to his left, clutching a space beneath his ribs. He looked like he'd been shot.

'We need to get you to a doctor,' I said.

He shook his head.

'Healy, you're—'

'*No!*' he spat, and started coughing again, so bad this time he pressed his sleeve to his mouth, like he was trying to force it back down. Eventually, it began to fade away, but his breathing became an odd, distressed buzz; an almost electrical noise, like a hum. 'I'm not going to a fucking doctor, okay?'

I didn't say anything.

East shifted, as best he could, on the chair. When I turned to him, his eyes were on Healy. He wasn't dangerous like Grankin or Korman, but it was hard to trust him. Whatever he'd felt for Gail, April and Abigail, however regretful he was for their deaths, he'd still been prepared to lie to them in the first place, snaking his way into their lives to preserve his own. He seemed to look at Healy with a mixture of bleakness and opportunity, seeing the material decline of this man and, with it, a chance to get out of here. Physically, Healy would be no match for him.

All he had to do was get the better of me.

I moved out of the shadows and across the room. He turned to face me just as I got to him. Pressing a hand to his shoulder, feeling fat and bone at my fingertips, I looked into his eyes – a partial reflection of my face coming back at me in the lenses of his glasses – and I said quietly, 'I'm going to take the gag off.'

He nodded.

'But, before I do, we're going to establish a rule.'

Disquiet in his face.

'I'm going to ask you some questions, and if you lie to me – even once – I'm going to leave you tied up and gagged in here, and my friend is going to do what he wants with you.' I paused as he looked from me to Healy. 'I don't think you're a bad person, Calvin. I just think you're weak. You're involved in something you don't know how to get out of. But I saw that little home movie you made.'

Panic. His eyes switched between us.

'I saw the video,' I went on, fingers pressing harder into his flesh. 'I know you don't want to be involved in this. So you're going to confess to me, and I'll tell you why: right now, I'm the only

394

barrier between you and my friend here. He doesn't give a single shit about your life. You completely ruined his, so why should he?'

He glanced at Healy.

'Give me the truth,' I said, 'or I walk.'

Tears glistened in his eyes.

'Calvin?'

A moment more of silence – and then, finally, a nod of the head. I ripped the duct tape away from his mouth and dropped to my haunches in front of him. He tried to bring a hand to his face, where specks of blood had formed among a thin covering of stubble, but then remembered his wrists were tied behind him.

'If I talk to you,' he said, 'I'm a dead man.'

'You'll be a dead man if you don't.'

He looked at me.

He was scared now. I wasn't going to kill him, any more than I was going to let Healy do it – but East didn't need to know that.

'Okay,' I said. 'Let's start at the beginning.'

# CHAPTER 47

'Stourcroft came to the museum the day after it opened in 2001.' Calvin East's voice was soft, frightened. He kept his gaze fixed on me, only occasionally looking out across the darkness of the room, to where Healy stood, leaning against a broken, burnt wall panel. Outside, the rain had stopped. There was no sound now. Only East.

'She phoned the museum, got put through to me, and asked if she could speak to someone. She told me she was writing a book about the history of the pier. Until Mr Cabot hired me, I was working boring insurance jobs, so being interviewed by an author in your first week at work . . . well, that was exciting.'

'So Stourcroft came in – then what?'

'We talked about the pier. That was it. I organized a separate interview for her with Mr Cabot, which was the main reason she'd got in touch. Given his history with Arnold Goldman and Wapping Pier, she obviously wanted to speak to him. Mr Cabot was happy about it, because he'd just opened the museum, and – at that time – he still had plans to refurbish and reopen the pier too, so it was all good publicity.' East stopped, the tip of his tongue touching dots of blood at the side of his mouth. 'Stourcroft sent us a copy of the book when it came out in 2002, with a thank-you note inside, and I didn't hear from her again for eight years. Then, in 2010, she called up out of nowhere, saying she had some new questions for me.'

'She was planning to revise the book.'

'Right. I didn't think anything of it. In fact, we were all really happy about it, because it was more publicity for Wonderland. But then she arrived and the interview started, and . . .' He paused, his eyes red from tears, a lack of sleep. 'The interview was different this time. She was much more guarded, aggressive, and she was asking all these left-field questions. She asked me who had access to the pier itself, the promenade, and I thought, "Why would she want to know that?"'

'Who *does* have access to it?'

'These days, only Mr Cabot and me. But back at the start of 2010, when Stourcroft came in, there would have been three of us. Mr Cabot, me – and Vic.'

'Victor Grankin?'

He nodded. 'Vic handled security at the museum, until Mr Cabot fired him for stealing a box of wood varnish from the store. That was the night they were all . . .' He swallowed. 'The night the family . . . the night it all happened.'

Out of the corner of my eye, I saw Healy flinch.

397

'Say it,' he called out.

East glanced at him.

'*Say* it.'

East's eyes pinged back to me: pleading with me, fearful. I held up a hand to Healy, then leaned in closer to East. 'Okay, so let me get this straight, Cal—'

'I want to hear him say it.'

I looked at Healy. 'This isn't the time.'

'He can't even say the fucking words.'

He came across the room towards East. The gun remained where it was, on top of the satchel on the floor, but then I realized Healy was holding something else: the serrated bread knife I'd left next door. Before I could stop him, he had a chunk of East's hair and was yanking his head back, the knife against his throat.

'Say it.'

East's eyes were filling with tears.

'*I wanna hear you say it!*'

'The night they died,' East moaned, saliva on his lips, tear trails carving a path down his cheeks. 'The night they died, they night they died, the night they—'

'Healy,' I said quietly, forcefully. 'That's enough.'

It took a couple of seconds for him to snap out of it, hypnotized by East, his voice, the words coming out of his mouth – and then he stood down. He glanced at me, face pale, eyes dark, before returning to the far side of the room. In his wake, East started sobbing.

I gave him a moment, looking across at Healy. He stood there staring back at me, unapologetic, unmoved. I wondered briefly whether he even cared about any of this – about building a clear picture of motivation and reason – or whether none of it mattered to him. Perhaps there was no point to this. Perhaps he was too far gone: invested too heavily in revenge, clinging too faintly to life.

As East began to calm down, I ripped my gaze away from Healy and returned it to the man we were holding captive. He was dressed in the same clothes he'd left home in earlier, just dirtier, shabbier, blood at the collar of his shirt. His glasses – too big for him – had slipped down his nose, finger-prints marking the lenses.

'So let me get this straight,' I said to him. 'Until Cabot sacked him after the summer fair in 2010, Grankin had full access to both the museum *and* the pier?'

'Yes.'

'How did he even end up in that job?'

East leaned his face into his shoulder and wiped his nose on his shirt. 'I was put in a children's home in Chingford when I was eight. St David's. My mother died of pneumonia, and I never knew my father. That was where I met them.'

He paused. Earlier on, out in front of the pier as the tourists watched him, he'd spoken with confidence. Now, it was like listening to a child trying to form words he was scared of. There was something else that I'd noticed for the first time too: although he spoke eloquently, it didn't sound like it came naturally to him, but through practice. The evidence of the boy he'd hidden was still there, a hard east London inflection that he sometimes failed to hold back.

'You were talking about the children's home,' I said.

He nodded. 'That was where I met them.'

'You mean Grankin and Korman?'

'Yes. I met Vic first. He was almost six years older than me, but he seemed immature for his age. Even at thirteen, his English was awful because he'd come over from Estonia and his parents were from Moscow and didn't speak anything but Russian. Even so, the home had this old, broken table-football game, and because we were the only ones that ever played on it, gradually, I got to know him a bit.'

That tallied with what Task had told me earlier: Grankin's parents emigrated from Estonia in 1974, died a year later in a car crash, and he'd grown up in care.

'Korman arrived about eighteen months after,' East continued. 'He was two years younger than Vic, three years older than me, but he was . . . different. He hardly ever used to talk, except to us. He said his name was Paul, but the people at the home used to call him Ben. Sometimes he'd tell us to call him other names, and he wouldn't respond to us unless we did. He'd just stare at us. Vic was pretty rough and ready. I mean, he could get violent. But Korman . . . he was worse. Much worse. He didn't like being around others. He'd disappear for days, sometimes *weeks* at a time, and then – all of a sudden – he was back, watching you, and you didn't even realize until he stepped out of the shadows. After a while, one of the other kids at the home started calling him "Dracula", because he had this weird way about him.' East stopped, his expression rippling with the anxiety of describing Korman. He looked down into his lap. 'That kid was killed in the toilets a week later. Someone used a shard of glass to cut his neck, and just let the kid lie there and bleed out.'

'It was Korman?'

'No one ever admitted to it. But I knew it was him.'

'Okay,' I said. 'Go on.'

'Anyway, Vic was never the easiest person to get along with, but we were friends – of a sort, I suppose. Once Korman arrived, though, everything changed. Vic abandoned me, basically. I was suddenly the outsider. And when Vic turned seventeen – and Korman was almost fifteen – the two of them walked out of the home, and they didn't come back. This was 1984. They took all their things with them, and left. I never saw Vic again for sixteen years.'

'Until 2000?'

'Right.'

'What made you get back in touch?'

He shook his head. 'I didn't. Back when I worked

insurance, I lived in this crappy place in Nunhead, and one Sunday, in November 2000, the buzzer goes.'

'It was Grankin?'

'Yeah. Sixteen years of radio silence, and all of a sudden he's standing on my doorstep, acting like no time has passed at all. I remember thinking it was odd, but then Vic was never ordinary. He had a nasty temper on him. He could be vicious if he wanted. It was just lucky I was never on the receiving end.'

'Where had he been for all that time?'

'He wouldn't tell me – or, at least, talked around it – and, instead, he starts asking me if I'm still into history. I told him I was. I'd always been a big reader growing up. Books were my escape in that place. Vic used to tease me, and call me "The Professor", but I never used to mind. There are worse things to be called. So Vic hands me this advert he's cut out of the newspaper, and says, "I think you should apply for that." I unfold it, and it's an ad for a job as a museum curator.'

'At Wonderland?'

'Yeah,' East said. 'We'd gone sixteen years without as much as a phone call – and then he turns up out of the blue and tells me I should apply for a job.'

Healy stepped in, frowning. 'That didn't strike you as weird?'

'Of *course* it struck me as weird,' East replied, his voice still tearful, at points barely audible. 'But

I *hated* working in insurance. So we talked a little more about it, and he said to me, "Put on your CV that you used to work for Arnold Goldman, at his casino on Brompton Road." I looked at Vic, and said, "But I didn't. That's a lie," and he fires this look at me, the same sort of look he used to have sometimes, back when we were growing up, and he says, "Put down that you used to work with Goldman. The guy who runs the museum and the pier now, he used to work for Goldman. He'll like that." So I ummed and aahed about it, about whether to lie like that, but eventually . . . I decided to do it.'

'Okay,' I said. 'And then you got the job?'

'In the interview, I made up a load of crap about meeting Arnold Goldman, about how he'd always been a hero of mine, and Mr Cabot bought it. He started going off on a tangent, reminiscing about Goldman, about how he owed Goldman so much, about how he was such an inspiration. I felt bad that I'd lied to him.'

'Do you think Cabot was in on it?'

'With Vic?' East said. 'No. No way. He gave me the job because I pretended to know Goldman, and because I was cheap. The pay's *terrible*. I've had three rises since 2001. Mr Cabot's a good man, a good boss, but he's not benevolent.' His head tilted in my direction, as if he didn't want to have to make eye contact with Healy. 'But then, after I started at the museum, I began to think back to Vic's visit more and more, and it would

403

bug me. I mean, why reappear after all that time just because he saw a job I'd like? There had to be something more to it.'

As I watched him, eyes alive with the memories of what had happened, I remembered the photograph of him I'd seen in the museum, caught on the edges of a shot taken at Wonderland's opening ceremony in 2001. He'd looked nervous then, meek. He wasn't much different now, thirteen years on. Perhaps Calvin East was always destined to be a victim, bent and shaped to somebody else's agenda.

'So what *was* going on?' Healy said.

'Nine, ten months after I started at the museum, I left work one night and Vic was outside. I hadn't seen or heard from him since he came to my house. He said he wanted to buy me a drink, and a steak. I didn't want to go – it just didn't feel right – but Vic grabbed me by the arm and basically frog-marched me to the Tube. Thing is, when he wanted to be, Vic could be good company, really funny, and he was good company for a while that night. He made me laugh. By the time we got to this restaurant in Soho, I'd forgotten what I was even worried about.'

He rolled his head, his glasses sliding to the bridge of his nose, and looked out beyond me, into space. 'He leads me to this booth in the corner, and there's someone there already. And by the time I realize who, it's too late to back out.'

'It was Korman,' I said.

A funereal pause; a nod of the head. 'He said hello to me, shook my hand, asked how I was, started this normal, routine conversation – but his eyes were saying something else. *That's* the real Korman. He looks at you, and his eyes . . . they don't communicate with the rest of him. They aren't *part* of the rest of him.'

I glanced at Healy. The aggression had momentarily gone from his face, replaced by a clear recognition of what was being described. To anyone else, in other circumstances, East's description of Korman would have sounded absurd. But not now, to us. Healy and East had both suffered at his hands.

'When he looks at you . . .' East turned to me. There was a dried tear track on his face, skewing off left. 'It's like looking into the eyes of the devil.'

He held my gaze for a second and then turned away, back in this moment, tied to a chair in a gnarled and twisted house. And yet I sensed that, in a strange way, he saw this as better than being in that booth with Korman and Grankin.

'What was Korman doing there?' I said.

'He came to observe. After all the niceties, all the catching up, he just sat there, watching me. Vic did the talking for the rest of the night – all these stories from St David's – and Korman said nothing. He sat back and to the left of me, so I had to physically turn in order to see him. And when I did, there he was: staring at me, totally silent, this half-smile on his face. Then, after an hour, he got up and left. Just like that. No goodbye, nothing. I didn't think about it at the time, but I see it for what it was now: he was getting the measure of me. He wanted to see if I was still the same person he knew in St David's; to see how weak I was.'

'Where's this going?' Healy said, impatient, on edge.

I glanced at him. He still held the penlight in his hand – clutched in his balled fist – shining it in East's direction. In the silence, a faint breeze escaped through the gaps in the house, whining as it passed into the room and out on to the landing, and then there was nothing again.

Just the three of us.

'After Korman left the restaurant,' East went on, leaning forward in his seat, its frame creaking as his arms locked behind him, 'Vic asked me if I wanted to earn some more money. I thought he meant freelance work. So I said yes. Of course I said yes. I was dirt poor, living in that airless hole in Nunhead. I asked him what the job was, and he said it was more of a favour. He needed me to go in to work, talk to Mr Cabot and persuade him to hire Vic as his security guy.'

'So he could get access to the museum?'

'Right. Except I didn't know that back then. He palmed me off with some excuse about needing to get his business off the ground, about building a client base. He said, "I let you know about that curator's job, now it's your turn to do something for me." I couldn't figure out his motivation, and he could see I was hesitant. So he gets out his chequebook and says, "This'll help sweeten the deal."'

'He writes you a cheque?'

'For two grand. Two thousand pounds just for going in to see Mr Cabot and floating the idea of using Vic's company. I said to Vic, "But what happens if he says no?" and Vic says, "We'll cross that bridge when we come to it." So I go in the next day and speak to Mr Cabot, and start to play on his insecurities, telling him how it would be a disaster if any of the penny arcade machines were stolen, how they were irreplaceable with insurance money – and finally, I started to realize.'

'Realize what?'

Guilt seemed to claw up his throat like a virus, his Adam's apple shifting, a tear blurring in one of his eyes. 'I started to realize what a good liar I'd become.'

'This is bullshit,' Healy said.

I looked at him. 'Healy, let's just—'

'No, let's *not*,' he fired back. He gestured to East with the knife, the blade glinting in the dull light. 'He hasn't even *talked* about them yet. He's sitting there spinning a yarn that doesn't even matter. Korman, Grankin, we know they did it. He should be telling us where to find them, not spinning some history lesson.'

I didn't say anything in reply, and – in the quiet – we eyed each other, so much passing between us:

407

a history littered with exchanges like this, moments where I'd been forced to subdue him, sometimes physically, dragging him back from battles he'd never had any hope of winning. It would be even harder now. As far as the rest of the world knew, he was in a cemetery in north London. That made him unaccountable to anyone, unencumbered by the rule of law. If he picked up the gun and shot East through the head right now, there would be no fallout. There was no trail back to him.

As I thought of that, my mind returned to Craw, to the idea of picking up the phone to her, of passing off the chaos of this case, of giving her Korman and Grankin's names; and, as I thought of the alternative, of *not* picking up the phone to her, a kind of premonition took hold, utterly clear to me: Healy, face-to-face with Korman and Grankin, and this journey ending exactly how it had begun – in blood, in death. *This is going to spin out of control if you let it.*

*Call Craw.*

*Call her now.*

'What about Gail and the girls?'

Healy's voice brought me back into the moment.

East looked at him, but didn't reply.

Healy stepped forward, simmering. 'What about Gail and the gir—'

'We're almost there now,' East said, cutting him off, a bleakness to his voice that doused Healy's fire. 'But you'll want to hear about the machines first.'

'Machines?'

'The ones in the museum.'

I looked from Healy to East, and said, 'What about them?'

He looked between us. 'Gail's dissertation was about forgotten Victorian architecture. I don't know if you know that already, but it was. Part of it was about the pier. She let me read it once. In it, she said she believed the pier had some undiscovered story to tell, a hidden secret of some kind. She didn't know what; neither do I. I don't even know if Carla Stourcroft did, despite everything. But I think maybe they were right.' He paused, a blink of fear. 'And I think it's to do with the penny arcade machines.'

# CHAPTER 48

East turned from me to Healy and back to me, then took a long breath, as if readying himself for what was to come. 'About five months after Mr Cabot hired Vic to run security, Vic comes to my office and says we should go for a drink. So we head to this place in Wapping, and there's no sign of Korman this time – just Vic and I – but exactly the same thing happens. Vic gets out his chequebook and says, "How would you like to earn some more money? All you have to do is turn a blind eye to some things."'

I looked at him. 'Meaning what?'

'I asked him that. I said, "I don't want to be involved in a burglary." But he said, "It's not a burglary. We won't be stealing anything. There'll just be a subtle change, here and there. Nothing serious." I told him I couldn't agree to anything that was going to get me fired, but he said Mr Cabot would never find out. I asked him again what was going on, and he said, "You'll probably never notice." It still sounded like something that was going to get me the sack, so I thanked him for the drink and told him I couldn't do it . . .' A pause. Sad, anguished. 'But then, as I got up to go, he touched me on the arm to stop me, and he handed me a cheque.'

I nodded, said nothing.

'Ten thousand pounds.'

'That's how much he paid you this time?'

'Yes.'

'And what happened?'

'Like I told you, Stourcroft was on the right track.' He glanced at Healy. 'So was Gail, in her dissertation. The second time I met Carla Stourcroft, in early 2010, it was clear she thought something was going on at Wonderland. Gail eventually thought the same too. I found her dissertation in the flat when we were dating—'

'You weren't dating her,' Healy snarled.

East looked at him. 'I never wanted—'

'I don't give a fuck what you wanted.'

Silence, vibrating with the threat of violence.

I held up a hand to Healy and said, '*Specifics*, Calvin.'

'Korman and Grankin . . .'

East faded out. He was leaning forward, arms uncomfortable behind him, muscles and bones starting to stiffen. I considered freeing his wrists, cutting the duct tape and letting him talk to us without being bound. But then I looked across the room at Healy, gaunt and pinched. Fire burned as clearly in his eyes as if we'd set the room alight. He had a knife and a gun – and nothing else to live for.

As if on cue, he stepped away from the wall – fuelled by the mention of Gail and the girls – and said to East, 'Korman and Grankin *what*?'

East glanced between Healy and me.

'Come on, Calvin,' I said. 'You took another ten grand of Grankin's money, and he asked you to turn a blind eye to what was going on. Which was what?'

The chair creaked again under his weight, as he shifted position. 'He was right. Nothing got stolen – but strange things would happen. I remember, one day, about three months later, I was walking through the museum, across the first floor, and I noticed two of the penny arcade machines had changed.'

'Changed how?'

'They'd swapped positions with each other. It was these two old bagatelles, which are kind of like non-electrical pinball tables. They were almost exactly the same design. Most people – even Mr Cabot, who knew all those machines so well – wouldn't even notice. But I was in there doing tours every day. I noticed them.'

'You think it was Grankin?'

'It had to be.'

'Why would he bother swapping them around?'

'I don't think he swapped them. I think he removed them, and when he brought them back again, he couldn't remember which one went where.'

'Removed them? Why would he do that?'

'I checked both of the machines over, inside and out, to see if anything had been altered or updated – but pulleys, springs, mechanisms, they were all still in place, exactly as they should have been. It was just the finish that had changed.'

'Finish?'

'The finish on the cabinets. They'd both been freshly varnished.'

'You're saying he removed them in order to *varnish* them?'

'Yeah. But they hadn't been done well.'

'What do you mean?'

'I mean, from early on, Mr Cabot entrusted me with looking after the machines, but always, *always* underlined the importance of using the same brand of wood varnish – Hoberman's. It's super-expensive – like, forty-five quid for a pot – but it gives the perfect finish and it's the only varnish that should ever be used on machines as old as the ones in the museum. Usually it goes on so smoothly, if it wasn't for the marginal colour change, you'd have a hard time even seeing it. I get why Mr Cabot pays so much for that brand. But the finish I found on those two bagatelles, it wasn't smooth at all.'

'What was it like?'

'It was kind of globby. Careless.'

'Did Cabot ever notice?'

'No. Like I said, he didn't have the time to attend to all the machines himself; the museum, the car workshops he still owned, they were keeping him too busy. So he passed the job of maintenance to me. He told me, if there was ever something more complicated, I should consult him about it – but basic stuff he was happy for me to handle. I wanted to tell him what I'd found the first time I saw it. I felt terrible lying to him. I felt frightened that he would find out what was going on, about these machines being varnished without permission . . . but I was even more frightened about what Vic and Korman would do to me.'

He swallowed, tried to speak, but then his words trailed off.

A brief memory sparked, of the conversation I'd had earlier with Ewan Tasker. *During the summer fair, Cabot told police that Grankin had stolen thirty-six 250ml tins of wood varnish from him.* That was eight years *after* this – East had noticed the machines swapping position in 2002, Cabot didn't sack Grankin for stealing the varnish until 2010 – but clearly the two events were connected. The question was how – and *why*. *Why* was Grankin revarnishing the cabinets?

'What else?' I said.

'About four weeks later, I was taking a tour group around and saw that something was wrong with one of the fortune tellers. They're these old machines about six feet tall, set inside a wooden cabinet, with a kind of puppet character behind glass in the top half that tells your fortune when you insert a coin.'

'What was wrong with it?'

'It had a small scratch down the side.'

'It wasn't like that before?'

'No,' he said. 'No way. Mr Cabot had spent his life preserving those cabinets when they were out on the pier. He used to joke to me that he never got married because he couldn't love anything more than his arcade machines. The only reason he never noticed was because the side with the scratch on was hidden from view.' He paused, looking between us. 'But I noticed. I could see where the cabinet had been removed. Vic hadn't quite lined it up with where it had sat before. I could see scratches on the floor.'

'Did he revarnish that one as well?'

'Yes. Just like the others.'

I glanced at Healy, then back to East. 'Why would Grankin be doing that?'

'I don't know,' East said, 'but it was definitely him. A couple of days after that, he came to my office and asked me out to lunch, and we hadn't got a minute from the museum when he said to me, "When we paid you that money, we paid you to keep quiet." It was like he *knew* that I'd noticed.' A long silence. 'We never even went out to lunch. He just turned right around and headed back to the museum.'

I tried to imagine the reasons that Grankin would go around applying fresh varnish to machines in Cabot's arcade – *and* doing it on the quiet. When I looked across at Healy, the same unanswered question was in his face.

'There was one other time, four years later,' East went on. 'This must have been towards the end of 2007. Vic came to my office and asked me if I fancied some lunch, so I headed out with him, and we actually went to a restaurant this time. Except Korman was there. I hadn't seen him at all since that meal we had in Soho at the start, back in 2002. He didn't say anything.'

'What do you mean?'

'I mean, he didn't speak.'

'At all?'

East squeezed his eyes shut, as if trying to exorcize the recollection from his head. 'He literally sat there in total silence for the entire time.'

'Why do you think they took you out like that?'

'I asked myself the same question, and remembered what had happened the last time – how Vic invited me out, and then all he did was warn me to keep my mouth shut. So I went back to the museum and looked around the arcade.'

'Something was wrong with one of the machines?'

He nodded. 'Except it wasn't just one of them. It took me a while to find them, but I found them eventually. There was a very minor crack on the glass of one of the strength testers that I never remembered being there before. It had been revarnished too. So I checked the rest of it. Nothing else had changed, inside or out – it was just the varnish. But then I looked up and saw another machine. A phonograph. That had been revarnished as well.'

'Just revarnished? Nothing else?'

'Nothing else. He never made any other changes.'

I glanced at my watch. *Two-thirty.*

We'd been going an hour, and now East was getting tired, emotional again, his eyes shining in the glow from the penlight.

'What happened after Grankin got sacked?' I said.

East went quiet for a moment, eyes on the floor. 'A few months after he got fired – I don't know, maybe November, sometime towards the end of 2010, after Gail and the girls were gone – Vic turned up at my house. I'd started to think – *hope* – that I wasn't going to see him again, but he came in, acting like nothing had changed. He said, now he wasn't employed at the pier, there was going to be a new way of working. By then, when the arcade machines needed servicing, I was bringing them home – with Mr Cabot's permission – and working on them in the garage.'

'What did Grankin want?'

'He told me that, before I brought a machine home to service it, I had to call him to let him know which one.'

'Why?'

'He didn't tell me. I tried to stand up to him. I asked him why he was going around adding varnish to all these machines, why he was trying to *hide* the work he was doing, but he wouldn't even respond to me. So, eventually, I said to him, "I refuse to lie to Mr Cabot any more . . ."'

His words fell away.

'He grabbed me by the throat, and he squeezed, and he said, "Do you want me to tell Ben you said no? Is that what you want me to go back and tell him?"'

'He called him Ben?'

'Ben, Paul, Gray, Korman, I don't know who he is, what he is. I don't know anything about him, and I've known him since I was nine. He used to change his name all the time at St David's, and wouldn't answer unless you called him by it. He's had many names over the years.' His voice cracked; emotion, fear, twisting the shape of it. 'But then that's what they always say about the devil.'

Healy had edged closer. 'So he asked you to call him before you brought one of these machines home for repair,' he said to East. 'Then what?'

'The first few times he didn't do anything. I'd call him up the day before I planned to take a machine out, he'd listen to me describe the machine that needed servicing, and then he'd put the phone down. But, finally, about ten months later, I called him after that strength tester – with the crack in its glass – had packed up, and he told me to hold off taking it home for twenty-four hours. Next day, I bring it home, and he's waiting there for me, and he says, "I'm taking this away for the night," and started loading this machine into the back of his car.' He stopped, shrugged. 'And that's exactly what happened. He brought it back to me the next day with a new coat of varnish on it. The finish was pretty much perfect this time. It had gone on smoothly. No bumps. He definitely used Hoberman's on it, I guess from the batch he stole from Mr Cabot.'

'How many times has this happened?' I asked.

'Since 2010? Twice. Once for that strength tester, and then once about a year ago when the coin slot packed up on the fortune teller.'

'The one with the scratch in the side?'

'Yeah. He arrived at my house and took that one away, revarnished it and then returned it a day later. That's the weird thing.'

'What is?'

'He's only interested in the wooden cabinets, because they're the ones he can varnish. You can't varnish the metal ones. But that's literally *all* he's doing. He's not changing them, or bolting things on, or repairing them. He's just recoating them.' East looked between us. 'And he's only doing it to the same five machines.'

# CHAPTER 49

Out of the corner of my eye, I could see Healy shaking his head. It looked like he was about to say something. 'Wait a sec,' I said, as much to Healy as to East, 'wait a sec. Calvin, this doesn't make any sense. Why would—'

Healy cut me off: 'No. No, this is shite. I'm done listening to—'

'I liked Gail.'

Healy stopped instantly.

East's eyes moved between us, and then they dropped to the floor. A hint of a smile for the first time: sorrowful, forlorn. 'I suppose I was predisposed to liking her because of how interested she was in the pier, in the history of the city, in her choice of dissertation. I got a call from her in the middle of 2009, months before Stourcroft came back to me for the second time. Gail came in, she interviewed me, asked me questions, and then she left. I gave her my card, in case she had anything else to ask, and as she was leaving, she said she'd requested an interview with Carla Stourcroft too, but hadn't heard back from her agent. I remember what I said to her, as clearly as I'm saying it now: "Oh, Carla's very knowledgeable. She'll give you lots of good stuff."'

A solemn hush hung over the room.

'I never thought for a second,' East said quietly, 'not one second, that the interview Gail eventually did with Stourcroft would lead where it did. How could I know?' He looked up, tears filling his eyes again. 'How could I know it would end so badly?'

'You pretended to date Gail, Calvin.'

I said it without emotion, but the implication was clear: maybe he didn't know at the start, but he knew at the end. He knew it was all a pretence, a lie.

I glanced at Healy, knife in one hand, torch in the other, and gave him a subtle shake of the head. *Hold off. We're almost there.*

His eyes lingered on me, his body as rigid as iron now, fuelled by the knowledge – the dread – of what was coming.

'Stourcroft came in to see me the second time, in January 2010,' East said. 'She didn't outright accuse anyone of anything, she just said she had information that might not paint the museum, or the pier, in the best light, and that she wanted to speak to Mr Cabot. So, after she was gone, I went next door to see him, and he's in there with Vic. A few weeks before, a TV company had been in touch about using some machines in a period drama they were shooting, and Mr Cabot had been pretty excited about it. He'd got Vic in to

421

organize the transport.' He stopped, a deflation to him. 'I didn't want to tell Mr Cabot in front of Vic, because I knew – whatever Stourcroft had got a whiff of, whether it was the machines, or the pier itself – it *had* to involve Korman and Vic somehow. So I made something up on the spot, and then told Mr Cabot I'd catch up with him later. But, after he was finished, Vic comes into my office, just walks in there and closes the door, and I can see on his face that he knows.'

'He knew you were holding something back?'

'Yeah.'

'So you told him?'

He shot me a look like I'd accused him of something, a flash of anger in his face. 'You don't get it,' he said. 'You don't know what he's like, what Korman's like—'

'We know enough.'

I didn't say anything else, dropping to my haunches in front of him again. He glanced at me, glasses back at the tip of his nose. He knew his failings better than anyone. My silence was my reply.

'I told him,' he muttered.

'You told him what Stourcroft said?'

He nodded: culpable, unable to take it back.

I held up a hand to Healy, telling him to wait, clearly seeing now where it had gone from here. 'Did Grankin begin tailing her after that, Calvin? Is that it?'

He didn't reply, just nodded again.

I pushed on: 'He begins tailing her, and when Gail finally gets to interview Stourcroft, Grankin sees the two of them together and starts looking into Gail as well. He finds out that part of her dissertation is about the pier. Maybe he even got inside her flat and *saw* the dissertation, but I doubt he saw enough to worry him. Gail was academically clever, but she wouldn't have been battle-hardened like Stourcroft. Stourcroft was a lecturer, a journalist, a writer. She could smell a big story on the wind. She knew how to protect it.'

East was bent almost double now, the top half of his body at forty-five degrees, anchored in place by the binds at his wrist. He was motionless, quiet. Off to his left, coming around closer to him, Healy stood, half covered by darkness.

'After a while,' I continued, 'just to be on the safe side, I think he gets you in a room with him, and orders you to start making friends with Gail. Just in case Stourcroft puts any more ideas in Gail's head. Just in case Gail knows anything she hasn't put in the dissertation. And you're so shit-scared of him and Korman, you do what he asks. You weasel your way into their lives.'

I paused, but I knew I was on the right track.

'Did you pretend that you *also* thought something might be going on at the pier, Calvin? Was that how you got Gail to believe you were a good guy, that you weren't involved in anything bad?'

He nodded.

'But the thing is, you liked her – didn't you?'

He nodded again.

'You liked the girls.'

A flicker of emotion in his face. I remembered the video he had of them, how they'd behaved with him, laughed, how they'd played Scrabble and stolen some of his vowels. I could hear them giggling, could imagine how – for brief snatches of time – he might have forgotten what he was doing there, with them. I leaned in even closer, so he could see my face. 'Why kill those two girls?'

No response.

'Why did they kill the girls, Calvin?' I said again.

Healy stepped closer, unable to get down on to his haunches or his knees, not without effort, not without the creak of old, defective bones. So, instead, he brought the knife forward, placing the serrated blade flat against East's cheek. I glared at him as East drew a sharp breath, but Healy just looked back, eyes a void. This was the moment he reconnected with that family: their life, their death, his dream.

'You're going to tell us,' he said to East, 'or I'm going to cut your throat. Why did they kill those two girls?'

East took a moment to compose himself, the cold blade still pressed at his cheek. 'Vic would call me three times a week, checking up on what Gail and I had been talking about. The night before they died, I went to see Gail after work, and we stood chatting while the girls went and played on the swings at the park.'

Out of the corner of my eye, I saw Healy baulk, neck muscles tightening, veins worming their way up his throat. This had been his dream. This had been his life for eleven weeks. Now it was someone else's reality.

'I had no idea what was going to happen to them,' East said, voice shrill. 'I swear I didn't. We got on. I wasn't lying when I said I liked her. I really did like—'

'Don't,' Healy said, teeth clenched.

'Okay,' East replied, panicky. 'Okay, I'm sorry.'

The change in the mood was palpable. Healy was like an animal in a pen now, chewing through its cage. East swallowed, glancing at me, looking for help.

'What happened, Calvin?' I said.

'Okay,' he repeated. 'Okay. So we're out at the park, and Gail suddenly changes the subject and tells me that Carla Stourcroft called her. Straight away, my heart drops. Up until then, Gail had been safe. She was no threat to Korman or to Vic. But Stourcroft . . . she was like a contaminant, dragging Gail into this—'

'She didn't drag Gail anywhere,' I said to him. I kept my voice measured, but I let him know what I thought of his opinion. 'She knew there was something rotten going on. She was doing her job. The rest of the world deserved to know what—'

'No,' East cut in. 'She screwed it up for every—'

'Shut the fuck up,' Healy said, pushing with the flat of the blade.

East swallowed again.

'Let's hear it,' I said.

His eyes moved to me from the floor, but his head – pressed against the knife – was still. 'Stourcroft thought she was being watched, that someone was following her. She told Gail someone had been inside her house. It wasn't broken into, ransacked, but she'd got home and things were in the wrong place. So she was phoning Gail to tell her to be careful. Gail asked her why someone would even *want* to follow them, and Stourcroft gave her the basics: she had a witness who had seen someone out on the pier in September 2007 – and she'd tied this person to the disappearance of a couple at a fancy-dress ball the same month.'

Healy and I exchanged a look. *Neil and Ana Yost.* They were pinned to the wall next door, their disappearance like a tsunami: it hit Stourcroft, Gail, the girls – and in February 2014, when Healy had gone looking, it had hit him too.

'Stourcroft told Gail that she believed one man linked both events,' East continued, looking ahead, a prisoner walking to his execution, 'and she believed he was Russian. I knew she was talking about Vic. I knew it in a second. I didn't know anything about him being seen on the pier in 2007, anything about that couple, but I knew she was talking about Vic.' He stopped again, and this time a tear broke free. 'She said, "Do you know anyone at the museum like that?"'

'And you told her you didn't,' said Healy.

426

More tears ran out from under East's glasses. 'You lied to her.'

Healy was silent, paralysed, looking at East with a mix of regret and disgust. The rest of East's sentence remained there, unspoken, like an echo: *And when Grankin rang me to check in on Gail, like he did every week, three times a week, I told him what she'd said, I told him that it wasn't Gail who was the problem, it was Stourcroft. I sat there and begged him for Gail's life.*

'But it wasn't enough,' East wept. 'It wasn't enough,' he said again and again, his words perishing the moment they came out, hollow and worthless. 'He called me while I was *there*, at the flat with them. I went outside and finished the conversation, and when I came back in, Gail had prepared dinner for us all. I sat down with them to have dinner, looking across the table at Gail, trying to pretend nothing had changed. The girls went off to bed, we had a bottle of wine, and I was going to tell her to run, to take the girls and run – I swear I was – but then someone knocked on the door, and Gail went and answered it, and . . .' He swallowed, eyeing Healy, then me. 'It was Korman.'

A ripple passed across the room.

'What?'

'She invited him in,' East said.

'He was at the flat the night before they were killed?'

'He was there, in the middle of their bloody flat, yards from where the girls were sleeping. I hadn't seen him for a couple of years, and in that time he'd grown his hair long. He had this beard. He'd dyed everything blond.'

'Did Gail know who he was?'

'No. As she came back in with him, she said, "It's one of your friends, Cal." That's what he'd told her: that he was a friend of mine. He'd told her his name was Samuel.'

He watched me, seeing if I remembered our conversation at the museum. I did. We'd looked out of the window and down to the paved area in front of the pier, to the spot where Samuel Brown had dumped one of his victims in 1674.

*The Devil of Wapping.*

Straight away, I recalled something I'd read in the murder file, about how two of the cameras at Searle House hadn't been working for months. Korman must have come from the *other* direction the night before – on foot, from the Tube. They'd arrived by car the following night because he'd needed a fast getaway – that was why he'd headed out in the other direction. If Healy's team had been able to catch him on film the night before the murders, they might have got clearer shots of him. This whole thing might already have been over. Korman and Grankin might have been rotting in jail.

'He stood there in the living room, talking to Gail,' East was saying, 'putting on this show of normality, telling her how he and I were such close friends, and how he'd been dying to meet her. I was just pinned to the sofa. I couldn't move. "Calvin said that, if I was ever in the area, I should come and say hello." That's what he told her. Gail being Gail, she was so sweet about it all. She was just so . . . so . . .' A shudder passed through him, cutting him off; and then a short, dreadful wail, like the cry of an animal. 'She was so sweet,' he said, his speech soft and slurred. 'She stood there and listened to all his bullshit; invited him to have a drink with us. And all the time, I knew. I knew what he was doing there.'

He was scoping it out.

Gail.

The flat.

That was why she let him in the next evening, why there was no sign of struggle or a break-in. He was East's friend – so why *wouldn't* she trust him?

But East knew the truth. He knew it then. He knew it the next day, when they were all dead. And he knew now, here in front of us, as tears spilled down his face: 'Vic turned up at my house the next morning and told me I was going to be his alibi for the night of the fair, but I knew what he was really telling me. They were gone. They were all gone. I said to him, "*No*. No, I will *not* be your alibi! What the fuck have you done, you animals?" – and he grabbed me by the throat and squeezed so hard I thought I was going to pass out. He said, "You're going to do this for me, or

429

you die too . . .'" He was sobbing now. 'I tried . . . I tried to fight back—'

'Why did the girls have to die?' Healy's voice was steady, flat, as if shell-shocked.

I was still on my haunches, but now I got up and took a step towards him. He didn't move an inch, not even his eyes, his gaze fixed on the side of East's face, the flat of the blade still pressed against the cheek. I took another step closer, my hand up.

'Healy,' I said quietly.

But he didn't look at me.

'Why did the girls have to die?' he repeated, the same way as before. Not a single tonal shift. Yet in his face there was movement: a wince, the weakness of his body trying to contain the strength of his anger; four years of searching for answers, for reasons, nearly a half-decade where his life had been laid to waste by the actions of these men. 'Why did Korman have to kill the twins?'

'I don't know,' East begged. 'I don't know.'

'*Why?*'

'He doesn't know, Healy.'

For the first time, he looked at me. 'He doesn't know?'

'He says he doesn't know.'

He stood there facing me, so much playing out in his eyes. For a moment, I thought he was going to sink the knife into East's throat. His hands twitched, his thin fingers rolling along the handle of the blade.

But then he opened his fingers and the knife fell to the floor with a clang. The penlight followed from his other hand.

And he left the room.

# CHAPTER 50

I gave him ten minutes and then went to find him.

He was sitting at the table downstairs, crying.

As I moved in behind him, into the darkness of the living room, I expected him to try to recover himself, to disguise his sobs, but he didn't. His back was to me, and he was hunched, fingers pressed to both eyes, trying to stem the flow.

Eventually, I felt I had to attempt to comfort him – but when I reached out to one of his shoulders, he shrank away and a part of me felt a strange sense of relief that something of the old Healy still lived.

'East just told me that he had no idea about Korman's antiques shop in Camden,' I said, 'not until the day of your heart attack. He says he got a call from Grankin at work, and Grankin ordered him to leave early and head to that address, and he had no idea why. He says that day was the first time he even knew it existed. Korman and Grankin must have been on to you. They must have seen you watching East.'

He didn't respond.

There were other questions too. Why had Grankin got so sloppy when he stole those tins of varnish from Cabot? Had he *wanted* to get sacked? Was it an attempt to bolster his alibi, playing further into the idea of him being there, at the summer fair, the night of the murders? He and Korman had made no mistakes until then – it seemed out of character to leave traces of varnish on the carpet of his office. And why even revarnish the machines in the first place?

'The sun'll be up in four hours,' I said.

This time he looked back at me, and in the lack of light, in the way the shadows wrapped around him, it was hard to make out much beyond the whites of his eyes.

'Why didn't they just make us *all* disappear?'

I frowned. 'What do you mean?'

'I mean, they made that couple disappear into thin air. Why not do the same to me? To Carla Stourcroft? Why not do the same to Gail and the girls?'

'Making people disappear is hard.'

He shrugged. 'Is it?'

He meant all the people I'd been employed to find over the years.

Maybe he even meant himself.

In an ideal world, Korman and Grankin would surely have wanted to do that: to make it clean, to leave no trace of their victims. They would have had the opportunity too. Carla Stourcroft was a smart, ambitious, single-minded woman – but she had the instincts of a journalist, one who could be drawn out, lured somewhere remote, with the promise of a source or a tip-off. Yet they hadn't done that. Instead, they'd made her death look like a bungled robbery.

Healy was the same. He'd been following Calvin East for weeks, watching the patterns of his life repeat, and then Korman had snared him by changing the routine. By ordering East to leave work early, telling him to get on the Tube and head up to Camden, he knew Healy would follow. A suspicious ex-cop, focused on the only case that mattered to him, wouldn't let it go. He'd want to find out why East's plans had altered. And when he got to the market, Korman instructed East to lead Healy into the quietest part of it, and then Korman had gone on the offensive: a short, devastating act which would ultimately look like a heart attack. I wasn't sure what made me more nervous: the fact that he'd been able to do it so quickly, so effectively, without anyone seeing him – or that he'd been able to detect Healy's physical weakness in the first place.

I didn't know enough about Neil and Ana Yost to say exactly how they fitted in, but it was clear they'd been preyed upon by Grankin this time, and if they'd been talking to him the night they disappeared, his lies had plainly been convincing enough for them to leave with him. Gail and the girls were always going to be harder, their physical location making them trickier to move. It wasn't just seventeen floors of a tower block Korman had to negotiate, it was seventeen floors of a tower block with a woman and two eight-year-olds in tow. Moving Gail – silently, in fear of her life – was one thing; moving two eight-year-olds without them speaking, or making any sound, was much more difficult.

In the end, Korman and Grankin had been devious, and incredibly smart: different crimes – two missing people whose bodies had never been found; a family killed where they lived; a robbery-murder – and then an overweight man suffering a heart attack, couldn't easily be connected. It wasn't good luck. It wasn't chance. They'd done it that way on purpose. If Korman and Grankin had dealt with them all in the same way, there'd be a pattern. Someone, somewhere, would have noticed.

But no one ever had.

Not until now.

'I don't understand why Stourcroft didn't raise the alarm,' Healy said. 'She was killed almost a month after Gail and the girls, but she never said anything to anyone. She must have seen what had happened, but she never went to the police. Why the hell didn't she pick up the phone to them?'

I thought of the obituary I'd read in East's house. 'Because she wasn't in the country at the time. She was visiting her sister in Australia, and only landed back in London on 5 August. Korman and Grankin hit her the next day.'

'She didn't watch the news while she was out there?'

'It wouldn't have been on Australian news channels. I doubt it would have been reported in their newspapers either. How often do homicides in Sydney or Melbourne get reported here?'

It all made sense. Korman had killed Gail and the twins, and then they'd done the same to Stourcroft. They'd done it before she even realized what had happened while she'd been gone, before she got the chance to find out.

It was all planned perfectly.

I looked back at Healy. He was wiping a sleeve across his cheek, some of his composure returning. Outside, the rain started up again.

'Are you ready to go?' I said.

He nodded.

'I need to walk back to East's place and get my car, so you sit tight here – I shouldn't be longer than forty-five minutes.'

'And when you get back – what then? What are we going to do with East?'

In my hands was Healy's roll of duct tape.

'We're going to take him with us.'

# CHAPTER 51

We moved north through dark London streets. The rain had stopped again, but it was damp and cold outside, and the heaters of the BMW had to work overtime.

Healy sat beside me, wrapped in his coat. I could smell sweat on him now, the odour of clothes that had gone too long without being washed. He spent the journey staring out of the window, exterior lights occasionally forming a ghostly reflection of his face in the glass. In the back, East lay flat, in a foetal position, his wrists and ankles bound, a fresh bandage of duct tape over his mouth. I looked at him occasionally, but he didn't make eye contact, just stared off into the back of Healy's seat, quiet, numb.

At 5 a.m., we reached Wapping.

The high street was silent, still to wake from its slumber. Most of the old warehouses were flats now, rather than businesses, and that meant the approach to the museum was lightless, windows black, curtains pulled. That was good and bad: most people would still be asleep, but not all. Some residents would already be moving around in the

437

shadows of their homes, able to see us, but not be seen.

I found a space two hundred feet away from the museum, under trees, and switched off the engine. Turning in my seat, I watched East's eyes flick to me. A flash of panic now, his body squirming, rolling into the seat, pressing against it.

'Calm down,' I said.

He looked from me to the back of Healy's head.

I removed a bunch of keys from my coat and held them up to him. Along with five hundred pounds in cash for the non-existent chair Healy was willing to sell him, and his mobile phone, they had been the only things East had on him. We'd been through the phone's address book and Recent Calls list with East back at Healy's hideout, asking him to show us Korman and Grankin's numbers. They were listed under aliases: Grankin was Vic Smith; Korman was Paul Gray. But Korman never called him directly – *ever* – and Grankin always called from the landline at his house, up in Whitehall Woods. They'd also instructed East to wipe his phone clean after every use – calls, email, Internet.

Yet taking possession of the phone would, at least, give us a clearer idea of when East's absence might be noted by Grankin and Korman – and how closely he was being watched. Would they call East when he didn't turn up for work this morning? Or would they fail to notice until later on? Or tomorrow? Or two days' time? I didn't think too hard about the other possibility: that, somehow, they knew already.

I held up the key ring. 'Which of these is for the pier?'

There were ten keys in total. I started to go through them, one by one. At the eighth, East gave a nod of the head. It was a copper-coloured Yale. With the tenth, he nodded again. One for the gates, one for the pavilion.

Removing them from the key ring, I pocketed the others as well as East's phone, then got out of the car and spent a couple of minutes checking the area immediately around us, and on the approach to the museum. Much further down, I could see a lorry bumped up on to a pavement, hazard lights going. Otherwise, there was no sign of life. Again I felt a shiver of alarm: *What if they already know?* I pushed the question away, checking again for a tail, for any sign we were being watched.

Returning to the car, I slipped in at the wheel, reached back to East and tore the duct tape away from his mouth. He winced in pain, his eyes watering.

'When do you think Grankin will call you next?'

'I don't know,' he said feebly.

'How often do you speak to him?'

He shrugged, as best he could. 'It depends.'

'On what?'

'On when he needs my help. I hadn't seen him for a while until last night – he came to my house and got a penny arcade machine from me.'

439

He was talking about the two he'd had in his garage, one of which Grankin had taken away. I realized a couple of things now that hadn't seemed important at the time: the one Grankin left behind had been metal, the one he'd taken was wood; and the one he'd taken was a bagatelle.

'The machine he came and got last night,' I said. 'Was it one of the machines you noticed had been swapped around, back in 2002?'

East nodded. It was just like he'd said: for twelve years, Grankin had been taking the same five machines, varnishing and revarnishing them, over and over again. Healy glanced at me, clearly as perturbed as I was by the strangeness of such an act.

I looked across at the museum, thoughts continuing to turn over. Right at the edge of the old paper mill, I could make out what looked like the periphery of the pier. Or maybe it wasn't. Maybe it was just a trick of the dark; something to tempt me, to draw me closer.

I turned back to East. 'When did you last go inside the pavilion?'

He shook his head.

'You don't remember?'

'No,' he said.

'Take a guess.'

He spent a couple of seconds trying to think. 'Maybe eighteen months back. Mr Cabot had concerns about the pavilion roof four years ago, so he went up with a couple of people from the council. But it looked like it was about to collapse a year and a half ago, so he got in a building inspector to take a look, and some repairs were made to it. I asked him if I could tag along that second time, just so I could have a look around the place. We spent most of the time outside, though. It's not very safe in there now – and it's too expensive to fix.'

'Nothing set off any alarm bells?'

'Inside the pavilion? No.'

'No sign of anything suspicious?'

'No,' he said again.

*So what had Grankin been doing in there?*

Carla Stourcroft's witness, Winston Cowdrey, had seen Grankin out on the pier in September 2007 – that was over seven years ago. I thought of Cowdrey, looking out from one of the flats dotted around us, and hoped he'd managed to remain off Korman and Grankin's radar; then returned my thoughts to what East had just said: *There was no sign of anything suspicious inside the pavilion.*

Maybe whatever Korman and Grankin were using the pavilion for had long since finished. If there had been anything inside – anything bad – Cabot would have noticed. East would have too. I looked at him again, watching for any lingering sense he'd lied to me – but we were past that now.

He was done lying.

I returned the tape to his mouth. He didn't resist, just meekly accepted it. Getting out, I opened the boot of the car, grabbed a torch and wedged it into my belt, and then – with one last look around me – started pulling East out of the car. I checked again that there were no eyes on us, and then half walked him, half carried him to the boot, bending him into the space as gently as I could, on to a tatty blanket.

I heard Healy get out.

'We'll be back,' I said to East.

He looked up at me, anxious, scared.

'And when we get back?'

Healy. They were the first words he'd spoken since we'd left Camberwell. He was standing next to me – raincoat zipped up, hood covering his baldness – looking down at East with disgust in his face. The truth was, I hadn't yet decided what I was going to do with East – but now wasn't the time to argue over it.

I slammed the boot shut. 'Let's go.'

# CHAPTER 52

Beyond the gates, the pier waited.

As we passed the rusty ticket booth, and moved to the paved area, it began raining hard, drifting in off the Thames. There was no security lamp on the back of the museum, and not much in the way of illumination from nearby flats, and yet – even with our torches off – it was possible to see enough. On the other side of the river was the glow of south London, pockets of light scattered in every direction along the fringes of the Thames. They painted the angles of the pier a smoky grey, almost backlighting it, its lines visible in the shadows of early morning, its legs planted in the murk of the river. The closer we got to the gates, the more prominent the sounds of the water became, fading in like a song.

I undid the padlock, pulled it from its loop and checked behind us. Healy was watching too, eyes scanning the buildings close by. Electrified fencing hummed above us as we passed through – and then, thirty seconds later, we were inside the gates, the padlock back in place, the pavilion ahead of us.

443

Briefly, Healy glanced at me.

There was no expression on his face, but something shifted in his eyes, a clear unease. The pavilion lay at the end of three hundred feet of slowly decaying wooden slats, a rectangular building with a huge domed roof. On either side of us were the stalls, boarded-up former shops from which people in period costume had once sold candyfloss and ice creams. On some of them were faded reminders of what they'd once been called, but most were way past that, their façades little more than bleached wood, rinsed of colour and form by years of hard weather.

We moved as quickly as we could, the rain getting harder. The promenade felt soft underfoot, the slats bowed or, in some cases, missing entirely, the gaps not big enough to fall through, but oddly disorientating. It wasn't just the slats either: a third of the way along, some of the fencing, which hemmed in the promenade, had fallen away, washed out to sea at some point long forgotten. A rust-speckled bench was on its side in front of the gap, ripped from the metal plates it had once been secured to, and tossed around by the wind. A central glassed seating area – modelled after the one on the Grand Pier at Weston-super-Mare – had been destroyed too, most of the glass now gone, the intricacies of the metalwork caked in mould and salt.

Forty feet short of the pavilion, I became aware that Healy was no longer at my side, and looked back. He was struggling, his movements slow, laboured. As the rain and the wind pressed at him, he drew his coat tighter around himself like a second skin, revealing his contours, meagre and unimpressive. *It was a mistake bringing him out here,* I thought, his pale face looking out from the hood, seeing me waiting for him, waving me forward. I did as he asked, but the unease didn't shift, a feeling that became more pronounced as I reached the red doors of the pavilion.

Above me, the front of the building climbed into the early morning, walls stained by age and abandonment. Windows remained intact at regular intervals, except for two which had been boarded up. Selecting the second key and springing the padlock, I grabbed one of the doors and heaved it open. Its hinges squealed. The smell of old wood, damp and rot wafted out of the pavilion, and I could make out a painted arch about seven feet high, just inside the doors. It said:

GOLDMAN'S VICTORIAN ARCADE
WELCOME TO A LITTLE PIECE OF HISTORY!

A grinning clown in a Victorian top hat looked out from the middle, the words *Goldman's* and *Arcade* either side of him. It was hard to see anything beyond that.

I remembered then that I hadn't come alone, Healy's feet slapping against the promenade behind me. When I turned back, my eyes were drawn past his sparse silhouette, to the distance we'd travelled. The rain had got so hard, it was difficult to make out the northern banks of the Thames now, our departure point obscured, the museum too, the warehouses of Wapping drifting in and out of the mist. It gave me the sensation of being out to sea, unanchored to anything, rain and water everywhere. Maybe this explained how I'd felt the day before, looking along the promenade. I'd seen a loneliness to the pier, a sense of isolation. As Healy moved level with me, out of breath, eyes on me – trying to get a fix on my thoughts – I turned back to the doors, to the darkness within, and recalled something Calvin East had said to me when I first met him: *They say the ghost of Samuel Brown haunts this part of the river, and possibly the pier too.*

I'd always believed in a different kind of ghost: heartache and loss and regret. But, even so, it was difficult to stand here and not feel *something* – a vibe, an anxiety – as the pier moaned in the rain.

'You all right?' Healy said, hoarse, fatigued.

I looked at him. 'I guess we'll see.'

I led us inside.

# CHAPTER 53

There was no sound under the pavilion roof. The roar of the rain, so powerful outside, ceased to exist the minute I pulled the doors shut behind us. Without our torches on, even as our eyes adjusted to the dark, it was impossible to see anything. No natural light escaped in at all, nothing from buildings on the other side of the river, no angles, slants or corners; it was all hidden in the shadows.

I flicked my torch on.

The interior was long: a single, high-ceilinged room with a mezzanine on the left, built on pillars. There was some sort of structure on top, difficult to make out from where I was, but – that apart – the layout was straight up and down.

As I edged forward, I could see the echo of the original arcade in discoloured squares on the floor. They ran in long rows, from the front of the pavilion to the back, each square marking out where a penny arcade machine had once stood. Underfoot, tiny chips of glass glinted in the torchlight, crunching softly, and as we inched forward, I thought of Gary Cabot, of how he'd spent his youth here, of what it must have looked and sounded like in its prime. There had never been anything electrical in here, save for necessities like lights. That meant the machines wouldn't have been generating noise. The sounds inside this place would, instead, have come from period phonographs, from the brass band Arnold Goldman had employed, from conversation and laughter. But all that was gone. Years later, it didn't have a voice.

The pier lay silent.

Healy started moving to the right.

As the darkness began to thicken and congeal, so the smells of the pier got stronger; a long room besieged by rot and damp. At the centre of the pavilion, it grew even darker and more suffocating, and I started to feel a little unsettled, my mind playing tricks on me. Despite the predictable shape of the building, it felt almost as if the walls were closing in, sharpening to a point, funnelling me into a dead end. It was an absurd, irrational fear, but the more I pushed it away, the harder it rebounded, until a thought struck me: *I haven't slept for almost twenty-four hours.*

I stopped where I was, legs heavy, eyes gritty, head humming with noise. Taking a series of long, deep breaths, I tried to bring some calm to my system, clear it, reboot it, begin again.

I directed the torch ahead of me.

Four white plaster pillars – crumbling and dirty – were thirty feet away, the mezzanine on top, penned in by a three-plank wooden fence. On the other side of the room was Healy's torch, a light-house beam cutting through the night.

I headed up the mezzanine stairs.

Somewhere above me, I heard the flapping of wings, a bird taking flight, but at the top the pier fell silent again, and I realized where I was: above me was a painted arch, a smaller version of the one at the main doors, the same clown in a top hat. This time it read *Goldman's Spectacular Mirror Maze*, and beyond were the traces of what once would have stood here. With the mirrored panels now inside the museum, all that was left were the emaciated frames that had housed them, like a forest of metal trees growing out of a dark, stagnant pond.

I headed in, walking among them, checking the frames and the floor on which they stood, and ended up on the left-hand side of the mezzanine where I shone my torch off the edge of the platform. It took me a moment – but then, below me, I saw something, seared into the wooden floor.

*Burn marks.*

I headed back down to where the marks were. They were rings about two feet in diameter. The floor had been scorched so badly, it had actually been partly eaten away, creating a half-inch trench. Inside and outside the circumference of the circle, though, the pavilion's slats remained unaffected.

'What are you looking at?'

Healy was behind me now, shining his penlight across to where the circle marks were. I dropped down and ran a finger along the ridge of one of the burns, crackling as it travelled, gathering up a fine layer of dirt.

Except it wasn't dirt.

'What is it?' Healy asked.

'It's ash.'

I directed my torch past the burn marks, towards the back of the pavilion. The light crept further into the shadows on the left-hand side and – ten feet further down – picked out a structure built against the wall. It was a stage about six feet across, with iron trellising enclosing it. As I got closer, it became clearer, and I saw a sign hanging from the trellis: *The Amazing Mister E!* Beneath that: *Card tricks! Sleight of hand! Illusions! You won't believe your eyes!*

Whoever Arnold Goldman had employed as a magician was long forgotten – other than by a peeling, faded sign on the stage he'd once used – but there was something else there too, right at the edge of the platform, on its side; something that didn't belong in this love letter to Victorian England.

It was a broken cassette recorder.

# CHAPTER 54

There was nothing else but the recorder.

I picked it up off the floor, turning it over in my hands. It was red, scuffed and damaged, with five buttons in a row on the front: Rec, Play, Rew, FF, Stop. On the back, the clip-in lid that secured the batteries in place was gone, the batteries too, but next to that was a small manufacturer's logo and the words *Made in China, 2006*. It might have been ancient technology by modern standards, but the unit itself was only eight years old. So what was it doing here?

I shone my torch out, illuminating the spaces around us. Everything was a pattern on repeat: old wood, collapsed structures; the continuous unfurling of the pier, its blemishes, its disrepair, hidden by the dark.

The stage we were on wasn't a circle but a hexagon, five sides of it finished in iron trellising, the sixth open and leading to the steps down. When I looked at Healy, I could see we were both thinking the same thing.

Neil and Ana Yost.

The tape recorder was made in 2006. They'd

451

disappeared in 2007. Was this where they'd been brought? Had Korman and Grankin audio-recorded them?

For what reason?

Healy came up on to the platform and moved across it, looking at it under the glow of the penlight. 'There's nothing up here,' he said. He meant blood. Hair. Trace evidence. He meant obvious signs of a murder having taken place.

'Not any more there isn't.'

'You're not saying you think that they're dumped in here somewhere?' He directed the torch out, into the spaces around him. 'East said Cabot has been up here at least a couple of times trying to sort out the roof. He had people from the council in. Building inspectors. Workmen. You don't think any of them might have noticed two dead bodies? Korman and Grankin wouldn't be that careless.'

'I agree,' I said. 'I don't think they disposed of them in here.'

'But you think the Yosts were kept in here before they were killed?'

'Maybe not for long, but Grankin was employed by Cabot, so he'd know if Cabot had any plans to come to the pavilion. I think they brought the Yosts here, killed them, and then left the bodies until it was the right time to get rid of them.'

'And when was it the right time to get rid of them?'

'Well, we're on a river.'

He understood. 'But bodies wash up.'

'Maybe they had access to a boat. Maybe they chopped them up and took them down the Thames. Maybe all the way out to sea. I don't know.'

'And that?' he said, pointing to the cassette recorder that I still held in my hands. 'We're not in 1988 any more. If they wanted to record something, why not just put it on video – or on a phone?'

'I don't know,' I said, shaking my head. But then I started to become aware of something else. An odour. 'Can you smell that?'

Healy glanced over, sniffed the air, but didn't say anything, and I caught the same whiff of something for a second time. 'Smell what?' he said finally.

'You can't smell it?'

He shook his head, then ran his torch across the stage again. I paused there for a moment, unable to put a finger on what it was I thought I'd smelled, before shining my light out beyond the stage. Even though it was cool inside the pavilion, I could feel sweat running down my back, my T-shirt sticking to my skin. My head pounded, but I was unsure whether it was a headache or exhaustion now. When I paused for breath, when I stopped moving the torch, I felt light-headed, briefly unbalanced, white dots in front of my eyes.

'What the hell is that smell?' I said.

Again, Healy sniffed the air, and again he looked at me blankly. I placed the cassette recorder back down and moved off the platform, struck once more by how dark it was, shadows hemming me in from all sides, and – as I moved – the smell hit me again, even stronger than before. I turned back the way I'd come.

*What the hell is wrong with me?*

I rubbed an eye, drifting for a few seconds, and remembered blacking out at the museum.

'Raker?'

I looked at Healy.

'Are you all right?' he said.

Spinning on my heel, I began retracing my path in, past the stage again, the rings burned into the floor, the stairs to the mezzanine, the rows of discoloured squares, to the main doors. Every step I travelled, the air became thicker with the smell. It wasn't the odours I'd inhaled as I'd come in – not the rotten wood, the damp, the musty stench of a forgotten building – it was something else. *Clear your head.*

*Clear your head.*

*Clear your –*

'Raker?'

Healy's voice carried across the stillness of the pavilion. For a second, I'd almost forgotten he was here. I tried shining my torch in his direction, but it only reached to the halfway point between us. I couldn't see him. He was just words.

'What's going on?'

'Wait a sec,' I said, my attention split between him and another prickle of recognition. *That smell.* A second later, goosebumps scattered up my arms, as if my body had skipped ahead of my brain.

'Raker?'

'Yeah, okay, just give me a secon—'

In an instant, it came to me, hard like a punch to the throat. *That smell. I know what that smell is.* Immediately, I looked towards the mezzanine, even though I couldn't see it. 'Healy,' I said. 'Healy, get down here. We need to go.'

'What?'

I grabbed one of the main doors.

'Why?'

'Get down here,' I said. 'Get down here now.'

I heaved it open and looked out.

*Holy shit.*

The smell seemed to rush past me, drawn into the darkness, knocking me off balance like it was something solid and powerful. I took another step forward. The rain had stopped, the sky had cleared, the pier already drying out.

Halfway along the promenade, huge mushroom clouds of smoke billowed up into the grey-blue of early morning, the stench of burning wood carrying across to me, beyond me. But it wasn't that I'd been able to smell. It was the trail of liquid, starting outside the doors of the pavilion and snaking back along the wooden slats, towards land.

*Petrol.*

Someone had set the pier on fire.

# CHAPTER 55

With no rain, there was nothing to stop it. The fire raged, vicious and ruthless, eating away at the pier's old wooden frame, gaining ground all the time. I looked from the flames to the trail of petrol, which stopped inches from the main doors. The exterior of the pavilion had been doused in it too, the walls shining with it, the promenade glistening under my torchlight. Someone had wanted the entire thing to burn – and everything inside. That meant Healy and me. That meant every trace of whatever had gone on here.

I shouted for Healy and then rushed back inside, through the darkness, towards him. He was walking gingerly down the centre of the building, bony hand gripping the penlight. I saw him look towards the open door at the other end of the room.

'What the hell's going on?'

'We're in deep shit,' I said, and grabbed him by the arm.

We were halfway back across the pavilion when he saw. Black smoke was starting to drift in through the doors, coming in on a faint breeze. An hour

456

before sun-up, night was beginning to give way to morning, but it wasn't the changing light that allowed him to see what lay ahead, it was the violence of the fire, the size of it, flames licking at the promenade as it rode the petrol trail towards us.

He hesitated, slowing down.

'We have to go,' I said, hand back on his arm.

He shrugged me off. 'Go where?'

'In ten minutes, this place'll be a memory.'

'Go *where*, Raker?'

I looked through the doors.

He was right.

There was no going back the way we'd come. Behind the crackle of the fire, there was the sound of the pier moaning, its archaic structure giving way, the criss-crossing struts beneath the promenade bending and burning. Pretty soon, they'd be falling away to the sea, the walkway toppling like a domino set.

Even if we'd been able to bypass the fire – which we couldn't – there was no safety out there: on the other side of it, the pier had already been seared, the boards we'd walked, the fences on either side of us, now blackened and brittle.

'Follow me.'

'Are you *listening*?' Healy said, a sudden panic in his voice. I paused for a second, taken aback, remembering what he'd said to me when we'd still been at the house in Camberwell: *Being in that coma, it took my survival instinct away. It took everything away. I didn't want to live.* But now I realized that wasn't true – or not entirely. He didn't want to die here, just the same as me. He wanted to live.

He wanted to survive for now.

I felt a strange sense of relief, even here, even in this moment, as we stood at the end of a structure that was about to plunge into oblivion; and then something cracked, a deep, creaking sigh, and the whole promenade seemed to pitch right.

Grabbing his arm again, I used torchlight to direct a path to our left, out around the side of the pavilion, where coin-operated binoculars stood sentry, ancient, corroded. Ahead of us, at the rear of the building, I could see half of the bandstand, its roof sagging. Tiles had fallen away and gathered in a pile at one side of it, and the platform under the roof – where Goldman's brass band had once played – had begun to cleave apart, softened by years of rain and sea spray.

Right in the corner, behind the bandstand, a metal gate had been built into the fence. It was open, flapping in the wind, revealing a ladder down to a small wooden jetty, slathered in seaweed. As I got to the gate, I peered over: one side of the jetty was completely gone, ragged boards reaching out like fingers into the centre of the Thames. Small boats would once have used it to dock here.

But not now.

I looked at Healy, a hand pressed to the fencing, out of breath, his gaze fixed back across his shoulder. The fire was hardly visible from here, disguised by the pavilion, but we could hear it: the cacophony of snapping wood, like trees falling one after the other. And there was something else too, distant, fading in.

*Sirens.*

'We need to go.'

Healy looked from me to the gate and started shaking his head. 'You want me to *swim* back to shore? Are you kidding? *Look* at me. Do I look ready for that?'

'Would you rather die?'

He peered over the fence, down to the water, then along the fringes of the pier, to the museum. Something crashed, a doughy moan like the last breath of a giant, and then – for the first time – we both saw it: the fire was at the pavilion, clawing its way around to the side, a monstrous, unstoppable force of nature.

'We'll get hypothermia,' he said.

'I've got a spare change of clothes in the car. As soon as we get back, you can have those. You'll be fine. But we need to go right now.' I glanced at the fire, at the roof of the pavilion, all under attack. 'It's not just about the fire any more.'

He knew what I meant.

Sirens meant fire engines.

It meant police.

We started the climb down, me leading the way. At the bottom, I pressed a foot tentatively to the jetty, making sure it wasn't going to sink as soon as I stood on it, and then stepped off and waited for Healy. He was slow – much slower than I needed him to be – but I didn't say anything. Once he was off the ladder, I knelt and watched the patterns of the river, the direction the current was travelling in.

'There's all sorts of shite in there,' Healy muttered.

It was heading west to east, and it was fast, swollen by the rain. It meant, as soon as we got in, we'd get pulled towards the burning wreckage of the pier.

'Did you hear what I just said?'

I looked up at him. 'If we stay here, we're dead.'

A flicker of something in his face.

'Are you coming?'

He hesitated for a moment, then quietly: 'I can't swim.'

There was so much in those three words: another admission of failure; a silent call for help; and confirmation that I was right. For now, he wanted to live.

'Okay,' I said.

I stepped off the side of the jetty, into the water. It was cold – but not as cold as I was expecting. Immediately, though, I could feel the strength of the tide.

'Okay,' I said again, holding out a hand to him. 'We need to go.'

# CHAPTER 56

The crossing was brutally, relentlessly tough. As I swam on my back, dragging Healy behind me – an eleven-stone dead weight – I was fighting the current the whole way, the course of the water pulling me sideways, in towards the burning pier.

It took everything I had – every ounce of energy, every atom of willpower – not to be pulled under the collapsing promenade, but the river was eventually too strong: it drew us in towards it like a magnet, under it, chunks of scorched wood hitting the surface like bombs. Healy started to wriggle, panic setting in, and I had to tell him calmly to keep still. But I felt none of that calm inside. My heart was a fist against my ribs, striking so hard I could hear it pounding in my ears. Broken slabs the size of railway sleepers were falling from the sky, slapping the water, churning it up, the heat from the fire like a furnace.

But then, suddenly, we emerged on the other side, the storm of debris and heat fading as we continued east. I looked back over my right shoulder and saw a sandbank ahead of us. It arced out from the river wall, directly under one of the old warehouses, now converted to flats. There were lights on inside, but I wasn't near enough to see if anyone was watching. Instead, I heaved Healy closer to me, head to my chest, and started trying to steer us towards the sandbank.

It was hard, but I got there, hitting dry land at the very end of the bank. I dragged Healy up, out of the water, and paused there – doubled over – trying to catch my breath. Every muscle in my body ached. My lungs burned. My head was thumping so hard it made it difficult to see straight. I turned and looked at the pier, a quarter of a mile back up the river. The pavilion would be gone in twenty minutes, claimed by the fire. Half of it had already been consigned to history, the front slowly collapsing in on itself, like a mouth opening to scream.

Next to me, Healy started coughing.

He lay on his back, sounding even worse than me, despite the fact that I'd carried him the whole way. His clothes clung to his meagre frame, his raincoat like a sheet of cling film, revealing the underside of his ribs, his left hip bone, the clefts and angles of a body that – less than a year ago – was hidden beneath layers of fat.

'Korman did this,' he said.

I glanced at the pier again, and could see a crowd at the edge of the water now, their gaze fixed on the fire. They were starting to gather, people out exercising, walking their dogs, all stopping to look at the pier's atomized carcass; a monument from another time that soon wouldn't even be that.

'Yeah,' I said. 'This was Korman.'

'How did he find out we were here?'

I shrugged, still catching my breath. 'He knew we'd end up here. I didn't see him following us, but that doesn't mean he wasn't. He could have come in and killed us – but what if we'd escaped? Better to burn down the evidence first.'

'Leaving us alive is a risk.'

'Is it?'

'We could go straight to the police.'

'He knows we're not going to do that,' I said.

If Korman had followed us to the pier, he'd have seen Healy and me together, and he'd know Healy was alive. Right now, I was trapped.

Just another part of another lie.

# CHAPTER 57

A set of concrete steps led us off the sand-bank, up to a narrow pathway that ran between two old wharves. I stopped and looked out between the buildings. We were right at the end of Wapping High Street, the museum about a fifth of a mile along, concealed beyond a bend in the road. I knew what awaited us there, though: sirens were still going, blue light painting the warehouse walls.

'Stay here,' I said to Healy.

We were both cold, chilled to the bone by the water, by the coolness of the morning, but he'd begun to shiver, to shrink in on himself, and if I took him with me, he'd slow me down. I shrugged off my jacket and handed it over.

'This'll dry fast, and hopefully keep you a bit warmer.'

He put it on.

I scanned the street again. It was just after seven and people were already up, even though it was a Sunday morning, seeing what all the fuss was about at the museum. I was soaked, which made me easy to place at the scene, but I didn't have a

464

lot of options. In my car were the fresh, dry clothes I'd promised to Healy. More importantly, East was still in the boot. I had to get him, us and the car away from Wapping as fast as possible.

'I'll be back in five minutes,' I said to Healy, and then headed off, trying to straighten my clothes out as I went. There was no getting around the fact that I looked wet, that my shirt was sticking to me, my trousers too, but I sorted my hair out, made it look respectable, and moved as quickly, as casually, as I could.

At the Overground station, I crossed the street, avoiding a couple milling around at the entrance, but then had to stop at the junction for Wapping Lane: two fire engines were travelling in my direction, lights flashing, sirens blaring. Stepping slowly back from the pavement's edge, I kept on going until I was out of their line of sight, and then waited for them to take the roundabout and head east, down towards the museum. Once they were far enough away from me, I set off again.

There was a slight bend in Wapping High Street, left to right, and it wasn't until I got to King Henry's Wharf, about five hundred feet from the museum, that I realized two marked police cars had already cordoned off the area in and around the old paper mill. They'd parked diagonally across the road, three fire engines stationed between them. The fire crews were busy unfurling hosepipes from their trucks and running them alongside the museum and down to the banks of

465

the river, where the pier was burning to ash. Tape had been used to ringfence an area about one hundred feet in length. There was no access.

I double-backed and crossed Wapping Rose Garden, heading out the other side on to Green Bank. A few people passed me in the park, eyes lingering on me, on my soaked clothes, but I kept my head down and my pace up. Green Bank was busier than the high street, a maze of four-storey residential buildings fringing one side of it, and it became even harder not to be seen. Out of the corner of my eye, I saw one old lady on the opposite pavement actually stop and watch me. Twenty feet further on, I glanced back over my shoulder, and she was in the same spot, eyes tracking my movement, all the way down to the side street in which I'd parked. I tried not to let the idea of being ID'd distract me, and headed left, into the road.

Straight away, I stopped again.

At the other end, two uniformed officers were coming up from Wapping High Street, moving slowly in my direction. One of them had a notepad clasped in his hand, his eyes repeatedly returning to the page.

*They've got my registration number.*

Someone had tipped them off.

I zeroed in on my BMW, left illegally halfway along in a residents' parking bay. It was protected from view for the moment by a Sprinter van – but not for long. They were maybe only forty feet away from it, temporarily distracted by a second BMW, newer than mine, better and more expensive, but the same colour.

I moved fast, keeping to the edges of the pavement, using the van as cover. It was a risk: they couldn't see me, but I couldn't see them, which meant – if they picked up the pace even a little – they'd be on to me long before I got to my car.

Fifteen feet away, I sidestepped to my right, seeing they were still at the other BMW. I heard snatches of their conversation, one of them telling the other that it wasn't the model they were looking for, and then I finally reached my car.

The boot was unlocked.

It sat there, an inch open, rising and falling gently as a breeze rolled in off the river. Almost on cue, a thread of sunlight broke above the rooftops to my left, bouncing off the bodywork and exposing a sliver of what lay under the lid.

Calvin East.

But not as I'd left him.

He was in the foetal postion, his legs and arms still together – bound with the duct tape Healy had used before I'd even arrived at the house in Camberwell. There was blood everywhere, so much of it, it was hard to get an idea of exactly how he'd died. The blanket he'd been lying on was twisted around him, coiled like a python, the upper half of it – around his chest, and his throat – stained red.

Worse, he still had tape over his mouth.

He'd died here, alone, unable to scream. I felt a flood of guilt wash over me, for the needless loss of life, for leaving him here. Despite everything he'd done – his failings, his culpability, the hand he'd played in Korman and Grankin's awful crimes – he didn't deserve an end like this.

Static. The sound of a police radio.

Slamming the boot shut, I moved to the driver's side, the stark reality of my situation hitting home. They had the make and model of my car. They had my registration. They were only feet from me – and now I had a dead body in the boot.

I slid in at the wheel, started up the car, then swung the BMW out of the parking spot, into the road. I didn't look at the two cops, but I could see them react: a quick glance at the notepad, and then they were running towards me.

I put my foot to the floor.

The tyres squealed on the tarmac, and I accelerated away, gunning the car to the end of the street. In my rear-view mirror, I saw the two cops pursuing me, one of them radioing for back-up, the other slightly in front, sprinting full pelt.

When I got back to Healy, he was in the same place, pale face visible in the shadows between warehouses. Somewhere behind us, sirens started up again. He moved as quickly as he could, and got in. 'What the hell happened?' he said.

'East is dead.'

It was difficult to read him, hard to tell whether the news made him feel better or worse. He'd waited a long time for this moment, to see the destruction of the men who'd cost him everything he'd ever loved. And yet, now the first of them had fallen, he didn't look triumphant. There was no delight in this reprisal.

Maybe because it hadn't been at his own hands.

Or maybe because – now, in these moments – he realized something he'd always known deep down: that four years after he'd found the Clarks, three years after he'd buried his daughter, there was no victory in savagery, and no joy in death.

# CHAPTER 58

I called Melanie Craw from Wanstead Flats, three hundred acres of grassland in east London that bisected Leytonstone and Manor Park. Despite being only yards from the noise of the city, from the hum of early-morning traffic and the squeal of commuter trains, inside the car – with the heaters blowing, and the gentle patter of rain against the roof – we couldn't hear it. All we had was the view: grass and trees and birds, the blue smudge of distant roofs the one hint that we hadn't left the city entirely.

Wandering out into the long grass at the front of the BMW, I pieced my phone together again. I'd taken the SIM card and the battery out as soon as we'd left Wapping. When everything was assembled, I glanced back at Healy, his face peering out through the glass at me, one side of him completely in shadow. The dichotomy only seemed to accentuate his decline, pulling at the folds of his mouth and the hollows of his eyes, a pissed-off expression on his face. He didn't understand why I needed to call Craw, and I wasn't sure I was ready to tell him.

As the drizzle hit my face and my phone kicked into life, it buzzed three times in my hand. Three missed calls, all from Craw, all within ten minutes of one another. She'd phoned an hour after I'd left Wapping – and then again, and again.

I dialled her number and waited for it to connect. It rang for a long time without any response: nine, ten, eleven rings. I thought about hanging up, my finger moving to end the call. But then, a moment later, she finally answered.

'Raker.'

One word, but delivered with such weight. Sorrow, frustration, anger, disbelief. It threw me off balance, and I found myself looking back towards Healy, as if subconsciously reaching out for his support. Around me, the grass moved, swaying in the wind, its gentle whisper carrying off into the grey of the morning.

'Craw, listen to me—'

'What the hell's going on?'

A lorry rumbled past, heading north on the three-quarter-mile stretch of road that ran through the centre of the Flats. There was no pavement on this side so I'd bumped up on to the kerb, the car partly submerged by grass like a slowly sinking ship. Once the lorry was gone, the Flats became quiet again: the softly falling rain, the gentle *whoosh* of the grass in the wind, the buzz of the telephone call.

'You know I didn't do this,' I said.

'Is that what you called to say?'

471

'I wanted you to hear it from me.'

She didn't respond this time. I looked back at Healy, his eyes on me. 'Craw, listen to me,' I said. 'I'm being honest with you, I swear. We *were* on the pier—'

'Who's "we"?'

I stopped. *Shit.* 'I was on the pier, but I didn't burn it down.'

'You're lying to me, Raker.'

'I'm not.'

'Then who's "we"?'

My gaze returned to Healy. 'It's complicated.'

'It always is with you.' She said it calmly, which only made the comment sting even more. 'You're all over the wires, Raker. This isn't even my borough but you're still the first thing I heard about when I got in this morning. A witness said he saw two men on the pier before it burned down, and one of them was a guy in his early-to-mid forties matching your description. He said they arrived in a grey BMW 3 Series with your plates. Two officers . . .' She stopped. I could almost feel her anger, pulsing like an electrical charge. 'Two officers saw you *making a fucking getaway this morning.* They *saw* you, Raker. Are you even aware of what you're doing?'

'Who was the witness?'

No answer, just a derisory grunt.

'Did they give their name?'

'Even if I knew, I can't discuss witnesses with—'

'Make a few calls,' I said to her, cutting her off. 'Make a few calls to Tower Hamlets and ask them if he gave his name. Because I guarantee you: he didn't.'

A pause. 'So?'

'So, there *is* no witness.'

'They got a call—'

'Did he leave his name?'

Silence.

'It was the guy who burned the pier down, Craw – you know that as well as I do. It's a set-up. *Yes*, I was on the pier. *Yes*, that was me. That was my car. But you know the first time I realized that the pier was on fire? When I walked outside and the promenade was collapsing into the river. I *swam* back to shore. He coated that whole place in petrol and set it alight while we were still inside—'

'Who's "we"?'

I stopped, glancing at Healy again.

There was something of the past in him now, a hint of suspicion that was like a bridge, connecting one point in time to another. I thought back to that first meeting we'd had in January, looking out from a café in Hammersmith at rowers carving through the icy Thames, and wondered if either of us imagined it would end up here: him, a spectre, a memory given life; me, a man on the run, under suspicion again, defending himself to the one person left who might believe him.

'His name's Paul Korman,' I told her.

'Who?'

'This so-called witness. Or it could be Victor Grankin—'

473

'I can't hear this.'

'They were using the pier for something—'

'I don't want to *hear* it.'

'I'm trying to tell you the truth here.'

'And what do you want me to do with this information, Raker? Shall I march up to Bethnal Green CID and tell them we've just had a nice little chat?'

'Come on, Craw.'

'No,' she said, her voice quiet but sharp.

'Who else do they have?'

'Who else do *who* have?'

'That family.'

She sighed. 'This case isn't *yours*.'

'Then why did you help me yesterday? Why did you tell me about Healy? You *knew* I wasn't going to leave it there.'

No response.

'That family haven't got anyone else. This is it. I'm as good as it's going to get for them. The Met investigation is buried in a filing cabinet somewhere, and all this crap, this fantasy that Korman has reported to police this morning, it's all just a distraction. That's all him and Grankin are trying to do.'

'Because?'

'Because they know I'm getting close.'

Silence. I stopped and took a long breath. This was going nowhere good. I couldn't explain what I felt, couldn't express what I meant. In the years since I'd started tracking missing people, I'd seen something different from Craw, something worse: not just people trying to conceal the abhorrence of their crimes, but trying to scorch any trace of it from existence. When men and women vanished, *everything* was gone: there wasn't a body, there wasn't forensic evidence, there was no reason or motive, all you had was a mound of earth into which you dug and dug and kept on digging. And by the time you got that first glimpse of whatever was buried there, you were so deep into the earth, it was too late to claw your way out. All you had were these men, these devils.

The only choice left was to fight.

In the background, for the first time, I heard voices, slowly fading in. Craw covered the mouthpiece and said something short, muffled. The voices faded out again. She said, 'I'm going to have to tell my super about this call.'

'Do what you have to do.'

'Even if you're right, even if I believe you, they're going to tear into your phone records and find this conversation. I can't afford to get caught up in this.'

'Do you?' I said.

'Do I what?'

'Believe me.'

Craw didn't respond, a long sigh crackling down the line. I looked at the time. Just after 9 a.m. My head was so full of noise, for a moment I struggled to recall when I'd last slept. Was it yesterday? Or was it the day before? The distant sound of sirens stirred me from my thoughts, and I gestured for Healy to start the car.

'Do you?' I said again.

No response.

'Craw, do you believe me?'

It sounded like she was about to say something.

'Craw?'

'Yes,' she said finally. 'Of course I believe you.'

'Okay,' I replied, moving through the grass. 'I've got to go, but I need to tell you this. Someone needs to know.'

'I told you, I don't want to—'

'Please.'

A pause. 'What is it?'

'Tell whoever's running this case at the Met to get a forensic team into the museum at Wonderland and look at the penny arcade. Some of the machines in there . . .' I stopped, knowing how this would sound to her. 'Just look at them.'

'Look at them for what?'

'I'm, uh . . . I don't know exactly.'

'What the hell are you talking about?'

I glanced at my watch, remembering I was supposed to call Gary Cabot this afternoon. It seemed so long ago since I'd spoken to him at the museum.

'The man who runs the museum,' I said to her, 'is a guy called Gary Cabot. He got back from Dubai this morning. He'll be able to help you ID the machines—'

'Cabot won't be doing anything.'

That stopped me. 'What do you mean?'

'I mean, he was reported dead forty-five minutes ago.'

'Cabot's *dead*?'

'You didn't know?'

'No.'

'I only heard whispers from someone I know,' Craw said. 'But apparently a team from the Met went to tell Cabot about the pier, and they found his front door unlocked. They go inside, and he's face down in the kitchen with his throat cut. His dad's there too. Looks like someone's closing the circle.'

# CHAPTER 59

We'd stopped briefly at a supermarket in Stratford where I'd grabbed some clothes, and now I clumsily changed in the car, restricted by a lack of space in the front. I pulled on jeans, a T-shirt, socks, and laced up a new pair of boots, keeping my eyes on my mirrors. Sirens faded again as a police car headed off towards some other part of the city. But sooner or later they wouldn't fade out.

Sooner or later they'd find us.

'Are you going to tell me why you felt it necessary to stop here and call Melanie Craw?' Healy said, making it clear how he felt about taking this detour.

'She needed to know I didn't do it.'

A snort of contempt. 'Why the hell would she need to know that?'

I just looked at him.

'Are you *insane*?'

*I don't know*, I thought. *Maybe.*

'You *do* realize you just confessed to a police officer, right?'

'I know exactly what I did.'

'She doesn't give a damn what you *tell* her you didn't do, Raker. Your registration number is out on the wires. Those uniforms can place you in *this* car, *at* the scene. You get that, right? You see the deep level of shite you're in here?'

I turned to him. 'We're done talking about this.'

Looking out through the windscreen, I watched the rain hit the glass, and then thought of East, his butchered corpse still twisted up in a blanket in the boot.

Getting back out, I stood at the edge of the road and looked both ways, listening for any sound of traffic. It was quiet. Returning to the car, I opened the boot, grabbed hold of his body and hauled it on to the ground. He rolled slightly, concealed by the grass. Checking for traffic a second time, I dragged him off, deeper into the grass, until I got to an old, gnarled chestnut tree.

I covered him with the blanket.

DNA on the blanket and in my car would soon connect me to the corpse, so this wasn't about trying to disassociate myself from the body. The only way I could prove I hadn't killed him was by finding the person who had. Instead, by leaving him here, by putting in a call to police from the next payphone I found, I hoped, in some way, it might be better than carrying him around in the boot of my car, like a sack full of debris.

And yet, as I knelt down next to him, found two twigs and – using some vine from the tree – created a primitive crucifix, that rationale started to taste

479

a little sour. *This is no way for a person to be left. This is no better than having him in the back of my car.* I swallowed, again, again, unable to tear my eyes away from the shape under the blanket, my mind returning to Craw's words. *You're going to lie down in the dark, and you're going to eat the same pills Healy did.* Or maybe it wasn't going to be like that. Maybe it was going to be like this.

A brutal death.

Lonely. Discarded.

I placed the crucifix in the ground and headed back to the car. Slamming the boot shut, I slipped in at the wheel and reversed it back out on to the road.

'You're just going to leave him here?' Healy said.

I sidestepped the question. 'Gary Cabot's dead.'

'*What?*'

'Korman, Grankin – they're tying up all the loose ends.'

'I thought Cabot wasn't involved.'

'He wasn't. But he was still a danger to them. All the stuff East told us last night, whatever's going on at the pier, Cabot might not have been in on it, but – given enough of a push by police – he could probably have started putting it together for them. Grankin stealing those tins the night of the fair, whatever was going on before that, with the varnishing – Cabot was a smart guy. He'd have started connecting the dots. They couldn't risk that.'

I stopped, thinking of Joseph Cabot for the first

480

time, old and slow, blind, unaware. I imagined how his last moments must have been, the terror, unable to see what was happening, just the sound of it, until they turned on him. I felt a deep swell of sadness for him, for his son, for all the people cut down by Korman and Grankin.

And then the sadness began to harden.

'We have to find Korman.'

Healy rubbed an eye. 'What about at the market?'

'You mean his antiques shop?'

He nodded.

In everything that had happened, I hadn't given it a thought. Camden was ten miles west, back across London – a trip I didn't want to make. I picked up my phone, found the number for Gray Antiques and Collectables, and dialled it. It hit a generic BT answerphone message inside three rings.

Hanging up again without leaving a message, I went to my browser, found the number of a clothing shop in the next unit along from Korman's, and called them instead. After a couple of seconds, a female voice answered.

I spun a story about being from a data collection agency, employed by the management at Stables Market to get feedback from tenants. She told me she wasn't even open for another forty minutes, that she had things to do before it did, and questioned why I was calling on a Sunday. Slowly, though, I managed to talk her around, asking her about ways she'd like to see her working experience improved. When I finally ran out of things to ask, I said, 'I haven't been able to get hold of the man in the unit next door to yours.'

'Probably because he's never around,' she said.

'How come?'

'He just doesn't run that place like the rest of us run a business. I can go a couple of months without seeing him here. That unit just sits there, locked up, until he decides it's time to come back.'

'I see. Have you ever been inside?'

A long pause. 'Where did you say you were from again?'

'Chalk Farm Data Collection.'

I said it without hesitation, hoping it would be enough.

'I've been in once or twice,' she said.

'It seems pretty normal?'

'It's just an antiques shop.'

'What do you make of him?'

Another even longer pause, and this time I realized the conversation was getting away from me. Even so, I waited, knowing it was the last question I was going to ask her. 'He seems okay,' she said finally. 'You know . . . fine.'

But that wasn't the truth. The truth flickered in her voice, long enough for me to pick up on it. She didn't like him. She didn't want to be next to him.

He was strange. He put her on edge.

Somewhere deeper down, he scared her.

I hung up. 'He's not at the shop.'

'So?'

'So we need to find him and Grankin. If we find them, we can end this.'

'And how the hell do you plan to do that?'

'By knocking on Grankin's front door.'

# CHAPTER 60

**P**oland Gardens, the address Ewan Tasker had given me for Victor Grankin, was in Whitehall Woods, a thick knot of trees that straddled the London and Essex county lines and formed the southern tip of Epping Forest's nine square miles.

We left the car at a multistorey in Leytonstone, then got on the Tube and rode the Central line north to the station at Buckhurst Hill. It was two miles west from there to Grankin's house, a distance Healy claimed he would be able to do on foot – but we both knew that wasn't true. Grabbing a taxi, we made the trip in silence, the lack of conversation and the hum of the cab gradually pulling me away, until I could feel myself starting to drop off. It wasn't until we hit a bump in the road that I realized I actually had, waking to find us at a stop fifty yards from Poland Gardens, directly adjacent to a dreary, half-disguised caravan park.

Forest was everywhere, thick and opaque, fringing the sides of the two-lane road along which we'd travelled, and in my sluggish state I wondered for a moment whether we'd actually left London behind.

But then a mixture of adrenalin and dread kicked in and I led Healy away from the taxi and down towards the entrance to the road. The caravan park was built in a semicircle, almost cut into the tree-line, static vans sitting on breeze blocks in a line, all facing the road. There was an office at the front, a few cars in badly marked parking bays, and a waning plastic mesh fence beyond that, presumably being used as a boundary marker. As we walked, I saw flickers of Poland Gardens on the other side of the mesh, houses coming and going as the foliage seemed to blossom and dissolve, and then we were at the top of the road.

It was a cul-de-sac of five houses, the road in – one hundred and fifty feet of cracked tarmac, crumbling edges falling away on to the forest floor – bordered on the left by high fir trees and on the right by the caravan park. The foliage thinned out a little around the homes themselves, Whitehall Woods kept back by high property walls, but every-where else the forest was unrelenting, dense and hermetic. It was mid morning and the light was only just breaching the top of the trees, thin spears of it glancing off the first of the houses and glinting in its windows.

'Which one's his?' Healy said.

There were two houses on either side, facing each other, and then one on its own beyond the rest. I pointed to the one on its own. 'That's his,'

I said, and when I looked again, I saw for the first time that a faint *3* had been drawn on a steel dustbin sitting at the front of the building, rubbish bags spilling out of it. The windows of the house were dark and the tiled roof was littered with pine needles.

I tapped Healy on the arm and told him to follow me, and we headed back along the road and into the caravan park. I could see a man at a desk through the grubby office window, but he was leaning over, looking at something, and didn't notice us. As we got beyond the row of caravans, the forest seemed to close in, the canopy like a landslide of leaves.

At the plastic mesh fence, I checked there were no eyes on us, then stepped over it and on to an undulating forest floor covered in fallen pine cones. Healy did the same, but much more slowly, and then we were moving again, between tree trunks, across gnarled, twisted roots reaching out of the ground like fingers.

We passed along the back of the two houses on the right and then stopped, peering along the outside wall of the second one, towards Grankin's place. Our view was partly disguised by a nest of sycamore trees. Behind me, I heard Healy catching up, out of breath. He placed a hand against the wall as he got to me, and frowned, as if he couldn't understand why I was looking so concerned about him. I didn't say anything, returning my gaze to Grankin's house.

Around us, the forest's song faded in, leaves snapping in the wind, the *dmph, dmph, dmph* of rain against the canopy. 'Stay here,' I said to Healy, and before he could argue I left him catching his breath and moved further along the outside wall of Grankin's neighbour, using the trees for cover.

Through the gap in a copse of pine trees I spotted his rusty Citroën, parked on a tarmac driveway. The closer I got, the more I could see evidence of work having been done on the property: part of the exterior had been rendered at some point, the colour of the rendering darker than the colour of the paint elsewhere; there were piles of breeze blocks and red bricks close to where the car was parked, with lengths of wood for a timber frame extension on the ground next to them. As I looked at the piles of unused material, I remembered something Ewan Tasker had told me: *Grankin's been at the address in Poland Gardens since October 2010.* That was three months after he was given the sack by Gary Cabot. He was fired from his job, then went out and bought a house. Something didn't add up.

Keeping the other side of the treeline, I headed towards the rear of the property. There was a door on the side of the house, and at the back I found dark windows on the top floor that mirrored those at the front, and sliding French doors on the ground floor, leading into a shadowy living room. There was no fresh rendering on this side, unlike the front. The garden at the back was small and

487

unremarkable: a few pot plants, some flowers in the bed, a clean patio, all hemmed in by a five-foot brick wall.

So where was Grankin?

I returned to Healy.

'See anything?' he asked.

'Nothing.'

His eyes snapped to the house and it was clear he had the same anxieties as me. Instinctively, without realizing, his hands went to the pockets of the coat I'd lent him. In one of them was the gun he'd had at the house in Camberwell. But that was all we had. We'd left the bread knife on the table I'd found him crying at, alongside the candles and the old mattress, with the memories of the months he'd spent there, waiting to die. Was that what we were doing here now – waiting to die?

'Why don't I go in first?' I said.

He frowned. 'Are you kidding me?'

There had been sun and rain earlier, coming in from different sides of the forest. But now the sun disappeared behind a bank of cloud, the light altered and the house seemed to change subtly, a sudden narrowness to it as if it were closing in on itself, protecting what lay inside its walls. I looked back at Healy, and could see him watching me, trying to get a sense of what I was feeling, but what I was feeling was hard to articulate. I couldn't put it into words, not in front of him. All I knew was that I'd spent a lot of time around people like

Grankin, and the places they lived in. I'd become attuned to them. And I just knew this place was bad.

'Wait here until I call you,' I said.

Before he could reply, I made a dash for the house.

# CHAPTER 61

To the right of the property, indistinguishable pieces of old furniture had been dumped and were slowly decomposing: what could have been an armchair, torn and misshapen; a rusty sink; a wood panel from a wardrobe, split, broken. To its left an oak tree was growing out of the ground, its roots tearing through a concrete path – that connected the front of the house to the back – like it was paper. In its shadow was the side door I'd seen earlier.

It was set behind a screen made of blistered wood and pale green mesh, which swung out from the frame and then banged back against it every time a breeze passed through.

I paused at the very edge of the treeline, not breaking cover for the moment, listening for any sound of movement from the house. But the only noise came from the screen door, still knocking against the frame, and a soft humming from somewhere. I wasn't sure if the humming was originating from inside the property or out in the forest. Satisfied no one could see me, I made a break for it, pulling the screen back and trying the door.

It popped away from the frame.

Briefly, I thought about a retreat, unsure of what I was getting myself into. It wasn't just the house. It was Grankin, it was Korman, the things they'd done together. But then my head filled with images of the Clarks, the crime-scene photographs of two innocent girls in their beds, treated as if their lives meant nothing – and I made my way in.

The side door moved soundlessly, fanning back into the semi-darkness of the house. A hallway was directly in front of me, kinking left and connecting with the front door. Ahead of me was a long lounge-diner, the curtains pulled at the front windows; further on the right, out of sight from where I was standing, had to be the sliding doors I'd seen at the back. Beside me was a small cupboard, tucked in under the stairs. I quietly opened it; there was a vacuum cleaner and a bucket inside.

I inched my way forward, footsteps muffled by the carpet, which looked new. The house was immaculate. Fresh paint on the walls, pristine sofas in the living room and, as it came into view around the corner, on my right, I saw the kitchen at the back of the house looked new too: granite work-tops, white tiles. It must have been why all the old furniture had been dumped at the side of the house.

In the kitchen, the back door looked out on to the tidy garden. I tried it but it was locked. Removing a knife from a rack on the counter, I made my way along the hallway, towards the front door and the bottom of the stairs.

Looking up, it was hard to see anything at the top. Maybe a flicker of light; a TV playing without sound. Beside me, I could see the banister was brand new, the gloss paint reflecting back my face. Gripping the knife, I started the ascent.

Immediately at the top was a bathroom, small and plain. Next to that was a spare bedroom, nothing inside. Literally no furniture at all, except for two built-in wardrobes on the left. The third door was where the light was coming from.

As I processed that, I became aware of something else: the extractor fan was still whirring in the bathroom. He'd used the toilet, or the shower, or both.

And he'd done it recently.

*He's in the third room.*

I was squeezing the knife so tight, I could feel sweat popping out from my palms, breaking a trail across my skin. When I reached the third door, the floorboards moaned, a deep, unwelcome sound that echoed through the house.

But everything remained still.

Edging around the door, I looked in at his bedroom. It was dark, curtains half pulled at the windows, the TV on mute and throwing out grey-blue images of mountain scenery. The bed was unmade, the duvet pulled back, as if Grankin had been getting ready to sleep. On the bedside table was a set of keys.

But no Grankin.

*He's not here.*

I walked around the bed and looked out at the street.

*So where the hell is he?*

Checking each of the rooms again, including the built-in wardrobes, I found nothing and headed back down.

In the living room, I went through his DVD collection, through a small pile of magazines, through the tedious detritus of his life – a few photographs of him in his twenties, on a trip back to Estonia; old receipts; electricity bills he'd paid long ago – and then finally found something worth stopping for: his laptop.

I booted it up, keeping my eyes on the side door. He'd left the TV on in his bedroom. He'd been about to get into – or had just got out of – bed. The extractor fan was still going in the bathroom. He had to have been in the house only minutes before we'd arrived, and yet there was no sign of him. Why? Where had he gone? If he'd headed out, it must have been on foot because the Citroën was still here – so why leave the side door open?

The laptop buzzed once.

A password screen.

I powered it off, put it back where I'd found it, and moved through to the hallway. The side door and the screen were moving in unison now, wafting back and forth, clattering against each other as they closed. As they did, a hush settled across the house, and I became aware of a different sound: a soft, familiar humming.

I'd heard the same noise outside.

Was it the TV upstairs?

The fridge?

I realized there was something else too, not just the sound. There was an abnormality to the house that was only now starting to dawn on me. I looked around, at the fresh paint, the new decor, the elegant kitchen, and realized the house felt cramped, confined and oppressive.

Returning to the kitchen, I opened up the refrigerator, trying to find the source of the humming noise. There were a few basics inside – butter, milk, some out-of-date eggs – but not much else. The bottom half was the freezer. I checked the three drawers, which were full of pizza and frozen meat.

Then I noticed something.

Next to the fridge, poking out from under an electric cooker, was a footprint. It was so clear on the pale cream lino, I could see a manufacturer's logo. That wasn't all: dust, crumbs and dirt were gently drifting across the floor, out from under the cooker, blown there by a breeze.

But the breeze wasn't coming from the hallway.

Placing a hand either side of the cooker, I began rocking it back towards me, one side to the next. As I did, the humming got louder, the breeze cooler and stronger. Six inches clear of the wall, I stepped forward and looked behind it.

Grankin had cut a hole in the wall.

As I looked through the gap, I could see a space beyond it about two feet deep and at least six feet high, running right to left, and out of sight. And I finally understood why the house felt wrong; why it felt so constricting and closed in.

It was too small.

It was smaller on the inside than it was on the outside, because the work Grankin had done on the house hadn't been to improve it, or extend it.

It had been to reduce it.

He was hiding something in the walls.

# CHAPTER 62

Crouching, I stepped through the hole in the kitchen, into a narrow passageway, the grey concrete blocks of the exterior wall on one side, and the plasterboard of the new interior wall on the other. A high-powered LED lamp hummed above my head, clamped in place with a crocodile clip and making a similar noise to the one I'd heard outside. The lamp's glare bleached everything in a harsh, white light.

The passageway ran for about ten feet to my right, struts knitted together overhead, until it hit a vertical slab of older plasterboard, which must have been the hallway wall. In front of that, Grankin had set up a wooden trellis table, a penny arcade machine sitting on it, tins of Hoberman's varnish and paintbrushes as well. The penny arcade machine was the bagatelle I'd seen Grankin take from Calvin East's house the night before. Its back panel was open, but there was nothing inside, just the basic mechanical skeleton of the machine: all its pulleys and cogs and wheels.

In the other direction, to my left, the space moved through to the back of the house about the same distance. Chipboard panels had been placed on the floor, covering the entire length of this new extension – *except* for a space about three feet in diameter where there was no flooring at all.

Just a hole.

I felt a flutter of alarm, not just at the discovery of this hidden extension, not just at the thought of Grankin maybe being somewhere deeper inside, but at the way the house had begun to change. It put a hesitation in my stride, as if this place were some sort of living, breathing thing, able to react, change shape and adapt.

*You sound insane. Get a grip.*

And yet I couldn't dispel the idea entirely. I was tired, on edge, maybe not thinking straight, but these men, what they'd done, it was so abhorrent there *was* something of the unimaginable about it. So why *wouldn't* Grankin's home be like this? If a house reflected its owner, this was him: covert, elusive, unpredictable.

*Dangerous.*

I backed out and moved quickly to the side door, waved Healy towards the house, and then returned. A minute later, he entered the kitchen, his breathing heavy, wheezing gently. 'What the hell is this?' he whispered.

I put a finger to my lips, and listened.

No noise except the rain outside, the moan of the wind.

I looked towards the gap in the floor. It was like a sinkhole. When I began moving quietly along the boards, intent on finding out where the hole went, I felt them move and shift beneath me, like plates of sand. Behind me, Healy entered the space, heavy on his feet, ungainly, a crackle to his breathing that may as well have been a scream within the oppressive confines of the extension. I turned to him, gesturing for him to be quiet, and then stopped and looked down the hole.

It dropped away about six feet, and then dog-legged left. It was some sort of tunnel, a shaft, but not one that had been on the original plans for the place. *Grankin must have dug it out.* A metal ladder leaned against the hard walls of the hole, dropping away into the semi-lit chamber below. Another light – this one less powerful – was clipped to the bottom rung of the ladder, and shone off along the horizontal portion of the shaft, none of which I could see yet. I paused, momentarily uncertain.

And then I started the climb down.

At the bottom, I dropped on to my hands and knees and looked along the tunnel. Its length was difficult to judge, even though it was relatively straight. Forty feet, maybe fifty, the opposite end illuminated by a light that must have been secured out of sight, on one of the higher rungs of a second ladder propped there. Thick semicircles of metal sheeting had been placed all the way along, ensuring the shaft didn't collapse in on itself, but it seemed pretty secure, even without them.

A deeper sense of unease formed in me.

This went all the way under the garden, *beyond* it – but to where? Why not just walk to wherever this led? It must have taken months to dig out.

What was worth that kind of effort?

Hesitantly, I started moving on my hands and knees. Behind me, I heard Healy's heels chime on the metal ladder, but then the sound seemed to die, and the walls started to feel like they were closing in, like the shaft was changing shape, funnelling me into an even narrower gap.

Suddenly, I could feel my pulse quicken.

My heart was thumping in my ears.

I tried to focus on what was ahead, a brightly lit square about thirty feet further on – *the end of this, just keep going, just keep going* – but the faster I went, the worse my head started to buzz, white spots blinking in front of my eyes. I was sweating, panicked, unable to breathe properly, and then it started to feel like I wasn't moving any more, my knees, my hands, desperately pumping, trying to carry me forward, trying to gain momentum. *Keep going, keep going, keep goi–*

The shaft ended.

I looked up, expecting to see another lamp – but instead it wasn't artificial light that was illuminating this end of the tunnel. It was sky. For a second, I was unsure exactly what else I was seeing. It didn't help that I was struggling to calm down, my breathing ragged, clothes soaked through with sweat, frightened by whatever had come over me again. I'd felt like this in the museum, in the seconds before collapsing. I closed my eyes, trying to calm myself.

A noise – from somewhere above.

I looked up again, starting to become aware of rain dotting my face, of the sounds of Whitehall Woods. Wind, leaves snapping.

I started the climb, then paused halfway, heart fluttering. All around me was forest: countless trees, one after the other, heading in all directions, twisted roots breaking out of the earth; at ground level was a sea of fallen leaves, golden brown, orange, all of them woven together like a quilt; and then, as I continued to turn on the ladder, and looked behind me for the first time – in the direction we'd come – there was something else, right on top of me.

A fence.

Except this one wasn't like the thin plastic mesh fence dividing the caravan park and Poland Gardens.

This was an eight-foot steel perimeter fence.

It ran in a gentle arc, disappearing behind banks of tree trunks on the left and right of me. Grankin's house wasn't visible, even though it was only fifty feet away, its boundary, its back windows, its roof, all disguised behind a thick wall of fir trees and high brambles, of weeds and vines. It was why I never saw a hint of this fence, even when I'd been standing at the back of his property. I'd never seen the barbed wire around its top, the KEEP OUT! PRIVATE PROPERTY! signs. But I'd heard it. *The humming*. It wasn't coming from the lamp in the shaft – it was coming from the fence.

It was electrified.

*Grankin dug out the tunnel to get beyond the fence.*

I climbed up and out of the hole. As Healy emerged – breathless; slow, leaden movements – I looked deeper into the forest. As I tried to imagine why he would go to such lengths, I recalled again what Ewan Tasker had told me over the phone, about Grankin moving into the house in October 2010, just three months after getting fired from Wonderland – and, slowly, an idea came to me.

You didn't just *buy* a house, even if there was no chain. It took time. It took meetings, paperwork and phone calls. I'd wondered if Grankin had deliberately got himself caught, in order to provide a cover story for the night of 11 July 2010. Now I was starting to wonder whether this house may have been a part of it; that when he realized the house was going to be his, he realized he didn't need access to the pier any more, and he deliberately got sloppy. He stole those tins of varnish and waited to get caught – because not only would he have his alibi for the murders, but whatever Korman and he were doing could be better done here.

In the house. In this forest.

I looked at Healy, gesturing silently to him, asking him if he was ready. He had one hand on his hip and was breathing hard, wheezing, his startling loss of weight seeming more pronounced

501

among the giant trees. What had I done by bringing him here? What good was a gun if the man it belonged to couldn't react in time?

Pushing the thought away, I led us forward.

There were no ready-made paths, no hints of the routes Grankin may have taken. Any path we cut out, we cut out through a bed of low-level weeds, of overgrowth and contorted tree roots. I moved deliberately slowly, partly because I knew nothing of this forest, its contours and dangers, and partly because I wanted to reduce the noise we were making. Grankin could have been anywhere.

*He could be watching us now.*

The idea made me stop, Healy almost bumping into me. I scanned the area immediately around us, the trees so close in it was like being back in that tunnel. My heart rate increased again; my muscles hardened. We were barely any distance from civilization at all, and yet it felt like we were somewhere remote and uncharted.

'What?' Healy said softly.

To our right, there was a minor break in the trees, an oval-shaped gap that showed through to a sliver of open land. Was it a clearing? I pointed at it, telling Healy we were heading there, and we began to cross a dense patch of nettles and vines, pine cones crunching beneath our boots. The closer we got, the more I could see of what lay beyond the treeline: it looked like a field, full of knee-high grass, surrounded on all sides by a relentless, tangled barrier of trees.

But it wasn't a field.

It was a garden.

As we stopped at its edges, the front of a building came into view, ugly and grey, flat-roofed, double-storeyed with two wings. It was big and functional, like a cross between a police station and a Victorian grammar school, but its windows and doors had been boarded up. The forest formed a broken circle around it, revealing the remnants of flower beds that had once grown here, and a driveway. It came up to the front of the building, looped around and headed out again.

'What the hell is this place?' I said, as much to myself as to Healy.

He didn't reply, his eyes scanning the building for any sign of life, then settling on a warped, paint-blistered sign, half hidden by trees, at the bottom of the front steps. Moving a little further to my right, I tried to get a better view of it myself.

'What was it East said?' Healy whispered.

I looked at him. 'Huh?'

'He said he was put into a children's home in Chingford.'

I looked back at the building.

Healy nodded, his eyes returning to the sign at the front, rinsed of colour but the letters still visible.

*St David's Children's Home.*

'This is where Korman and Grankin grew up,' he said.

# CHAPTER 63

We waited, rain continuing to beat against the trees, drumming against the leaves, against the canopy. There were four huge windows on the front of the shell that had once been St David's Children's Home, all boarded up. What I was more interested in was an extension on the side of the building – a little newer, although still decades old – built in brick, with a slanted red-tile roof: it was half submerged behind a bank of big fir trees, but I could make out a set of grey double doors at one end.

One was slightly ajar.

I gestured for Healy to follow me, and we arced around, using the trees as cover. Forty feet short of the double doors, I stopped for a second time, taking in the view on this side of the building, waiting for Healy to fall in. As the wind picked up, the open door wafted out from its frame.

'Are you coming in with me?' I said to him quietly.

He frowned. 'What sort of question is that?'

He was weary, his shoulders rising and falling, and I thought I could see him shivering slightly.

'I don't know what we're going to find in there.'

He shrugged, his breathing slowly settling into a rhythm, and then looked at me, a shimmer in his eyes. 'It doesn't matter,' he said. 'All that matters is them.'

He didn't mean Korman and Grankin.

He meant Gail and the girls.

Before I had a chance to say anything else, Healy was moving past me and along the edges of the treeline, in the direction of the extension on the side of the building. '*Healy!*' I hissed, but he didn't stop. He broke from cover very briefly as he crossed to where the extension jutted out, and then found a spot, out of view, in front of the fir trees.

He looked back at me, focused, defiant.

I scanned the boarded windows, trying to see if anything had changed, if there was any indication that his movements had been detected, but there was nothing. Every window remained hidden behind slabs of wood. Out in the forest beyond, however, changes were harder to spot: leaves moved, branches swayed, rain drifted out of the sky in grey lines. I started to worry that the door might be a trap, left open in order to draw us in, while Grankin waited somewhere else.

Maybe alone, maybe with Korman.

Had he seen us approaching his house and made a run for it? I thought of how the TV was still on, the extractor fan going, as if Grankin had left in a hurry. And then I looked at Healy, still short of breath, my coat swallowing him up, even the gun big in his hands now, and had a moment of clarity: *I'm going to get us both killed.* I could look after myself, account for my actions, justify them, push the fear down and do what was necessary – but I couldn't do the same for him. I couldn't lead him in there, frail and vulnerable, incapable of defending himself.

I'd be leading him to his execution.

I couldn't do that with a clear conscience.

Getting out my phone, I checked the signal, then looked at Healy again, our eyes lingering on one another.

Then I dialled Craw's number.

Healy was still looking at me, almost enclosed by the fir trees, a frown forming on his face. He mouthed, *What are you doing?* I held up a finger to him, trying to tell him that he needed to trust me here.

Craw answered. 'Raker?'

'Craw,' I said. 'I need you to listen.'

'Where are you?'

'Just listen to me. *Please.*' I glanced up at Healy. He'd stepped away from the fir trees, the gun at his side. 'There's a guy called Victor Grankin. He lives at 3 Poland Gardens in Whitehall Woods. You have to tell whoever needs to know that *this* guy – and another man, possibly called Paul Korman, possibly Benjamin Gray – are responsible for the death of that family. They murdered the Clarks, they probably murdered a couple called Neil and Ana Yost too. You getting this?'

A pause. 'Let me get a pen.'

I waited, watching Healy.

Then she was back on: 'Okay. What was the name?'

'Victor Grankin, 3 Poland Gardens. I was in his house—'

'You broke in?'

'*Listen* to me,' I said. 'You need to send a team down.'

'Raker, it's not my borou—'

'Then find out whose borough it is, and call them. *Please*, Craw. I've got . . .' I stopped, eyeing Healy. *I've got Healy here, but not the Healy we knew. Not that version of him. Not any more. This version I can't protect. I can't protect him from Korman and Grankin.* 'Just send a team to that address, and to the former site of St David's Children's Home. That's literally next door to the place Grankin is in.'

'Why?' she said. 'What's at the children's home?'

'I think that's where these men are hiding out.'

'Why?'

'Because they grew up here.'

'"Here"? You mean you're there already?'

I glanced across what used to be the front lawn, to where we'd come from. The thick forest. Grankin's house, invisible, hidden.

'Yes,' I said to her. 'I'm here.'

A sigh, but no response.

'Just trust me, okay?'

'Are you in danger?'

'Not if you send a team down . . .'

I stopped.

'Raker?'

*Shit.* 'I've got to go, Craw.'

'Why?'

I looked across the front lawn.

Healy had disappeared.

# CHAPTER 64

Slowly, I pulled the grey door open.

Immediately inside the extension was a reception area, a wooden counter with a sliding glass window on the right, green linoleum on the floor, posters and notices still on a corkboard to the left. It had the vibe of a hospital ward, closed in and musty. Straight ahead were two security gates, one after the other, with a number pad embedded in the wall beside the first. Both gates were wide open.

I slipped inside and let the door fall softly back against the frame, the light dwindling. On the other side of the reception desk there was a small skylight, but most of what lay ahead remained in shadow, the corridor continuing beyond the security gates, both sides lined with identical grey doors, apart from a single red one on the left. That had been chained shut.

At the end was a staircase.

I hadn't brought a torch, because I hadn't been expecting to need one, so as I inched forward, I took out my phone, accessed the torch function and held it up in front of me. On the floor, I could see footprints, a mix of mud and leaves from the forest. *Healy*. They headed straight along the centre of the corridor, through the gates, in the direction of the stairs. As I followed them, I felt a mixture of anger and panic at his stupidity for trying to do this all by himself, alone and under-powered; at the idea of what may be awaiting him.

Midway along, I realized one of the doors to my left was slightly open, revealing an office. A desk had been turned over, as if toppled, chairs scattered too. A high window behind them looked over the long grass and knots of bushes on the lawn out front. Like a puddle of spilt paint, a little of the light from the room leaked out into the corridor, and I could see a series of signs hanging from the roof in front of me, pointing in different directions, to different parts of the building. Reception. Administrative offices. The North Wing. Something called the JJC Block.

Quickly, lightly, I headed up the stairs.

Another set of doors connected this newer part of the extension with what must have been the second floor of the original building. It was Victorian, polished marble floors, high ceilings, rooms and windows on either side. It was old, musty, airless, but it wasn't in a state of decay, and it made me wonder how long the home had been shut. Did it close around the time that Grankin moved here? Was that another reason for him choosing to buy the house in Poland Gardens?

I refocused, passing the rooms.

They each appeared to have catered to different age groups, the remains of their previous life still evident: in the first few, big foam shapes, toys, pens, drawings that had fallen away from pinboards; then bookshelves, DVD boxes and old board games in the ones further down. At the end, another staircase wound back down to ground level, but not before I spotted something in the last room on the left: an old table-football game, uneven on its legs, its levers rusted, the glass cracked. It was just like the one East and Grankin had played on as kids – or maybe *was* the same one.

My attention drifted back to the stairs in front of me, and I took a couple of steps forward, peering over the side of the banister.

Darkness below.

But then distantly, almost beyond range, I started hearing something. Inching down to the second step, I looked again, still unable to see anything, but hearing it more clearly than ever. What *was* that? I continued my descent until, halfway down, I stopped again, staring into the shadows – and, like an explosion of fireworks, goosebumps scattered across my skin, along my back, the edges of my shoulder blades.

Because I knew what it was now.

I knew that noise.

It was someone crying.

# CHAPTER 65

At the bottom of the stairs, the building cleaved off in two separate directions: to a dining hall, out of reach beyond doors that had been chained shut; and then the other way, into a long, straight corridor that ploughed even deeper into the bowels of the building. Midway down, on the left, there was an open door, light flickering on and off inside, its glow spilling out into the hallway. As it did, shadows shifted and twisted all the way along, making it look like the whole corridor was moving, its walls alive, doorways changing shape and appearance. There was no mains electric – which meant it must have been a torch.

The crying was coming from that direction.

I switched off the light on my phone and looked behind me, through the glass panels in the dining-hall doors, knowing – logically – that there was no way anyone could come at me from there. The doors were chained, and there was no one else on the stairs. Any trouble was going to be in front of me. But I still felt hesitant, panicked.

As I stared along the corridor, at the light

moving, at the gentle sound of sobbing, I closed my eyes again, trying to gather myself. I could feel the cut on my face throbbing, the pain of even older scars too, beneath my shirt. My head was hurting, my heart drumming in my ears. It was an orchestra, a wall of sound and doubt, and it felt like I was drowning in it. Before long, I started to worry that I was about to drop to the floor again, just like I'd done at the museum.

*Not here. Not now.*

*Please not now.*

I took a long, controlled breath, then opened my eyes again, searching the immediate area for something I could arm myself with. A voice played out in my head on repeat, warning me that I'd been drawn into this way too fast, but I ignored it and kept looking. Finally, tucked away out of sight, in a space next to the dining-hall doors, was an old broom. I grabbed it, removed the bristles and managed to break the damp wood of the handle in two. Shorter was going to be better: it wasn't the best weapon, but it was heavy enough – and now it had a sharp, splintered end.

I turned back, looking along the hallway.

Quickly, something seemed to shift in the darkness further down, beyond the open door, beyond the light and the sound of crying. Was someone there?

Was someone watching me?

If I'd been spotted, it was too late to back out, so I started moving forward, quicker than before, heart hammering against my chest. The corridor kept on going, a tunnel of doors, one after the other like a film rerunning, the same scene being played over and over again. Two or three were open, the vague shapes of bunks still inside, stripped of their mattresses. *These were all bedrooms.* This was where Korman and Grankin had slept, where Calvin East had tried to fit in. The further I got, the deeper I was drawn, the more the smell seemed to change. It became more ingrained, a blight, settling as I got to the building's core: old wood, mould, the tangy stench of iron.

I reached the room.

Inside were two sets of bunks against opposite walls, long since stripped of their mattresses, leaving just the frames and the wire springs. The room was small, windowless; a cupboard was at the back, open with nothing in it. A torch lay on the floor between the bunks, its light fanning out in a cone to reveal a cassette recorder like the one Healy and I had found on the pier. A tape was gently whirring inside.

The sound of crying was a recording.

It was a woman.

Automatically, I took a couple of steps closer, drawn to the noises she was making, hypnotized by the awful, guttural moans catching in her throat. My hands balled into fists, my muscles calcified.

It was Gail.

*Gail's on the tape.*

As she tried to speak, her accent clear even in

the few words she was able to get out, I realized it wasn't the tears that were halting her voice in her throat.

It was her injuries.

Korman had recorded her as she lay there dying on the sofa in her flat, bleeding out over her dressing gown, over the furniture, the floor. In the background, in the spaces beyond her last, whispered cries for help, I could hear the television.

Stomach tightening, I found myself inching further inside before I even noticed what I was doing, my boots hitting a pool of water, leaking out of pipes in the corner of the room. I picked the torch up off the floor and went to switch the tape off.

Then I saw a flash of movement.

It was behind me, right on the periphery of my vision, coming out of the darkness of the corridor. I turned, trying to see what it was – and my movement saved me. A knife was driven straight across the back of my jacket, where my ribs had been a moment before. The material snicked and tore and I felt knuckles brush against my spine, the momentum of the thrust carrying the fist, the blade, the person, into the space beside me.

I shifted further around, the jagged broom handle in one hand, the torch in the other. Flipping the torch on its head, so the lamp and the rubberized casing were facing up, I retreated towards the back wall, water parting beneath my feet.

As I kept going, I hit the bottom edges of the

bunk on the left, stumbling slightly, accidentally kicking the cassette deck across the floor, into the water. It turned on to its side, the lid of the tape deck flipping up, water running into it, into the machine itself, the recorder making a soft, fizzing sound as the electrics fused. I stopped as my boots hit the wall, watching as my attacker inched forward himself, into the dead centre of the room.

Victor Grankin.

He was wearing a grey mask.

It was *the* mask, the one he'd worn the night he'd waited for Korman outside Searle House – right down to the crack on the left-hand side. He stood there, tall, thin, blinking inside the eyeholes, dressed in black tracksuit trousers and a black T-shirt, mud-streaked canvas shoes on his feet.

In his fist was a hunting knife.

He adjusted the mask, pushing it harder against his face, as if trying to fuse himself with it, his eyes glinting in the low light, and then inched towards me. His feet hit the pool of water, knife in front of him, swiping it through the air right to left, its serrated edge making a whipping sound; a thick, brutal noise.

He must have heard us approaching, seen me out in the forest around his house, then made a break for this place. Why?

*The recording of Gail.*

He'd used it to draw me in, trying to distract me long enough to put a knife between my ribs.

And the only reason to do that was because there was something else hidden here that he didn't want me to find.

He looked around him.

'We used to sleep in this room,' he said, seven inconsequential words that seemed to carry so much threat. His accent was heavy, even all these years on, deadened slightly by the mask. A few more steps, the hem of his trousers soaking up the water. 'Did you like the tape?'

He was trying to force a mistake out of me.

I said nothing, gripping the broom harder.

'I thought you might like it. I knew you'd be drawn to it, like a – how do you say? – moth to a flame.'

When I gave him nothing, he started making a grotesque noise, a gurgling sound: Gail struggling, choking to death, her last moments, every lost word.

'You'd better get used to that sound,' I said.

'Yes?' He stopped, eyes fixed on me. The mask gave him a weird, alien look: only a faint hint of moulded lips, of definition in the cheeks. 'Yes?' His gaze flicked from me to the remnants of the broom handle, then to the torch. 'You are going to end my life with those things?'

'I'm going to try.'

'I never realized you were a killer.'

'It's over,' I said.

He laughed. 'For you maybe.'

'The police are on their way.'

A flicker of panic in his eyes. I didn't actually know if the police were coming or not. I didn't know whether I'd given Craw enough to work with. I'd had to hang up on her when I saw Healy had already come inside. But she had Grankin's home address now. I'd told her about St David's. She'd said she believed me.

And then I thought: *Healy.*

*Where the hell is Healy?*

Grankin pulled me back into the moment, another step closer, swiping the knife from side to side, just a blur in his hands. There was ten feet between us. 'The police are not coming,' Grankin said.

'They are.'

'You wouldn't call them.'

'I would.'

'You would expose your lies?'

'To expose yours?' I nodded. 'Absolutely.'

His eyes narrowed, the knife dropping away slightly. For a second, it was like he was standing down, finally cognizant of the fact that the end was coming.

But he wasn't standing down.

Rocking from one foot to the other, he came at me, his sudden change of pace catching me on the hop. He was lithe and he was fast, devious, aggressive. I felt the knife disturb the air in front of me as I moved sideways, arching my body, the tip of the blade slitting open my jacket at the arm. As his momentum took him further towards me,

I rolled back on to the balls of my feet and swung the broom handle. It clattered into him somewhere around the waist, knocking him off balance, and he staggered sideways into the frame of the bunk on the opposite side of the room. The metal vibrated, its legs scraping against the tiled floors, water splashing up.

For a second, I thought I had him exposed, his back half-turned to me, the knife in front of his body, incapable of getting to me before I got to him – but as I swung the lump of wood at him, he ducked, the underside of it brushing the top of his head. The force of my swing carried me towards him. Knowing he couldn't get the knife out from in front of him in time, he used his elbow instead, jabbing the point hard into the base of my throat.

It was like being shot.

I stumbled back, winded, spots in front of my eyes. My head was a mess of static, my legs weak, my sense of perception gone. I reached out for the other bunk bed just beside me, but it wasn't there. I grabbed air, the bed another foot and a half away from where I expected it to be. With nothing to hold me up, I lurched forward, hitting the floor. Water spattered my face, my mouth, my skin.

I rolled over on to my back.

My vision was blurring in and out, but I could see enough: Grankin moved into view, knife out in front of him, looking down at me. He placed a hand on the mask and lifted it away from his face, perching it on top of his head. It was bound to his skull with a piece of old string. He had the torch in his other hand now, which I'd dropped without even realizing, and was using it to blind me, to toy with me, shining it into my eyes and then away again. I could feel my jacket soaking through to my spine, the back of my trousers too. I tried to shift myself up on to an elbow, but it was like I was paralysed. I was an animal, dying in the headlights of the car that had struck it.

'Is that it?' Grankin said.

He shuffled in over me, feet planted hip distance apart, fingers re-establishing their grip on the knife. His neck tilted to one side, almost looking at me with pity, and then he leaned forward, pursed his lips and let his saliva drop into my face.

'You are pathetic,' he said.

He drew the knife back, ready to strike.

But he never got the chance.

# CHAPTER 66

Something clicked.

Freezing exactly where he was, Grankin turned. I followed his eyeline, across the room to the darkness of the hallway – and then Healy stepped into the edges of the torchlight, gun aimed at Grankin. He moved slowly, cautiously.

'Oh,' Grankin said calmly, glancing at me. 'I didn't know if you'd brought him or not.' He straightened, looking Healy up and down, then raised his hands above his head, the knife still in his left. 'You should put on some weight, friend.'

Healy just stared at him.

'Where did you go?' I said.

'I thought I heard a noise.'

'Ah, look at you two.' Grankin smiled. 'Is it love?'

'Drop the knife,' Healy told him.

Grankin frowned. 'Or what? You are going to shoot me? You are going to leave my body here for the police when they come?'

Healy's eyes flicked to me. 'You called the *police*?'

I sat up, my system starting to settle.

'*Raker?* You called the police?'

'Yes,' I said. 'I called the police.'

'Why?'

I looked at him, unsure what to say.

'*Raker?*'

'There's something wrong with me,' I said, hauling myself to my feet, wet, aching, unsteady. *I thought I was calling them because I couldn't look after you.*

*But it wasn't you I couldn't look after.*

He frowned, stepping towards me.

*It was myself.*

'There's something wrong with you?' Healy said.

'I think I might be ill. I don't know. It doesn't matter now.'

'What do you mean, "ill"?'

'Colm,' Grankin said almost delicately, moving fractionally in Healy's direction, 'why don't you see if that cassette recorder on the floor still works?'

Healy glanced at it.

'No,' I said. 'Ignore him.'

'See if it still plays,' Grankin continued.

I tried again: '*Healy.*'

He was frowning now, confused, half an eye on the tape. This was exactly what Grankin wanted: a loss of focus, a lapse, a mistake.

'Healy,' I said again, calmly, quietly.

He looked from the tape to Grankin. 'Why?' he said, jabbing the gun at Grankin's face. 'What's on the tape?' He eyed me, looking for the answer. 'Raker?'

'He's baiting you,' I said.

'About what?'

I held up a hand. 'We need to talk to him.'

'What's he baiting me about?'

'He's trying to force you into a mistake.'

I could see Healy's jaw tighten, almost contract, as he gritted his teeth. He stepped in closer to Grankin. For the first time, from the angle he was at, he saw the mask on Grankin's head. It seemed to send a jolt of electricity through him.

'What's on the tape?'

'We need to talk to him,' I said again.

'Gail's on the tape,' Grankin whispered.

Healy was instantly silenced. Grankin took another step towards him, capable now of reaching up and grabbing the weapon.

'You . . .' Healy said faintly, shell-shocked. 'You recorded her?'

Grankin inched forward.

'You *recorded* her?'

'Yes.'

'The night she died?'

'Yes.'

'Healy,' I begged, watching as Grankin tightened his grip on the knife. 'This is what he wants. Don't you see that? *Focus.* We need him. We need his answers.'

'You recorded her dying?'

'*Healy.*'

'Yes,' Grankin said. 'We recorded her dying.'

'Why?' Healy muttered. 'Why did you do that to her?' Tears softened the words spilling out of his mouth, his eyes filling up, saliva bubbling at his lips.

'Because.'

'Because *what?*'

Grankin shrugged. 'What does it matter now?'

A tremor seemed to pass across the room, like the floor had shifted beneath us. Grankin glanced at me, as if this were some sort of performance – and then, in a flash, reached up, clamped his hand on to the barrel of the gun and tried to direct it away from his face, jabbing the knife in hard.

'*Healy!*'

The roar of the gun going off.

A blink of light.

And then Grankin was staggering backwards, half hitting the bunk on the way, his balance gone, his control. He smashed into the wall and fell forward, dropping to the floor like every bone in his body had turned to liquid. Healy stepped in towards him, gun facing down at him, the front of his clothes torn, traces of blood evident where the blade had nicked his stomach. But if he was in pain – if the wound was deep, if it was serious – he didn't notice, or didn't care. He was muttering to himself, sobbing, inconsolable. He leaned over Grankin and pushed the gun into his skull, pressing it into his eye.

'Why did you kill the girls?' he said softly.

Grankin's blood washed out into the centre of the room, the bottom side of his face a mess of gore and bone, his wound slowly being submerged by the lake of spilt water. It ran into his eye, his nose, his mouth, the hole in his head.

'Why did you kill the girls?' Healy repeated, but this time he could hardly form the words. '*Why did you kill the girls?*'

I took a step towards him. 'Are you hurt?'

He looked back at me, surprised, confused, as if he'd forgotten he wasn't alone. In his head, in this room that Grankin had once called home, it was just the two of them – and now a gunshot, an act of self-defence, had robbed Healy of the answer he craved. Looking at me again, he lifted the gun up, away from Grankin, and I glimpsed the wound at his stomach: a cut, a swipe of a blade, but not deep.

'Why did he have to kill the girls?' he said.

'Healy.' I held up a hand. 'It's okay.'

'Why did he have to kill them?'

'Healy . . .'

'*Why did he have to kill them!*' he screamed, his voice carrying out into the corridor of the building – an echo, repeated over and over, in search of an answer. When none came, when I couldn't offer him anything, his eyes filled with tears and he began sobbing.

Their custodian.

Their avenger.

A man they had never known in life – but who had loved them all the same.

# CHAPTER 67

We left Grankin's body where it was and moved back out into the corridor. Healy was completely silent, the tears gone, the gun returned to his jacket, this shell of a man reduced to something even less: a machine, pale and broken, propelled by whatever remained of the power that still held him upright. I'd tried to console him as we stood there between the bunks, but he hadn't responded, had hardly been able to look at me. When he did, I realized I didn't know what to say to him.

I'd looked for a phone on Grankin's body, but he'd had nothing in either pocket. Whatever he'd come here to do, he'd come here to hide it, and he'd come here to do it quickly.

'Healy, I want to take a look further down.'

He stared at me.

'Are you coming with me?' No movement, no reaction; he just continued to look at me, through me, something of him gone. '*Healy*. Listen to me.'

Except I still didn't know what to say to him.

'Come on,' I said, and led us away from the room.

The corridor ran on another sixty feet, but it didn't seem as closed in now, or as intimidating. I had the torch, which helped, but the further we got, the more daylight seemed to be escaping past the boards at the windows, binding together in the centre of the hallway. Eventually, we reached a set of double doors, one partially open, and through the gap I could see the corridor kinked left, back around towards the reception area and the extension, a sign pointing the way.

In the opposite direction were toilets.

I slipped through the gap, shone the torch left, towards the reception area, and saw another door, this one coloured red. I'd seen the same one when I'd first entered the extension. It had been chained from the other side. That meant there would be no short cut back to the extension this way. We'd have to go out the way we'd come in.

I turned to Healy again. 'You said you heard a noise earlier?'

He looked at me blankly.

'*Healy*,' I said, trying to rouse him. 'You said you heard a noise when you were out front?' I waited. Eventually, he nodded. 'So you followed the noise in?'

He shook his head. 'I didn't come inside,' he said quietly, eyes still wet. He looked from me to the red door. 'I checked around the back, because I thought the noise had come from out there. But there was nothing. Then I came inside.'

I swung the torch around, lighting up the

entrance to the toilets: male and female doors, and some sort of janitor's cupboard. Edging forward, I saw that the door to the Ladies was ajar, propped open with a chunk of brick. I gestured for Healy to follow me, placed a hand against the door and slowly opened it fully. Using the torch, I could see a row of six cubicles and a set of wash basins. A hand drier was attached to the far wall, and some of the old piping was exposed, plasterboard broken, edges fraying and crumbling.

'Watch the door,' I said to Healy.

He stirred, frowned. 'What?'

'Someone else might be here.' *Korman.* 'Just watch the door, okay?'

The smell in the room was unpleasant – stale urine, damp, rust – but I kept moving forward. Halfway in, I glanced back at Healy, standing there in the door, swamped by a jacket too big for him. His eyes were focused on the hallway, but his mind was somewhere else: on Grankin, Gail, the girls, on the gravity of a single moment. As I turned, I noticed something for the first time, hidden in shadow beyond the cubicles.

Two oil drums.

The drums were empty, dry, the paint on the inside stripped away. Their lids – two big circular discs – were propped against them, at the side. I reached in and dabbed a finger to the interior, but no trace of anything came back on my skin.

Both drums were spotless.

A memory formed: I was back on the pier, in

the moments before Healy and I were forced to make a run for it. I'd found a cassette recorder there, like the one Grankin had left in the bedroom – no tape, no batteries, but the same make.

And I'd found burn marks.

I knelt down in front of one of the drums. *These are what left the rings on the floor of the pier.* There had been two circles scorched into the wooden slats of the pavilion, their circumference matching the size of the drums. I shifted one of the drums out from the wall, looking at the piece of board it had been placed on. The board had the same ring burned into it: same size, colour, measurements.

Korman and Grankin were still using them.

Just not on the pier.

I turned on my haunches and directed my torch out across the rest of the room. Were they burning bodies in here? There was no smell of seared flesh, no lingering stench of decomposition. But as I continued to breathe in, the faint smell of disinfectant came to me.

*Bleach.*

'Wait here,' I said to Healy, but this time I didn't have to move fast to avoid an argument. He just nodded and remained there, half lit from one side by a row of four thin windows – all set behind wire – high above the basins in the toilets. There wasn't much light escaping into this part of the building, but there was enough. I gripped the torch and headed next door, to the men's toilets. They were set out in the opposite way to the Ladies, cubicles on the right, basins and the high windows on the left. In the same corner as next door, in the shadows beyond the cubicles, my torch picked out a fat plastic tube, on its side. As I got closer, I saw what it was.

A portable pressure washer.

Grankin had been in the middle of using it, the tiles of the bathroom still slick with water. That was why he'd made a break for it when he'd spotted us outside his house. *He'd come here to wash down the walls.*

I edged closer.

There was blood in the water – not much, but some. It swirled around on the surface of the puddles like coils of red dye, gradually running into a drain beneath the basins. In between some of the tiles, blood had stained the grouting, but it had been rinsed to a very light pink over time, and you had to look hard to see it. There was the smell of bleach here too – even stronger than next door – and when I went to the pressure washer, I found out why: setting it upright, I unscrewed the cap, and the smell hit me instantly. He'd mixed bleach and water.

Then my attention switched again.

I could hear a noise outside: faintly, distantly.

*Shit.*

It was sirens.

# CHAPTER 68

Grabbing Healy by the arm, I hauled him out of the toilets and back into the corridor, hurrying past the endless doors in the direction of the staircase. As we passed Grankin, I looked in at him: his legs were visible, one of his hands too, stretched out beside him, like he'd been reaching for something. The water was everywhere, a lake stained pink, his knife like a boat beached in the middle. I'd called Craw and got the police involved because it had seemed like the right thing to do at the time. Now I didn't want them here. Not yet. Detectives and forensics would have a field day: not just with Grankin and the knife, but with whatever Healy and I had left behind. *Should I go back and wipe it down?*

There wasn't time.

I needed to get Healy out of here.

Moving more quickly now, I led the way back up the stairs, past the playrooms on the first floor, and then descended into the extension. Once I got to the grey doors, I paused, peering through the gap, listening to Healy move in behind me.

Everything looked quiet.

531

But that still didn't settle my nerves.

I gestured for Healy to follow me, and we headed out, the cold starting to bite, the rain still coming down. Checking the rear of the building, and finding a series of empty parking spaces, I returned to the front of St David's, looking off in the vague direction we'd approached it. What had once been the garden, play fields for the kids who had called this home, was now an untidy mess of weeds and long grass. Among the trees on the far side somewhere, hidden from view, was the eight-foot electrified fence, and the hole in the ground that led back to Grankin's house.

*Our only way out.*

I glanced at Healy and suppressed a murmur of panic. He was looking at the floor, at the grass around his ankles, adrift, lost. There was no going back the way we'd come, not with the police almost at the house, and – if they'd listened to Craw, if they'd heard the part about the children's home – they'd be coming through the main gates any moment too, somewhere down at the bottom of wherever the driveway led. We were trapped here, hemmed in. I'd tried to do the right thing – but all I'd ended up doing was boxing us into a corner. We'd left a body behind. Healy was supposed to be dead. Worse, he didn't even seem to be aware of what was going on, or the scale of our problems. His muscles were still propelling him, but his mind hadn't moved.

Part of him was still inside the home.

I grabbed his arm to try to rouse him – the kind of physical contact he normally would have hated – and he followed me down the driveway, through the knot of trees that arched around it, and on to a gentle slope. It snaked down the side of a shallow hill, enclosed by the forest, but – beyond the twisted branches and thick canopy – I caught glimpses of something up ahead: a road.

At the bottom of the driveway was a brick wall, separating the road from the property boundaries, an eight-foot main gate built into it. Either side of the gate, set atop the wall, was a stone eagle. I slowed down, signalling for Healy to do the same, and looked off through the woods: the electric fence connected at either end of the brick wall, starting at road level and ascending the slope on my left and right, until it eventually looped around the children's home. On top of the brick was more electric fencing – this time a three-wire variant – but there was none on the gates themselves. Instead, two CCTV cameras were set into the brick beneath the stone eagles, focused on the gates, the pavement and the main road.

Close by: more sirens.

I glanced at Healy, standing beside me, one foot on the driveway, one in the mud at the side, his eyes sunken and hollow, looking down towards the gate. Blood had run out of the gash in his jacket, on to his leg, his trousers gathering at the ankles where they were too big for him, his hairless head shining wet with rain. He looked at me, seemingly aware for the first time of what was happening.

We were about to be caught.

Arrested.

In two minutes, this was over.

As the sirens got louder, I pulled at his arm again and headed right, down to the gates. He followed. Cars whipped past, even more of Epping Forest visible on the far side of the road. I shrugged off my jacket and, as Healy caught up, I handed it to him. 'Put this on over yours,' I said.

He looked at me, confused.

'But put it on back to front.'

It took a second for him to catch up, but then he got it: the cameras. I was going to hoist him up and over the main gates, and he was going to use the hoods on both coats to hide his identity: by wearing mine back to front, he could disguise his face. It was thin enough for him to see through – or at least to see enough until he was clear of the cameras.

'And you?' he said.

'Hurry.'

'And *you*?'

Sirens, getting louder and louder.

'Just put it on, Healy.'

He put my jacket on over his, but the wrong way round, like he was slipping into a straitjacket. When he was done, I zipped it up at the back. He looked absurd, but I didn't care. Instead, I moved him into position at the gates, dropped down behind him, and then told him to place a foot into my locked hands.

The vague flash of a blue light.

'Let's go, Healy.'

I heaved him up and felt him fumble around for a grip, but then he came away, almost toppling on to me. Saying nothing, I grabbed hold of his foot again and pushed even harder. This time, I could sense a weight adjustment, as if he'd got hold of something. Pushing again, I felt him become even more secure, his foot slowly leaving my hands. I stole a look up. I couldn't see the strain in his face, but I could see it in his skin: in the veins in his hand, his fingers like claws.

He was on top, one leg over the other side.

More blue lights.

I stepped up to the gates, looking along the road. I couldn't see them, but it sounded like they were right on top of us.

'Make the jump, Healy,' I said. '*Now.*'

Still clinging on to the top of the gates, he swung down, one arm losing its grip, one still holding on, and then – finally – let go, crumpling into a heap on the other side. I saw passengers in passing cars glance at us, and spotted a couple across the street, framed by a mix of fir and horse chestnut trees, talking to one another, yet to notice.

'Run,' I said to him.

'What about you?'

'Just run, okay?'

'But you're—'

'*Healy.* You can't get caught. You need to go.'

'I . . .' He hesitated. 'What am I going to do?'

'Lie low. I'll find you.'

He didn't react.

'Are you listening to me?'

A long pause. 'Yes.'

For a second, he sounded emotional again, but it was hard to tell for sure. Through the hood of my coat, I could see the outline of his face: a hint of a nose, a chin. Nothing else. The sound of the sirens suddenly got louder than ever, ripping across the afternoon in a series of shrieks. *They're here. They've entered the street.* He looked up to where the cameras were focused on him: I was safe on my side of the gate, out of view, undocumented; every second he lingered, more of him was committed to tape, more evidence, more for the police to work with.

'Go, Healy,' I said.

He stepped back.

A second of hesitation.

And then, at last, he walked away.

# CHAPTER 69

Over the next hour, everything changed.
I watched from the back of a marked police car, the radio buzzing in front, voices drifting in and out, as St David's came alive. A uniformed officer stood just outside my door as a succession of vehicles arrived: more marked cars first, then two plain-clothes detectives in a blue Volvo, and then – once a team had been into the building and found Grankin – forensics arrived in a white Iveco van.

As the techs pulled on their white boiler suits and sorted through their equipment, an Asian man in his late thirties, smartly dressed in grey trousers and a black tie, with a stab-proof vest, made his way over to me. He talked in hushed tones with the PC – a mumble of conversation – and then opened my door.

'Mr Raker?'

I looked up at him.

'I'm DCI Bishara.' He placed a hand on the roof of the vehicle and looked across at the building. 'So, it's a bit of a mess in there. Is all of that your work?'

I shook my head. 'No.'

'Which bits are you?'

'None of it.'

He glanced at me. 'You found it like that?'

'Yes.'

He didn't say anything else, his eyes taking me in: the cut on my cheek; my clothes, still soaked through; the mud caked across my hands from Healy's boots.

'Okay,' he said.

It was obvious he didn't believe me.

I didn't blame him. He probably had someone back at the station doing a background check on me right now. It wouldn't take him long, if he didn't have that information already, to find out what had happened in Wapping this morning. He'd know that I'd made a break for it.

He'd know about my history.

The only saving grace, for now, was that I'd left the car a couple of miles away. If they'd had the chance to go through that, they'd have found East's blood all over the boot. As I looked past Bishara, to where uniformed officers stood on the edges of the treeline, I realized how much trouble I was in. This whole place was a lockdown. My prints were all over Grankin's house. They were all over the room in which he'd died. If Healy was smart, he'd dump the gun somewhere it would never be found, making it impossible to tie me directly to the murder. But, even if he was lucid enough to do that, and do it properly, I was still cornered.

'Sit tight for a couple more minutes, okay?' Bishara said, and then pushed the door shut without waiting for an answer. He said something to the uniformed officer, and then I watched him make a beeline for the forensic team at the van. A couple of minutes later, the two techs headed inside the building, leaving Bishara to talk to a woman in her forties, who I assumed was the scene-of-crime officer.

I started thinking about Healy, about where he might be now, and then – from behind me – Bishara appeared again, passing the car and following the SOCO down to where the uniforms were lined up. Somewhere in the forest beyond them was the tunnel that Grankin had dug out. They would already have found it, because a Met team was already in his house, but the SOCO seemed to be filling Bishara in on what she knew, perhaps had even seen, gesturing to the trees, pointing with her finger in the direction of the tunnel. Bishara nodded, not interrupting, only speaking again when the SOCO started leading him a little way into the forest.

They disappeared for a moment, swallowed by branches and leaves, but then reappeared. Bishara beckoned to a couple of officers to follow him, and they headed back in, keeping to exactly the same route set out by the SOCO.

I waited.

In the silence, I started to drift, exhausted, drained. My body ached all the way down to my bones, my head hurt, my cuts, my bruises. I tried to stay awake by counting the hours since I'd slept, and then – to keep it going – worked back through the events of the last month, trying to pinpoint a night when I'd slept the entire way through. I couldn't remember. That was what scared me. I couldn't actually *remember* sleeping through the night. I'd forgotten what it even felt like.

Before I was aware of it, my head rolled against my shoulder and I lurched awake, looking out into the memories of St David's garden: the long grass, the weeds, the tangled bushes, the density of the forest that penned it in.

Moments later, a forensic tech appeared from the treeline, hood up, mask on, carrying an evidence bag in either hand. I felt a moment of panic: *What has he found?* He wouldn't have brought whatever it was all the way through the tunnel and out this side, so it must have been something he'd found in the forest. But what? *What had we left there?* Had Healy dropped something? Had I? I tried to focus on the bags, to get a sense of their shape and size, but then the tech moved behind me, past the boot of the car and around towards the front of the building.

I rubbed at my eyes. They were gritty, dry, painful, and when a single shaft of sunlight broke through the clouds above the trees, shining directly into the back seat of the car, I closed them and gave in: I let the fatigue take me away, like a boat

540

washing out to sea. I felt my shoulders relax, my head drop back and my body shut down.

Darkness.

But then I was awake again.

Someone was shouting.

I blinked myself into consciousness and tried to clear my head. It was just after 3 p.m. I'd been asleep for twenty minutes. Glancing out across the garden to the treeline, I saw that there were no officers there any more. The one stationed outside the car was still here, but only just: he'd stepped away from the back of the vehicle, eyes fixed on movement at the far end of St David's, close to the extension.

I knocked on the window. He didn't respond.

'Hey,' I said.

Nothing.

I looked again, down to where the forensics van was parked up, its back doors open. I could see flashes of movement to the left of it, between the van and the side of the building. Briefly, I made out two officers, one radioing something through, but then they were gone, sprinting through the doors of the extension.

'Hey,' I said, tapping on the glass.

This time the constable glanced at me.

'What's going on?'

He was young, panicked, nervy. His eyes lingered on me, almost flickered, as if caught between telling me to shut up and keep quiet, and wanting to share.

'What's going on?' I said again.

He looked from me to St David's, then back to me again. But as I was about to knock on the glass a third time, I noticed something behind him.

Black smoke.

It was creeping out through the gaps between the window frames and the boards on the bottom floor, through the holes in the brickwork there. It escaped up towards the sky, towards the sunlight, in thick, twisted cords.

The building was on fire.

*Just like the pier.*

'Hey,' I said, hammering on the glass. 'Let me out.'

He shook his head. 'Quiet.'

'Listen to me—'

'No, *you* listen,' he replied, jittery, unconvincing. 'Shut up.'

I was about to come back at him again – but then, from the grey doors of the extension, a forensic tech emerged, the one I'd seen come from the forest earlier. He no longer had the evidence bags with him.

As he exited, he removed his gloves, pocketed them and headed across to the van, shutting both the rear doors. He didn't get above walking pace the whole time. Instead, as he reached the driver's side and pulled that door open, perching one foot on a ramp next to the tyre well, he looked back along the length of the van – hood up, face mask still on – as if he were checking something on its side. But he wasn't looking at the van.

He was looking at me.

It was Korman.

# CHAPTER 70

'Hey,' the constable said to Korman. 'Hey, what's happening?'

I knocked on the glass. 'No!' I shouted. 'No! He's not with the police!' But the PC didn't even turn, just waved a hand in my direction, swatting me from his thoughts. He took another couple of steps closer to Korman, flicking a look to his left where smoke continued to leak from the cracks of the building.

He asked Korman something else, a repeat of the same question, but the officer was too far away from me now, his voice subdued by the distance between us.

With the outside of my fist, I thumped at the rear window so hard, I could feel the echoes of it travel through my body, but the officer was saying something else to Korman now, Korman's eyes still on me even as he was being addressed. I had a flashback to the CCTV film of him exiting Searle House – after he'd killed the girls, after he'd stabbed Gail and then stood there recording her final moments – and started to feel light-headed: all the rage and the suffering and the need for revenge blinking like a strobe behind my eyes. Korman finally stepped off the foot ramp on the side of the van, eyes switching from me to the officer.

'No!' I screamed. 'Don't approach him!'

*Do something.*

*You've got to do something.*

I rolled back, on to the base of my spine, and launched a series of kicks at the passenger window, pounding against the glass with both feet. The third time, it cracked, splitting from top to bottom, zigzagging open like ice on a frozen lake. I saw the officer stop, level with the back of the van, but Korman just looked at him, saying nothing. Listening.

*Those eyes.*

I kicked again and the glass shattered, exploding into a shower of crystal chips that spilled out across the inside seat and the grass outside. As the sound travelled, the constable looked back, Korman just inches away, eyes still on him, even as he turned – and I realized that, without intending to, I'd made a mistake.

I'd diverted the PC's attention.

Like a trap springing shut, Korman grabbed the PC at the back of the neck, smashing him face-first into the side of the van. I scrambled on to my hands and knees and threw myself through the window, nicking myself on a fang of glass still lodged in the window frame. As I hit the ground, I looked up: Korman had yanked the baton out of the officer's belt and whipped it into its full extension. He swiped it around the officer's head, blood flecking against the flank of the van.

The PC dropped to the floor.

'Korman!'

I scrambled to my feet, Korman – bent over the officer – looking up at me. He wasn't out of breath; in fact, he hardly seemed affected at all, even by me coming towards him. All I saw was a minimal twitch of the head, left to right, eyes moving to the building, to the smoke plumes drifting out from its belly, thick and gnarled and as dark as oil. A second later, one of the boards fell away from somewhere close to where the toilets were, charred black on the inside; through the open window, I could see the fire ripping through the room, licking at walls, at the ceiling.

As Korman shuddered out of his stillness, tossing the baton to one side, I heard voices, Bishara calling my name, the sound of people coughing, emerging from the inside of the building. Officers spilled out, holding evidence bags to their chests, Bishara gesturing towards me, shouting at me to stay where I was.

Footsteps.

Korman was making a break for it.

Instinctively, I headed after him.

'Raker! Stop!' Bishara shouted, and without even looking back I heard officers take off after me. As Korman emerged from behind the van, Bishara shouted a second time, 'That's him!' They were talking about Korman this time.

*They know he's a fake.*

He'd compromised himself.

My movements softened as I hit grass, and then my boots slapped against the concrete of the driveway again, Korman pounding down the slope at full pelt about twenty feet in front of me. There was a uniformed officer stationed at the open front gates. As he saw us, he took a couple of steps in our direction, holding up a hand, asking us to slow down. Korman kept going, the officer's hand straying to his equipment belt, fingers gripping his baton. He told Korman to stop, but Korman accelerated instead, the shift in speed deceptively quick; as the officer was bringing his baton out, Korman smashed into him, sending the PC pirouetting off into a bed of leaves, head crashing into the base of a tree.

Somewhere, close by: fire engines.

The sound got louder as we hit the street, a long, two-lane road with high trees on either side. Korman didn't stop, wheeling out right. I followed, dodging between passers-by, people looking at us, at him, at the cops giving chase even further back. Gradually, the gap started to close, Korman finding it hard to keep running in the forensic suit, the boots dragging, pulling at his heels, weighing on him. He tossed the mask aside, the hood whipping off his shaved head too, and for the first time he glanced back at me. A second, maybe less – and then he was focused on the road in front of him again, finding acceleration from somewhere, a reserve of energy that I simply couldn't call upon after almost two days without sleep.

As the gap started to widen, the pavement ended and I was pursuing him along the edges of the road, trees closing in around us. It felt like we were leaving the city, all sound seeming to die away, the sirens, the rumble of vehicles, people, birdsong. Up ahead, the road gently curved to the left, Korman following its arc. I had no idea where we were, my direction shot, the lack of signposts and the endless trees making it hard to get a sense of anything – of location, of what lay ahead. I looked behind me at the cops giving chase, but they were lost around the curve of the bend – and then back to Korman.

But he was gone.

I stuttered, slowing instinctively – and then accelerated again, faster this time, trying to see if he'd got beyond the bend in the road. When I got there, I saw the route extended another five hundred feet, meeting a T-junction.

He'd vanished.

Movement in the trees to my right.

I looked back, unable to see the cops yet, then made a sideways dash, off the road and beyond the treeline. My surroundings immediately greyed, like a light being turned down, the canopy trapping the darkness. The forest went on in all directions, impossibly huge, the ground soft beneath my feet, spongy, where the rain had yet to dry out. The whole thing was carpeted in pine needles, cones and fallen leaves. I looked from tree trunk to tree trunk, trying to spot flashes of white. Korman should have been easy to see here, the brightness of the forensic suit like a beacon beneath a ceiling of branches. But there was nothing. As I moved further in, trying to avoid placing my feet where they would make a sound, I couldn't see any sign of him.

*Beep beep.*

I stopped.

What the hell was that?

Looking back the way I'd come, I heard fast footsteps out on the road, the brief shadows of the three cops who'd been chasing me fading in and out, lost on the other side of the trees. Moments later, a sharp flare of sound, deadened by the forest: fire engines heading one way, towards the home, police sirens coming the other. *Bishara has sent a car after us.* They'd realize soon enough, if they hadn't already, that we'd come into the woods, but, as a flash of blue painted the trees at the edges of the road, the car passed my position – for now, at least – and the forest settled.

*Beep beep.*

I tuned back in. The sound was coming from in front of me.

I moved slowly, gingerly, reaching down to pluck

a fallen branch off the bed of the forest. It was damp, rotten at either end, but it would do. Off to my left, I could see traces of the police car's flash bar, still smearing some of the leaves blue; to my right, in front of me, it was just trees. Infinite trees, unfurling into a sepia fog.

I gripped the branch even harder, my stomach tightening, churning. How had he disappeared? Why wasn't I seeing him? My head was starting to hurt, the pain washing in like a tide, the same place as before, pounding right behind my eyes.

And then I saw something.

Lying on the floor of the forest, in the space between two huge fir trees, was a mobile phone. It beeped twice, the display illuminating the immediate area.

*Did he drop it?*

I scanned my surroundings, more cautious than ever now. But there was no movement, no sign of Korman. The place was silent. No wind. No rain. I inched in closer, keeping my eyes on the trees circling me, gripping the branch with both hands, one over the other. A couple of feet short of the phone, it beeped again.

This time I could make out a message.

### Pick me up.

Spinning on my heel, I looked deeper into the forest, anticipating some sort of trap, but everything remained still. If it was a trap, I started to realize, it wasn't one where he was going to attack me.

*But he can see me.*

I bent down and picked it up, looking around in every direction as I did so. Where was he? In my hand, the phone erupted into life.

*Beep beep.*

A new message.

Incoming call in 3 secs.

I'd barely had a chance to process that when the phone started ringing. I looked at the number: another mobile, but not one I recognized.

I hit Answer.

Silence.

Turning the whole time, trying to find him in the maze of timber, I started becoming aware of a soft sound on the line.

*His breathing.*

'I have your friend, Healy.'

My heart sank.

But then I tried to think logically: did he *really* have him? How was it even possible? *This is a trap.* I started shaking my head. 'No,' I said. 'No, you're lying.'

'I saw you give him a foot up,' he replied. He was talking about me getting Healy up and over the gates to St David's. 'I saw him take off. Before I headed to Victor's house, I grabbed him. He's sick and slow. It wasn't hard.'

'No,' I said again, but less certain this time.

A crackle on the line.

Korman was moving.

I heard footsteps and then the clunk of a van door opening, the quality of the call changing, softening, background sounds dying.

'Say something,' Korman said.

'Hello?'

It was him. *Shit, it's Healy.* He sounded in pain. He was distressed, tearful. His *Hello?* hung there in the quiet, a single word carrying the weight of so much.

'What do you want?' I said, anger building.

'I will kill him,' he replied calmly, matter-of-factly, his accent difficult to pin down, his words pronounced, precise. 'Do you want to see him alive again?'

'What do you think?'

A long drawn-out pause. 'Then do exactly what I tell you.'

# CHAPTER 71

I got the mainline train down from Chingford to Liverpool Street, then walked the two miles south to Wapping. Maybe I was paranoid, or tired, or both, but as soon as I emerged on to the concourse at Liverpool Street there seemed to be police everywhere, and I figured that, if they recognized me, I had a better chance of making a break for it if I wasn't trapped inside the Tube.

When I reached Wonderland, it was silent and dark. At the side of the old paper mill, police tape still flickered and twisted in the breeze coming off the river. I ducked under it and moved into the shadows, along the side of the museum. It was just before 7 p.m., a chill in the air, winter lying in wait, and as I looked out across the back of the building, the wind picked up again and seemed to pass right through me: my skin, my flesh, my bones.

There was even more police tape at the banks of the river, cordoning off what was left of the pier, out in the water. It was basically unrecognizable: a twisted, scorched series of legs, fanning out into the Thames; a piece of broken, faltering promenade midway along, great mouths of space everywhere else; skewed, crumbling slats hanging off like fingers; and then the pavilion, its roof collapsing in on itself, as if sucked into its centre, its walls gone, exposing an interior of blackened shapes, melted and indistinguishable.

The museum, untouched, now stood alone.

Ahead of me, its rear doors – the same ones that Calvin East had emerged from the first time I'd been here – were ajar. Not much, but enough. Korman had told me he'd leave them like that. Yet I didn't move, keeping my eyes on the back of the building. Why had he asked me to come here? Returning to the museum was a risk, for him as much as for me. The police and the fire crews were gone, finished for now, but they would return. They'd spent the day walking the halls and offices of the museum, trying to discover the reasons why Gary Cabot and his father had been murdered, why the pier had been awash in petrol and set alight. I doubted they'd found anything. So for police, this was still a work in progress.

That made it a dangerous place to be.

I moved quickly, my steps punctuated by the wash of the Thames against the river wall, and slipped in through the gap. It took me a couple of seconds to get my bearings, as I'd come in through the front of the building the first time.

But then I saw where I was.

The entrance foyer was ahead of me, and a door marked *Journey through Time* was on the right –

the room of photos, documenting the history of the pier.

The entire place was disconcertingly quiet.

Cautiously, I started moving.

At the foyer there was some dull low-level lighting, tiny lamps dotted around the base of the payment kiosks; and, beyond those, a night light in the restaurant, a muted yellow-green rinsing out across a room full of empty tables and stacked chairs. Part of the dining area was tucked away out of sight, but I knew Korman wasn't going to be in there. I knew where he would be.

*The penny arcade.*

I started the ascent. At the top was the arch that led to the pavilion-like façade, windows looking out on to painted seaside scenes, the old machines enclosed by a white picket fence. Five rows stretched out in front of me, the middle one leading to the next set of stairs, wooden slats whining gently as I moved towards them. Like the ground floor, every-thing was lit, just not well: above each window, a night lamp glowed, turning the place a pallid yellow. It was strange, unsettling, blobs of light reflecting in the glass of the cabinets, making it look like movement on either side of me. Every so often I'd stop – heart hammering, braced for impact – and then realize there was nothing there: just light and shadows and stillness.

The spiral staircase, corkscrewing up to the next floor, was iron. I hadn't noticed it yesterday, but

I noticed it tonight: as I stepped on to it, my feet made a soft *ching*. A second later, there was a brief noise above: a creak, a weight shift.

*He's seen me.*

I looked up, craning my neck.

At the top of the stairs was the Oracle, the same fortune-telling machine that I'd looked at previously. Inside the cabinet, the puppet was lifeless and slack, bent my way, its dead eyes peering past me into the half-light.

Gripping the railing, I began climbing, legs suddenly heavy, muscles stiff and unresponsive. I thought of the first time I'd been here, of standing among the machines on the second floor and feeling like I was in the middle of a graveyard.

*I'd thought of it as a kind of mausoleum.*

Maybe, tonight, it would become that.

I reached the top.

Directly in front of me, halfway along a canyon of machines, was Healy. He was tied to a chair, bound and gagged, head slumped sideways. A floor lamp had been placed next to him. There was blood on his face. Beneath the light, he looked ghostly, emaciated, both jackets on the floor, his sweater, his shirt, his shoes and socks removed too. He sat there with his body revealed, unconscious but alive. I could see the rise and fall of his chest, muscles shifting, ribs exposed.

I'd begun to accept how he looked, my eyes not lingering on him as often, not hypnotized by the sparseness of him, or his lack of force. But it was

556

hard to take my eyes off him now, off this version of him, his shirtless torso like a sack of bones, his skin so thin it was barely able to disguise them. He was so small.

I wanted to go to him, but I didn't. Instead, I reached into my pocket and removed the phone I'd found on the floor of the forest, holding it up to the dark. I tried to watch for signs of movement ahead of me, but it was just a sea of arcade machines, different shapes and sizes, rolling out into the shadows at the other end of the floor. The shop, off to the right, was closed up, its shutters down. The mirror maze I could see only glimpses of, its panels reflecting back a dull glow.

There was no Korman.

But I knew he was here.

I placed the phone on the floor in front of me, keeping my eyes up ahead, doing exactly as he'd asked during our call. He wanted the phone he'd left for me, to make sure it didn't get in to anyone else's hands. I turned three hundred and sixty degrees and then lifted my shirt up, revealing my stomach and chest, and did the same again. He wanted to see that I wasn't carrying any weapons with me. Maybe he even thought I might be wearing a wire, even though the idea of me working with the police was laughable. I let my shirt fall back into place and stepped forward.

'What do you want, Korman?' I said.

Healy didn't react, clearly not awake, and for a

moment I stood there, looking off into a maze of machines.

Slowly, something started to shift.

To my right, across Healy's shoulder, there was movement – and, from behind a hexagonal wooden pillar on which six bagatelles were mounted, Korman finally emerged. He was dressed all in black, his body another part of the shadows, but his head – the pink of his scalp, the colour of his cheeks – was different, his skin reflecting back the colour of the standing lamp. He stood there, on the edges of the light, and stared at me. His eyes were dark, small like bullet holes, and it gave him an odd look, as if I were seeing right into his head.

'I've done what you asked,' I said.

His eyes shifted from me to the phone, and he took another series of small steps forward, until he was behind Healy.

Softly, he placed a hand on Healy's shoulder.

I felt myself flinch, readying for whatever he was about to do. But he did nothing. He just stood there, looking at me, one hand on Healy's shoulder, one at his side. I refused to look away, even though it took everything I had not to. There was nothing in his eyes to focus on: no colour, no substance.

'I've done what you asked,' I repeated.

No response.

'Are you listening to—'

'You carry a lot of scars.'

He was talking about my back, about injuries I'd been left with on another case, a long time

past. So much had happened since then, I sometimes forgot they were there, sometimes went
weeks, even months, without thinking about the
men who had carved them into my body. They'd
been like Korman, lightless and savage, and when
I'd faced them down, I'd done the same as I was
doing now: I'd maintained a façade – even while
the fear chewed me up inside.

'So what now?' I said.

Again, he didn't reply.

'It's a risk coming here.'

'I suppose it is,' he replied, his voice quiet,
benign.

'So why choose this place to meet?'

'Where else was I going to go?'

'You have the whole city.'

'Not any more.'

He meant not after today, after we'd uncovered
Grankin's house within a house; after Korman had
been forced to breach a crime scene and flee from
the police. Korman had disguised himself well,
cloaked his existence in a series of different names
and former addresses. But now, as Grankin's life
unravelled in the full glare of a police hunt, it was
only a matter of time before they closed in on
Korman. He could see that. He could see the stark
reality of being on the run. So in a strange way,
despite the obvious risk in returning here, maybe
this *was* the smart place to be. Because it would
be one of the last places anyone would think to
look.

'I've done what you asked,' I said for a third time. 'So what now?'

He nodded again, his head minutely shifting, the rest of him utterly still. 'Now I want you to see something.'

# CHAPTER 72

I watched him, unnerved, unsure of where this was going.

He lifted his hand away from Healy's shoulder, then stopped, touching the side of Healy's face instead, gently, almost tenderly, fingers crackling against stubble. Slowly, he moved from the neck to the cleft between shoulder blade and collarbone, as if massaging it, and then further down, all the way to the centre of Healy's chest, where his hand stopped, fingers settling like the legs of an insect.

He was covering Healy's heart.

Korman hadn't yet taken his eyes off me, but this time he did, his gaze shifting into the shadows, to the machines around him, his hand still in place on Healy's naked chest. 'Why did you have to ruin everything?' he said.

I looked at him, uncertain what the right response would be.

When I gave no reply, he slowly returned to me, as if shaking off the remains of a dream, head dropping at an angle and rolling from side to side. Quietly, he said, 'Which of you shot him?'

He was talking about Grankin.

'It doesn't matter now,' I said.

'It matters to me.'

I shrugged. 'Why murder that family?'

A frown, as if the question were irrelevant.

'Why kill people? Why burn everything down?'

He remained there, unmoved. 'I've always liked fire. I like the way it twists and contorts, how it changes things, reduces them. After Calvin told us about you coming to see him at the museum, I knew you would return to the pier eventually. I waited for you, and then set that whole place alight. I sat there for a while and watched it burn. It was beautiful.' His tone was confusing: soft, a little melancholy; so at odds with the brutality of his crimes. 'I didn't expect you to die out there, but I hoped – after making my anonymous call to the police – that you'd get caught. Even if you told them who I was, what then? I'm a respected businessman with no history of trouble – at least on paper. A man with your track record; your friend here, who convinced the world he was dead. You'd both be revealed as liars. Who would believe you over me?'

For the first time, I noticed Healy's gun: it was placed on top of one of the penny arcade machines to Korman's left.

'But I underestimated you,' he went on, the first flash of resentment in his voice. 'I didn't realize how much you knew. When Victor called me this morning and told me you were at the house, I was on my way back from taking care of Cabot. I couldn't get up there in time to help Victor. But, whatever happened, I knew St David's had to burn to the ground. I had to make sure we didn't leave anything behind.'

'Except you did.'

He frowned, eyeing me.

'The blood on the walls of the toilets, the oil drums.'

He shrugged.

'There'll be DNA on them.'

'And what difference will that make?'

A weird answer, one I couldn't interpret. There was no viciousness to him, no ferocity, no sense of irrationality: he spoke flatly, even serenely, as if he were discussing something unimportant. It made me even more uneasy somehow, more perturbed by him. I'd come in expecting him to be unstable and crazed, a heightened version of Grankin: his insidiousness, his cruelty, channelled into something even worse. As I thought of the scene he'd left behind at Searle House, his violation of a family, I knew he *was* those things. But it didn't seem like it – not here, not now.

'How did you even get inside St David's?'

He shrugged again. 'You saw me in my forensic suit.'

'So you just wandered in?'

'I got there at the right time. It was chaos at the house, people coming and going. I used the confusion to take the tunnel through to the forest.'

'But where did you get the suit from?'

'I swiped it from the back of a forensics van.'

'Just like that.'

He was still. 'I've become good at blending in.'

He seemed entirely unconcerned by what forensics might find. So why had Korman risked everything to return to the children's home? If he didn't care about the evidence he and Grankin may have left there, why bother taking the risk to go back and burn it down?

It wouldn't be long before the Met started to realize he and Grankin were working together, that Calvin East had been involved too – three histories entwined from the early days at St David's, all the way through to their alibis the night the Clark family were killed. But, without returning to St David's, he'd have had a head start on the police. He could have made a break for it, left the country, found somewhere to dig in and lie low.

Instead, he'd compromised himself – for what?

Korman moved slightly, staring at me, dragging me out of my thoughts. He was aware that I was trying to piece it all together. He wasn't going to share his reasons, and he wouldn't be tricked into a confession, but then something else caught my attention, something I might be able to use: very quickly, he glanced at Healy, still out cold. It was as if he was checking up on him.

*Because he is.*

He was waiting for Healy to wake up.

Whatever his reasons for asking me here, whatever

564

it was that he wanted to show me, he wanted to show us both: he wanted Healy awake, fully cognizant.

'Aren't you worried about what the police might find?' I said.

His eyes narrowed, as if he sensed that I was getting close to an answer, an animal aware that his surroundings had changed. I was reminded of Healy's description of him in the moments before the heart attack; how Korman had zeroed in on his weakness, sniffing out its scent: *He punched me square in the chest, right on my heart, over and over. It was like a jackhammer.*

'There'll be evidence Grankin didn't wash away,' I said again, but he didn't respond. 'The fire won't have destroyed everything.'

This time he considered it. 'It'll have destroyed enough.'

'Why did you go back in?'

Again, no response.

'Why did you go back in?' I repeated – and then a thought struck me hard. *The night he and Grankin were caught on film at Searle House.* It had looked like Korman had changed his appearance – *and Grankin had no face at all.*

The mask.

'You went back in for Grankin's mask.'

There was nothing in his face now, no expression, no movement at all, as if he'd deliberately closed himself down, a sudden blankness that was quite eerie. I didn't know if he was calm or enraged. And yet the more I thought about it, the more it made sense.

'The fire was just a distraction,' I said, attempting to put myself there, to imagine it. 'You went in, disguised as a forensic tech, and grabbed the mask. But people started to realize they didn't know you, or recognize you. They realized there was an extra body in the forensic team. So you set the place alight to try and give yourself some time. But it was too late by then.' I paused, recalling Bishara as he'd left the burning building, gesturing towards Korman: *That's him!* 'They realized that you started the fire.'

Nothing. No reaction at all.

'Why did you have to go back for the mask?' I asked.

He looked down at Healy, his fingers still pressed to the centre of Healy's chest, where they'd been the whole time. 'The heart is such a wonderful piece of engineering. Chambers, arteries, valves. I know the heart hasn't got anything to do with emotion, with *feeling*. We don't feel sad because our *heart* is sad: it's just the brain telling us, it's chemicals, it's a cold, biomechanical process. But, sometimes, it's easy to forget that. When I walked into St David's today, with my evidence bags, my bottles of petrol, I felt something here.' He pushed his fingers hard into Healy's chest, forcing him sideways; he was still unconscious, his body straining against the duct tape, so he wouldn't feel anything. But this wasn't about punishing Healy,

566

it was about using Healy to get at me. 'I knew, unless everything went perfectly, that I would have to use the petrol. So I suppose, when I did, what I felt was a kind of sadness that this was all about to end.'

I glanced at Healy, at his chest. *Be careful.* 'But what you were doing was killing people,' I said evenly, calmly, trying not to aggravate him.

He remained stiff, apathetic.

'You killed two eight-year-old girls.'

'Yes,' he said.

'That's it? "Yes"?'

He sniffed.

'Why did you kill them?'

'It's okay to kill their mother, but not them?'

I felt a twist of anger.

'That's what you're saying, isn't it? That you're willing to overlook the fact that their mother was stabbed nine times, if I just give you the reasons why those two girls had to die as well.' He looked at me. 'Are their lives more important?'

'They were *kids.*'

'Kids can be duplicitous too.'

That stopped me. 'What are you talking about?'

He didn't reply immediately, glancing down at Healy, at his hand, and then he said, 'If you're looking for someone to blame, you should blame Stourcroft. If she hadn't written her book, none of this would have happened. That family, those girls, would still be alive. Your friend here might still be fat and angry, and chasing his tail on the *one that*

567

*got away.*' His eyes widened at that last part, the words carrying the edges of the ruthlessness that really drove him. 'All of this,' he went on, voice steadying, slowing up, 'it's not down to *us*. It's down to that woman's book.'

'No,' I said. 'It's got nothing to do with that.'

'Really? But you've read the book?'

'None of this is down to a book about a pier.'

Instantly, something changed, his hand finally moving away from Healy, his mouth forming an *oh*. A smile broke at the corners of his mouth, sly, crooked. 'I think you need a change of perspective,' he said.

'Meaning what?'

He didn't reply.

I was confused, thrown.

He slid in front of Healy, his smile gone, and reached around to the back of his belt. Suddenly, he had a knife in his hand. It was almost exactly the same as Grankin's: a darker grip, more teeth on the blade, but the same length and size. Now I knew why he wasn't interested in the gun to his left; why he hadn't even looked at it. He preferred knives. It was how he'd accounted for Stourcroft, for Gail, the girls.

I moved towards him.

We were fifteen feet apart, surrounded by rows of dormant penny arcade machines. 'Don't come any closer,' he said, quiet, still. 'You come any closer and I will kill your friend, and then I will kill you. Is that clear?'

*Something's changed.*

He was almost distracted now, eyes moving across the room, inching from one machine to the next. I could see a hint of grey in his irises, the light either side of him settling around the top of his cheeks. There was none of the menace in him I'd seen so clearly and briefly a second ago. When his gaze returned to me, his nose wrinkled – as if disgusted – and I recalled the very first thing he'd said.

*Why did you have to ruin everything?*

'What's going on, Korman?'

Behind him, Healy twitched.

Korman picked up on it, Healy's bones popping and creaking as he shifted gently on the chair. Re-establishing his grip on the knife, Korman began to retreat. I followed him, trying to lessen the gap between us, in case he went on the attack. Healy was barely conscious, vulnerable, and I needed enough time to get to him. But Korman didn't use the knife on Healy. He just stopped moving and said, 'I'm glad you've woken up.'

Healy opened his eyes, groggy, looking straight ahead at me, and then to his side, where Korman was still watching. 'You . . .' he said, voice full of fluid, and started coughing, hacking up lungfuls of air, saliva spilling from his lips. When he was finished, he glanced at Korman again. 'I'm going to fucking kill you,' he muttered.

Korman didn't say anything.

Healy shivered, arms trapped behind him, trying

569

to shake himself out of the haze. 'I'm going to *kill* you,' he spat again, stretching the binds. Muscle and veins showed through as he tried to lean towards Korman, tried to get to him, a dog straining on a leash. *'You're gonna pay for what you did!'* he screamed, but the effort was too much for him and he descended into another coughing fit.

Korman watched him, half turned towards me so he could keep me in his sights, then turned completely in my direction, looking down at the slats between us, the wood worn by years, by thousands of passing tourists. As Healy calmed down, Korman's attention shifted to the machines again, looking at them the same as before, his eyes lingering on them, almost doting on them; how a parent might look at their child.

'This is what I wanted you both to see,' he said.

I studied him, his face, the knife in his hand, trying to figure out where this was going – but then, before I'd barely even processed it, he'd turned the knife around, the blade facing along the inside of his arm.

I leaped forward, arms out, trying to stop him.

But he wasn't going for Healy.

He drove the blade into himself, the knife entering his stomach, just below the ribs. The impact sent him stumbling, one step, a second, and then he regained enough self-control to grip the handle and give the weapon a violent twist. There was a terrible sound of flesh tearing, a hiss of pain, and then he dropped to his knees, the

570

impact sending a tremble through the slats, the room seeming to list. He looked up at me, knife embedded in his body, blood running out of him like a tap, and finally it came: the smile Healy had described seeing after Korman left him dying on the floor in Stables Market; the person Calvin East had been so scared off, silent and frightening, haunting him through the corridors of St David's. Here was the man who had taken the lives of two eight-year-olds.

This was what he wanted us both to see.

Quickly, I closed the gap between us, but then I stood there, looking down at him, unsure what to even do. I had so many questions for him, and there was no time left to ask them. The smile faded from his face, his expression drooping, but his eyes remained alive for a moment more, confirming what this was.

One final act of cruelty.

There would be no answers to my questions, no closure for the families his actions had torn apart, nothing for Healy even after everything he'd sacrificed to get here. There would be no journey to the centre of whatever it was he and Grankin had done, no clues about how long it had been going on or how many had suffered; only the burnt, twisted traces of whatever hadn't gone up in flames, and the worthless scraps I could pick out from the memory of this last conversation.

I grabbed him by the collar, pulling him towards me, his body jerking as he tried to hold himself back.

'No,' I said. 'You're going to tell me what you know.'

But it was over.

Whatever tiny flicker of light had ever existed in him fizzled out, and his eyes started a slow retreat into the void. The corners of his mouth, still turned up in the echoes of that last smile, began to drop – and then there was nothing.

I let him fall to the floor.

'No,' I heard Healy say. 'No, no, no.'

He was sitting awkwardly, head looking one way, at Korman, body facing the other, trapped by its binds. One of his eyes teared up, the tear breaking free as he glanced at me, at Korman, just repeating the same thing over.

'No. Not like this. *No!*'

I didn't know what to say to him, because this was worse than anything I could have imagined for Healy. This was an ending filled with the tragedy and emptiness of revenge – except the vengeance wasn't Healy's, and it never would be. The real vengeance belonged to Korman. He'd denied Healy his retribution, denied any of us the answers we'd so desperately sought, and now all that was left was a promise: the one Healy had made to the girls, as he'd knelt there between their beds, the day he'd entered their bedroom.

And the certainty, now, that he could never honour it.

# CHAPTER 73

After a while, I picked up Korman's knife and cut away Healy's binds, dropping the knife to the ground again. Blood settled around it, around Korman, gathering like a cloak. But Healy didn't move to him, or get out of the seat. He just sat there, muttering the same thing, tears marking his cheeks, skin bleached white beneath the floor lamp, narrow bands of fat gathered at his belly as he leaned to one side.

I thought about trying to comfort him, about trying to find the words to tell him we'd fix this, but I wasn't sure what those words were, or whether there was anything left to fix. The answers were lying in a pool of blood on the floor.

Instead, I left him to gather himself, and scanned the arcade, across the tops of the machines, out to where the glow from the floor lamp made little impact. As I did, I recalled the look on Korman's face as he'd done the same thing. In the seconds before he'd killed himself, what had been that expression on his face when he'd looked out at the arcade? Sorrow? Affection? I rewound further, to everything Calvin East had told us about the weird things that would happen here: cabinets changing position, cracks appearing in glass, cases being revarnished.

*And always the same five machines.*

I started moving slowly along the middle, in the direction of the mirror maze. There were a hundred machines here, maybe more than that, beginning in straight lines, then becoming messier and less ordered the further I went. The centre row maintained its linearity, all the way down to the maze, which was why I hadn't been so aware of the layout the first time I'd been in. But I could see it clearly now as rows intersected, lines of travel merged, the room becoming a tangle of walkways, nooks and alcoves on either side of me as the space accommodated bigger machines with different dimensions – the height of the fortune tellers and laughing sailors; the width of pushers and puppet shows.

I stopped. *What the hell am I doing?*

What I should have been thinking about was getting out of here. Korman was dead, and now we had to clear up whatever part we'd played in this. That meant getting rid of Healy's blood, wiping down surfaces, the chair he'd been tied to. If the police returned here in the morning, we needed them to find Korman, for the forensic team to determine it a suicide, and for no trace of us to be left here. After that, I'd have to figure out the rest.

Should I hand myself in?

Or should I wait for them to come to me?

I started making my way back to Healy, who was hunched and shrugging on his clothes, when something caught my eye, off to the right.

Making a detour, I passed from the middle row into a tangle of different machine types, all set in a rough circle. Among three matching kineto-scopes – Victorian motion-picture viewers – ornate and beautiful, with polished brass peepholes, was a strength tester, set inside a wooden cabinet. On the glass at the front, there was a crack, right in the corner.

*This is one of the machines that East described.*

I checked it over, running my fingers across the varnish. I wasn't sure how the finish was supposed to feel, or what difference a tin of Hoberman's might make, but nothing felt strange about it. It was smooth to the touch, and professionally applied. When I went around to the back of the cabinet, I found a rear door, about two and a half feet high, with a handle attached.

I pulled at it and it popped open.

Inside it was empty. I bent down, getting on to my hands and knees, and leaned closer, moving my hand around the interior, checking surfaces for anything that didn't feel right. There was nothing. My fingers glanced off pulleys and cogs, the work-ings of the machine, but mostly the strength tester was just a tall, empty box, like a coffin.

'Healy,' I said.

He looked up, eyes shifting slowly.

As I waited for him, I continued moving through

the arcade, circling the machines, weaving in and out of the chaotic aisles, keeping my eyes on the cases. Once he'd arrived, I returned to the strength tester. 'You remember how East talked about the same five machines being varnished over and over again?'

He looked dazed, eyes moving sluggishly around the room. He glanced at Korman. 'We should leave.'

'We will,' I said, trying to keep my voice measured. He wiped his eyes with his sleeve and then stood there, as if he hadn't heard anything I'd just said. I tried again: 'Once the police turn up tomorrow and find him, we're not going to have another chance to look around this place.'

He glanced at the strength tester a second time.

'Healy?'

He nodded.

'You listening to me?'

He nodded again.

'There are five machines they care about, one of which is this strength tester. We're also looking for two bagatelles that are almost exactly the same design as one another, but there'll only be one here tonight, because the other one is back at Grankin's place.' I paused, remembering how it had been hidden inside the false wall. 'The other two machines are a fortune teller with a scratch down the side, and a phonograph. You getting this?'

'Yeah,' he said.

'I'm not sure how we identify the phonograph, because I've seen about three of them already tonight – but let's try, okay?'

Without saying anything else, he turned and headed across to the other side of the arcade, moving through the sea of cabinets, expressionless, remote. I wasn't sure how much he was taking in, but he seemed to belong in this moment somehow: a ghost of a man wandering through a forest of archaic machines, surrounded by the façade of a long-forgotten pier. All of it, Healy included, was just a vague hint of something that had once been better.

I carried on moving through the rows, before eventually double-backing on myself and returning to the strength tester. There were countless bagatelles, countless phonographs too, but it wasn't until I crossed the middle row, to Healy's side of the room, that I finally found something.

'Here,' I said.

He came over. Among a group of bagatelles was an empty space where another one should have been.

'The one we saw in Grankin's house must go here.'

But Healy was frowning now, looking over at the other side of the arcade.

'What?' I asked.

'They're in the same position.'

I glanced from him to where he was looking. 'What do you mean?'

'The one we saw in Grankin's house had a design with three red circles on the front. Did you notice that when we were there?'

I tried to remember.

He gestured across to the other side of the arcade. 'There's one with three red circles on it over there, not far from the strength tester you were looking at. I saw it earlier on. The one that Grankin had in his house, and the one over there, they've been placed in the same position – just on opposite sides of the room.'

He was right: the one that normally occupied the empty space, and the near-identical bagatelle on the other side of the room, mirrored one another's position exactly. They were the same distance from the middle aisle, in a straight line across from one another. Had they been purposely placed like that?

I returned to the one that was still here, opened its rear door and checked it over. Just like the strength tester, there was nothing unusual inside.

'We're still missing a phonograph and a fortune teller,' I said, but as soon as the words were out of my mouth, I'd found them both: they were among a crowd of machines between Healy and me.

'They're all in a row.'

Healy looked at me. 'What?'

'The machines – they've all been placed in a row.'

The phonograph was different from the others. It sat atop a wooden plinth, about two feet in length and a foot high – no rear door, just a slide drawer built into the plinth itself. I opened it up. There was nothing inside. When I checked the fortune teller with the scratch – a smaller version of the Oracle, which I'd seen on my way up to this floor – it was exactly the same: empty. None of the machines was directly adjacent to one another – there were other cabinets in between – though they'd been placed roughly the same distance apart. No one would notice the pattern unless they knew what they were looking for. But because we *did* know, it was absolutely clear: they were in a straight line. If the missing bagatelle had been here and not at Grankin's house, we'd be looking at a deliberate pattern – the only five machines Korman and Grankin had ever cared about, all purposely placed in a row.

'Why have they done that?' Healy asked.

I shook my head, still trying to piece together the evidence I was seeing, when something Korman said bubbled to the surface.

*You need a change of perspective.*

'Raker?'

An idea started to form. I ran my fingers across the surface of the fortune teller, which was closest to me, and then over the surface of another, random machine to the right of me. Something was different. The finish on the fortune teller was good, smooth – but was marginally darker, and it was harder to the touch as well, with a texture like chalk.

'Raker, what's—'

'Hold on a sec,' I said, and removed my phone from my pocket, my adrenalin starting to fizz. I checked my camera app, going through its settings, and when I saw that it had the option I needed, headed over to where Korman had placed the floor lamp. Following the lamp's cables, via an extension lead, to the nearest plug point, I found the switch that would turn everything off.

Healy was watching me.

'I'm going to turn off the lights,' I said.

'What? Why?'

The arcade was plunged into darkness. Using the glow from my mobile phone, I returned to the fortune teller and selected the camera option I wanted. Slowly, I levelled the phone's lens at the back of the machine.

On-screen, the fortune teller lit up.

'What are you doing?' Healy asked.

I directed the phone towards the rest of the floor, towards the phonograph and the strength tester; to the bagatelle and its matching empty space on the other side of the middle aisle.

They were all a luminous pink.

Even the empty space was marked with the remnants of it: the outline of a square where the bagatelle normally sat.

'They used infra-red paint.'

'What?' Healy stepped towards me. 'What are you talking about?' he said, watching my phone screen now, seeing for himself what this arcade really was.

'They mixed infra-red paint with the varnish,' I said, as much to myself as to Healy, 'and it reacted. That's why the revarnished wood has slowly got darker over time. That's why it feels harder to the touch. They made a mistake with the two bagatelles, right back at the start, by getting the mix wrong – it's why East said it was gloopy and careless. But they never got it wrong again.'

It seemed so obvious now: Korman and Grankin had chosen wooden machines because, unlike the metal ones, they could revarnish them. But they'd also selected the machines based on their location, revarnishing the same cabinets over and over again to maintain a line of five beacons, all in a row. The missing bagatelle, the fortune teller and the phonograph on the left of the aisle; the remaining bagatelle and the strength tester on the right.

Except the row wasn't *quite* perfect.

Because the pattern seemed unevenly weighted – three machines on the left, two on the right – my eye was drawn to a point roughly in the middle, between the centre aisle and the bagatelle on the right, where a sixth machine was sitting. If it had been revarnished like the others, if it had shown up under infra-red, it would have fitted perfectly into the pattern, turning five machines into six. It would have made things even – three on the left, three on the right. It would have finished everything off.

But it hadn't been varnished.

It had been left untouched.

I took a step closer. It was a tall, thin cabinet, some kind of puppet show, its name written across the top in letters that dripped blood: *The Haunted House*. A coin slot on the side had a plate above it – *Do you dare bring the Haunted House to life?* – and, through the glass, there was a domestic scene: four small puppets – two parents, two kids – sitting at the kitchen table. Waiting in the wings, crudely visible through long slots at the side of the cabinet, were ghosts, which would pass back and forth across the kitchen – the family reacting accordingly – once a coin was inserted.

'What the hell is this place?' Healy said.

I looked from him to the machine, then back to him. 'I think it's a map.'

# CHAPTER 74

I switched on the lights again, and the map disappeared. To the human eye, the varnished machines were virtually indistinguishable from the ones around them: a little darker in shade, the finish a little drier and firmer to the touch – but you'd have to look hard to see the difference. The only reason we'd even been able to find them in the first place was because of what Calvin East had told us.

The Haunted House was the largest of the six cabinets by a long way, about five feet high and three feet wide – and it sat in the space where, if Korman and Grankin had completed their row of revarnished machines, the fourth point on the line would have been. It seemed obvious why they hadn't revarnished this one, though: it was too big to move, too cumbersome, too heavy; the chances of being caught taking it out of the museum, too great.

But I wondered if there was another reason.

It sat among a group of others of about the same size, almost disguised by them. Its rear panel was incredibly difficult to get at: not only was it against a pillar, but there was no access to it from either side because of the location of adjacent machines. That, presumably, was the point. However, while under infra-red there was no evidence of varnish having been applied to this cabinet, I could see scratch marks on the wooden slats of the floor, made by the machine's feet, where it had been levered out and then back in again.

'Give me a hand here,' I said to Healy.

With no space at the side of the machine, I bent down and pulled from the bottom, while Healy tried to heave it from the top. It was clumsy, difficult work, and we kept getting in each other's way. Eventually, I told him to stand back, and – with a series of jerks – I managed to get it far enough out from the pillar to squeeze in behind it.

Manoeuvring into the space we'd created, a network of cobwebs and dust at ankle level, I tried the rear door of the machine. It was locked.

I looked back at the other machines in the row, starting to get a sense of what was going on here. 'Korman removed something from them.'

'What?' Healy said.

He was standing behind me, shadowing me, partially reanimated by what he'd seen on the phone. 'The other machines,' I replied, 'the revarnished ones in this row, their rear doors have been left unlocked. Because Korman removed something from each of them.'

Healy looked along the row, then back to the

Haunted House, seeing where I was going with this. 'And the reason this one is locked . . .'

'Is because he put whatever he took out of *those* into *this*.' I glanced across at Korman. 'Can you grab his knife for me?'

He seemed reluctant to go back to the body at first, but then retreated down the middle row. Once I had the knife, I slid the tip of the blade in through the gap between door and frame, and began prying it open. Eventually, the panel started to bend.

With one final heft, it popped open.

Inside was a small sports holdall, zipped up, padlocked. I removed it and shuffled out from behind the cabinet, to where Healy was standing. Puncturing the holdall with the blade, I cut along the top, adjacent to the zip, and opened it out. For a moment, I wasn't entirely sure what I was looking at.

It was a series of five opaque plastic sleeves, all ziplocked. When I opened up the first, a wristwatch spilled out into my hands. The face was a sickly yellow, faded and discoloured, and it wasn't working. The maker, Wirrek, I'd never heard of. When I turned it over, I found a manufacturer's mark, a series of numbers, and then an inscription: *To our darling Edward. With much love. Mum and Dad.*

I set it aside and opened up the next sleeve.

A gold chain with a crucifix attached.

In the third was a cigarette lighter, silver and

ridged. I flipped it open. The spark wheel still turned, but there was no flame. I looked for any identifying marks, but all I could find were scratch marks on the underside of it.

I placed it down on to the floor, next to the wristwatch and the chain, and opened the fourth sleeve. Inside was a waistcoat. The last sleeve felt lightest of all – and, when I opened it up, I wasn't even sure that there was anything in it.

But then something fluttered out.

I reached down and picked it up.

'What's that?' Healy said.

It was plain, flat and stiff, like a piece of yellowing card. I turned it over. On the other side was a drawing: a bluebird carrying a heart, with the name *Life* in a scroll under it. The drawing had faded over time, its lines smudged.

I handed it to Healy.

He took it, examining it, turning it over again – and a sudden realization bloomed in his face. It wasn't a piece of paper. It wasn't a drawing.

It was a tattoo on a flayed piece of skin.

'Who the hell do these belong to?' Healy said, looking from the skin to me, to the holdall on the floor – and then he started frowning. 'Wait, you've missed something.'

I looked back at the bag.

Right in the corner, hidden beneath the folds, was another item. I reached in and grabbed it – but as soon as I took it in my fingers, as soon as

I had it halfway out of the holdall, I knew what it was.

We both did.

It was the grey mask that Grankin had been wearing.

# PART V

# CHAPTER 75

Forty-eight hours later, I'd struck a deal with the police.

The alternative was admitting to nothing and building a lie, but as soon as I contacted Bishara and arranged to hand myself in, I realized there were too many ways to slip up, and he was too smart. Sooner or later, he'd find some area I hadn't considered, an anomaly, and because he and his team were good at their jobs, and I was bone-tired and depleted – barely functioning after two days with no sleep, and a month of insomnia – the lie would reveal itself, and then everything would collapse. So I admitted to fleeing the scene in Wapping, putting it down to panic after finding East murdered in the back of my car; and then I admitted to leaving his body on Wanstead Flats, uncertain now of the reasons why I'd chosen to do that. Had I seen it as some sort of moral act? Had I really believed that there was something better and more principled in leaving him out there like that – exposed to the elements – rather than driving him around the city in my boot?

I wasn't sure any more.

I couldn't think straight.

Yet I maintained enough of a spark to know what I had to play with. If the police wanted the whole story, they'd have to come through me. For better or for worse, I had answers they didn't yet – not everything, but enough. With my help, they could join the dots, knit everything together, and there'd be something close to a complete picture. Without my cooperation, they'd carry on the search, never having the opportunity to call on Korman and Grankin, and particularly on Calvin East, who'd revealed so much about the life of the arcade, its machines, its secrets.

The only lies I told them were to safeguard Healy.

I assured them that Grankin was dead before I ever arrived at St David's, and pushed a theory that Korman was cutting off every avenue back to whatever it was they had done together. It was an obvious but logical route to take, not least because Korman had already accounted for Calvin East, for Carla Stourcroft and Gail Clark, even for Gary and Joseph Cabot, who thought the pier had just been a tourist attraction – and the twins, who knew even less than that. It made sense to Bishara, to Sewinson too, a petite detective sergeant on his team, who had a hard south London accent laced with steel and mistrust, and who asked most of the questions. After all, if Korman was prepared to kill himself, why *would* he leave Grankin alive? There was no logic in ignoring a loose end.

When they asked me if I knew who the person was who'd been caught on CCTV camera, scaling the front gates of St David's minutes before police arrived, I said I figured it was Korman; that he'd done a loop and come back around to the house at Whitehall Woods to grab a forensic suit. When they asked me why, if that was the case, he didn't just burn the place down before he left, I told them it was because he would have been spotted and cornered that way. Police were only seconds away by the time he jumped the gate. In using a forensic suit, in taking his time, he'd almost been able to walk in and walk out again.

Every time I tried to protect Healy with a lie, I thought of him, of what he might be doing, and how he might be dealing with the fallout. He was somewhere safe for the moment, holed up in a hotel not far from my house. But while I could protect him from other people, at least for now, I couldn't protect him from himself. That was what worried me most. He'd barely spoken in the hours after we'd left the museum. At the hotel, he'd gone to the toilet and locked the door, and I'd been able to hear him sobbing. Before I'd left to hand myself in early the next morning, he'd told me that it wasn't over, not until we found out why the girls had been killed. But I wondered, with Korman and Grankin dead, if we would ever know – and whether, in some ways, it might even be better that way.

The other thing I had to sidestep was an eye-witness account from the day the pier was set on fire. At first, I thought they were still pushing what Korman had anonymously called in, but then realized it was a genuine eyewitness living in one of the flats surrounding the pier. She claimed to have seen two men out on the promenade in the minutes before it went up in flames. 'Maybe she meant she saw me and, sometime after, she saw Korman,' I said to Bishara and Sewinson.

'She said she saw two people at the same time,' Sewinson replied.

I nodded. 'Maybe Grankin was there too.'

'So you're saying she saw Korman and Grankin?'

'I was alone.'

She eyed me, face neutral.

'I don't play well with others,' I said, attempting a half-smile. It was met with absolutely no response at all. Ultimately, I wasn't sure if they believed me or not, but I hadn't once deviated from the account I'd given them, so they couldn't accuse me of changing my story. A couple of times I saw them trying to trap me, clever attempts at backing me into a corner and forcing me to come to a different conclusion, or present a different set of circumstances. But I managed to head them off, and after a while there became fewer gaps for them to come at me through.

Eventually, they couldn't find any gaps at all.

My solicitor had always been Liz, my former neighbour, my ex-girlfriend, but when she moved out, it was because she wasn't coming back, not for me, nor for anything I became involved in, so

I took the name of a solicitor the police gave me, and called him. He was an earnest man in his fifties, starchy and humourless, but he did what I needed him to. He listened to me, advised me, worked with the Met to draft an agreement where I wouldn't be charged if I provided information that helped progress the investigation and close the case, and – after I signed it – he remained there in the room, taking notes, as I recounted everything I knew.

# CHAPTER 76

Eventually, the flow of information went both ways.

'After you gave us the name of Korman's antiques shop,' Bishara said, 'we raided it. Ninety-nine per cent of the stuff in there was legitimate antiques.'

'But not all of it?'

Bishara shook his head. 'Not all of it.'

'What else was there?'

'You ever heard of "murderabilia"?'

I had. It was the term used to describe antiques or collectables that were connected or related to violent crimes, or formerly owned by murderers themselves. It might be poetry written by killers. Artwork. Possessions. Diaries. *It could be watches, gold chains, cigarette lighters or waistcoats.*

*It could be flayed skin.*

'Korman was a collector?'

Bishara nodded. 'He had a storage area behind the counter, which he kept covered with a carpet. We found some knives inside, mounted in frames, which we can assume Korman bought or acquired somehow. We found other things too, yet to be catalogued and analysed – including some pricey medical equipment . . .' Bishara stopped. 'We think some of it was stolen from the Dead Tracks.'

Its name froze the blood in my veins. My experience in Hark's Hill Woods, nicknamed the Dead Tracks by locals, had brought me into contact with the man that had murdered Healy's daughter; a man called Glass. He was in prison now, but the ripples of his awful crimes continued onwards in the hands of collectors like Korman. It made a certain kind of sense that Korman would find a fascination in Glass: the two men had never met, and never would – but they were both responsible for destroying the same person's life.

It also confirmed now why Korman didn't have to run his business like everyone else, only opening when he wanted to work, and closing it when he didn't – because his bottom line was being bolstered by a lucrative sideline.

Bishara gave me a moment more and then continued, quietly, solemnly: 'We found DNA belonging to three separate people inside the oil drums.'

My stomach clenched.

'Two, we haven't been able to ID yet,' Bishara said.

'And the third?'

'We think that belongs to Ana Yost.'

The idea sickened me, but it didn't surprise me. And, as I mulled it over, I started to line everything up.

'David?'

I looked at Bishara. 'I was just thinking, Grankin must have got Neil and Ana Yost out to the pier somehow. Maybe he told them he worked there and he had a set of keys. Maybe they were all drunk after the fancy-dress ball. Maybe they saw it as a dare. However he did it, Korman was waiting there, and he killed Neil and Ana, and then stuffed them into the drums and turned them to ash. Then Korman and Grankin just waited for the right moment.'

'The right moment?'

'To remove them again. No one was going to think to look for the Yosts on the pier, so Korman and Grankin could just bide their time. Once they felt the coast was clear, I think they came back at night, most likely by boat, loaded the drums on and then scattered what was left of Neil and Ana into the Thames. There wouldn't have been much. Maybe the teeth, because they don't burn, even at a thousand degrees Celsius – but how are you going to find individual teeth in a river that's two hundred and fifteen miles long?'

'So who are these other two we've found traces of in the oil drums?'

'Other victims.'

'Are you saying we're dealing with a pair of serial killers?'

'If we are, it'll be serial *killer* – singular. Korman was the killer. I'm not sure Grankin was. Or, at least, he didn't kill for pleasure. Gail Clark, the twins, probably Carla Stourcroft too – they were all murdered by Korman.' I stopped, and let my thoughts align. 'When the two of them bought the house in Whitehall Woods, they switched locations: they stopped using the pier as a kill site, and started using the children's home. It wasn't just for symbolic reasons, although that was part of the appeal – it was safer at St David's too. If Grankin had been desperately trying to hose blood off the walls, I'd suggest whoever it belonged to was killed recently. Maybe the DNA in the oil drums is theirs.'

I swallowed, tasting bile in my throat.

'What about the audio tapes?' Sewinson asked. 'You said you found a cassette recorder on the pier, and we found one in St David's too, on the floor of the room in which Korman killed Grankin. There was a tape there too, but it's ruined. No chance of recovering anything. Any idea what they were recording?'

'No,' I said.

'Why put something on tape in the first place?'

'I don't know.'

'Why use such old technology?'

'I don't know,' I repeated, and it wasn't a complete lie: I hadn't been able to work out why Grankin would record Gail dying, why Korman and Grankin might possibly have recorded the Yosts' deaths too, and why they'd used an old-style tape deck and not a camera or a phone. But I couldn't tell Bishara or Sewinson that. I couldn't tell them that Gail's last moments had been captured on tape, because if I admitted that, I admitted I was in the room when it was playing, and my lie about Korman being the one who'd killed Grankin would be exposed.

'Have you found any other tapes anywhere?'

Sewinson didn't reply. In the seat next to her, Bishara's head had dropped. He wasn't keen on talking about anything to do with what had happened at the children's home, because then we had to start talking about the fire, and that was where he found himself exposed. He'd allowed Korman to breach a crime scene and then set that crime scene alight. It wasn't Bishara's fault, but – along with the SOCO – it was his responsibility. I sensed part of the reason he'd chosen to take the deal with me was because he saw a way of advancing the case more quickly. But it was hard to see how he walked away from this unharmed, given the way it would play out in the media. Someone had to be hung out to dry.

I turned my mind back to the museum instead, to Korman's suicide, to the holdall. 'What about the items I found in the museum?'

'The holdall?' Sewinson moved forward in her seat, flipping through a couple of pages to some notes she'd made. 'They're with forensics.'

'I think the mask will tell us,' I said.

Sewinson frowned. 'Tell us what?'

'The reason Korman returned to St David's.'

'I don't follow.'

'The reason he took such a risk in coming back to St David's, in disguising himself, was to get inside and retrieve the mask.'

'And you know this how?'

'It's a hunch. But the mask *meant* something to Grankin, because he was the one that wore it – and it must have meant something to Korman if he was prepared to put everything on the line to get it back. It's got something on it, or *in* it, that would have created trouble for them.'

'Such as?'

'I don't know. DNA evidence, the type of plastic it's made from, the crack in it – *something*. Something big enough for Korman to take that risk.'

Sewinson didn't look convinced.

'What about the skin?'

'We're waiting on forensics,' she said blandly. 'We've got a lot of evidence here, Mr Raker. You've got to respect the fact that it takes time to—'

'If there *are* other victims, do you think they all ended up the same way?' Bishara asked.

Sewinson glanced at him, surprised at the change of direction, or maybe the fact that he was entertaining my opinion at all. They'd kept things pretty close to their chests, with Sewinson especially circumspect. But if it wasn't clear before, it was crystal clear now: Bishara wasn't interested in dancing around the edges of the case for all the reasons I'd suspected. If he was going to get sent out to be publicly flogged, he was going to do it armed with everything he needed.

'Yes,' I said. 'Burning them is how they got rid of them.'

'Why not do the same to Gail, to the girls, to Carla Stourcroft?'

'Gail and the girls, Stourcroft, they were never supposed to be a part of this. But because of the way Stourcroft and Gail started looking into the pier, they *became* a part of it. They weren't chosen, they just became something that Korman and Grankin had to deal with. Psychologically, they didn't see the Clarks and Stourcroft as the same as the others, if there *are* others – plus, by doing it the way they did, by mixing it up like that, they didn't create a pattern.'

'But there already *is* a pattern if there were others,' Bishara countered. 'If they were luring people in, and then killing them, there's a pattern.'

'A pattern of disappearances.'

'But a pattern all the same.'

As he watched me, I got the sense he was trying to lead me somewhere. 'I'm not sure I get where you're going with . . .' But then I stopped, looked at him. 'You don't think you're going to get any matches on the rest of the DNA in the oil drums.'

Bishara started nodding before I'd even finished my sentence. 'We've got DNA belonging to three separate people. I think there's a reason Ana Yost is the only one that has popped up on the radar so far. I mean, think how long Korman and Grankin could have been doing this. When did they first start using the pier – when it closed in 1993? Or was it later, when Grankin took on the security there? Whenever it was, apart from the Yosts, not a single red flag has gone up in all that time in relation to people disappearing in the same way they did. Why?'

I thought about it – but not for long. How did you make sure your victims were never identified? 'The other victims are illegal immigrants.'

'Bingo.' He looked at Sewinson, then back to me. 'We found the remains of a smashed cassette tape in a rubbish bag at the back of Grankin's house and managed to recover about twenty seconds of usable audio from it. It's not much, but it's enough. It has the sound of a man screaming in Romanian on it.'

If the majority of victims were here illegally, there would be no record of them, and no indication they were missing. In the end, except perhaps for Neil and Ana Yost, Korman and Grankin had taken untraceable people to a lonely place and they'd reduced them all to ash. But, if that was true, why did Korman and Grankin take the Yosts? Taking Neil and Ana represented much more of a risk than taking someone no one even knew was in the country.

'What about the infra-red map?'

Sewinson returned me to the moment.

I looked at her. 'What about it?'

'What was its purpose?' She came forward at the table. 'Why even go to the trouble of creating it in the first place? It's not like they were going to forget where the holdall was.'

'I don't think it's *only* a map,' I said, giving voice to a theory I'd been kicking around. 'I think it was like an altar to them. To further the analogy, it's what they worship. The museum, its machines, is the church. I think they stored each of the five items in the five machines that were repeatedly varnished – the watch, the lighter, the chain, the waistcoat, the skin – and they kept the mask inside the bigger one. The mask was the centrepiece. That's why all the rear doors were open on the five smaller machines, and why the one on the Haunted House was shut: because when the walls started closing in, Korman returned to the museum and transferred everything to the holdall and locked it inside the centrepiece, hoping it would never be found.'

I stopped, recalling how Korman had looked out at the arcade before killing himself. *The way a parent looked at their child.* 'I think the arcade meant something to them. They had some attachment to it. Korman knew the Haunted House was the best one to hide everything in. It's difficult to get out from the pillar. It's boxed in. The back panel is hard to prise open. It makes sense.'

'Why bother going to the trouble of hiding them if all he was going to do was kill himself?' Sewinson said.

'I'm not sure.'

'And the items represent what?' Bishara asked.

'The mask, I don't know. Grankin wore it the night Korman killed Gail and the girls. He wore

604

it to the fancy-dress ball when he took the Yosts.'
I paused, trying to piece it together. 'Maybe it's
the one thing that links everything.'

'Everything?'

'Every life they've taken. I don't know, I'm
stretching here, but maybe the mask is part of
their MO – something they bring out for every
kill – while the five other items stay where they
are, in the machines at the arcade. The mask was
Korman and Grankin's present, something they
continued to make use of. The other items were
their history, something they left on display; a
reminder.'

Sewinson nodded. 'The other items are from
their first kill.'

'Maybe.'

'But we've done a database search for those
missing items.'

'There's nothing?'

She shook her head. 'Nothing.'

I thought of East again, of how Korman and
Grankin had paid him off, and of how they'd
continued to manipulate him. He'd talked to me
about not finding anything inside the machines
when he'd looked – but, while Grankin worked at
the museum, he must have been watching East
the whole time, shifting the items around when
needed, and returning them to their rightful place
when East was done. Over time, Grankin got better
at transporting the cases too, so that meant no
more scratches or cracked glass, and nothing to

raise suspicions in East. In the end, it didn't matter that Grankin had to get himself fired to secure his alibi for the night the Clarks were killed – he might not have been at the museum any more but, by then, East had stopped looking for abnormalities on the machines. He'd long since accepted his fate.

As if thinking the same thing, Sewinson said, 'They were taking a hell of a risk leaving those items in the arcade like that.'

'I don't think they were.'

'They left evidence right there the whole time.'

'Exactly. You can apply the same theory to the pier and St David's. These are places we pass every day but don't look inside. We don't access them, even though they're in plain sight. Korman and Grankin knew that. They knew, as well, that if they controlled Calvin East, they controlled this place they'd created as a celebration of their work. East would have been the only one who might have found out the truth about what they were hiding, because Gary Cabot had long since given up repairing machines. That was why Grankin kept such a tight rein on East, and which machines he was taking home to repair.'

There was a heavy silence in the room as we all thought about the way the machines had been removed and varnished, used to create a map; the way the very centre of the map, the holdall, appeared to contain items taken from yet another victim, as yet unknown. The innocent people

Korman and Grankin had chosen had spent their last days facing a version of hell they could never have imagined might exist. And after that, they were consigned to oil drums, and their ashes scattered on water, on land, wherever they would never be found again.

Now there was really only one question left, and I thought of Healy again as I asked it: 'Why did they kill the twins?'

Sewinson had started writing something, but now looked up at me. Next to her, Bishara pushed aside his coffee. 'Their mother was killed in the room next door,' he said. 'They were a loose end.'

'Is that what you call it?'

He opened out his hands. 'You know what I mean.'

'Korman referred to them as "duplicitous".'

'Who?'

'The twins.'

Bishara frowned, glancing at Sewinson. 'What did he mean by that?'

'I don't know,' I said.

'Korman was a psychopath.'

I nodded, letting Bishara know that he was right, and that I should probably just forget it. But I couldn't forget it. It was playing on my mind, because it was playing on Healy's mind. I'd tried to convince myself that maybe it was better not knowing, that the answer might be worse than the question.

But the argument rang hollow.

Those girls were joyful, innocent – I'd seen it myself on Calvin East's home video. They weren't deliberately duplicitous. They were eight years old. And that was what I couldn't let go.

# CHAPTER 77

The evening I finally got home from the station, I collapsed on the bed and slept for almost fourteen hours, lying there – fully dressed, on top of the sheets – unaware of the thunder that passed across the sky, or the breeze drifting through the open window. For a while, I was unaware of the doorbell going at 9 a.m. the next day either, until my phone started buzzing in my jacket pocket, vibrating against the edge of my hip bone. I stirred, at first incapable of pulling myself out of the fugue, before finding enough energy to locate the phone and answer it, eyes still shut.

'Hello?'

'It's me.' *Craw.* 'Are you home?'

'Hold on.'

Slowly, I swung myself around in bed and made my way to the front door. She was standing there, under the protection of the porch, rain jagging out of the sky behind her, dressed in a long black raincoat, grey trousers and black heels. I saw her look me up and down, my clothes crumpled, my hair standing on end, a mix of amusement and pity in her face, and then – without me saying anything – she stepped up, into the house, brushed past me and headed for the kitchen.

'You look like you need a coffee,' she said.

I pushed the door shut. 'I need a shower first.'

After I was done, I returned to the kitchen, and she was standing at one of the windows, looking out at the front garden. Her car, a red Mini, was parked where my BMW would have been if it hadn't been parked in a forensics lab.

'Morning,' I said, rubbing at an eye.

She turned. 'Morning.'

She'd clipped her fringe back from her face on the left-hand side, and it had now become long enough at the back to tie into a small ponytail. It gave her slender features a different slant, revealing more of her eyes and cheekbones. I'd spoken to her once since handing myself in, from a payphone inside the station, a conversation that had lasted thirty minutes, and in which I'd told her everything I'd found out. For half an hour she'd just listened, silently, on the other end of the line. Afterwards, I wasn't sure why I'd been so candid. She couldn't help me then, and she wouldn't have been able to help me if I'd been charged, and much of our relationship had been built on an unspoken under-standing that we might never feel comfortable giving so much of ourselves away. Yet I'd told her all the same. Perhaps a part of me was just sick of holding on to everything.

'How are you feeling?' she said.

I shrugged and picked up the coffee that she'd left for me. 'I didn't land you in trouble, did I?'

I'd called her twice before I'd handed myself in – once from Wanstead Flats when I'd still had Calvin East in the boot of my car; and once from St David's. The second time, she'd called Bishara, her equivalent in the borough of Waltham Forest, and told him he needed to get a team down there. As a result, Craw's commanding officer would have wanted to know why it was her I'd chosen to contact.

'I said we had history,' she said, smiling.

'Well, that's not a lie.'

'They know about Dad, and what you did for me last year. They don't approve of it, but they know. They assume you chose to call me because of that.' She eyed me for a moment. 'So you didn't answer my question: how are you?'

I shrugged again. 'Why did they kill those girls?'

'Life meant nothing to those men.'

'That wasn't the reason why.'

'It's *a* reason.'

*Kids can be duplicitous too.* 'It's not *the* reason.'

She studied me. 'So what's next?'

I perched myself on one of the stools.

'Raker?'

'I don't know,' I said. 'Maybe nothing's next.'

'You're just going to let it go?' She said it with an even expression, but it was clear she didn't believe me. When I didn't respond, she said, 'I don't know if you're looking for advice, but I'm going to give you some anyway. Why don't you see what Bishara comes up with? Forensically, I mean.'

'I don't think he'll be calling me in a hurry.'

A half-smile. 'I'm sure he won't.'

She didn't say anything else, although there was a hint of something in her face. 'Are you offering to help me?' I said.

In her pocket, her phone started ringing.

She took it out, looked at the display and said to me, 'I've got to go.' But she didn't make a move to leave. 'Look, I know Bishara a little. We went on a course together after he moved down here. We spent four weeks in each other's company, and after a month you get the measure of someone. He's a clever guy, and he'll pull this investigation together, and everything that needs to be ticked off *will* be ticked off. But the reason why those girls were murdered . . .'

I got where she was going. 'That won't get ticked off.'

She didn't commit either way, but it was obvious that was what she'd been driving at. 'It's a four-year-old case that's been tainted by a disgraced detective.'

'The girls don't have to suffer because Healy—'

'I'm telling you how it's viewed at the Met. That's all. What you've got to understand is that no one's going to prison for this. There's no conviction on the line here. Korman, Grankin, they're dead. Bishara's got the Clarks, the Yosts and Carla

612

Stourcroft to deal with, before you even get into who the DNA in those barrels belongs to. He's got techs inside those machines at the museum, he's got a fire-damaged pier and a half-gutted children's home. He's got the very real prospect of a suspension in the pipeline too. Fact is, he doesn't have time to find out *why* the girls had to die – however wrong that seems to you. I mean, maybe there *is* no why. Korman was a depraved psychopath. Is it so surprising that he'd kill them as well as their mother?'

I understood the logic, but it still didn't feel right.

'So are you offering to help me?' I repeated.

She didn't reply immediately, glancing at her phone again, at whatever was on the display. 'I'll keep you up to date with things I feel are relevant.'

'Which means what?'

'Which means exactly what I just said.'

I stared at her. 'It's not even your borough.'

'But I know people there.'

'And you're prepared to do this why?'

'Because otherwise you're going to be chasing around after Healy's ghost until there's nothing left of you. And because I'm a parent too, and I can't let this slip through the cracks. I think you're right, basically. Maybe you've *always* been right.' She pocketed her phone. 'Those girls deserve an answer.'

# CHAPTER 78

After Craw left, I made some calls.

The first one was to Gemma, to see how she was. She didn't cry this time, her tears for Healy all used up at his funeral, but it was hard to hear the emotion in her voice and sit there in silence, knowing the truth about her husband's fate. I thought of him a couple of times, as she referenced things they'd done together – days when their marriage had seemed viable, even good – and pictured him in the place he was now: a bland hotel room half a mile away, alone and in pain.

'Thank you for everything, David,' Gemma said to me as the call began to fizzle out. 'Thank you for finding out what happened to Colm, for all your help with the funeral – for bringing Liam and Ciaran, *me*, some sort of explanation.'

My lies stung even more now, sitting right in the centre of my chest, the truth so close to the edges of my tongue, for a moment it felt like I was about to tell her. But I didn't. I muttered some conciliatory words, said goodbye, then sat there at the windows of the living room, remorseful, troubled, watching the rain.

Eventually, I hauled myself up, made some lunch and then spent an hour chatting to Annabel on Skype. It was a relief to see her, to hear her voice, to think about something else. After ten minutes of filling me in on what had happened at work, and then another fifteen talking about a parents' evening she'd been to for Olivia, she stopped, a slight frown on her face, and I knew what was coming.

'I know I keep saying this, but—'

'I'm fine, sweetheart.'

She smiled. 'You look tired.'

'That's just old age.'

The smile drifted away. I felt a bubble of annoyance at not being able to deter her, and frustration that I'd been so easily read. I knew her question only came from concern, but I didn't want to get into the case with her, because then I'd start having to lie to her, and I feared that would be even harder to hide.

'I just haven't been sleeping well,' I offered.

She nodded. 'Because of Healy.'

I couldn't look her in the eyes as I replied, 'Yeah, him. But, you know, not just that. Some work stuff, people, relationships . . . Plus I miss seeing you both.'

'Why don't you come down?'

'I promised you both that you could come here.'

We'd planned for them to stay for the week during Olivia's half-term, but all that had fallen by the wayside after I'd found the body beneath Highdale.

That moment seemed so far away now: the warm weather, thinking Healy was dead, realizing that the truth was just another well-concealed lie. Maybe that was what was making me look tired, and adding to my fatigue: all the deception.

And not just other people's.

'I'm fine, though,' I said to Annabel. 'Honestly. Last night I slept for almost fourteen hours. I'm back on track. Maybe I can come down to Devon in a couple of weeks and see you. We can go crabbing. Last time, I *trounced* you both.'

She laughed. 'You certainly did not.'

'I did.'

'I caught two more than you.'

'Lies!'

'Even Olivia hooked more than you did.'

'Double lies!'

And so it went on, our conversation slowly changing course as I put on a show for my daughter that settled her anxiety and let her know that I was fine.

I maintained my smile for her until after I'd quit out of Skype, and then – as the last frame of her left a ghostly mirror-image on the screen – I let the smile drop away, and sat there staring at my laptop, wondering where I went next.

# CHAPTER 79

The answer was Neil and Ana Yost.

That night, as I lay sprawled on the sofa, the room lit only by a small lamp on a side table, I realized that of everything I'd uncovered, everything I'd found out, I knew least about them. They were just more victims, seduced by Grankin, their fate hidden by shadows, what I knew of their lives beginning and ending inside the lines of a newspaper story pinned to the walls of a half-melted house.

I put in a search for them, and discovered the same newspaper stories I'd seen already: picture-perfect accounts of a beautiful couple in their twenties, two weeks into marriage, who'd attended a fancy-dress party and never come home.

Collating as many links as possible, including the subsequent search for them, I remembered Bishara's theory: that if there *were* other victims, they'd be illegal immigrants, to prevent them from being missed, and to make identification even harder. Yet that wasn't who the Yosts were.

Something about that didn't sit right with me.

Did the fact that Korman and Grankin took a

risk with the Yosts suggest that, in their eyes, Neil and Ana were more like Gail, Stourcroft and Healy? Were they people who could have cost Korman and Grankin their secrecy, through knowing that something was going on at the pier, at the museum? Were they people who were cut down before their investigations could go any further?

The idea was a good one, but as I went through what I could find of their history, I couldn't see anything to support it. Neil Yost had just qualified as a vet, Ana worked as a campaign manager for an advertising agency in Holloway. I couldn't find a single thing to connect them to Wapping, let alone to the pier. They lived in Ruislip. His parents were in Durham; hers were from Hounslow. The fancy-dress party they'd attended the night they vanished had been a charity gala, raising funds for disadvantaged kids. Why had Grankin made such an effort to be there that night? What had put Neil and Ana on his radar in the first place? I couldn't see any clear lines connecting the Yosts to either him or Korman.

And yet he'd been there all the same.

I started to wonder whether, perhaps, he'd met them there by chance and just acted on impulse. Maybe he'd got them back to the pier, put them in front of Korman, but Korman hadn't liked it, had seen the risk in deviating from their usual choice of victim. It made a certain kind of sense, because – in all of this – Korman was the driving force, the dominant power. He was the real killer.

I continued working through the stories about the Yosts, making some notes, but as the coverage began to wane, so the same old details were repeated: their recent marriage, their dream honeymoon in the Maldives, what eyewitnesses at the party had said about the man in the mask and the fact he'd had an accent. After a while, even the tragic disappearance of a beautiful, newly-wed couple couldn't keep either of them on the front pages.

I picked up my phone and dialled the number of the spare I normally kept in the bedroom. It wasn't in the bedroom now. It was half a mile from my front door, in a hotel room on Uxbridge Road.

'Hello?'

'It's me,' I said.

Healy sounded groggy. 'What time is it?'

'Almost 11 p.m.'

There was a risk in putting Healy into a hotel, a chance he might be seen. I felt the risk was lessened by the fact that it was my name in reception, my name on the booking, and I'd told him not to go out unless he absolutely had to. If I was concerned about anything, it wasn't him being there. It was him being alone.

Was he still suicidal? Would I turn up there in a week and discover that he'd *really* swallowed the pills this time? Four days after Korman had killed himself in front of us, Healy was still living and breathing – and yet I hadn't been able to relax. It wasn't just the idea of him taking his own life which continually nipped at me, it was the thought of what we would do if he went the other way and decided to embrace this new existence, to start again. He would always be in the shadows, worried about being exposed. He'd made an irreversible choice – one where he could never maintain a normal life again.

'I've been thinking about Neil and Ana Yost,' I said.

'What about them?'

'Why were they selected?'

'What do you mean?'

'Police have got traces of two other unidentified people in the oil drums. That's two other victims, potentially. Then there's whoever the items in the holdall belong to. The identities of all those victims have been well hidden. On the flip side, you've got Gail, Carla Stourcroft and you, people who were in the process of making, or about to make, waves for Korman and Grankin. You all suspected that something was going on at the pier. So you were dealt with, but in a different way. It was short, sharp. A murder. A murder-robbery. An assault that you weren't supposed to wake up from. You were never part of the fantasy.'

'Murders.'

'What?'

'Mur*ders*. It wasn't just Gail.'

He was right, of course: there were two other

deaths, perhaps the hardest to take of all, impossible to forget, unexplained, essentially unsolved. It made me wonder what was worse: not seeing the killer face justice – or not knowing his reasons.

*Kids can be duplicitous too.*

Healy cleared his throat. 'Are you saying that, despite how they were killed, you think they've got more in common with Gail, Stourcroft and me?'

'It's a theory I'm kicking around.'

A pause. 'I can take a look in the box.'

He was talking about the box that Carla Stourcroft's husband had passed to him when Healy had pretended to be with the Met. We'd returned to the house in Camberwell after I'd finished at the police station, and removed everything – the box, the handwritten notes that Healy had stuck to the walls, the transcript.

Now the box was in his hotel room.

'Is there anything else in there you haven't been through?' I asked him.

'No.' He sounded despondent. 'Anything on the pier, anything related to it, related to the disappearance of that couple, I put on the wall. Everything else is just Stourcroft's personal belongings.'

'And you've been through those too?'

'Yeah. Her husband said it was mostly stuff he cleared out from her office. A lot of old paperwork, framed book covers, desk junk – pencils and calendars, all that sort of shite. I'll take a look at it again – but I wouldn't go expecting much.'

'All right.'

'I'll talk to you tomorrow.'

I hung up and closed the laptop, feeling tiredness kicking in again. When I closed my eyes, I saw photographs, frozen moments in time that I might never be able to erase: a mother, nine stab wounds in her chest, her life leaking out across a sofa; and two girls, skin so pale and flawless, reduced to statues in their beds.

My phone woke me up.

I started and felt my laptop fall off, on to the carpet. As I opened my eyes, sunlight blinded me, arcing through the windows of the living room, bathing me in winter sun. I sat up and swung around, checking my watch, confused, bleary.

7.32 a.m.

I'd been asleep for eight hours.

My phone continued ringing. I stood, unsure for a moment where I'd left it the night before, then saw it buzzing on the floor next to me. I scooped it up.

*Craw.*

'You keep waking me up,' I said, after I'd answered it.

I'd tried to lace my voice with some humour, but maybe it was too early in the morning for that. Craw didn't respond to the joke – and I heard a door close.

'Craw?'

'Are you functioning?' she said.

'Barely.'

'Well, you'd better clear your head.'

I frowned. 'Why? What's the matter?'

'You're going to want to hear this.'

# CHAPTER 80

'I've just got off the phone to someone I know in Bishara's team,' Craw said. She spoke in hushed tones, clearly squirrelled away in a room where no one would be able to hear her. 'He says they've had forensics back on the items you found.'

She was talking about the waistcoat, the lighter, the gold chain, the watch, the flayed skin. The mask. I headed across the room to where I'd left my notepad.

'What did they find?' I asked.

'The wristwatch was made by a company called Wirrek. You probably know that already. Their name is on the watch face. You ever heard of them before?'

'No. Never.'

'That's because they went out of business in 1956. The watch is an antique, made in 1943. The cigarette lighter is even older – maybe 1940 or '41. The manufacturer's mark has been rubbed off because of its age, but my guy says the forensic team managed to narrow it down to an American company called . . .' She paused, presumably checking what she'd written. 'Purridean. Looks like these lighters were popular with GIs. The assumption is that it got left here by a US soldier after the end of the Second World War. The gold chain and the waistcoat are much harder to put a date on, but the flayed skin . . . that tattoo is old. The ink's old. The skin has been coated with some sort of preservative, a mix of chemicals that you can't even get on the market now because most are carcinogenic.'

'What about the mask?'

'This is where it gets weird: the mask has got a label inside that says it was made by a company called Barrington Games – they were a toy company.'

'"Were"?'

'They closed in 1958.'

'So the mask's old too.'

'Right.'

'What's so weird about that?'

'No other companies make masks like that any more – not from that same material, or to the same design. However, Bishara's team found a business card in Grankin's kitchen for a company called Masquerade – they're a high-end fancy-dress and party company based near Spitalfields Market. They also happen to make custom-order masks for rich people with too much money. Bishara sent one of his detectives to speak to the manager, and this woman says that they've been repairing the same mask, for the same person, on and off, for the last twenty-one years. I'll do the maths for you: twenty-one years means the first time this person came in was in 1993.'

The same year the pier closed.

*The same year Korman and Grankin started using it as a kill site.*

'Did she ID this person?'

'It was Grankin. Bishara's people showed her a picture, and – straight away – she said it was him. She said that, every couple of years, he'd always bring the same mask in with him and have her work on it, trying to secure it, touch it up, whatever else – basically trying to stop it falling apart due to age. First time he came in, she saw the crack on the mask and said to Grankin that she'd try and close the gap and fix it. But he told her no. He said he wanted the crack on the mask. He said that was what made it unique.'

I paused for a second, thinking. Clearly, the mask represented something important to Grankin – but what? Why have it repaired, year after year, but not its obvious flaw? Why not just buy a new one?

'Look,' Craw said, 'I've got to run.'

'All right. Thanks for this.'

But, seconds after she'd hung up, my mind was already moving, returning to something Korman had said to me. I grabbed my laptop, his words still clear.

*I think you need a change of perspective.*

I thought he'd been talking about the arcade,

about seeing it in a different way, through a different lens. Maybe he *had* meant that. It had certainly, perhaps inadvertently, led me to the holdall and the mask. But maybe he meant something else too. Maybe he meant that the pier and museum were a sideshow; that they led to something else. Something even worse.

My phone erupted into life again.

This time it was Healy. Last night, he'd agreed to go back through Carla Stourcroft's possessions, double-checking the box her husband had passed on.

'There's nothing in here,' he said, once I'd answered.

'Nothing? No more notes?'

'You've already seen all her notes.'

And they were all indecipherable, written in a bespoke pseudo-shorthand that she'd developed to keep them private. I hadn't been able to translate them.

'You're absolutely sure?' I said.

'Positive.'

'There's nothing else in the box at all?'

He sighed, his breath crackling down the line, and then started to list everything in a bored voice: 'Photos of her family. One with her husband. One with her kids. One with husband *and* kids. A certificate from the Institute of Leadership. A 2009 desk calendar. Some screen wipes. Two pencils. One copy of *South of the River* by Carla Stourcroft. One copy of *From Richmond to Regent:*

627

*London's Parks from A to Z* by Carla Stourcroft.
One copy of *Invisible Ripper*—'

'Okay, I get it, Healy.'

'It's just junk.'

I shifted my thoughts forward, trying to carve a path through everything I'd found out from Craw, from Bishara and Sewinson before that – and then something struck me about the holdall I'd found in the arcade. *There were five items inside.*

Five *different* items.

'The stuff you just listed,' I said.

'What about it?'

I pulled my laptop towards me.

'Raker?'

But I was hardly hearing him now.

I put in a new web search. It took me to an account of five murders, long past, that I'd never given a second's thought to. And yet, the whole time I was working this case, the whole time I was trying to find the men who killed the Clark family, all five deaths were within sight of me, waiting to be brought back into the light. Edward Smythe. Gordon Gregory. Eric Bale. William Simpkins. Abel Dimas.

*I think you need a change of perspective.*

'Raker?'

'We've been looking in the wrong Stourcroft book.'

'What?' I could sense Healy shift. 'What are you talking about?'

I felt dazed, light-headed, like a punch-drunk boxer reaching for the ropes. 'This isn't about *A Seaside in the City* at all,' I said to him. 'It's about *Invisible Ripper*.'

# CHAPTER 81

The answers had been there the whole time.
*Right in front of our eyes.*
'What are you talking about?' Healy said.
'The five items in that holdall. They don't belong to one victim. They belong to five.' I looked at their names again. 'Edward Smythe. Gordon Gregory. Eric Bale. William Simpkins. Abel Dimas. The items are Eldon Simmons's trophies.'

This time, Healy was silent.

'There's an inscription on the back of the watch,' I said, needing to talk it through as much for myself as Healy. '"To our darling Edward. With much love. Mum and Dad." That's Edward Smythe. He was Eldon Simmons's first victim.' I turned back to my laptop, scrolling down the page, skim-reading as much as possible. 'Gordon Gregory, the second, was from Maryland, and stayed in the UK after the end of the war. His friends told police he loved and cherished his Purridean lighter – but, when they searched his belongings, they couldn't find it anywhere. Because Simmons had taken it. The third victim, Eric Bale, had a crucifix lifted from him that his father had

630

given him. The fourth, William Simpkins, was found with skin missing from his right arm where a tattoo of a heart with the inscription *Life* had been cut out. And the waistcoat belonged to Abel Dimas, the last victim.'

'Let me grab the book,' Healy said.

As I heard him moving, returning to Stourcroft's box of possessions, to the copy of *Invisible Ripper* she had in there, I tried to imagine why. Why had Korman and Grankin become so consumed by Eldon Simmons's work?

'Do you know much about the case?' Healy said, when he came back on.

'Simmons? Not really. Why?'

'I'm sure there was some story . . .' He stopped, sucked in a breath, sounded frustrated with himself. 'Ah, my memory's shite, but I'm sure there was a thing in the news a few years back about him. Some retrospective on his arrest. Back in the fifties, they slapped the cuffs on him in some boarding house in White City – but something was wrong with it.'

'Wrong with the boarding house?'

'No, with Simmons's arrest.'

He paused, and I heard him flicking through the book. While he was doing that, I managed to find a brief Internet account of the Ripper case: after killing five men between August 1951 and May 1952, Simmons was found living in a tatty boarding house in west London. A neighbour called the Met and said he'd seen Simmons bringing home a succession of men, one of whom left with blood all over his face. When police went to talk to Simmons, they found a knife hidden under sheets in his wardrobe. It had traces of blood from two of the victims on it. Simmons was arrested and charged, before being sentenced to death. He was hanged at Holloway Prison in March 1953.

'The arrest seems pretty clean,' I said to Healy.

'Hold on, I'm trying to find the chapter here.'

Suddenly, the doorbell rang.

I tore my eyes away from the laptop and looked across the living room. From where I was sitting, I could see all the way down the hall. A silhouette was out on the porch, absolutely still, the shape distorted by the frosted glass.

'I'm going to have to call you back,' I said to Healy.

'Why?'

'Someone's at the door.'

'Just ignore it.'

He was right: we were on the cusp of something. I glanced at the silhouette again: petite, slim and motionless. It looked like a woman.

'Okay, got it,' Healy said.

'What does it say?'

I could hear him muttering to himself, skim-reading the chapter that dealt with Eldon Simmons's arrest. 'No, it's not this,' he said.

'What do you mean?'

'This is the same thing everyone knows – about

the police finding a knife in his bedroom, his arrest, his death. No, it was something else. What *was* it?'

'Was it something you saw on TV?'

'Maybe.'

'In the papers? Online? Where?'

'I can't remember.'

'Think, Healy.'

'I *am* thinking.'

But then the doorbell rang for a third and fourth time. When I looked up again, the woman started knocking on the door.

'His sister,' Healy said.

I tried to tune back in. 'What?'

'That's *it*. I remember now. I got it wrong – this was much more than a few years back; maybe the mid eighties. Anyway, before she died, his sister was trying to clear his name. I think Simmons had some minuscule IQ, and she claimed he was forced into signing a confession by the cops. She said the knife was planted in his room, and the Met and the courts never bothered looking at anyone else because Simmons was homosexual – and back in 1952, being gay was still a crime. His sister was the one that coined the name "Invisible Ripper".'

Off the back of that, a thought came to me. 'Has the book got an index?'

'A what?'

'An index – at the back.'

'Uh . . .' I heard pages being turned. 'Yeah. Why?'

'Is there a listing for Neil or Ana Yost?'

'Why would there be a listing for them?'

'Just have a look.'

I listened to pages being turned. 'No. Nothing.'

'Is there an Acknowledgements page?'

'Where are you going with this?'

'*Is* there?'

'Yeah, it's here. So?'

'Any mention of them there?'

A long pause. 'Shit. Yeah, there is.'

'What does it say?'

'"I'd like to thank the family of Eldon Simmons for their cooperation in the writing of this book, and for making their archive of material available to me. In trying to clear his name, the work of his sister, Moira Silke, and her daughter Ana Yost – both, sadly, gone – can only be admired."'

'Ana Yost was related to Eldon Simmons,' I said.

As we both took that in, I backed out of the true crime website I was on, and put in a search for Moira Silke, Simmons's sister and Ana Yost's mother. She'd died in 1986, from liver disease – leaving Yost to carry on the campaign to clear her uncle's name.

'She must have had something,' I said, almost to myself.

'What?'

'Yost. She must have had something, some new piece of information that was going to clear Simmons's name. That was why they got rid of her.'

'Who? Korman and Grankin?'

'Yeah.'

'But why would they even care what she had?'

'Maybe it implicated them – or whatever they were involved in.' I tapped out a rhythm on the laptop, shifting my thoughts forward again. 'What else does it say about the neighbour in there?'

'Eldon Simmons's neighbour?'

'Yeah. The one that tipped off the police about him.'

'Uh, hold on.'

The doorbell rang again.

I tried to ignore it, keeping my eyes focused on the laptop, even though I was finding it hard to concentrate. When I looked up, the woman was still standing there, face on, waiting for me to answer.

'He never left a name,' Healy said.

'What?'

'The neighbour. They traced the call to a phone box on the same street that Simmons lived on – but they never found the person who made the call.'

'Did they actually interview his neighbours?'

'Yeah, but it was a boarding house. People came and went.' Then Healy stopped and, quietly, started talking to himself, reading something back. 'Wait a second, wait a second. It says here that "a witness at the time told police she thought she might have seen the neighbour, from down the street, making the call".'

'Did she give a description?'

'No. Too far away. But she said his face was "pale and smooth".'

'"Smooth"?'

'Whatever that means.'

I thought about it for a moment, trying to line everything up, but then that word came back to me: *smooth*. Smooth, featureless, plain. *Just like Grankin had looked in the mask, the night he'd waited for Korman outside Searle House.*

'The neighbour was wearing the mask,' I said. 'It's the same mask that Grankin's been wearing.'

'*What?*'

The doorbell.

Again. Again.

'I'll phone you back in a second,' I said, pissed off now.

Ending the call with Healy, I set the laptop and the phone aside, and made my way to the front door. Halfway along the hall, I could see the woman shift as she saw me coming towards her, through the glass.

I grabbed the door and yanked it open.

'What is it?' I said sharply.

But it wasn't a woman. It was a man, small, a hood up on his parka, the front edges of it over-hanging his forehead and casting shadows across his face.

I stepped back, startled, placing a hand against the wall, steadying myself. The man on my door-step, a gun concealed in the folds of his coat, came forward.

It felt like the room turned on its axis.

This was why police never found Eldon Simmons's neighbour, the man who had tipped them off. This

636

was why Simmons's family thought he was innocent. This was why Ana Yost vanished, this was the real reason why Carla Stourcroft was killed, this was why Gail Clark was slaughtered in her home. Because, eventually, at different stages, they all began glimpsing the truth.

The Invisible Ripper didn't die in 1953.

The pier, the museum – they just became his hiding place.

'Hello, David,' Joseph Cabot said.

# CHAPTER 82

'You look surprised to see me,' he said softly, his east London accent still strong, his words croaky and hoarse. He glanced out into the road, left then right, his milky eyes sluggishly switching direction, and I realized his vision was impaired badly, probably irreversibly – but he wasn't totally blind. He just pretended he was. It was smart and it was devious – after all, who would suspect a blind man in his late eighties of anything? As if reading my thoughts, he pushed the gun towards me and said, 'Are you going to leave an old blind man out in the cold?'

I stepped back.

He checked again, up and down the street, and then came inside, moving easily, fluidly. Everything at Wonderland had been a show. He was old, slight, liver-spotted, but he wasn't delicate or immobile. As one of his eyes began to water, he pushed the front door shut behind him and backed me into the living room. He entered, his eyes narrowing as he tried to focus on my photo frames, and then on my laptop still open on the table, poised on a shot of Eldon Simmons.

As we stopped, I tried to process everything. *Craw had told me that he was dead.* Or had she? He sat on one of the sofas, gesturing for me to take the opposite settee, and I tried to remember exactly what it was she'd said. *Cabot is face down in the kitchen with his throat cut. His dad's there too. Looks like someone's closing the circle.*

She'd never actually confirmed Joseph Cabot was dead, just his son, and I'd never thought to ask about them again, to question it, to follow up on it. Healy and I had just swum for our lives from a burning pier. I'd fled a crime scene with a body in the back of my car. I'd gone for twenty-four hours without rest, a month without sleeping a single night through. I was dealing with the idea that I might be ill, that a sickness might be taking hold of me, coiling inside me like a tapeworm. I'd just assumed they were both dead, that Korman was taking care of anyone who could put him and Grankin anywhere close to the museum and the pier, instead of the reality: Korman killed Gary Cabot, but only injured his father.

A deliberate act.

Because they were all working together.

'You let Korman kill your own son,' I said.

He sighed, resting his elbow on the arm of the sofa. The sleeve of his coat sneaked a little way up his arm, and I could see evidence of bandaging, part of the injuries inflicted by Korman. They'd been clever: cutting the outside of Cabot's arm would make it look like defensive wounds. He could spin a story out of that.

He gestured to the laptop. 'Is that Eldon Simmons I can make out?'

I glanced at the stories I'd been reading, and then back to him. As I did, he came forward, gun levelled at my stomach, watching me. 'I only got out of hospital yesterday,' he said, 'so it was only then that I was able to appreciate all your fine efforts. But this works out well, because you don't know how long I've been waiting to *talk* to someone about this, about all I've achieved – and the fact that *you* get to sit there and listen to me before I'm done. This is so perfect.'

'Before you're done?'

He didn't reply. As I went to repeat myself, my phone burst into life, buzzing next to me on the sofa. It was Healy.

Cabot raised the gun off the arm of the sofa. 'Leave it.'

I ignored the phone as it continued towards me – then it snapped back into silence. I looked at him again. 'What did you mean, before you're done?'

'Why did I let him kill my own son?' he said, sidestepping the question. 'Actually, you might be interested to know that Gary wasn't my son. He was two years old when I married his mother, and then she died in a car accident when he was fifteen.' He shifted on the sofa, his spare hand straying to his left knee. There was a momentary distance to him. 'I never had any plans to be a parent. Not at the start. I never wanted to get married either, for reasons that you can probably imagine.'

He nodded at the laptop.

'Women weren't really my thing.'

'But you married Gary's mother anyway.'

'It was a good cover story,' he said, eyes still focused on the laptop. 'It looks like you've been reading about the neighbour. What was it they said about me? I had a "smooth face"?' He stopped, a flicker of a smile. 'I always liked wearing that mask. The way it felt. I liked the anonymity it gave me, the way that anonymity hands you so much power. Victor developed a fondness for it too. He was a simple boy, really, and I think – by my allowing him to wear it – he saw it as a way to get close to me; maybe to gain my approval. Benjamin, Paul – whatever you prefer – he didn't like it as much. We all have our quirks, things we adopt, ways we like to get things done. Life's a rich tapestry – isn't that what they say?' He shrugged. 'Now you understand why Ben had to retrieve it for me.'

'Because your DNA is all over it.'

'Correct.' He pointed to the laptop again. 'It won't say it on there, but after Simmons's sister died and young Ana took up the reins, things got a little hairy for a while. Ana was insatiable, absolutely obsessed about clearing her uncle's name, and she somehow managed to track down the witness that claimed to have seen Simmons's "neighbour" at the phone box that day. This witness even remembered seeing me hanging around Simmons's place in the hours before the arrest. However, the witness was just a girl, barely ten years old at the time, so the police never placed much credence in her statements back then – which was just as well.'

'For you maybe – not for Eldon Simmons.'

'That's true. This girl also described the neighbour as having "something wrong with his leg" – what police referred to in their reports as "a kind of nervous tic". Basically, a predilection for playing with his left knee.'

I paused, looking at him, at his other hand: it was on his knee as we spoke – and, as I saw it, a memory formed. *He'd been doing the same thing the day we met in Wonderland.* It reminded me of Healy, in the weeks and months before his heart attack: his hands, his fingers, drawn to the weakest part of his body.

Cabot began massaging the joint with his thumb and forefinger. 'I went to France in 1944, after the D-Day landings. I was only eighteen at the time. Got shot through the thigh by a German sniper in Caen on my second day.' He pointed at a spot just above his knee, on the outer edge of the thigh. 'Forty-eight hours of war, followed by a lifetime of pain. Does that seem fair to you?'

'It would have been fairer if you'd died out there.'

A smile, there and then gone. 'When we took Ana and her husband that night in 2007, we went to their house afterwards and removed any evidence she'd gathered from that witness. We got there before Ana had a chance to pass any of the paperwork on to Stourcroft. I mean, this was before Stourcroft had even started the *research* stage of *Invisible Ripper* – although the two of them had discussed the idea of a book. We found emails between Ana and Stourcroft to that effect.'

'And no one suspected anything?'

'What do you mean?'

'Ana Yost's disappearance. No one looked in your direction?'

He smirked. 'Do you know what Ana did for a job, David?'

'She was a campaign manager.'

'At an advertising agency and PR firm where her clients included Russian oligarchs, abortion clinics, those great believers in human rights Kazakhstan, and the Israeli government. Where, on a list of potential suspects, do you think the police would have placed "person who may have committed five murders in the early 1950s that someone else already confessed to, and was hanged for, and who has crawled out of the woodwork sixty years later to silence a woman who has no new evidence"?' He stopped again, something insidious moving across his face. 'Still, you should have seen Ana's eyes when I introduced myself to her.'

I felt sick listening to him.

Before I could ask him why they'd killed the Yosts in the way they had, he said: 'We had some good fortune too. In the time between Ana and Stourcroft first agreeing the idea of an Invisible Ripper book in 2006, and Stourcroft coming to research and write it in early 2008, the witness that saw me at Simmons's house back in 1952 – with my mask and my "nervous tic" – suffered a stroke. She couldn't talk, and it wasn't going to get any better for her. We thought we were in the clear.'

'But you weren't.'

'No. We may have got rid of the paperwork before Ana had a chance to pass it on to Stourcroft, but what we found out later was that Ana had mentioned to Stourcroft *verbally* that Simmons's neighbour had had some kind of knee problem – only once, but once was always enough for Ms Stourcroft.'

It took me a moment to catch up. In 2008, the year before Carla Stourcroft published *Invisible Ripper*, she'd interviewed another contemporary of Eldon Simmons's, Winston Cowdrey, at his flat in Wapping. They'd talked about the years Cowdrey had spent living in the same building as Simmons, and Cowdrey had mentioned seeing someone on the pier – in a mask.

Stourcroft must have felt like she'd been gut-punched. A year before that, Ana Yost had disappeared from a party, after talking to a man in a mask. Now a man in a mask was out on Wapping Pier. She wouldn't have been able to see all the links then, but, if nothing else, she wanted to find out what was going on at the pier, a place she already knew so much about from writing *A Seaside in the City*. So, in 2010, after publishing *Invisible Ripper*, she returned to see Calvin East, sniffing another story on the wind: that the man in the mask was responsible for the disappearance of Ana Yost; and that the pier had a secret.

Something else fell into place for me too. 'She saw you,' I said. 'The second time that Stourcroft went to the museum to see East, in 2010 – she saw you there.'

'Correct. I was sitting in Gary's office, waiting for him to take me home, when I looked up and spotted her in the corridor, talking to Calvin. She was just staring at me. Eventually, I realized why: I was playing with my knee again.'

That was the moment Stourcroft started to put it together.

What Ana Yost had told her. What Cowdrey had seen. She was a year too late to put it all into *Invisible Ripper* – if, at that moment, she even knew what *it* was. But she looked at Cabot and saw a flicker of history; the outline of *something*.

And that was what got her killed, what got Gail killed too: the two of them had shared all that Stourcroft knew during the interview Gail did with her; Stourcroft thought she was being followed, that she'd set something in motion, and warned Gail to be careful. But she didn't go to the police, maybe because she didn't have enough evidence, maybe because Cabot was an old, blind man, and – although unnerved by the idea of who he might be – Stourcroft couldn't see where the immediate threat was coming from. She knew that, if she was going to bring the story to the world, if she was going to do it properly, she needed time. She needed all her ducks in a row, the facts laid out for everyone to see. So she carried on piecing her investigation together, working the angles, and she carried on with her life at the same time – other paid work, family events, social get-togethers, holidays. But she never had a clue how close they were to her. She never understood that her existence was being measured in weeks, not years. Korman, Grankin and Cabot were just waiting for the right time to strike. As soon as she left for her Australian holiday in July 2010, they took care of Gail and the girls. As soon as she was back, they killed Stourcroft at the market.

And the whole thing was about a man stopping the world from finding out who he really was: a murderer six decades ago – and a murderer now.

'What do you want?' I said.

He glanced at the gun. 'Isn't it obvious?'

'You're going to shoot me?'

'I can just about make out enough of you, even with my sight the way it is. I could hit you from here if I wanted. But I don't – and you'll find out why soon enough.' It was a strange answer, one that made me think again of something he'd said earlier: *You get to sit there and listen to me before I'm done.* 'An empire falls a lot faster than it's built, David,' he went on. 'How does it feel to take down an empire? You're destroying a sixty-three-year legacy here.'

'You call what you did a "legacy"?'

'Of a sort.'

'It's murder. It's savagery, pure and simple.'

'Different perspectives,' he said ingenuously. His voice barely got above a murmur: it reminded me so much of those final moments in the arcade, listening to Korman. 'A few things are slotting into place for you now, am I right?'

I studied him, trying to keep my face neutral.

But it was true. Now, finally, I understood why Korman and Grankin had recorded the deaths of Gail Clark, of Neil and Ana Yost, of others whose identities still remained a mystery. It was proof. It was so they could take them back to Cabot and he could *hear* them taking their final breath, even if he couldn't see them.

And there was the map.

Maybe it was a kind of church to Korman and Grankin. Maybe the holdall and its contents *were* the altar to them, to Cabot as well. But it was practical too: since he was barely able to see any more, the luminosity of the pink light was the only way the Invisible Ripper could quickly and efficiently find his way back through the maze of penny arcade machines, to those original trophies.

'Sixty years is a long time to hold on to a secret,' he said, using the gun like a pointer. 'Like I said, sometimes you get tired of keeping things quiet.'

I looked at him, letting him know what I thought of him. 'Are you even aware of what you've done?'

'Oh yes,' he said, cogent, resolute. He watched me for a moment. 'I should probably tell you that I started dating Gary's mother the year that Eldon Simmons was arrested, and then we married in 1954, the year after he got the noose. I want you to know these things. It's important.'

'Why?'

'I knew I was in the clear by then,' he continued, ignoring me, 'but I didn't want to take any chances. As soon as anyone smelled gay on the wind back then . . . well, it turned into a witch-hunt. That was why I set Simmons up: I had a close call with the fifth one. Abel Dimas. He was this beautiful Spaniard I met in a bar way before I got close to killing anyone. I suppose I was working up to him, always thinking about him. I didn't want to mess it up. I planned the whole thing *so* carefully, and when I finally got him back to this hotel, when I got him alone, I wanted it to last.' He paused. It was hard to make out the detail in his eyes, his irises pearly, their direction unclear. 'But he was a screamer. He screamed a lot, even through the gag, and when I'd finished with him, and I left, I started to panic. Even though I wore that mask, I thought, "I could have got caught. I need to start over. I need to be better at this." So I hid.'

Simmons was his hiding place.

His marriage was. Gary Cabot was.

'I'd started working as a mechanic in the day,'

he went on, 'and then – at night – I'd go off and do my own thing while Gary and his mother were at home. I told her I was doing extra shifts. When I finally opened my own garage, that was when it got easier. We used to have a scrapyard next door to us, and they had this furnace, and that was when I first thought about getting rid of bodies that way. Reduce something to ash, and what are you left with?'

There was a disconcerting calmness to him.

'How many?' I said.

'How many what?'

'How many have you killed?'

He shrugged again.

'You don't even remember?'

'No,' he said. 'After a while, you lose count.'

To him, this was just a methodical unveiling of facts. He could have blandly been reading off a menu.

'Do you know how much ash an average human male leaves after you cremate him?' Cabot asked. 'Six pounds, give or take. All that blood and bone reduced to a pile of dust . . .' He cupped his spare hand. 'Until the eighties, when DNA came in and we had to be more careful, there was no better way of making someone vanish.'

'"We" being you, Korman and Grankin?'

He looked down at the gun, cloudy eyes studying it. 'How could I let my own son be killed,' he said. It wasn't a question, just an insipid repetition of what I'd asked earlier. 'That was just the thing. I didn't ever really *see* Gary as my son, I just saw him as someone I had to share my life with. Someone who would help hide me from view. That doesn't mean I didn't feel anything for him. Sometimes, I'd try so hard to look at him through a father's eyes, especially after his mother died. I tried to influence him. I tried to shape him the way I wanted him to be. But he was fifteen by then, too well adjusted, too rational and wise, and I'd say things to him sometimes, catch myself off guard, and he'd look at me, and it was like he could see all the way into me; like he could see my history and who I was, in my face. That was when I realized I had to focus my attention elsewhere.'

I frowned, unsure of what he meant.

But then, all of a sudden, I was back inside the dark, abandoned corridors of St David's, making my way through the extension, passing signs pointing out different parts of the building. *Reception. Administrative offices. The North Wing.*

*The JJC Block.*

'The Joseph J. Cabot Block,' I said.

Keeping the gun levelled at me, he began to unbutton his coat, letting it fall open. 'Very good. I'd opened four garages by 1980, the money was rolling in. I was a successful, upstanding member of society. But I was getting on. I could feel my bones beginning to creak, I was slowing down, my eyesight was getting worse, and I started to think, "What am I going to do when I'm too old?"'

'You mean, too old to murder people?'

He ignored me. 'Gary was twenty-eight by then. He'd started taking over the running of the garages and had plans to open more. He was an accomplished businessman. He was making me more money than I knew what to do with – but he couldn't give me what I *really* wanted. He was just like his mother: so strait-laced and buttoned down, so uninteresting. I used to look at him when he was in his twenties and see nothing of myself. I'd literally made no impression on him at all. I mean, I'd deliberately kept my . . .' He paused, trying to come up with the word. *Excesses. Brutality. Depravity.* 'I'd kept it all hidden from him. He obscured me. I hid behind him. He was my suit of armour. And some days I hated him for that.'

He started to drift slightly, the gun inching a little to the left. But then he snapped out of it, and we were back in my living room, his eyes settling on me.

'So I started a career of philanthropy.'

'You invested in St David's.'

'Correct. I put money in, and I attended dinners there, and the more of my pounds they took, the more I got invited back. I started watching these kids they had there while I was standing around at garden parties and summer barbecues, and they were all so boring, so samey and colourless. All of them except for one. One of them *always* caught my eye. In 1982, he would only have been eleven, but it was so clear what he was, even back then

651

– everything I didn't see in Gary, I saw in this boy.'

'Korman.'

'Yes,' he said, wistful, forlorn. 'Through him, I learned that I *did* want to be a parent, after all. He taught me about fatherhood, about caring for something; and I taught him to survive, to control, to kill – and how to keep on doing it.'

# CHAPTER 83

Cabot's breath rattled in his chest.

'Korman was his mother's maiden name,' he said. 'Benjamin Paul Gray. As the years went on, things just developed. I offered to help the home with him, to take him out; try and settle him down. He was the weird kid there that no one could get a handle on. He'd vanish, and the staff wouldn't be able to find him anywhere, and then he'd just return out of the blue.' He stopped, and I recalled something that East had said: *Korman would disappear for days, sometimes weeks at a time, and then – all of a sudden – he was back, watching you, and you didn't even realize until he stepped out of the shadows.* Cabot said, 'Do you want to know where he would go?'

'He was staying with you.'

'Right. We'd go places.' A long pause. 'Learn things.'

The temperature in the room seemed to drop. There was so much in those last two words, his tone loaded with over sixty years of cruelty and bloodshed.

'And Grankin?'

'Victor wasn't as talented as Ben. But he had a

drive, a focus, and because he wanted to belong, he was pliable. I figured he would prove useful.'

I thought about the three of them: Korman and Grankin had left St David's in 1984 – Korman still only fourteen, Grankin seventeen – and never returned. Now I knew why. Cabot had taken them in, hiding them from sight, cultivating them, developing them, brainwashing them. That went on for nine years, his own health deteriorating. By the time 1993 arrived, he was sixty-seven.

'Why the pier?' I said.

'We'd taken Gary there as a kid. He loved it. The machines fascinated him. We lived in Whitechapel at the time, so he'd make us take him down there most weekends. When it closed in '93, all it did was sit there. No one claimed it: this big, ugly, empty vessel. And then I remember being down there with Gary a few months after it shut, and he said to me, "If it didn't cost so much, I'd love to buy it and restore it." He was about the only person who was *ever* going to want to do that. Even Arnold Goldman couldn't get it to work. It was a failure. It was just going to sit there – unused – until it got demolished.'

'Not unused by you.'

'No,' he said. 'For us, it was the perfect hiding place.'

I studied him, his eyes moving around the room. They shifted fast enough, even if they didn't see much.

'Ben saw a kind of purity in the penny arcade

machines too,' he said softly, 'but for different reasons from Gary. Gary saw his childhood. He saw a chance to recapture it and invest in something. Ben saw decay and dysfunction, a place that reflected him and his tastes. The things we hid there, to him it was part of the elegance and artistry of it all.'

I watched his eyes shimmer.

'My sight had got really bad by 1993,' he continued, noticing my gaze. 'I could make out shapes, like I can make you out now, but all the detail was gone. I was almost seventy, yet I still had the taste for it. Everything I'd taught Ben over the years, from when I first took them out of that home in 1984, it was all leading up to this point. Technique. Strategy. He'd watched me, and he'd learned from me, but this was when I had to let him go. I knew I would compromise him and Victor if I went with them to the pier. I *wanted* to go, believe me, to see what it was like in there, to see our new home. But not only did they have to get someone *on* to the pier, they had to get them off again. I would have slowed them down.'

'Why take the Yosts to the pier and not Gail, or Carla Stourcroft?'

He shrugged. 'Circumstances. We needed to make them disappear as quickly as possible once Victor got them away from that gala. They were all drunk – or, at least, Victor pretended to be – which helped, so they were up for a dare. The pier made sense. All the others we could take our time with – they weren't supposed to be in the country, so no one was looking for them. People would be looking for the Yosts – but no one would be looking for them on the pier.'

'You must have been so proud.'

A twitch of a smile on his face as he reacted to my contempt. 'I wanted to enjoy those moments, which was why I used a tape recorder. I started in the days when digital recordings were just science fiction, but I never made the switch. You have more control over a single tape than you do over a digital file, out there on the Internet, leaving a footprint. I'd listen to the tapes I'd made, the tapes Ben made for me after he took up the mantle, and then – when I was done – I'd hide them among my music collection. In lieu of taking trophies, I chose them as my new keepsakes. It was only in the last couple of days that I told Victor to get rid of them all for me.'

Something else clicked into place: why Grankin had the tape of Gail's last moments. It was Cabot's. Grankin was in the process of destroying all the tapes, from *decades* of murders, but had held that one back. Perhaps he'd seen it as a way to draw Healy and me in; a way to destabilize us. It had almost worked.

'The pier was such an inspired choice,' Cabot said. 'Ben would tell me the whole pavilion smelled of seared human flesh – but no one ever went inside.'

My phone started going again. Healy, for a second time.

656

'You have persistent friends,' Cabot said.

Ten seconds later, Healy hung up again.

'Why are you telling me all of this?'

He tilted his head slightly, shifting in his seat, a hand drifting to his knee. 'You ruined everything,' he said, echoing what Korman had told me, a mix of anger and sadness in his voice.

'Korman made the decision to kill himself.'

He studied me, his face like the grey mask he'd once worn: expressionless, barren. But, still, something lingered in it; something put there after my comment about Korman. A hint of pain, a flash of remorse.

And then I got it: '*You* told him to kill himself.'

'In taking his own life, Ben was the victor.' He watched me with those eyes, inscrutable, empty, but I knew exactly what he was saying: *He agreed to kill himself in order to save me, his teacher, his father. The police were closing in. They would eventually find the link between us. So he hid the trophies in the holdall, and killed himself. He did it for me – and he did it because it meant your friend Healy never got the revenge he so desperately wanted.* 'Ben saw the beauty in that final act. Do you think your friend saw the beauty in it too, David?'

I didn't say anything.

'Did he cry?'

I glanced at my phone's display:

Missed call: Spare mobile

657

'Did he sit there and *cry*, David?' He smirked. 'Ben became the son I always wanted. I'm devastated he's gone. But you know something? Doing it like that, in front of you, in front of your pathetic little friend, it was worth it. I love that the choice was taken from you.'

I remained still, unmoved.

But I was burning up inside.

His eyes shifted a little, amused, as if he could sense I was suppressing my hatred for him. 'Why the twins, David? Is that what you want to know – *why?*'

But then his whole expression changed, brow creasing, the skin – dotted, blemished, marked by age – furrowing at the edges of his face like folded leather. For a moment, there was a hint of genuine anguish in it.

'It was such a shame that Gail Clark had to fall in with Carla Stourcroft,' he said. 'It became so complicated once they'd begun chatting. Stourcroft filled that woman's head with ideas.'

'You're confusing ideas with the truth.'

'If we'd let it run, it just would have got bigger and bigger, and more difficult to resolve. Stourcroft was smart. In the end, she would have figured it all out.'

'So you sent the son you never had to murder a couple of innocent eight-year-olds?' I looked at him, absolute revulsion in my face. 'How did that help?'

His eyes narrowed. 'Let me tell you a story.'

'You've already told me more than I ever—'

'It's about April and Abigail.'

His voice was flat and detached, the words delivered with no emotion – and yet the room seemed to congeal at their names being spoken aloud.

'After Gary realized his miserable little dream and bought the paper mill and the pier in 2000, I knew the pier was going to be harder for Ben and Victor to access, because Gary was going to take an interest in it. That was when we went to Calvin East. He was weak and scared, and easily manoeuvred. I made sure I was whispering in Gary's ear the whole time, pointing him first towards Calvin as curator, and then towards Victor as security.'

'What's this got to do with the girls?'

He held up a finger. 'Spring 2010, the house in Whitehall Woods came on the market. I was extremely well off by then. So I put in an offer. I knew Ben and Victor would appreciate the symbolism of returning home, to the place we all first met – and, with St David's closed and boarded up, I knew, on a practical level, that the children's home would be a much safer environment to carry out our work. That was part of the reason Victor got himself fired – it meant we had an alibi in place, of course, but the fact was, the pier exposed us. When we first started using it in 1993, Wapping was a shell. By 2010, there were flats and apartments everywhere. We didn't need the pier any more, all we needed was the museum, and our map – and we had Calvin to help with that.'

'I'm not interested in any of this.'

'Do you believe everything is connected?'

I studied him.

'Events, decisions, people,' he said, his left eye filmy and wet. 'Are you like me? Can you see all the parts clicking into place?'

'What are you talking about?'

'We installed Calvin as curator at the museum because he was a coward and could be controlled. I mean, it wasn't for his qualifications. I don't even know if he finished *school*. But the irony was he became very well respected by some of the local academics, who thought he really had a connection with kids, and he made learning enjoyable. So the schools would come back, year after year, to the museum, and he'd give them the tour, and they'd have some money to spend in the arcade, and everyone went away happy.' He paused, obviously trying to see if I'd got ahead of him. 'You can see now where this is going, can't you, David?'

'The girls came to the museum.'

'Correct. Autumn 2009, they came with their school. I was waiting in reception for Gary to take me home, and I watched these two twins, so different from one another. One of them was quiet and watchful; the other was loud, showing off to all her friends. And then the show-off looked over at me and saw my eyes. I couldn't react, because I was supposed to be blind – but I watched her whisper something to her friends and start to point at me, and they all started laughing.'

I was incredulous. 'Are you *listening* to yourself?'

'No,' he said. 'You misunderstand me. I wasn't upset that they laughed at me. So what? They were just stupid girls. But I could tell, straight away, that the show-off – April, I later found out – was trouble. She had a furtive edge to her.'

'She was eight.'

'She was sly.'

'She was *eight*, you fucking lunatic.'

'Actually, I think she was seven at the time.' He lifted the gun off the arm of the sofa, reminding me it was there. 'But, anyway, my point is, later on the next year, when it became clear that Gail Clark might create problems for us, I asked Ben to take me down to Searle House. I don't normally go on field trips like that, but this was a family; there were young kids. I felt it necessary to take a look.'

'So suddenly you developed a conscience?'

'Not really,' he said. 'But we were getting reports back from Calvin about how Gail didn't know anything, that there was no reason to go after her, and the more reports we got back like that, the more it began to concern me. It felt like he was protecting them more than he was protecting us. So we dropped by, on the way back from signing the contracts for the place in Whitehall Woods. Do you see how everything connects, David?' He waited for a response that never came, but didn't seem perturbed by my lack of reply. 'When we pulled up, I looked over to the park, and there

661

they were. *Right there.* Those same two girls. I said to Ben, "I recognize them," and he looked over and said to me, "Probably because they're Gail Clark's daughters." But it wasn't that. I mean, I knew she had girls, just not that they were twins. *The* twins. When I saw them there, when I realized they were the same girls I'd seen at the museum, the same one that laughed at me, it was like the universe had snapped together.'

I shook my head. 'You're insane.'

He took a breath, the exhalation whistling through his nose. 'The quiet one was just sitting there on the swings, going back and forth. The other one was with a crowd of other kids, doing some stupid dance, showing off again and making a spectacle of herself. I disliked her immediately.'

'She was a child.'

'She was trouble.'

'She was a chil—'

'I went over to them,' he said.

I came forward on the sofa. 'What?'

'After their friends disappeared, and it was just the two of them left, I felt compelled to go over. Ben advised against it, but I wanted to speak to them.' He paused. 'The quiet one sat there, swinging back and forth, watching. She was humming to herself, but she stopped when I got there. The other one, she spotted me first and came forward, all bold and brash, and she said to me, "I recognize you." So, I said, "Where do you recognize me from?" She tells me she recognizes

662

me from the museum. "You've got weird eyes," she says, and I tell her that's rude, but she doesn't seem to give much of a damn either way.'

I thought about the video I'd seen of the girls, playing Scrabble with East, laughing, joyful. This picture of April Clark he was trying to build wasn't who she was: she was just a child, innocent of any label he put on her, any brush he tried to tar her with. She'd laughed at him because she was unaware of social etiquette; she'd commented on his eyes because she didn't understand them. She'd shown off because she was eight: her entire life was still in front of her, the world lying in wait, ready to teach her. He'd robbed her of that.

Cabot pursed his lips; an expression of distaste on his face. 'She says, "Why are you here?" and I replied that I was an adult, and I could go wherever I wanted – but she just kept looking at me. Staring. I said to her, "You need to learn some manners, young lady," but she just keeps staring.'

'She didn't mean anything by it.'

'How do you know? Were you there?'

My whole body was like a furnace. I looked from the gun to him, imagining my fingers at his throat.

'I told her to stop staring, but she just kept doing it, all brash and brazen, hands on her hips, so I stepped closer to her and said, "Did you hear me? Stop staring at me." But she didn't. So I went even closer, my weird eyes right up close to her face, and I said, "I can hurt you." And she looked past me, to the car, to where Ben was, and she said, "I know you're a bad person. I saw a picture of you on my mummy's computer. I heard her talking about you on the phone."'

I swallowed.

He looked at me. 'Stourcroft had sent Gail Clark a picture of me.'

It was so hard to listen to this, my fingers digging into the sofa, my chest on fire. I wanted to tear him to pieces.

'After that, she went and grabbed her sister's hand and they ran off, back to their desperate little flat. I returned to the car and I said to Ben, "She's got a photo of me. She's seen you. She's mannerless and crude, but she's devious. If we let this drift, if we let that photo sit there on that PC, they'll be in a police station before we know it, telling them everything. The mother, the daughter, all of them."' He looked at me without contrition. 'So I said to Ben, "When it comes to dealing with the mother, you'd better make damn sure you take them all."'

My head thumped.

My skin crawled.

And then: a noise from the kitchen.

# CHAPTER 84

We both looked along the hallway, before Cabot seemed to notice his attention had been diverted, and whipped the gun back around. 'What's that?' he said. I'd barely had a chance to move, and silently cursed myself for not trying to go for the gun. He was agitated now, disquieted. 'Go and see what it was.'

I got up. Once I was past him, he hauled himself to his feet, old bones creaking, hand planted for support. I heard him move in behind me as I walked along the hallway, heading to the kitchen, on the right.

A plate had shifted on the rack, moved by the breeze coming through a partially open window. Everything else was exactly as I'd left it this morning. Out through the window, I could see Nicola, my neighbour, on her driveway. Beyond, an old couple walked past, the woman wheeling a trolley. A scene of domestic normality outside, while, inside, a man – who'd killed for so long and so often he couldn't even remember how many had suffered at his hands – was holding a gun at my back. I turned and found him behind me.

'It's just a plate,' I said.

He watched me for a moment, the opacity of his eyes even starker this close in, and then he began backing up, gun steady in front of him. I followed.

'I think maybe we've got to the end,' he said, and the finality of his words sent a shiver through me, navel to throat. 'I'm fascinated by you, David. I've read all about you, about your history. I think, perhaps, in different circumstances, you might even have been able to appreciate the similarities between us.' His feet shuffled back, in sequence, like a machine on a factory floor. 'You probably see this as some sort of victory – me coming here, telling you everything. But why would I willingly give you the inside track on sixty years' worth of secrets?'

He finally stopped, a smile breaking across his face.

'The victory isn't yours, David. It's mine. By a process of elimination, the police will come to realize my DNA is on that mask, then they'll find me all over that house in the woods, inside St David's – it's over for me. But I'm not going to jail. I'm too old for that. So I've burdened you with everything I've done, because I want you to sit there and chew on it after I'm gone. I know you'll do that. That's who you are. I want you to remember how we got away with it, and you couldn't do a damn thing about it. And if you come at me, if you try and hand me into the police today, I'm going to tell them about your friend Healy.' The smile turned briefly into laughter – gluey and vile – and then all emotion fell from his face. 'I was never going to *shoot* you, David. Why would I do that when I have you exactly where I want—'

A blur of movement.

It came from the left, from the direction of the bedrooms, careering into Cabot and taking him with it – crashing into the table, the table legs scraping across the floor, chairs spinning out from under it. Cabot's gun was thrown across the carpet. And then, a second later, it all shifted into focus.

Healy.

I could feel a breeze coming from my left; hear the soft whistle of wind drawn from one side of the house to the other. *The bedroom window was open too. Healy had caused a distraction in the kitchen and then made his way around.*

Suddenly, I was back in the moment.

Cabot was face down, Healy on top of him, two gaunt, shrunken men, dazed in the corner of the living room. I wasn't even sure if Cabot was breathing or not. Healy had a knee in his spine and a hand at the back of his neck, pushing his face into the floor. Except the closer I got, the clearer it all became, and I realized that it wasn't a hand that Healy had pressed against Cabot's skull.

It was the point of a blade.

'Healy,' I said. 'It's okay.'

He looked back at me for the first time, tears pouring down his face, saliva on his lips. *He heard the end of what Cabot was saying. He heard him talking about the girls.* My heart dropped at this portrait of him, so derelict and ruined. Cabot shifted a little, twitched, but Healy didn't move. He just kept staring at me.

'Healy, it's okay,' I said again, almost whispering it.

He shook his head.

'Healy . . .'

He started shaking it faster.

'We can sort this out,' I said.

He tore his eyes away from me, released the knife and rolled Cabot on to his back. The old man started to cough, his ribcage juddering like a faulty engine. Once he'd calmed down, Healy slowly moved the point of the blade in against the craggy folds of his neck.

'They were innocent,' he sobbed.

It took Cabot a couple of seconds to find Healy, to see his outline against the shadows around them. When he did, he said, 'Are you going to kill me now?'

Healy whimpered.

'Go on,' Cabot said. '*Do* it.'

'No, Healy. That's not who you are.'

More tears.

'Do it,' Cabot spat. 'They *deserved* to die.'

Healy reacted instantly. At first, I thought he'd put the knife straight into Cabot's neck. But then, as Healy wailed in pain, I saw only a single trickle of blood, and realized Cabot was still alive. The knife had gently pierced his skin.

Healy muttered something.

'You're pathetic,' Cabot said.

Again, Healy said something.

*What is he saying?*

He said it again, muted, indistinct: '. . . you.'

I took a step closer.

'What did you say to me?' Cabot sneered.

Healy straightened slightly.

And this time I heard him.

He tossed the knife aside, watching the surprise in Cabot's face, and then leaned right in, looking Cabot in the eyes. He didn't want Cabot to miss anything.

He wanted him to see the words on his lips.

And with tears streaking his face, his voice crippled by four years of chasing this man, by four years of misery and misfortune, by four years of losing his daughter and almost losing himself, Healy grabbed Cabot's collar, lifted him up off the floor towards him, and quietly, fearlessly, he said three words.

'I forgive you.'

# CHAPTER 85

I sat in the car surrounded by long grass and the colours of autumn, rain dotting the windscreen, and watched the silhouette of Joseph Cabot totter out across Richmond Park, into the loneliness of a clearing.

As daylight drifted out of the sky above him, I saw more plainly than ever why he'd come to me, why he'd chosen to tell me everything, why – even when he'd failed to force Healy into taking his life – he still believed he'd won.

It was because of this.

Because I had no choice but to let him walk away.

He'd explained it to me himself: if I handed him in, he would tell the police about Healy. I'd turned possible scenarios over in my head, had thought about pretending Cabot had lost his mind, that he'd confused me mentioning Healy with Healy actually *being* there – because how did a man come back from the dead? But, while Cabot was many things, he wasn't muddled. He was, in fact, extraordinarily lucid. One moment of doubt on the Met's part, about what I was telling them, and they'd

670

start looking exactly where I didn't want them to: at Healy's death, at the circumstances behind it.

All that Cabot had said to me made sense now: *I've burdened you with everything I've done, because I want you to sit there and chew on it after I'm gone. I know you'll do that. That's who you are.* He told me I'd ruined his life, the life of Korman, the son he'd adopted as his own – and now this was his revenge.

This was the victory he'd spoken of.

He stood there for a moment, like a blemish against the approaching dark, and looked back at me, a flicker of doubt in his face. He knew his DNA would get him caught. He knew he'd spend the rest of whatever life he had left rotting in a prison cell. Yet here, at the finale, he seemed unsure whether he could go through with it.

But then his expression changed, hardening, as if a realization had suddenly taken hold: that there would be no triumph in backing out, and no triumph in showing me he was scared. So he reached into his jacket, removed his gun and put it into his mouth. He made sure I was watching. And, a couple of seconds after that, he closed his eyes and pulled the trigger.

Birds scattered from the trees.

Then there was silence.

After his body crumpled to the floor, vanishing among the sea of grass, I became conscious of my headache again: pounding, massaged by the anger I felt, the bitterness that he'd got this ending where he never faced judgement for his crimes – at least, not in this life. He was right: I *would* chew on everything he'd told me, because that *was* the person I'd become. He'd gone out on his own terms, and I'd find that hard to let go. It would eat away at me, and maybe it wouldn't come to the surface now – but it would come to the surface eventually.

As I drove home, my thoughts turned to Healy, to his forgiveness of Cabot at the end; to the moments afterwards, when he'd told me the reasons he'd come to the house.

'I knew something was wrong,' he'd said.

'How?'

'I know you. We were right in the middle of something big, and you told me you would call me back.' He'd shrugged. 'When you didn't, it worried me.'

That had stuck with me, the idea that he might know me like that, the way I thought, the way I was programmed. It played into what Craw had told me about Healy and I being the same; and it made me think about something Joseph Cabot had said, perhaps the only rational thing that had ever come out of his mouth.

Everything was connected.

When I got home, it was pitch black. I wandered up the driveway alone, Andrew and Nicola visible through the living-room window next door, sitting beside one another on the sofa. My eyes lingered on them for a second, on this snapshot of a life I didn't have, and then I let myself in to my own house, silent and dark except for the hum of the television and the light it gave off. A news channel was playing softly.

It took me a while to see him, sitting in the corner of the room.

As the fallout from another suicide bombing painted the edges of his thin, pale face, he turned to me, standing in the lightless hallway, and said, 'Is it done?'

I nodded. 'Yeah.'

It was hard to know what else to say.

I made my way through to the bedroom, showered and changed, and then returned in the darkness I'd left behind. He was in exactly the same place, half disguised by shadows: minimal, solitary, forgotten about by the rest of the world.

'Are you sick?'

The question seemed to come completely out of the blue, his voice quiet. But then I started to recall the moments before he'd shot Grankin, when I'd told him the reasons I'd asked Craw to send the police. *There's something wrong with me. I think I might be ill.* I'd become worried that I couldn't protect us both.

'I blacked out,' I said eventually.

He turned towards me.

'I've been having headaches. Panic attacks maybe. I don't know.'

'Are you going to see someone about it?'

673

His voice wavered briefly as he asked, and something stayed there, in the contours of his face. I thought it was concern to start with, but then it seemed to solidify and become more defined – and I realized it wasn't that at all. It was fear.

He didn't want to be left on his own again.

'I've got a doctor's appointment tomorrow morning,' I said. 'I don't know if they'll find anything. It's probably hard to locate obsession.'

I smiled, but he just nodded.

'We need to talk about what happens next,' I said.

He shifted again, returning his eyes to the television.

'You're going to have to leave London.'

If I was expecting a reaction, I didn't get one.

'It's too risky being in the city.'

'And where am I supposed to go?'

'You can lie low at my parents' old place in Devon. No one will look for you there. In the winter there's no one around, so just keep your head down until I figure this out. I know it'll be hard – especially as you make friends so easily.'

This time, a hint of a smile formed at the corners of his mouth.

'This'll work out,' I said softly, but the smile gradually fell away from his face, and when he looked at me, it was obvious he didn't believe me. 'I mean it.'

'Okay.'

'But you need to understand something: there's

no going back to the way it was before. Family, friends, this city – it's all history. I know people who can help us – but they're going to be wasting their time if you aren't one hundred per cent clear on what you're going to be.'

'And what am I going to be?' he said.

'You're going to be someone else.'

# SOMEONE ELSE

179 days, 16 hours, 44 minutes *after*

That night, after falling asleep in front of the news, he dreamed.

They were on the swings as he approached. They didn't see him at first, their backs to him – talking to one another, laughing about something – but as he came around beside them, April turned, and then Abigail, and they began to slow up, the arc of their swinging getting smaller and smaller until, eventually, it stopped altogether.

'Hello,' he said.

They stared at him blankly.

'Do you remember me?'

Nothing.

'Don't you . . .' He began to feel hesitant. 'Don't you recognize me?'

They both took a step back.

He held up a hand, telling them to stop. 'It's okay. I was the one that helped you paint the mural in your bedroom. Do you remember that? I played tag out here with you . . . I played every day after school for months. You must remember that.'

They didn't react.

He stopped, swallowed, trying to think of other things they'd done together. 'I used to take you both to school, and I'd kiss you goodbye at the gates. I took you on the Tube. We used to play with Charlie. You remember Charlie, right?'

He looked around for his dog, Charlie, expecting it to be shadowing him like it always had – thinking he could use it to reassure them, to remind them of who he was – but the dog wasn't here. It was gone. It was part of another life.

He started to panic.

'Please,' he said, unsure what to say now, the twins stepping further away from him, from the swings, April looking off towards Searle House, as if she were about to make a break for it. She reached out for her sister's hand, taking it in hers. 'It's okay,' he repeated. 'Please. Please don't be scared of me.'

The girls looked off across the grass again, to the place in which they both lived, moving in unison, their gestures mirroring one other. They seemed to grow paler as they became more afraid.

I'm frightening them, he thought. How can they be frightened of me?

'Please,' he repeated, voice breaking up. 'Please tell me you remember me.'

The two girls stood there for a long time, gazing at him, expressionless and mute, the breeze passing through the park's trees.

'I loved you girls.' Tears filled his eyes. 'You were mine once.'

Instantly, as he spoke those last four words, a change bloomed in their faces, like sun burning through cloud. The alarm, the confusion, it vanished, becoming nothing but a memory, and smiles began breaking across their faces – first April, then Abigail – as if he were only now coming into focus for them.

'Oh, we so hoped you would come back,' April said excitedly.

He swallowed again, his heart starting to swell.

Abigail let go of her sister's hand. 'We missed you so much.'

And as he wiped the tears from his eyes, April ran across to him, tapped him on the arm and shouted, 'You're it!' – and the two girls took off across the grass, in the direction of Searle House, squealing with delight.